Into the Atlas

Aya Amrani Adventures

Book One

Zack Hacker

ALSO BY ZACK HACKER

Cut Reality

THE MAGIC'S EROSION SERIES

Those Who Watch From Afar

A Fading Future *(coming soon)*

THE AYA AMRANI ADVENTURES

Prequel: Beneath the Andaman

Into the Atlas

Within Galata's Shadow

Amidst Angkor's Silence *(coming soon)*

Sign up for Zack's email list at ZACKHACKER.COM for a free copy of the Aya Amrani Prequel, Beneath the Andaman.

INTO THE ATLAS

ZACK HACKER

Enjoying the journey?

- Leave a short Amazon review. It's the best tool to help new readers discover Aya's quest.
- Join the mailing list at zackhacker.com for your free copy of Beneath the Andaman, the Aya Amrani prequel.
- Continue Aya's journey in Within Galata's Shadow.

PART ONE

ONE

THE BRITISH TOURIST was just what Aya needed. Drunk, loud, and in a fluorescent yellow tank top. A walking distraction. His complaints about the restricted dig site had already drawn the nearest guard's attention twice in the past hour, each time pulling the armed man away from his patrol to shout cautions.

Aya watched from beneath her headscarf as the tourist gestured wildly at his companion, pointing toward the excavation site their guide was describing. His voice carried across the thin desert air, demanding to know why paying customers couldn't see the *real* treasures inside.

It took thirty seconds for his tirade to reach its predicted crescendo. Another thirty seconds, and the guard marched over for the third time and threatened to remove him. It was the opening Aya needed to slip past.

If only he knew how rare the treasures that he was missing really were.

The otherworldly expanse of the Wadi Rum desert stretched endlessly across southern Jordan, approaching the

Saudi Arabian border. Its ancient silence was broken only by the sounds of scattered visitors who made the place one of Jordan's most-visited tourist destinations.

For three days, Aya Amrani had moved among them, memorizing the rhythms. Morning tour groups clustered around guides until afternoon heat drove everyone to shade, and the final evening exodus returned everyone to their glass igloos or traditional tents. Guard rotations changed every two hours. There were blind spots in the eastern fence. The tomb's entrance stood in the middle of it all, a narrow shaft hidden within the main excavation chamber.

Fifty meters away from her now, the forgotten Moabite Queen's final resting place lay protected by nothing more than a section of chain-link fence and a single remaining guard.

Heat shimmered off the red sand, distorting the air above the dig site. Aya's loose cotton dress clung to her skin against the desert wind, and she pulled her scarf closer to shield her face from the dust and sand. Plus, it helped her to disappear.

Years of practice had taught her the art of invisibility, but her features remained a liability. Dark eyes that lingered in memory. Full lips that drew second glances. The kind of face that made witnesses reliable.

A businessman from Dubai had already approached her that morning near the visitor center, his Arabic polite but persistent until she'd deflected him with careful words about waiting for her husband. Time was running short until she had to leave Jordan behind, or else she risked being remembered and tied to any crimes in the area.

The whispers that had originally led her to Jordan spoke of a tomb unlike any other, one that housed the sacred artifacts of the last Moabite Queen, including her crown, which Aya had been hired to locate. The Queen had been a priestess-queen whose civilization had rivaled Egypt's mysteries, and whose secrets lay buried for centuries. Now they were nearly exposed again within UNESCO's careful excavation.

Three months of following rumors through antiquities dealers and grave robbers had brought Aya here, to this moment when the official dig had finally reached the burial chamber's depths.

Desert wind kicked sand against her ankles. Somewhere in the distance, a low moan echoed across the dunes. The hair on her arms stood despite the heat, feeling the sensation of ancient eyes watching from shadows that shouldn't exist in the blazing afternoon sun.

"Just the wind," she murmured, reassuring herself.

The eastern fence, with its now convenient blind spots, rose before her. The chain-link was topped with razor wire. Warning signs in Arabic, English, and French declared the area restricted under Jordan's Antiquities Law. Behind the barrier, a single guard leaned against a concrete post, thumbing through his phone with the lazy attention of a man working a double shift.

"Hello," Aya called softly.

The man's head snapped up, his hand moving instinctively toward the rifle slung across his shoulder. When he saw her, alone and clearly lost, his posture relaxed.

"*Hadhih almintaqat kharij alhududi,*" he called back over the wind with authority.

Aya approached with hesitant steps, her hands visible, palms slightly raised. "I think I'm lost," she said, uncertainty coloring her voice. "Everything looks the same out here."

"English?" He studied her face, looking for signs of trouble. "This area is off-limits, miss. Tourists stay with guides. Dangerous to wander alone."

Her expression shifted, not quite a smile, but something softer. A look she'd perfected over two years of working alone, ever since her former partner had abandoned her, and Aya had to learn every aspect of the job herself. It was the kind of expression that made men want to help without understanding why. "I must have wandered too far from my group. Could you point me in the right direction?"

He gestured broadly toward the tourist area. His gaze traveled from her face to the curves outlined by her flowing dress. "That way. Stay on the marked paths."

She moved close enough to see the slight dampness at his collar from the afternoon heat. "*Shukran*," she said. "Thank you. You're very kind to help. Not everyone would take the time for a lost traveler."

Her fingertips brushed his forearm, the lightest touch, there and gone, as she adjusted her headscarf again. A motion she'd learned from Amina, a practiced dance where her former partner would create the distraction while Aya moved unseen. But that was before the betrayal. Now she played both roles, seduction and infiltration compressed into one solitary expertise. The fabric of her dress pulled taut across her chest with the movement.

"Just doing my job," he said, but his voice had lost its official edge.

"Guarding such an important site must be fascinating work. All this history right beneath our feet."

The guard glanced around, confirming they were alone. His grip on his rifle loosened as he leaned toward her. "Sometimes. Most days are quiet, and I miss being stationed in Amman, but the archaeologists found something interesting this week. They won't say what, but now I have to work double shifts. They're talking about bringing a full army unit here to secure the site and stop tourism to the area soon."

Perfect. Confirmation wrapped in complaint.

"Really?" She held her smile steady, letting interest sparkle in her dark eyes. She touched her collarbone, fingers tracing the edge of her neckline. "Perhaps you could tell me more about it? Over some tea, maybe out of the sun?"

She watched him war with himself, duty against desire, protocol against the promise in her voice. His eyes moved from the dig site to her mouth, then back to her face.

"I really shouldn't leave my post," he said, but any conviction had already been drained from the words.

Aya leaned closer, dropping her voice to a conspiratorial whisper. "Just for a moment? I promise it'll be worth your time."

He swallowed hard, scanning the empty desert one final time. "All right," he said. "But we have to be quick."

"Wonderful," she said. "Lead the way."

The moment he turned, years of prior training compressed into fluid motion. Her elbow found the pressure point at the base of his neck. He folded without sound, and she caught him before he could fall, closing her arm around his neck and counting to ten before easing him gently behind a rocky outcrop where afternoon shadows would hide him until evening prayers.

"Sleep well," she whispered.

Her lock-picking set emerged from her boot like an extension of her hand. The lock was a military-grade mechanism, standard issue. Sturdy enough to deter tourists, simple enough for someone who'd learned her trade amongst the best art thieves and antiquities dealers across Europe, Africa, and Asia.

Her reflection caught in the scratched plexiglass of the entrance sign: dark eyes shadowed with exhaustion, face drawn tight with three days of careful performance. The loneliness of her life hit her sometimes, in moments when her instincts still expected backup that would never come.

She shook her head. It didn't matter. Soon she'd have

answers. Soon she'd hold what the Moabite Queen had hidden for millennia.

The lock yielded with a soft click.

A stagnant silence swallowed her footsteps as she slipped beneath the earth, following ancient passages toward whatever secrets lay waiting in the dark.

COOL AIR ROSE from the depths, carrying scents of limestone and something older, burned to ash centuries ago but still clinging to carved walls. The excavation team's lights cast wavering shadows across faded murals.

The queen gazed from the carefully decorated walls, hands raised toward the heavens that were mapped in astronomical signs. Warriors flanked her, but she commanded more than armies. Star charts spread beneath her fingers. Hieroglyphs spiraled around her figure in patterns Aya recognized: loyalty, divine power, the bridge between earthly rule and celestial authority.

This was no simple monarch. The fragments Aya had studied spoke of a priestess-queen who preserved knowledge during the upheavals that toppled neighboring kingdoms. While other rulers left only their names carved in stone, she had been a keeper of secrets, technology, and wisdom that died with her civilization.

One glyph stopped Aya cold, and she leaned in to analyze it further. A falcon wreathed in flames, its design unlike anything in her research. Whoever this queen had been, her story remained unwritten.

As she straightened, the familiar weight of Aya's father's

journal pressed against her ribs through the fabric of her bag. Without conscious thought, her hands found the weathered leather binding, pages brittle beneath her fingers. Muscle memory guided her to a sketch that had puzzled her since she found the notebook.

The falcon motif matched his drawing exactly.

Falcon of the Sands, his careful script read in the margin. *Connection to the Moroccan legends? Possible link to Idris Flame. Coordinates suggest Atlas Mountains.*

For a heartbeat, the scholar in her stirred. The girl who'd sat cross-legged in dusty libraries while her father traced connections between civilizations, following mysteries that spanned continents. The desire to understand, to follow where his research had led, tugged at something deep in her chest.

She snapped the journal closed, shoving down the familiar guilt. This was what her life had become: stealing pieces of history instead of preserving them. She knew each artifact she stole for Léglise's network represented knowledge lost to the world, stories silenced forever behind the walls of billionaires' mansions.

The excitement that had once thrilled her about dangerous jobs had dulled to hollow routine, each theft another betrayal of everything her father had tried to teach her. But she needed this score. It was one last job before she could step away from Léglise entirely, before she could afford to stop worrying about chasing another paycheck, to reevaluate her life.

Before continuing on, she pulled out her phone and captured the falcon's intricate detail with a few quick shots. The significance would have to wait.

At the chamber's heart, a stone sarcophagus rested beneath a canopy of crumbling gold filigree. Smaller offerings lay scattered around it—ceremonial weapons, clay jars, jewelry dulled by dust and time—but the pedestal before the sarcophagus drew her attention like a magnet.

The Crown of the Moabite Queen caught the lantern light, hammered gold gleaming through millennia of burial. Gemstones reflected dazzling light like trapped stars. She had found it.

Modern equipment threaded through the ancient chamber like veins of the present, laying claim to the past. Blue LEDs traced the pedestal's edges: weight sensors, pressure plates, connections to monitoring systems that would scream her presence to the excavation team the moment she disturbed their prize.

Aya crouched beside the sandstone base, fingers hovering over the circuits. Her jamming device, a slim tool disguised as a battery pack, beeped softly as it detected the network connection and spoofed it. She had minutes, maybe less, before they noticed the interference.

The device clicked through its calibration sequence while her heart counted each second. When the blue lights dimmed, she finally exhaled and reached for the crown.

Gold warm as living flesh filled her hands. The falcon at its center spread obsidian wings in eternal defiance, carnelian flames frozen in stone around its form. Beauty and danger, history and greed, all distilled into a weight that made her fingers tremble.

The crown's underside revealed what she'd feared most: a hair-thin wire that connected it to the pedestal's base. A silent alarm, the backup to the weight sensors. She traced its path before drawing her surgical blade.

"Of course. It is UNESCO." Her words echoed off the stone walls.

The wire parted with barely a sound. No klaxons, no flashing lights. Yet.

Her father would have been mesmerized by what she was holding. His voice drifted up from memory, warm with excitement as he'd shown her pottery shards in his study at their home in California: "The treasures of the desert aren't just gold and jewels, *binti*. They're whispers from the past, waiting for someone to listen."

She wrapped the crown carefully, its weight settling in her bag like a guilty conscience. This wasn't listening; it was plundering. The irony wasn't lost on her that she'd become everything he'd warned against. Still, her method paid a lot better than university grants. Plus, no matter who she worked for, the artifacts would be taken to some far-off museum in Europe or America, completely detached from the local culture that created them.

Her contemplation was shattered with an electronic chime.

Red light pulsed along the floor in waves, and alarms shrieked through the ancient stone while the cameras she'd deactivated whirred back to life, tracking her movement.

"Fantastic," she spat, already sprinting toward the ventilation shaft she'd identified during earlier, exterior reconnaissance of the dig. Blocked partially by a collapsed pillar, the archaeologists had been using the shaft for supply deliveries.

If she could get out unseen, it was a mile through the desert to her hidden cache: water, fresh clothes, a motorcycle with enough fuel to reach the capital city, Amman. If she could make it out of this chamber, the night belonged to her.

Her boot soles skidded on loose debris as she dove into the narrow opening. Metal rungs had been hastily attached to the wall, and they bit into her palms as she hauled herself upward. Below, Arabic shouts already mixed with pounding footsteps, while searchlights began flickering across the shaft's mouth.

The desert sunset blazed across her vision as she emerged onto the surface, crimson sky meeting crimson sand in a seamless canvas of fire, but she had no time to appreciate the beauty. Behind her, voices grew closer.

She ran toward the first waypoint she'd memorized, a distinctive rock formation shaped like a sleeping camel. From there, the desert's maze would unfold exactly as she'd planned.

Wadi Rum's labyrinth of stone towers and hidden canyons would serve her well in exactly this type of moment. Her days of careful study had mapped every outcrop, every dead end, every shortcut through the natural mazes.

At the camel rock, she veered left into a narrow canyon that would force her pursuers into single file.

The canyon opened onto a broader valley where tourists sometimes wandered. If she could reach the main road beyond the next ridge, passing vehicles would provide cover for escape.

As she ran, bullets sparked off stone ahead of her, the impacts sending rock fragments spinning through the air. She lunged left, feeling the heat of a round pass inches from her shoulder.

She pushed harder, legs burning as she sprinted toward the next waypoint. *Apparently, this crown is worth even more than I expected*, Aya thought.

Two

Emerging onto a plateau, Aya found herself exposed against the sky. The guards were gaining ground, their silhouettes moving with the confidence of men who knew every stone and shadow of this terrain. She needed a distraction.

A cluster of precariously balanced rocks ahead caught her eye. She accelerated, muscles burning as she pushed toward the formation. Behind the largest boulder, she crouched and studied the stone's foundation.

A few calculated kicks to the smallest support stone sent physics into motion. The rocks tumbled in a chain reaction, dust and debris billowing up to swallow her pursuers.

"That should slow them down," she said.

She allowed herself a moment to catch her breath, but the reprieve lasted only seconds. From the swirling dust, one guard emerged, rifle raised, his face lined with determination.

"Persistent, aren't we?" she called out.

"Drop the bag," he barked. "Now."

Aya tilted her head, the faintest hint of a smirk playing on her lips. "You're making this much more dramatic than it needs to be."

"Drop it!" He stepped closer, taking aim.

The familiar rhythm of pursuit and escape kicked in. Aya lunged forward, her long legs sweeping out in a clean arc that took his feet from under him as he attempted to fire. He hit the ground hard, rifle clattering into the dirt meters away.

Before he could recover, she planted her boot against his chest. The guard, winded and struggling, tried to roll away, but she stepped back and let him scramble to his knees. When he lunged for her, she delivered a sharp front kick to his chest, sending him sprawling backward. His head struck rocky ground with a dull thud. He went still.

She glanced at him as she adjusted her bag. "Please stay down," she warned, and was pleased to see he was unconscious.

More voices echoed through the rubble as additional guards navigated the rockfall.

Scanning the horizon, Aya spotted salvation: a plume of dust rising in the distance. Tourist Jeeps returning from sunset tours, their occupants oblivious to the gunfire and chaos ahead.

Perfect timing.

She adjusted course toward a series of sandstone arches that led to the main trail. The convoy was approaching a bend where she could intercept if she pushed herself hard enough.

Aya summoned her remaining energy and sprinted across the open ground. The guards' voices faded behind her, drowned by approaching engines.

She reached the trail just as the first Jeep rounded the corner, then stumbled onto the path with deliberate disorientation. The vehicle screeched to a halt, and the bearded driver looked at her with immediate concern.

"Are you all right?" he called in lightly accented English.

"I'm fine, but I got separated from my group." She kept her voice steady. "And I think someone's following me."

The driver's grip tightened on the steering wheel, his eyes darting across the horizon. "Out here? That's very unusual. Get in!"

She flashed a grateful smile and let him help her into the passenger seat. Behind them, two couples were focused on photographing the scenery, though she caught their curious glances in her peripheral vision.

"You're a lifesaver," she said. "I don't know what I would have done."

Her emergency pack and motorcycle were lost now. Another expense to add to this job's growing costs, but acceptable losses given the alternative. She wouldn't be reaching Amman tonight.

As the Jeep lurched forward, she glanced back. The guards had reached the trail but stopped, either uncertain of her direction or unwilling to open fire around tourists.

Aya removed her headscarf and ran her fingers through her dark curls, already shifting her appearance. The first rule of escape: become someone else as quickly as possible.

"Looks like you had quite the adventure," the driver said while navigating the winding road.

"You have no idea," she said with a soft laugh. "This place is full of surprises."

She clutched the bag where the crown rested, both triumph and burden. In the moment when she'd lifted it from its pedestal, the old rush had surged through her veins, reminding her how good she was at this work. Maybe too good. No matter who claimed the crown, she reminded herself, it would end up as a trophy in some foreign place where it didn't belong. At least her way paid the bills.

The driver glanced over. "You're sure you're alright?"

"I'm fine," she answered quickly.

Sunset continued to paint the desert in fiery shades, and Aya imagined the ancient sands swallowing her footprints, hiding evidence of her passage. She pushed the guilt away. One step at a time.

The Jeep rejoined the convoy as they wound back toward the visitor center. Aya engaged in careful conversation, transforming into just another enthralled solo traveler. She shared embellished stories of supposed train travel through Siberia, fishing adventures in Oman, and learning to dive in Honduras, each more captivating than the last. The tourists around her relaxed, initial suspicion giving way to camaraderie.

They arrived at Wadi Rum village as full darkness fell, bringing cool twilight air. Aya thanked the driver warmly and offered him forty dinars, but he waved her money away.

"My pleasure," he replied. "Welcome to Jordan, *marhaba*."

She moved with purpose, seeking distance from potential trackers. Her tent was compromised now. She needed to reach the nearest city, Aqaba, and rendezvous with her chartered plane to get out of Jordan and back to Paris.

The small, touristic village teemed with evening activity: vendors hawking handmade goods, children chasing through narrow spaces, travelers sharing stories over shawarma. She merged into a group heading toward the village center, fatigue threatening to overwhelm her as adrenaline faded. But rest would have to wait.

She wove through the crowd, conversation creating comforting white noise around her. Market stall lights cast kaleidoscope colors across her path. Spices, textiles, and trinkets competed for attention, but she headed for a quiet corner near the marketplace's edge.

Beside a stall overflowing with handcrafted jewelry, she found momentary refuge. Silver bracelets jingled, necklaces strung with amber beads glowed in lamplight, and earrings adorned with turquoise stones caught the flicker of nearby flames.

She gripped her bag tighter, the crown inside heavier than its physical weight. Each job seemed to chip away at something essential, leaving fissures that grew harder to ignore. She hadn't always been a thief. Once, she'd followed her father's footsteps as an archaeologist. But disillusionment had led her here, and the question remained whether she was any better off.

The falcon symbol tugged at her thoughts. Her father's journal mentioned specific coordinates in Morocco's Atlas Mountains. Had he been following this same trail years ago? Was the crown connected to his research? After delivering it to Léglise, perhaps she could investigate further.

She shook her head. First, she needed shelter for the night and transportation to the city come morning.

At a small teahouse, she settled into a corner table and ordered mint tea. The warm cup between her palms steadied her as she observed other patrons, locals and tourists alike, all oblivious to the stolen treasure in their midst.

She had the crown. Now she just needed to escape.

AYA LINGERED at her corner table for another hour, scanning the teahouse for any sign of pursuit. She poured the last drops from her pot of tea, grateful for momentary peace. The warmth seeped into her palms, grounding her as her mind raced with escape plans for the following day.

A commotion outside shattered the calm. Uniformed men

moved purposefully through the market, their organized sweep unmistakable. The guards had expanded their search.

She kept her head down, watching them in the reflection of a decorative mirror on the wall. Time to disappear from the streets entirely.

Slipping a few bills under her teacup, Aya exited through the café's side door into a narrow alley. The market's bustle faded as she navigated the village's passages, seeking shelter somewhere that wouldn't require extensive documentation.

The Wadi Rum Guest House sat tucked away from the main thoroughfare, its weathered sign advertising rooms for hikers and backpackers.

After securing a room with minimal conversation or question, Aya found herself on a small terrace overlooking the desert. The night sky stretched above the near-Martian landscape, stars shimmering like scattered jewels.

The view stirred memories of her father's stories about traveling through Morocco before moving to America and meeting her mother. As evening deepened, an unfamiliar clarity settled over her thoughts. Perhaps thirty was the right age to hang up this life in the shadows. No serious injuries beyond a few scars, no police record to follow her. She could walk away clean if she chose.

She extracted the crown from her bag, unwrapping it carefully. The onyx falcon gleamed in her room's dim light, its craftsmanship extraordinary even after centuries. *What secrets did it hold?* she wondered. *More importantly, what did her father know about it?*

But soon, thoughts of Léglise and his enormous wealth flooded her mind as she examined the artifact. She made a silent vow. *Existential crises can wait. If I'm going to make changes, I need to secure this payday first.*

She rewrapped the crown and stowed it away before settling in for what promised to be restless sleep.

As she lay down, sleep wouldn't come. She tried to read her father's notebook, squinting in the dim light. His entries from the final year of his life grew increasingly cryptic, neat handwriting deteriorating into rushed scrawl. Strange symbols crowded the margins—some resembled modified Tifinagh script, others looked Turkish, all interwoven with his personal shorthand that she'd never learned to read.

Whatever he'd discovered in those last months, he'd felt compelled to protect it behind layers of code. She traced a dense section, recognizing only fragments. "The key is not singular," she could make out, followed by indecipherable symbols and what might have been coordinates, though she couldn't be certain.

She'd need help decoding this. Someone with expertise in historical linguistics and cryptography. The thought made her uncomfortable, but some puzzles were too complex for solitary effort.

The notebook closed with the whisper of aged paper. Tomorrow would bring its own challenges. After that, perhaps she could afford to chase her father's mysteries into the Atlas Mountains.

If she was brave enough to trust someone again, she thought.

THREE

The following morning, Aya stood at the regional airport outside Aqaba waiting for her charter to depart, arms folded against the terminal's air conditioning. Behind her, a pair of tourists laughed over Wadi Rum photos on their phones, their voices grating against her raw nerves.

She withdrew her father's notebook again for a distraction, picking up where she left off the previous evening. Her fingers found the charcoal sketch that had haunted her thoughts: a stylized bird encircled by swirling lines, next to an arrow pointing toward "Atlas?"

Beneath the sketch, she noticed something she'd missed in her exhaustion. Several pages had been glued together, the edges barely visible where the adhesive had yellowed with age. It was unlike her father to damage his notes this way.

She worked carefully at the separation, revealing dense paragraphs written in the mixed cipher she'd glimpsed the night before. "*Morocco*" appeared frequently in plain text, but everything else remained locked behind his code. One section bore a date: "*March 2012 - First Contact?*" followed by heavily encrypted text. Another margin note read: *"If something happens to me, remember our word games. The personal is the key to the historical."*

Her hands trembled as she held the separated pages. "What the hell is all this? He'd been at it for years, decades."

She sank onto a nearby bench, boarding announcements fading to background noise. In all the years since his death, she'd carried this journal like a talisman, never giving it too much thought, not even knowing these secret pages existed.

"First Contact?" The phrase sent ice through her veins. Contact with what? With whom? The date, March 2012, was just months before his death, when a dig site collapsed in South America.

She squinted at the cipher, trying to force meaning from the symbols. A memory surfaced: sitting cross-legged on his study floor, watching him transcribe Tifinagh characters while explaining how ancient peoples encoded their most sacred knowledge. "Some secrets are too dangerous for plain text, *habibti*," he'd said, ruffling her hair.

The deteriorating handwriting suggested urgency, maybe even paranoia. This wasn't the careful scholar who'd raised her. This was someone running out of time. And it was time for her to board her flight.

Aya forced herself to stand on unsteady legs. Whatever her father had discovered, whatever had made him hide these pages, it connected to the crown in her bag. The matching falcon symbols couldn't be a coincidence.

She clutched the journal against her chest for a moment before carefully returning it to her bag. The secrets it held had waited over ten years; what was another day or two?

Walking up the private jet's stairs, she forced her mind toward practical concerns. Paris. Philippe Léglise. The crown would buy her freedom to chase normal things, maybe even her father's mysteries, without the pressure of rent and survival.

But as the plane's engines spooled up for takeoff, an uneasy voice whispered that some discoveries changed everything, whether you were ready for them or not.

AS HER PLANE began its descent into Le Bourget Airport outside Paris, Aya pressed her face to the window, watching scattered clouds drift over the city below. Her father would have loved this part of her life: flying over Europe, chasing stories in every corner of the world. "One day," he'd promised her as a child, "we'll see it all together." But that day had never come.

She pushed the thought away. Whatever dreams he'd had for her didn't matter now.

Her phone buzzed with a message from Léglise's aide. *Change of plans. Meet at 29 Avenue Rapp, 7th arrondissement. Urgent.*

Aya frowned, pulling her trench coat tighter. The meeting was supposed to be in a private room at a bar in Le Marais, her preferred location for secure, untraceable exchanges. Now Léglise wanted her in one of Paris's most upscale neighborhoods.

She hated this part: the vagueness, the invisible strings. Jobs always came with complications. For some reason, her instincts whispered that this one carried something worse.

She typed back: *This wasn't the arrangement. What's going on?*

Paris's cool air struck her like a physical blow after the

searing desert heat as she stepped off the private jet onto the tarmac. The Falcon 7X gleamed behind her, sleek lines catching airport lights.

Her phone buzzed again. *Increased scrutiny on our operations from unwanted parties. Safer location. Trust me. Can't be seen in public right now, need to inspect the artifact personally.*

"I don't have much choice," she muttered. "I need to get paid."

The knot in her stomach tightened as she slid the phone away. Léglise had discovered her in Guatemala years ago when she'd been a desperate, talented upstart chasing relics from Mayan ruins. He'd recognized her potential, plucked her from squalid smuggler circles, and molded her into a first-rate operative.

There had been a team at first, veterans of antiquities trafficking who answered to his vast network of buyers. They'd trained her in stealth, infiltration, and fencing artifacts. Léglise himself had paid for her first forged passport, taught her the difference between petty theft and truly lucrative "acquisitions," and landed her the Florence job where she'd met Amina.

Still, their relationship was purely transactional. She knew little of the man beyond his smooth reassurances: trust his methods, do the job well, and never worry about money again.

Over the years, they'd pulled off countless scores. Aztec gold in Costa Rica, hieroglyphic tablets from Abu Simbel, Renaissance manuscripts from under Dutch museum security. Léglise had always honored his agreements.

But this felt different. This wasn't how he worked.

A polished black Mercedes waited outside the terminal, its driver holding the door open. Stern-faced with a shaved head, he exuded the controlled tension of private security. The car's interior carried scents of leather and expensive cologne.

As the S-Class glided through Parisian streets, she watched the city blur past. Cobblestone gave way to grand boulevards, wrought iron balconies overflowed with geraniums, and the Eiffel Tower's lattice loomed in the distance as they approached the 7th arrondissement.

They pulled up to an Art Nouveau masterpiece, the building's façade glowing in the late afternoon light. "Madame," the driver announced, "while you are here, I will take your luggage to your hotel. When shall I return?"

"*Merci*. One hour should be plenty." Aya studied the building as she exited. Too quiet and too empty for this time of day.

Inside, the lobby radiated opulence: cool marble underfoot, air thick with lilies and beeswax, a chandelier scattering fractured light. A lone man stood by the elevator, posture rigid. He nodded as she approached.

"Miss Amrani. This way, please."

"*Allons-y! Après vous*," she replied with a tight smile.

They rode the elevator in silence to the fifth floor. The soft mechanical whirring filled the confined space while she observed her escort. His stance was rigid, gaze fixed forward, but his right hand lingered too close to his jacket pocket. Weapon, perhaps. Or just nerves.

The elevator jerked slightly as it slowed. When the doors opened, she stepped out quickly, her hand brushing the concealed blade beneath her coat.

The apartment beyond was spacious, with floor-to-ceiling windows offering panoramic views of the Seine. "Nice upgrade from a smoky bar," she said.

"Monsieur Léglise will see you shortly," the man said before disappearing down a hallway.

The room was luxurious in Léglise's typical style: Persian rugs, antique furnishings, and modern art carefully curated to impress. She'd seen enough of his properties to recognize the pattern.

A door opened, and the familiar figure entered. Large, impeccably tailored, silver hair slicked back, sharp blue eyes appraising her with predatory intensity.

"Aya Amrani," he greeted. "Always good to see you in the flesh."

"Monsieur Léglise, a pleasure," she replied smoothly.

He extended a hand. "Please, have a seat."

They settled into opposite armchairs with a low table between them. Aya placed her bag carefully at her feet, noting the subtle changes in his demeanor. More guarded, something unsaid. In past deals, he'd been content with cramped cafés and dim back rooms, regaling her with boring stories over drinks. Now he had private security. She wondered what had prompted this upgrade.

"I must apologize for the sudden change in venue," Léglise said. "I've begun some new public-facing work, transitioning away from any unsavory business toward something more respectable. These circumstances require discretion, as I'm sure you understand."

"Discretion is my specialty," Aya said, gaze unwavering.

"Indeed." He folded his hands. "Do you have it?"

Aya nodded, reaching into her bag to retrieve a protective case. She placed it on the table and opened it, revealing the crown nestled against black velvet. The Crown of the Moabite Queen remained as commanding as ever.

Léglise's eyes widened. "Magnificent."

"I always deliver," Aya said, watching him closely.

Her fingers lingered on the case's edge as she hesitated before sliding it toward him. The onyx falcon stared up at her, and for a moment, strange reluctance seized her. Part of her wanted to ask Léglise about the Idris Flame, why this particular piece warranted such elaborate exchange, but she swallowed the questions.

His gaze tore from the artifact to meet her eyes. "You do. And I always honor my agreements."

He gestured, and another man appeared. Tall, veins prominent in his thick neck, carrying a sleek metal briefcase. He set it on the table, opening it to reveal stacks of crisp Euro notes.

"Your payment, as promised," Léglise said.

The air grew heavy. The room felt wrong. The men moved too synchronized, too rehearsed.

Aya closed the artifact case, leaving it on the table, and placed her hands casually on her lap, inches from the tactical blade concealed beneath her coat.

"Pleasure doing business," she said evenly. "If that's all…"

Léglise's lips curved into a smile, but his eyes remained cold, calculating. He leaned forward, manicured nails clicking softly against the table. "Your reputation precedes you, Miss Amrani, but reputation can be a double-edged sword. Whispered secrets in the antiquities trade have a way of cutting both ways, "and we do have one issue to attend to."

FOUR

Aya met Léglise's gaze, working to keep her voice steady. "My reputation is built on going unseen, unheard. You know that, or we wouldn't be having this conversation."

His smile didn't waver, but his gaze sharpened like a predator sizing up prey. "Perhaps. But one can never be too careful."

Aya forced a smirk, though her hand drifted inside her coat. Despite their years of working together, she suddenly knew she wouldn't be meeting with her driver as planned.

Léglise followed her movement, distrust flickering across his face as he leaned forward and dropped his voice to a whisper. "One more thing, Miss Amrani."

"Yes?"

"Who else have you told about this item? About our relationship?"

"I think you know I operate with the utmost confidentiality."

His sudden suspicion felt personal, as if someone had poisoned him against her.

"Of course," he conceded. "But in our line of work, trust is a rare commodity. I'm not sure I fully believe you, especially after our rendezvous was compromised. There was quite a commotion in your wake in Jordan. Far too many people talking in the antiquities world."

"Philippe, you know how loyal I am," she replied coolly. "We have a solid foundation of trust."

Léglise shook his head. "Regrettably, foundations crumble. In the last year alone, the Art Loss Register has seen a ten percent increase in stolen antiquities reported worldwide. Museums are increasing security funding, and task forces are growing. Our world's window is closing at the most inopportune time for me. I can't afford loose ends."

Aya said nothing but stared.

"I know what you must think of me," he continued. "That I'm just another high-society collector with expensive tastes. But I'm past mere collecting, Aya. Far past it."

He turned away, lamplight catching the sharp lines of his jaw. "I've financed acquisitions over the years, paid you well to procure them. But I've heard enough chatter about certain relics to realize they're more than trinkets to line a study." His gaze danced over the crown, then back to her face.

"Objects imbued with something greater. Call it supernatural, if you will. They fascinate me and those I'm working with. Money can't buy real power, not the kind that lingers through centuries. That's what I'm after. And I'll spare no expense to attain it."

He paused, letting the weight settle.

Apprehension rose in Aya's chest. Supernatural powers were new territory for Léglise. Pure fantasy. But the intensity in his eyes gave her pause. Was this why the crown mattered? Because of the falcon symbol?

"So, you see, my dear, this last job wasn't just another

contract. It's a doorway to something beyond mere treasures. And if we're not careful, it might devour us both."

Léglise's closest security guard shifted his weight, hand moving toward his jacket.

"So what's the problem?" Aya asked.

"Just precautionary measures. Perhaps a problem for you," Léglise said, rising from his seat. "People have been contacting me, people who know the details of our arrangement. I fear you've gotten too close, and I can't risk you talking. I need to know every contact you've spoken to, no matter how insignificant."

"There's no one. How many jobs have I done for you?"

"Yes, but this world is changing. New players are entering, making things complicated. My new associates don't tolerate complications, Aya. They've invested too much to see it jeopardized by a single thief's loose tongue."

"I'm just here to get paid, Léglise."

"Well, then, if you can offer me nothing, I have no choice. I can't risk them questioning my loyalty." Léglise glanced past her shoulder, nodding to the guard.

Aya's hand finally tightened around the concealed dagger. "I see. Well, if that's how you feel, I'll just—"

In one fluid motion, she flipped the table toward Léglise. The artifact and cash scattered in an explosion of sound, Euros fluttering like wounded birds as the table slammed into him. Simultaneously, Aya drew her dagger, blade glinting in the lamplight.

The large guard lunged, but Aya was faster. She side-stepped, delivering a deep slash to the back of his knee. He stumbled, screaming.

She used the moment to grab her bag, along with a fistful of cash, leaving the crown lost in the chaos as two more men in suits blocked her path. She feinted left, then rolled right as one swung a baton. Coming up behind him, she struck the base of his skull with her dagger's hilt, dropping him.

The second man grabbed her arm, but she twisted free, using his momentum to hurl him into a decorative console table. It shattered in a cascade of wood and glass.

"Don't let her escape! Capture her!" Léglise shouted,

Aya bolted, mind mapping the layout. She darted into a study with large windows overlooking the street. Behind her, footsteps thundered.

"Nowhere to run!" a voice taunted.

She locked the door and scanned the room. Without hesitation, she swung a chair at the window. Glass cascaded like rain, night air slapping her face as she stepped onto the ledge. Below, the alley spread wide, an unforgiving drop.

The door frame exploded into splinters as her attacker charged through, baton raised.

Aya dove behind a massive oak desk to hide. Her pulse hammered as she glimpsed Léglise's laptop on the desktop. The screen was black, but a USB drive jutted from the port, tiny blue light blinking.

A printed label was attached that read "HRF Atlas Project, Morocco."

So what was Léglise working on before her arrival? Quickly, she snatched the drive, stuffing it into her jacket. If she survived, maybe it would explain why he'd turned on her.

"*C'est terminé, salope,*" her attacker spat, gaze darting between the shattered window and the balcony ledge beyond.

"Searching for something?" Aya hissed from behind him.

He spun, swinging desperately. Too late.

Aya's blade flashed in the dim light. She aimed low, slashing his thigh, eliciting a pained cry. He staggered, clutching his leg, and she seized the opening to knock the baton from his grip.

As it clattered away, she smashed her dagger's pommel

against his head. He collapsed with a sharp groan. Aya retrieved her bag and sprinted from the room before he could recover.

She navigated the apartment's labyrinthine corridors, pressing herself against the wall of a dimly lit lounge. She hadn't planned for this level of betrayal.

Hushed voices grew nearer in the hall. Peering around the corner, she counted three men sweeping the area, weapons drawn.

"Spread out. She couldn't have gone far," one ordered.

Her gaze lingered on a decorative wall display: an array of antique swords mounted artistically. A faint smile touched her lips. At least he had cliché, old-money taste.

Silently crossing the room, she selected a lightweight saber, testing its balance. Not ideal, but better than her knife.

A shadow loomed behind her. Without turning, she sensed the incoming attack. She sidestepped as a baton swung past her head, displaced air sharply in her ear.

Spinning, Aya brought the saber's hilt down on the attacker's wrist. He yelped, dropping his weapon. She followed with a swift kick to his chest, sending him crashing into a glass curio cabinet.

"One down," she muttered.

The commotion alerted the others, and Léglise's two remaining men burst into the lounge, eyes locking onto her.

"Good fight, but end of the line," the taller one said.

Aya raised an eyebrow. "You boys really should reconsider your employer."

They charged simultaneously. Aya parried the first one's punch with the saber's flat, then pivoted to deliver a sharp elbow to the second man's jaw.

Pain exploded in her side as the taller man landed a glancing blow with his baton. Feigning greater injury, she waited for him to advance before sweeping his legs.

The other man recovered, grabbing her from behind in a tight grip. Aya struggled, the saber slipping from her hand.

"Got you now," he growled.

She stomped hard on his instep. He cried out, loosening his grip just enough for her to twist free. Snatching a heavy crystal vase from a nearby table, she smashed it over his head. He collapsed in a heap.

Breathing heavily, Aya assessed the situation. The tall man was stirring, and more footsteps echoed in the hallway. *Time to move.*

Racing toward the entrance, she noticed an exposed service stairwell, previously hidden behind a tapestry, which now lay unevenly after the reinforcements had arrived. *Perfect.*

Pulling the tapestry tight behind her, she took the stairs two at a time, descending into the building's depths. The sound of pursuit was persistent but growing distant.

FIVE

Exiting into the back alley, Aya clung to the building's shadows. Evening air hit her flushed skin as she pulled up her hood, concealing her face before merging with the bustling streets.

She slipped into the urban maze, aiming to blend in. The Pont Neuf teemed with tourists and lovers, their laughter echoing against ancient stone. Street musicians filled the air with melodies of Piaf and Aznavour, providing a soundtrack to her escape. She moved with the crowd's current, a shadow among shadows, pulse matching the city's vibrant rhythm.

Each stride lengthened the distance between her and Léglise's men. As she walked, she tossed her phone into a trash can.

Her side ached where the baton had struck, and she felt warm blood trickling down her arm from a cut sustained during the fight. Ignoring the discomfort, she focused on navigation, utilizing the city's labyrinthine layout to her advantage. Fortunately, Paris was a city she knew well.

She ducked into a small boutique, its vintage clothing

displays offering convenient camouflage. The shopkeeper glanced up but paid little attention as Aya selected a scarf and beret.

"*Bonsoir*," she greeted, quickly placing more than enough cash on the counter.

"*Merci, mademoiselle*," the woman replied with a warm smile as Aya hurried back outside.

Aya donned the accessories, altering her appearance just enough to evade casual detection and pass for another tourist in love with the city's twinkling magic.

"Time to disappear," she said.

She walked along the Seine, dodging selfie-taking tourists, dancing groups, and wine-sipping couples. Crossing Pont Neuf, she allowed herself a moment to watch the city lights glittering on the water's surface.

A small brasserie caught her attention, its windows glowing with warm amber light, beckoning like a sanctuary. The aroma of fresh bread and Gauloises cigarettes mingled in the air, a comforting blend. She paused, drawn by the promise of temporary respite.

"*Excusez-moi*," she called softly to the waiter collecting glasses.

The man looked up, startled. "*Oui*?"

"May I sit for a moment? It's been a long day," she said, allowing fatigue to seep into her voice.

He hesitated, then nodded. "*Très bien*. But we'll close soon. Can I get you something?"

"*Merci. Un café allongé, s'il vous plaît.*"

The waiter nodded and disappeared inside while she settled at an outdoor table, the wrought-iron chair cool beneath her.

Deep breaths replaced adrenaline as the throbbing in her side intensified alongside the burning of her arm wound. Hours of travel and pursuit were taking their toll. Now, her body protested the sudden stillness, bruises blossoming, muscles aching. She gingerly touched the cut on her arm; the bleeding had slowed, but it needed attention.

After her coffee arrived, the waiter returned inside to close down. Settling deeper into her chair, Aya reached into her bag for a compact first-aid kit. Not much more than bandages and alcohol wipes, but it would suffice.

She winced as she dabbed the wound clean with an antiseptic wipe, the pain sharp but grounding. Rolling out gauze, she secured it tightly around her arm before tucking the kit away.

No matter how much it stung, Léglise's betrayal stung more. More than she cared to admit. She'd anticipated the possibility but hoped professionalism would prevail. Instead, she found herself on the run again, her earnings reduced to a fraction of what was promised, only what she could grab in the chaos. But it wasn't just the money. It was the danger. The isolation.

Once, the amount of cash in her bag would have thrilled her. Now the allure of wealth and adrenaline felt tarnished. Each job demanded more blood, more fear, more skill, while returns diminished. The underworld she navigated was growing darker, more treacherous. Something was changing, and she needed out soon.

Léglise's words hung heavy, too. His new associates didn't tolerate complications. Who were these associates? What kind of reach did they have? Léglise had always been dangerous, but he operated within boundaries. These new players sounded different. Less predictable, more ruthless.

Paris had been her sanctuary for years, the one place she could breathe without constantly looking over her shoulder. She'd never taken a job in France for exactly this reason. Now that safety was compromised. She knew Léglise's network, the eyes he had throughout the city. Hotel clerks, taxi drivers, shop owners, any one of whom could be on his payroll. Paris might never be safe again, not until she understood what she was dealing with.

Soft rain began to fall, droplets tapping a gentle rhythm on the cobblestones. Aya tilted her head back, letting cool water wash over her face. A small comfort, a momentary cleanse.

She stood and grabbed her bag. Who could have turned Léglise against her? The question gnawed. She'd been meticulous as always: minimal contacts, coded communications, no loose ends. She hadn't betrayed him despite plenty of lucrative opportunities over the years.

Her mind cycled through possibilities. Could it be Amina? Her ex had connections throughout the black market and certainly held a grudge. Then there was Serhan, a fence in Kabul who'd tried to undercut her last year. He had reason to want her out of the game. Or someone from the Jordan dig could have connected her to Léglise somehow.

The rain intensified as she walked away, streets glistening under streetlamps. She slipped into a narrow alley as a stray cat darted past, disappearing into the shadows. Aya watched it go, envying its simplicity. She sank onto an old plastic crate, the reality of her situation settling in.

"Could've gone better," she muttered, a wry smile tugging at her lips.

Leaning against the brick, she felt icy drops splash against her skin, each a tiny shard of penance.

Egypt. Luxor. The last big betrayal. The wound that refused to heal. Amina's ghost lingered, phantom warmth in the cold night.

They had been thieves, partners, lovers, bound by hunger for the forbidden, for capturing secrets buried beneath sand.

Amina's fiery spirit and sharp mind had mirrored Aya's own desires. And her own darkness.

But in the heart of a crumbling tomb she could never forget, beneath the weight of two thousand years, Amina had abandoned her when authorities closed in, escaping with the prize while Aya faced arrest alone.

She'd vowed then: never again. Never allow herself to be vulnerable, to trust. She'd seen partnership as an asset, but in this world it was a liability. Yet a flicker of desire for another life refused to be extinguished.

Only thirty years old, and already weary of shadows, constant fear, gnawing loneliness.

Footsteps approached, and Aya tensed, preparing to fight. A young woman emerged carrying a bundle of flowers. She glanced at Aya with curious concern before continuing on her way.

Aya continued out of the alley, merging again with the city's flow. Streets were less crowded now, the hour growing late. The last trains would be leaving Gare du Nord soon, and she needed to be on one.

There would be revenge on Léglise. After that, maybe she could finally contemplate a future of comfort.

Mind steeled, she hailed a taxi.

Six

Thirty minutes later, Aya stepped from the taxi onto the slick pavement outside Gare du Nord. The towering station loomed above, its clock glowing against the dark sky. She winced as she shifted weight, pain radiating from her bruised side.

She wove through throngs of commuters, senses on high alert despite exhaustion weighing her down. Hurried people all around provided a familiar backdrop as she moved toward the storage lockers.

At the station's far end, she paused and glanced around, ensuring she wasn't being followed. Satisfied, she took the escalator downstairs to a row of luggage lockers and quickly pressed her code into the scuffed keypad. With a soft click, the door swung open to reveal a nondescript black backpack.

"Hello, old friend," she whispered, pulling it out and scanning the contents.

Inside were emergency essentials: a forged French passport bearing the name Amélie Laurent, a fresh burner phone, and substantial cash in euros, pounds, and dollars. Tucked in the back pocket were a notebook, toiletry kit, folded plain clothes, and a small collection of tools of the trade.

She transferred her current bag's contents into the backpack before zipping it and slinging it over her shoulder. Rising slowly, she merged back into the traveler flow and returned to the main concourse, seeking a quiet corner to regroup before boarding one of the day's last trains to Spain.

She found a small kiosk, tucked away from scattered crowds. The comfort of a warm pastry momentarily soothed her frayed nerves, as did the six exit routes she'd identified and four uniformed police in her vicinity.

The world around her moved with purpose: people embarking on journeys, reuniting with loved ones, chasing dreams. *Outsider again,* she thought, tapping the table.

Adrenaline had burned off, leaving only the weight of choices and consequences. She watched as couples, families, and friend groups made their way to trains, exchanged reunion hugs, and kissed temporary goodbyes. The pang of isolation cut deep. For too long, her life had been a series of transactions, each more hollow than the last.

Aya sighed and tried to focus.

She needed to crack the USB drive stolen from Léglise. *HRF Atlas Project, Morocco.* Whatever he'd stored could be key to understanding his betrayal, possibly providing leverage to strike back. Getting a laptop and examining its contents had to be her priority before leaving France. Knowledge was power, and right now she was playing in darkness while Léglise and his mysterious associates knew the entire board.

Suddenly, a buzzing sound came from her bag on the table. "How did they get this number?" she whispered, glancing around the station. This phone was supposed to be brand-new. No one should have been able to reach her. Someone had broken into her locker.

She pulled out the burner phone, realizing the plastic was already open, its seal removed. Her brow furrowed as she examined it. That shouldn't have been possible. The station's ambient noise faded as she focused on the message:

"We have a lucrative opportunity for someone of your talents in Morocco. Your reputation precedes you, and you'd fit in seamlessly undercover. Interested?"

Morocco. The word hit like a physical blow. Her mind instinctively moved to her bag, where her father's journal rested. The falcon symbol from the tomb, his cryptic notes about the Atlas Mountains, coordinates he'd hidden in cipher, the USB drive in her pocket. HRF Atlas Project, Morocco. Léglise's secret project had the same destination. This couldn't be a coincidence. Someone was orchestrating this, pulling strings she couldn't yet see.

Morocco had always been a shadow in her life. She'd grown up with stories of bustling souks, desert winds, and walking along beaches where the Sahara meets the sea. A mixture of nostalgia and unease. Her father's homeland, a place she knew only through his vivid stories and a handful of faded inherited photographs. Maybe that was why this unsettled her so much. For once, the destination felt personal.

She considered ditching the phone, but the message was too specific to ignore.

Her fingers flew over the keypad: *"Who is this, and how did you get this number?"*

Brief pause, then: *"We have our resources, and swapping a cell phone is hardly difficult. Let's say we're impressed with your work in Jordan, despite the complications. Time is of the essence. Are you willing to hear more?"*

She typed back: *"I'm listening."*

Almost immediately: *"There's an artifact in Morocco that*

requires your expertise to acquire. Compensation will be five times your usual rate. Details upon acceptance."

The figure was tempting, especially after her financial hit.

She leaned back, eyes drifting over the station's grand architecture. Travelers hurried past, each absorbed in their own world, while her mind replayed the latest betrayal. She was making an unfortunate habit of being double-crossed by those closest to her. First Egypt, now this.

Accepting another high-risk job so soon could be reckless. Yet the prospect of working in Morocco pulled at her. A chance to connect with her roots, perhaps find meaning beyond the next score. More importantly, to decode her father's hidden research and understand Léglise's Atlas Project, the convergence of both mysteries in one country.

But the questions remained. Who were they? How did they find her? Was someone still watching? Had she missed something?

Her phone buzzed again: *"We assure your safety and anonymity. Our network is extensive. This job could be mutually beneficial. And, beyond the financial rewards, a chance to strike back at Léglise, which I think may appeal to you."*

Aya set the phone down hard. They knew about Léglise. About the betrayal that had happened only hours ago. How could they possibly know? Unless they were watching the apartment, tracking her through Paris, or worse, connected to Léglise's mysterious new associates.

She glanced around the station again, searching for anyone too interested in her movements.

The urgency to leave France was real. Whoever was reaching out knew much and revealed little. She had no power in this relationship. Moreover, the need for money was pressing, especially if this was to be one last job.

Her fingers hovered over the keyboard before memories of her father resurfaced. The warmth of his voice describing Moroccan sunsets, bustling souks. She could still see him at their kitchen table, sketching ancient symbols while describing the call to prayer echoing across Marrakech at dawn. "One day, *binti*," he'd promised, "I'll take you to see where the desert meets the mountains. Where our family's stories began." But that day never came.

After hesitation, she typed: *"Why me? There are plenty of other thieves who could do this job."*

The response took longer: *"We chose you for several reasons, Ms. Amrani. Your skills are unmatched, but more importantly, your background makes you uniquely qualified. We knew your father, Hassan. We worked with him years ago. This job aligns with his research into ancient artifacts that can tap into forgotten energy sources. What he sought is connected to what we're after now."*

The message jolted her. *"Fine. I'm interested. What's the next step?"*

The reply was swift: *"Excellent. Proceed to Marrakech. Further instructions will await you there. Safe travels."*

No additional details. No contact names. Nothing.

She held the phone, her reflection in the darkened screen staring back. A woman at a crossroads.

Gathering her belongings, she stood to purchase her ticket, stretching stiffness from her muscles. She desperately needed recovery time, but the game was still afoot.

With no line at the ticket counter, she walked straight to the teenager working the booth. "*Bonsoir.* When is the next train to Barcelona?"

The clerk tapped his keyboard. "The last train of the evening departs in thirty minutes."

"I'll take two tickets, please."

He printed and slid them across the counter as she handed over the cash.

"*Merci*."

She walked away, slipping one ticket into her pocket and discarding the other in a trash bin to throw off anyone tracking her movements.

Walking through the crowd, a large FNAC sign caught her eye. She stepped inside, greeted by bright lights and displays hawking French bestsellers, wireless earbuds, and vinyl racks. At the back, an electronics section showcased laptops.

A salesman approached, polite but eager. "*Bonjour, mademoiselle*. Can I help with anything?"

Aya nodded. "I need a computer. Something decent, at least an i5 with 16GB of RAM." She glanced at a row of ultrabooks. "This HP should work, right?"

Her mind raced with anticipation, thinking about the USB drive. She'd spent years dismissing much of her father's theories as academic fantasy, but if Léglise was pursuing them with such ruthless determination and someone was going to such lengths to contact her, perhaps there was more truth than she'd allowed herself to believe.

"*Oui*, of course," he said. "Do you need a case? A—"

"Just the laptop," Aya cut in. "Sorry, I'm in a hurry."

He nodded and rang her up.

Eager to examine the USB drive, she hurried to platform 8 as the train pulled in with a screech. She boarded, finding a seat with a table near the back of the carriage.

SEVEN

AFTER AN UNEVENTFUL TRANSFER at Gare d'Austerlitz, Aya found a private compartment. The gentle sway of the carriage offered a semblance of comfort as her body craved rest, but work remained.

She drew the curtains halfway, allowing moonlight to cast patterns on polished wood and burgundy upholstery. The space was quiet, save for muffled train wheels grinding against tracks. She eased into the cushioned seat, knees brushing the fold-out table, scanning the understated charm that whispered of bygone eras. Under different circumstances, she might have appreciated the elegance.

She locked the door and retrieved the laptop from her backpack, booting it up. HP splash screen, Windows setup, pop-up prompts. Time to see if it was worth it.

She produced the USB drive from her pocket, its small metal body unassuming yet fraught with potential danger. Sliding it into the laptop's port, a notification flashed:

Drive Encrypted. Enter Password.

She scoffed. "Of course. Nothing can be easy."

From her own flash drive, buried in her backpack, she installed a lightweight cracking tool she'd used before.

The train rocked as it cleared the station, city lights blurring into darkness. Her finger tapped anxiously against the table while lines of code cycled through possible keys. Outside in the corridor, a distant voice announced the train's next stop, but Aya barely registered it, mind locked on the scanning text.

Minutes later, the tool beeped. A file directory materialized on-screen:

HRF_ExpeditionBudget.pdf
Morocco_Dig_Plans_Confidential.docx
SecurityContract_USAF_Overview.xlsx
Léglise_Comms_Archive Directory (LOCKED)

She bit her lip. Some documents were unprotected beyond the first encryption layer. A hesitant click on *Morocco_Dig_-Plans_Confidential.docx* opened it immediately, revealing pages of logistical details for an excavation site in the Atlas Mountains. She scanned it: "deep drilling," "secured perimeter," "artifacts," "funding authorized by Heritage Reclamation Foundation."

Heritage Reclamation Foundation. Her brow furrowed as she scrolled on.

Sections mentioned "proprietary energy interests" with vague references to an unnamed company. She noted a line about "requires additional U.S. military contractor support to ensure site security."

U.S. military? This was bigger than a normal artifact dig. More than Léglise losing his mind chasing myths.

She opened *HRF_ExpeditionBudget.pdf*. The header bore a crisp, official logo for the Heritage Reclamation Foundation, accompanied by fine-print disclaimers. A glance revealed staggering sums funneled into "Site Restoration" and "Security

Infrastructure." She spotted repeated references to an "H.R.F. & PES Joint Initiative."

PES. Another acronym.

Her stomach twisted. Budget lines soared into seven or eight digits. This was far beyond philanthropic archaeology. It looked more like a covert operation. No wonder Léglise had tried to eliminate her. He couldn't risk anyone tying him to this.

Encrypted files scrolled by: *MoabiteCrown_Expedition*, *ProjectAtlas_Heirloom*, *IDRIS_223*, among dozens of code-labeled folders. She felt recognition at "IDRIS," the word scribbled in her father's log.

"What are you after, Léglise?" she whispered. Opening another file, amidst partially decrypted symbols, text flashed:

early references to an artifact older than the Moabite era... rumored seat of power in the Atlas... possibly harnessing the "fire that does not burn"...

It again echoed her father's strange notes. She clicked deeper, scanning a half-decoded chart:

Coordinates... possible correlation to 8th-century Berber script referencing "Djinn of the Iron Gate."

She hovered over the *Encrypted_Directory* folder. Clicking did nothing; a second password prompt blocked her. She tried her script again, but it froze after a few passes. Whatever was in that directory was locked behind a stronger cipher, one her current method couldn't handle.

Suddenly, the screen flashed, a chunk of text lost in garbled code. She swore under her breath. The data was incomplete unless she could crack it.

Still, it confirmed one suspicion: Léglise was after something directly connected to what her father had searched for, or perhaps even found. The Falcon symbol, the Atlas Mountains, references to ancient energy sources. Her father had been tracking something, and Léglise had picked up the trail.

She sat back. If she wanted real answers, plus a shot at a payday big enough to let her take a break, she had to follow along, too.

She tried to focus on what she had learned. Heritage Reclamation Foundation wasn't just a nonprofit sponsor. They clearly had ties to some energy conglomerate, maybe this "PES," and were pumping money into a dig involving U.S. military contractors.

"This is huge," she breathed, the train's gentle sway punctuating her realization. "Léglise, you bastard. No wonder you sold me out. You're worried about competition. About someone figuring out what you're actually up to. It's not just about stealing artifacts. This is something else entirely."

The operation's scale suggested they weren't just after historical finds; they were searching for something with real power. If Léglise was willing to invest this kind of money and involve military contractors, he must believe the Idris Flame was more than myth, making his speech about the supernatural more than delusions of a deeply rich man.

The train rattled around a curve, lights flickering. She pressed a few keys, moving the partial documents she'd copied onto her own drive. At least she had enough to figure out her next move.

"Morocco," she murmured, shutting the laptop. "Fine. I'll see what's really going on in your so-called 'foundation,' Léglise. And if you thought Jordan was risky, you have no idea."

For years, she'd dismissed her father's theories about the supernatural as academic fantasy, too much Indiana Jones. The desperate grasping of a man who wanted history to be more magical than it was. But what if he'd been right? His notes could give her a crucial advantage. She needed to review them more carefully, cross-reference them with information from the USB drive. Maybe then she'd understand what he'd been involved in, whether his death had truly been an accident, and whether there was any truth to Léglise's newfound beliefs.

Fighting a yawn, she tucked the laptop into her bag, ensuring it was secure before dimming the compartment light. The train roared on into the night, carrying her and her newly discovered secrets steadily closer to the next battleground.

Paris had fully receded into the distance, its threats hopefully left behind. Yet she couldn't shake the feeling of being watched. Léglise had eyes everywhere, and she couldn't afford to underestimate him, not to mention her new, seemingly omniscient employer.

Right on cue, her phone vibrated, disrupting the quiet rhythm of rails. She hesitated before picking it up. Another message from the same number.

"In Marrakech, make your way to Djemaa el Fna at sunset. Among the storytellers and musicians on the right side of the square, our contact Omar will find you. He'll guide you from there."

Djemaa el Fna. The heart of Marrakech. A place she'd heard described countless times with vivid detail, an alluring chaos of performers, vendors, storytellers, musicians, tourists, and locals. A crossroads of old and new.

"Noted. Any additional details?"

A moment later: *"All in due time. Rest, Aya. You're on the cusp of something extraordinary."*

She frowned. The familiarity was unsettling.

Setting the phone aside, she gazed back out the window as the French countryside unfolded. Rolling hills bathed in moonlight, dotted with glowing farmhouses.

She reached into her bag and pulled out a small notebook containing contacts, codes, and encrypted notes.

If she walked away now, she'd always be looking over her shoulder. Léglise wasn't the type to forget or forgive. With his resources and connections, she'd never be truly free until she stopped him. The best way to do that was to beat him at his own game, find what he was looking for first, and use it as leverage.

This job offered her a chance to solve multiple puzzles at once: to understand her father's work, to get revenge on Léglise, and possibly to walk away with enough leverage and money to start a new life. One where she wasn't constantly running.

Flipping to a blank page, she began listing potential scenarios and contingencies, preparing.

As the train crossed into southern France, her eyelids grew heavy, but sleep eluded her. Instead, she reviewed the messages again, searching for hidden meanings or traps.

The repeated contact from her employer was both reassuring and alarming. They seemed eager, too eager, to secure her cooperation.

Her phone buzzed once more: *"We hope you can get some rest. You've earned it. Safe travels, Aya."*

A chill ran down her spine. Whoever they were, they were monitoring her closely. She stood abruptly, peering out into the corridor. It was empty save for the faint glow of overhead lights.

Returning to her seat, she typed curtly: *"I don't appreciate being watched."*

This time, there was no immediate reply. She locked the phone and tucked it away, resolving to be more vigilant. Pulling the curtains shut, she decided to catch whatever sleep she could before reaching the Spanish border.

She settled into the fold-out bed, and she recalled an old Gnawa song she'd liked as a child, a haunting melody of distant journeys. The train's rhythm echoed the tune in her mind, preventing sleep.

She opened her father's field log yet again, looking through other references to Morocco, scanning half-faded pages he'd scribbled years before. One note leaped out:

In 1352, the Moroccan historian Ibn Battuta wrote of an inexplicable "smokeless fire" that consumed entire caravans near the Atlas. Possibly referencing local djinn lore. Cf. Tifinagh inscriptions in Toubkal region?

Below it, he'd taped a small newspaper clipping. "*1935 Explorer's Diary Mentions Vanishing Lights, Disoriented Berber Guides.*" The words "*Test authenticity??*" were scrawled in red pen.

She turned to the notebook's final entries, dated just weeks before his death. The cipher had grown even more complex here, combining at least three scripts with mathematical formulas. One phrase jumped out, written shakily: "The djinn remember those who remember them." Below it, numbers were carefully noted, but the final digits had been replaced with symbols she didn't recognize. Her father had been paranoid about something or someone reading his notes. What had he been so desperate to hide?

Sighing, she opened Chrome on her phone, searching for any mention of "Ibn Battuta" + "smokeless fire." She found only cryptic references: hikers scared by uncanny lights at night, local tribes refusing to guide explorers after dusk. Nothing definitive.

She closed her eyes and images played in her mind while she focused on the train's rattle. Djinn, curses, and an unknown artifact in the Atlas. For the first time, the heist she was chasing felt bigger than a payday. It felt like stepping onto a path her father had glimpsed but never fully walked.

As the train slowed near the Spanish border, passengers readied their documents.

Aya pulled out her passport bearing the name Amélie Laurent. The forgery was impeccable, crafted by one of the best in the business, but borders were unpredictable, and any scrutiny could spell trouble.

A firm knock on her door interrupted her thoughts. She slid it open to reveal a uniformed Spanish officer, flanked by a French counterpart.

"*Buenos días. Pasaporte, por favor,*" the officer requested politely.

"*Oui, pas de problème,*" Aya replied, handing over the document with a steady hand.

The officer examined it briefly, comparing the photo to her face. "Purpose of your visit to Spain?"

"*Tourisme, avec mes amies à Barcelone.*"

He nodded, handing back the passport. "*Que lo pase bien.*"

"*Gracias.*"

The door slid shut, and Aya allowed herself a small sigh of relief.

Shortly after, the train resumed, and she pulled up a map of Marrakech on her phone. Tracing the winding streets of the old medina leading to Djemaa el Fna, she tried to visualize the chaotic energy.

For the first time in years, Aya felt genuine excitement about a job that wasn't tied to a heist or a payout.

Soon, the train rolled into Barcelona's Estació de França. The station buzzed with morning activity, the typical swell of tourists and locals weaving through the grand hall. Aya disembarked, keeping a low profile as she navigated toward the exit. She had a few hours before her flight to Marrakech.

She found a quiet corner in a small café off the main road, where old men sipped thick coffee at worn marble tables. A single overhead fan stirred the late-morning air, coaxing warmth from pastries on display.

When a young waiter approached with a cheerful "Bon dia," Aya mustered a polite smile and ordered a xuixo and a cafè amb llet.

The combination was sweet and comforting, a small indulgence in a life that allowed for few. Each bite crackled lightly in her mouth. She savored it momentarily before reviewing her plans.

As she checked her flight, her phone vibrated again: *"We trust your journey continues without issue. A car will meet you upon arrival in Marrakech."*

Whoever these people were, they'd broken into her emergency locker, replaced her phone, and now tracked her every movement. They operated on another level entirely.

"I appreciate the updates, but constant surveillance wasn't part of our arrangement. If you want my cooperation, the tracking stops now. I work alone, on my terms. That's non-negotiable."

She hit send, half-expecting silence. Instead, the phone rang, an unknown number flashing on the screen.

Against her instincts, she answered. "Yes."

A smooth, American-accented voice responded. "Miss Amrani, we apologize for any discomfort our communications have caused."

"Then perhaps you can explain a little more. Now."

"Of course. We represent a client with significant resources and a vested interest in ensuring your safe arrival. Monitoring your progress is a precaution, nothing more."

"You're tracking my phone?"

"Only for logistical purposes."

Her eyes darted around the café, paranoia creeping up her spine. "This is unacceptable. If you can track me, so can others."

"Our systems are secure. Your anonymity is maintained."

She considered ending the call but hesitated. "Why me?"

"As we said, your reputation precedes you. Your skills are uniquely suited to this endeavor. And, despite your famous looks, few in your line of work will be able to blend in so well within Morocco."

"Flattery won't placate me," she retorted.

"Understood. Perhaps this will. Upon successful completion, you'll receive not only the agreed-upon fee but also access to a network of resources that could elevate your standing considerably. Resources that include classified archaeological databases, historical records that never made it to public archives, and connections to scholars who worked with your father, Hassan Amrani. We know you've been trying to decode his final research. We can help with that."

Her grip tightened on the phone. "You mentioned you knew my father," she said carefully. "Prove it."

"March 2011. Your father contacted us about a discovery near Toubkal. He believed he'd found evidence of the Idris Flame. We provided funding for a future expedition in exchange for first access to his findings. Unfortunately, the cave collapse in Colombia happened before he could begin. But we have his preliminary reports, his correspondence, his notes. All of which could be yours."

The café seemed to spin slightly. They had pieces of the puzzle she'd been missing for ten years.

"Fine. But no more surprises. I expect full transparency when I meet this Omar."

"Agreed. Safe travels, Miss Amrani. We look forward to your success, and we are happy to remain hands-off to allow you to work."

The line went dead.

Minutes later, as she took a taxi to the airport, the sun was high overhead, turning up the heat in Barcelona.

EIGHT

Aya sat in the departure lounge of Barcelona El Prat Airport, waiting. Her flight to Marrakech was delayed, providing more time to contemplate the path she was choosing, allowing the desire for a different life to dig deeper into her.

Around her, Spanish chatter mingled with the click of rolling suitcases. A wide glass wall offered a view of tarmac lights gleaming against mid-morning haze. Groups clustered by café tables, their conversations colliding with overhead announcements of final boarding calls. Others hustled through the terminal with single-minded focus. She envied the simplicity of their concerns, delayed flights or lost luggage.

Near the window, a girl, maybe seven or eight, sat cross-legged on the floor, completely absorbed in a battered paperback. Her father dozed in the chair above her, his hand resting protectively on her shoulder even in sleep. The girl's lips moved silently as she read, lost in whatever world those pages contained. The quiet intimacy of the moment caught Aya off guard.

She remembered sitting the same way in her father's cluttered office at UC Berkeley, walls crammed with archaeology journals and half-labeled artifacts from distant digs, Hassan Amrani pointing to a dog-eared map pinned to the wall. "That's where I grew up," he said, tracing Morocco's coastline with careful reverence. "One day, we'll see it together."

Aya must have been the same age as the little girl then, clinging to her father's words in the wake of her mother's departure. She could still recall the hollowness of the house when her mother's footsteps vanished for good. No goodbyes, no explanation. From that moment on, Hassan poured every ounce of affection into Aya, bringing her along on research trips to Cambodia, Peru, Mexico. Summers became a blur of sun-scorched ruins and dust dancing in tropical light. While other kids attended summer camp, she listened to her father lecture about lost civilizations, ancient mysteries, his eyes shining with fervor and sadness at what the past had held, at what had been erased by time.

He taught her that history wasn't just in books, but lived in the soil beneath her boots, in the broken pottery she helped catalog at dig sites. At night, he'd regale her with folktales, describing the majesty of the Atlas Mountains and the bustling souks of his youth, how the most dilapidated doors could hold fantastical palaces or unlock forgotten stories. Yet despite the wonders of his homeland, Hassan spent more time in Central and South America, chasing university grants and fighting academic politics.

She saw the toll his work took: frustration over how indigenous artifacts were treated like currency for academic prestige, for funding. She remembered hearing him argue with colleagues about selling rare finds to donors and museums to boost departmental funding, lobbying for which American museum would get which South American artifact.

Still, in quiet hours, he'd circle back to Morocco, a land he missed yet never revisited, locked away by obligations and his broken marriage. She sensed it in the way he lingered over old photographs, or how his voice caught.

She had deliberately avoided the country since his death. Morocco represented not just her heritage but the loss of the person who connected her to it. Her father had died before he could show her his homeland, and visiting without him felt like reopening a wound that had never fully healed.

But now she had no choice. She would have to face not just Léglise and his mysterious operation, but the ghosts of her past as well. She shook her head, attempting to dispel the wave of nostalgia.

Her flight was finally called, and she boarded, settling into a seat by the window. The cabin lights dimmed as the aircraft taxied to the runway. She watched Barcelona fade away below, happy to be back in motion, free from her thoughts. Her seat offered a sweeping view of Spain's coastline. She watched neon sprawl dissolve into the inky darkness of the Mediterranean below.

A flight attendant passed, offering water and a faint smile. Aya accepted out of politeness but said nothing, mind churning with half-formed plans. The aircraft's engines vibrated steadily through the armrests. She exhaled, letting the droning lull her toward sleep.

As the plane began its descent two-and-a-half hours later into Marrakech Menara Airport, Aya awoke and looked out at the sprawling, flat landscape below. Warm light reflected off a uniform wall of terracotta buildings, framed by the mountain backdrop.

The captain's voice crackled over the intercom: "We'll touch down in Marrakech within the next couple of minutes. The temperature is currently thirty-eight degrees. On behalf of everyone here at Iberia, we hope you had a pleasant flight. Thanks for flying with us."

After a smooth landing, Aya exited the plane and was greeted by the inferno of dry air that accompanied Marrakech's summer.

Inside, the terminal was bustling with what looked like a dozen flights having arrived within minutes of each other, and the already long customs line snaked back and forth. She sighed. She'd already been on the go for ages and couldn't wait to be resting, recovering, and taking care of her human needs, but it seemed she was in for a long wait.

After nearly two hours, she reached the front of the line. The border officer, a younger man with a carefully sculpted beard and an air of self-confidence, beckoned her forward. She was ready with lies.

"Passport, please," he requested, his dark eyes already appraising her with an intensity that made her skin prickle.

She handed over her forged document, expression carefully neutral. The agent examined it slowly, too slowly. His fingers lingered on the pages, eyes narrowing slightly as he studied the stamps. Had Léglise already spread word? Were his contacts watching borders? The agent's gaze flicked between her photo and her face multiple times, expression unreadable.

"Amélie Laurent," he finally said, drawing out the syllables.

She tensed, ready to run if needed. Then his face broke into a slow smile. "A beautiful name for a beautiful woman."

Relief left her lightheaded. Not a trap, just wandering eyes. She almost laughed at her paranoia, but the feeling quickly shifted to irritation as he leaned closer to the glass barrier.

"Thank you," she replied curtly, wanting to move things along.

"First time in Marrakech, Madame Laurent?" he inquired.

"Yes."

"And the purpose of your visit?" He clicked his pen repeatedly.

"Tourism," she replied, meeting his gaze with a cool stare. "See the medina, go to the desert."

"Ah, excellent choice," he said, nodding approvingly. "Marrakech is the best city, you will love it. And where will you be staying during your time here?"

This particular brand of attention, thinly veiled flirtation dressed up as official questioning, was its own special kind of annoying. Still, she played along just enough to move through quickly.

She named Riad Sierra, a guest house her earlier Google search had yielded. She had no idea where she'd actually be staying.

"Very nice." He leaned in conspiratorially. "Perhaps I could offer some suggestions for your itinerary. There are many hidden places in Marrakech that tourists never see." He winked. "Or, if you prefer, I could show you around myself."

"That's very kind, but I prefer to explore on my own."

He held her gaze for a beat too long, then finally stamped her passport with a flourish. "As you wish, Madame Laurent. But if you change your mind..." he held out a small notepad. "Perhaps you could leave me your number? Just in case you need any assistance... or company."

With a sigh, she took the notepad and scribbled down a fake French number.

"Thank you," he said with a wink, smile widening. "I'll be in touch. I have a feeling it will be memorable."

She retrieved her passport, fingers itching to wipe away any lingering trace of his hand.

Stepping outside, she noticed a driver holding a sign with her alias. She hesitated. Accepting their transportation could be a risk, but refusing might raise suspicions. She'd already come this far.

She approached the driver cautiously. "I'm Amélie," she said.

The driver smiled politely. "*Marhaba, mcharfin*," he said. He gestured toward a waiting car in the lot.

As they pulled away from the curb, she gazed through the back window at the sprawling, flat landscape. The airport, a modern structure of glass and steel, quickly gave way to a scene both familiar and foreign. Palm trees lined the wide boulevards, fronds swaying gently in the warm breeze. Beyond them, the ochre walls of the medina rose like a mirage, their crenelated outlines shining against the golden sky.

Here and there, donkey carts, laden with goods, plodded patiently alongside sleek Bugattis and Maseratis. This was it, a return of sorts, to a place she had only ever known through story.

A surge of unexpected emotion welled within her. A bittersweet ache of nostalgia mixed with regret. She was home, but she was alone.

The architecture and dusty streets triggered another memory, unwanted but vivid. Cairo, three years ago. She and Amina in a lavish apartment overlooking the Nile after lifting the legendary King's Fang from a shrine in the Phi Phi Islands and narrowly escaping its trail of death. The view had been similar. Palm fronds swaying against ancient walls, modern chaos mixing with timeless architecture.

They'd spent those weeks drunk on success at Château Grand Marquis, their bodies intertwined on Egyptian cotton sheets as they mapped out an exit strategy. Amina would stand naked at the window, backlit by the Cairo sunset, outlining plans for their lives together. Aya could still picture her there, the full curve of her breasts catching the golden light, the flare of her hips as she shifted her weight, utterly unselfconscious and magnetic. "Mindanao," she'd whispered later, her hands holding Aya's waist. "Remote enough to disappear, developed enough for the lifestyle I think we've earned. One more job after we help Anastasia in Sofia. Then we're ghosts."

Two months after that supposed "last job" had ended, Amina had left her in a tomb in Luxor, taking the payday and their shared dreams with her.

"Here we are, madame," her driver said as they pulled up to a boutique hotel on the outskirts of Marrakech's medina. The entrance was adorned with traditional Moroccan tilework, while a warm glow spilled from the inside.

Aya stepped into the riad's courtyard and paused, momentarily dazzled. Marble floors gleamed under ornate brass lanterns, their light dancing across geometric mosaics of blue and gold. In the center, a fountain gurgled softly, surrounded by lush trees and perfumed air. Overhead, carved cedar latticework created a pattern of shifting shadows.

It was the kind of understated opulence she rarely encountered. Pillows embroidered with silver thread lined low benches, and discreet staff bustled in near-silence. Her boots felt coarse against the polished tiles, a jarring reminder of her days on the run, but she felt the stress begin to wash away. Her usual lodgings involved peeling wallpaper and flickering lightbulbs, not centuries-old artistry.

A smiling attendant in a neatly pressed uniform stepped forward. "Welcome to Riad Yacout, madame. Long journey?"

"It felt longer than it was," she said, forcing a courteous nod. She slipped her passport onto the desk, scanning the corners of the lobby for cameras. Her pulse quickened at the sight of an unfamiliar man in a pressed suit. A ridiculous reaction in a tourist hotspot she knew, but she couldn't shake the fear.

"Well, your room is ready, and all expenses have been taken care of already. This way."

Aya followed. "You mentioned the room was taken care of. Can you tell me by whom?" she asked.

"It was prepaid online. A note was also left for you," the receptionist replied, handing her an envelope.

She accepted the envelope, resisting the urge to tear it open immediately. Instead, she entered the room. It was a luxurious space adorned with local art and overlooking a massive, tranquil garden and swimming pool.

Once inside, she secured the door and opened the envelope. It contained a stack of blue 200-dirham notes along with a message: *Rest well, Aya. Tomorrow at sunset, Djemaa el Fna. Omar will find you. Trust in the path ahead.*

She crumpled the paper in frustration, then set her bag down before checking the room for signs of tampering or surveillance.

She moved systematically, scanning every corner, but found no unauthorized wiring, no gaps in the paneling, nothing suspicious. Her hosts had resources, but they either respected her privacy or hid their tracks better than she expected.

Finally satisfied, she took a long, hot, overdue shower to wash off Paris and the entire journey. By the time she was finished, steam hung in the bathroom air, and she slipped into the hotel robe.

She stepped out onto her balcony, the earlier inferno of heat replaced by a warm breeze that blew through her robe and dried the last of the steam clinging to her body. She felt tired but refreshed.

Leaning against the railing, she closed her eyes, letting the peace of the moment wash over her.

Then, a voice pierced her reverie. A lone voice that gradually swelled into a chorus, rising and falling in a haunting melody that echoed in every direction. The call to prayer echoed from mosques across the city. She opened her eyes and followed the sound, her gaze drawn to the Koutoubia Mosque, its 12th-century minaret a beacon against the twilight sky, bearing witness to centuries of Marrakech's history.

Moments later, as the call to prayer faded, she suppressed a chill.

This job was becoming more than just that. It was a crossroads, one that could potentially lead to unexpected places.

"Tomorrow," she whispered into the night, before retreating inside. "We'll see what secrets you hold, Marrakech."

NINE

THE SUN'S rays glinted off the tranquil pool surface in the center of the riad's courtyard. Aya was mere steps removed from the honking scooters, donkey carts, crowds of pedestrians, and perpetual chaos of the Marrakech medina, but the riad's door was a portal to somewhere completely different.

She reclined atop an overstuffed chaise lounge, stretched out as she soaked in the Moroccan sun. A sleek black bikini clung to her body, still dripping from a plunge in the pool, the dark fabric complementing her olive skin. Only the bandage on her arm suggested she was on anything other than a luxurious, pampered vacation.

Chilled, sweet mint tea served as a welcome counterpoint to the heat. The scent of jasmine and citrus blossoms filled the air. For a moment, she allowed herself to drift, tension beginning to ebb away.

After the chaos of Paris, her mind had been evaluating risks, planning her next move, processing what she'd discovered. The weight of it all threatened to cloud her judgment, and she couldn't afford that, not with so much at stake.

Sometimes the best strategy was to step back, to let the mind reset. A few hours of genuine relaxation would help her approach tonight's meeting with a clearer head. She closed her eyes again, feeling warmth seep into her muscles, loosening the knots of tension that had built up since Jordan.

"Beautiful day, isn't it?" A British-accented voice interrupted her thoughts only moments later.

Aya opened her eyes to see a tall man standing beside her, perhaps in his mid-thirties, with chestnut-brown hair that fell in artful disarray over a high forehead. He wore a light green linen shirt, rolled at the sleeves. There was a relaxed ease to him, a poise that hinted at more than a handful of adventures behind a calm, appreciative gaze that was fixed on her.

"It is," she replied plainly.

"Mind if I join you?" he asked, gesturing to the lounge chair beside hers.

She considered him, noting the hours she had before the meeting. Plenty of time, she told herself, though the nagging voice of caution was harder to silence. She pushed it aside, letting herself savor the moment.

"Suit yourself," she said. A distraction was what she needed.

He settled in and took a long drink from a bottle of water. "Name's Jude," he offered, glancing over at her.

"Aya."

He noticed the bandage. "Looks like you had a bit of excitement."

She glanced down briefly. "Just a scratch."

"Well, I hope it doesn't slow you down," he said.

"Not much does," she replied, tilting her head to study him.

He returned a smirk, and comfortable silence settled

between them. She could occasionally feel his curious eyes on her. Normally, she would discourage this attention, but the prospect of a fleeting distraction was appealing.

"Any plans for the afternoon?" he finally ventured.

"Not at the moment, but I do have a few ideas." She rolled onto her stomach, propping herself up on her elbows to accentuate the curve of her lower back.

"If you're interested, I have a suite with a remarkable view. We could have a drink up there."

His invitation was clear, and she found the straightforwardness refreshing.

"Why not?" she said.

"Great, after you."

They gathered their belongings and strolled through the riad's corridors. His suite was spacious and elegantly appointed, with ornate woodwork and an outward balcony overlooking the city's rooftops. The late afternoon sun bathed the room in geometric patterns through the carved wooden screens.

"Make yourself at home," he said, pouring two glasses of chilled white wine he'd pulled from the room's fridge. He handed one to her. "To chance encounters."

"To things that don't need explaining," she replied, clinking her glass against his.

They moved to the balcony, where a gentle breeze carried distant sounds of the outside world. The view was breathtaking: rooftops and minarets stretched out toward the horizon, where the Atlas Mountains rose above the city. Below, the hidden geometry of the old city revealed itself from above. Courtyards within courtyards, secret gardens tucked behind crumbling walls, passages that led to passages in an endless maze that had swallowed travelers for centuries.

"It's quite a sight," she said, sipping her wine.

"Not the only one," Jude said, his gaze meeting hers.

"Bold."

"Just honest."

"Is that so?"

"I have a feeling you're someone who appreciates honesty. And boldness."

She considered him for a moment. "Sometimes." She closed the distance between them, her lips finding his.

They moved back inside, the suite feeling richer now. The carved latticework threw shifting shadows across the bed.

As she stripped away his shirt, she focused on the press of his body, the subtle flex of muscle beneath her hands, the warmth of his breath skating along her collarbone.

A small shiver ran down her spine as his lips brushed her collarbone.

For a fleeting second, her mind rebelled, reminding her of the risks, of what she was and who she could never be. But as his hands slid down her back, the warmth of his touch drowned out the voice of caution.

His fingers traced the edge of her bikini top before untying the strings with one pull. She didn't plan the next move or weigh the risks, focused instead on the sensations that grounded her in the present.

His lips found her earlobe, the curve of her neck, breath hot against her skin. She arched into him, her body responding instinctively to his touch, trembling slightly.

With each moment, the noise of the city, of her life, faded into the distance, leaving only the soft strain of the bed's wooden frame and the whisper of her pulse quickening in her ears.

Her fingers dug into his shoulders, her breath coming in short gasps as she matched his rhythm. Her eyes met his, their shared gaze unyielding. Her back arched, a soft cry escaping her lips.

When they had both finished, she pulled away and dressed quickly.

He watched her, propped up on one elbow. "Why don't you stay longer? I have to fly out tomorrow."

"Unfortunately, I have somewhere to be today, but thank you for this."

A flicker of memory threatened to surface. The last time she'd let herself close to anyone. Amina. Egypt. She'd been foolish, letting her guard down.

She swallowed hard, brushing away the thought. Once burned, she had no intention of risking a second heartbreak or another job turned sour by personal entanglements. Still, she missed not being alone and savored the moments when she could fool herself she wasn't.

She turned and left the room before he could propose that they meet up again in London, the door clicking shut softly behind her.

BACK IN HER ROOM, heat still radiated from her skin after the brief indulgence. She closed her eyes as the warm evening breeze hit her face through the open balcony.

What am I doing? The question hammered at her.

Far below, the courtyard shimmered. Soft voices drifted upward, travelers swapping stories in French and English. She felt relief from giving in to her body for the moment and longed for more. But there were bigger things at stake.

Refocusing, she let her robe fall to the floor and began

preparing for the evening ahead and her rendezvous with Omar. She donned black jeans and a fitted dark blouse, then exited the room, bag in hand, leaving no trace of her presence beyond the neatly made bed, just in case.

Ten

As she stepped into the evening, Aya could still taste the lingering citrus of white wine on her lips, but the memory faded as she tied her hair back.

The sky was awash with orange and purple hues as the daytime's baking sun was replaced by radiating heat that rose from the streets and buildings. She navigated quickly, having studied the city map for hours earlier as she pretended to be a local.

The alleyways teemed with vendors hawking everything from rugs to kefta sandwiches. People finishing work for the day carried on animated conversations, and tourists marveled at their surroundings. She moved quickly through the crowd like a shadow, her eyes down but attuned to every detail.

Approaching Djemaa el Fna, the heart of the city, sensory overload threatened her composure. The square had shed its daytime demeanor, transforming under the twilight-soaked sky into something alive, timeless, and pulsing with energy.

Smoke billowed from a hundred food stalls, the scent of grilled meat and spices creating a haze that stung her eyes.

Orange juice vendors competed with their sing-song calls while snake charmers' flutes wove discordant melodies through the din. A circle of onlookers had gathered around a henna artist whose hands moved nimbly across a tourist's palm.

To her left, acrobats formed human pyramids, their bodies glistening with sweat in the lantern light. To her right, a story-teller gestured wildly while playing a three-stringed guembri, his audience hanging on every word of a tale that had probably been told in this square for centuries. The competing sounds—drums, bells, shouting vendors, haggling tourists, bleating goats—created a wall of noise that made tracking any single conver-sation impossible.

It was organized chaos that had functioned by its own rules since medieval times. Every performer, vendor, and hustler knew their role in this nightly theater as Aya tried to blend into a performance that had been rehearsed for generations.

She positioned herself near a stall displaying intricate metal lamps, scanning the throngs of people where her contact had instructed her to be. She noted potential escape routes through the crowd and the locations of onlookers.

"Well, well, well. You're a difficult woman to find. I've seen pickpockets with less grace—no offense, of course. You're far more accomplished than any of those hacks. And you look like you could almost be Moroccan," a voice remarked beside her.

She turned to face a man who had appeared at her side. His dark hair was cut short at the sides and curled slightly on top, as though perpetually tousled by a breeze. A neatly trimmed beard framed a face that blended charm with mischief, and his eyes darted around constantly without ever settling.

"Omar, I presume," she said.

He dressed simply—a linen shirt open at the collar and loose trousers rolled at the ankles—but something about his stance was unsettling, with one hip cocked, making him seem ready at any moment to dance, argue, fight, or run.

He inclined his head and adjusted a leather strap on his wrist, centering it perfectly. "And you must be Aya."

"You're well informed," she replied with a smirk. "And for the record, I am half Moroccan."

"*Smahli, mtsharfin okti!*"

She frowned. "I don't speak Darija, though. First time in the country."

"So you still need me after all." Omar laughed.

"Apparently. Alright, we've met. What's next?"

"Direct. I like that," he said. "Maybe we can talk somewhere more private."

"Lead the way."

Aya followed him, her skepticism tempered by curiosity. His easy charm and surefooted stride betrayed no nerves, but she wasn't about to let her guard down.

After weaving through a series of winding derbs, Omar stopped at a modest wooden door tucked between a pottery shop and a café that overflowed with tables, chairs, and the smell of thick espresso. He produced a brass key from his pocket, unlocking the door with a flourish. "Welcome to my humble workspace," he said, holding the door open for her.

She stepped into the cool interior, eyes adjusting to the low light. The riad was small but meticulously decorated, with a central fountain surrounded by mosaic tiles. A large table stood in the courtyard, its surface cluttered with maps and papers.

"Not bad," she remarked, setting her bag on a bench. "For someone who keeps a low profile."

"I like to think it's functional. Just enough, not too much," Omar said, pouring two glasses of mint tea from a pot he'd prepared before coming to meet Aya. He handed one to her and took a seat across from her.

"Thanks. Let's talk business."

Omar nodded, his manner shifting easily. He gestured to the scattered papers. "Our employer, who prefers anonymity, funds this expedition for one reason: the Amulet of Idris."

"An amulet, of course. Classic," she said, picking up a map. "Tell me everything."

"Some say it was a gift from the Djinn," Omar continued, his voice dropping conspiratorially. "Others claim it was forged by Idris I himself, symbolizing his divine right. It's said to hold secrets."

"And I'm guessing some believe it's cursed?"

Omar's grin widened. "Naturally. Every legend needs a little darkness, and it's steeped in legend. If true, it does truly date to Idris I, founder of the Idrisid dynasty, and is far from mere jewelry. Maybe it's a key to lost knowledge, or something more powerful."

"What kind of power?"

Omar rested an elbow on the table, a playful glint in his eye. "Not that I should lecture a legend in this industry. Word is, you've worked on six continents: an Aztec heist in Mexico, a cursed relic from a Peruvian temple, a lost statuette in Egypt that got your name whispered in black-market circles. Most people never do half that in a lifetime." He offered a wry smile. "I figure someone with your résumé already knows more about retrieving valuables than I can teach."

"Yeah, yeah, yeah. I might have a few ideas. But humor me."

"Sure thing. But, it depends on who you ask," Omar admitted. "Some say the Amulet holds ancient tech, some say alien tech. Others say it reveals the location of the Lost City of the Djinn."

"Real djinn?" Aya asked.

"But of course," Omar said, rocking forward. "The djinn

aren't just bedtime stories; they're woven into the fabric of Morocco's oldest histories, folktales, you name it. Beings of smokeless fire that existed before humans, capable of bending reality itself. Go to the djemma and gather around the old storytellers, you'll see."

He spread a weathered manuscript across the table, pointing to intricate illustrations of swirling, ethereal figures amidst Arabic text. "According to legend, when Idris I fled to Morocco in the 8th century, he didn't just build a dynasty through political savvy. Some legends say he formed a pact with the most powerful djinn in the Atlas Mountains, the beings that had guarded knowledge since before humans even existed."

Omar's finger traced the illuminated image of a medallion at the center of the page. "This Amulet was supposedly forged at the nexus point between our world and theirs, to serve as a key that opens doorways most can't even see. Some accounts claim it allowed Idris to harness energies that powered devices far beyond his time. Hell, beyond ours, probably."

He pulled out another document, this one with faded sketches of strange mechanical devices. "European explorers in the 19th century reported finding remnants of a 'lost city' high in the Atlas. There were structures with no visible means of construction, rooms that defied the laws of physics, and most intriguingly, evidence of what they described as a power source that generated heat and light without consumption."

Omar's voice dropped to barely above a whisper. "Word is, the French colonial authorities seized and classified these reports. But rumors persisted of technology that could harness energy from the djinn's realm itself. Limitless, clean power that would make oil and nuclear energy obsolete overnight. The economic implications alone..." He let the thought hang.

"Anyway, our employer believes the Amulet isn't just a

historical curiosity. It's potentially the most valuable energy technology on earth, hidden for centuries, and they're not the only ones looking for it."

Aya studied his face. "And you? What do you believe?"

"Anything with this much history and myth is worth pursuing," Omar replied. "Treasure, knowledge, or a hefty payday."

She set the map down. "So what's your role? And mine? Why bring me in?"

"I'm good at finding people and making deals. But I'm no expert in retrieval or infiltration," Omar said, patting his stomach with a hearty laugh. "That's where you come in. You've got the reputation—skilled, resourceful, fearless. One of the best."

She sipped her tea, trying to mask her interest. Omar's bombastic style aside, his knowledge of the artifact her father had spent years researching was potentially valuable.

"And this employer? Who are they? Be straight with me."

The banter drained from Omar's face, replaced by a solemn monotone. "I really can't say."

She frowned. "But you trust them?"

"Let's just say I trust their money. Morals optional, payment mandatory. I won't pretend I know their endgame; that's above my pay grade. But their checks clear and they've never crossed me."

She studied Omar, weighing his words against his body language. There was something disarming about him, a charisma that could easily lead one to underestimate his intelligence. But she recognized the sharp calculation behind his casual demeanor.

Despite her wariness, she found herself grudgingly drawn to his straightforwardness about their arrangement. No false pretenses about noble causes or grand ideals, just the simple clarity of a transaction for him.

"I know working for a faceless patron is unnerving," Omar said. "But they pay better than half the governments I've dealt with, and have a lot less oversight. We find the amulet, deliver it, and walk away wealthy. Whatever they do after isn't our problem."

"Unless it comes back to bite us."

He shrugged. "Possible. Reward outweighs risk. And what's life without rolling the dice?"

Aya hesitated.

"Keep glaring like that; it might scare the mosquitoes, and they're driving me crazy this summer," he teased.

She shook her head. "Fine. What's the plan?"

Omar grinned. "Step one? Survive. Step two? Improvise. Step three? Maybe impress you enough to keep me around."

"Can you at least try to be serious?"

"Sure thing, *okti*." He laughed and pulled out a weathered map from the bottom of the pile. "The amulet's rumored to be hidden in a remote part of the Atlas Mountains, near Mount Toubkal. No exact coordinates yet, but an archaeological team is actively digging where scholars think it might be, and I've got my best guide looking into it. Word is, they're already getting close to finding the artifact."

Her brow furrowed. "So we're dealing with professionals. Archaeologists, researchers, possibly hired security."

"Exactly." Omar traced a route with his fingertip. "They're not random explorers; they're organized, well-funded, and definitely not eager for visitors. They'll be on guard."

"Okay. We'll have to slip in unnoticed."

He gave a small shrug, eyes gleaming playfully. "Hence, you being here. This isn't just about a relic in a dusty cave. We have to outsmart a team that knows exactly what it's protecting."

Aya studied the map. "You really think we can find it and blend in enough to gain access?"

"With the right guide." Omar smiled. "Which is where Abdelatif comes in. A scholar, native to the Atlas region, intimately familiar with the terrain, folklore, everything."

"And he's agreed to help?"

"He will," Omar said confidently. "He cares about history. He also cares about money. We just have to be respectful and honest."

Aya smirked. "Respectful? Will that be a problem for you?"

Omar chuckled, leaning back. "Charm isn't a weapon; it's a shield. Sometimes it's the only thing between me and a really bad day."

"Okay, then once we get there?" Aya asked.

"That's your domain, mistress of mischief. Figure out infiltration."

She rolled her eyes but held back a retort. "When do we leave?"

"Two days," Omar said. "Time enough to finalize things and let Abdelatif sort supplies."

Aya nodded, mentally ticking off logistical steps. "I'll need gear."

"I know some places. No tourist traps, I promise."

"The sooner we're prepared, the sooner we can find what we're looking for."

There was an undercurrent of urgency in her voice. Every day that passed was another day Léglise's people might get closer, another day the answers about her father's research remained buried.

He grinned and led her back into the medina, weaving through the alleys, offering a casual hand-on-heart greeting to shopkeepers and passersby.

"You've got quite a network," Aya observed.

"Marrakech is all about who you know. A few favors, a few connections—you can get just about anything from anywhere."

They stopped at a discreet shop, its windows filled with hiking gear, compasses, and tarps. The sign above the door bore no name, just a simple mountain symbol etched in wood.

"Here we are," Omar said, holding the door open. Inside, the air smelled of leather and old parchment.

Behind the counter stood an older man with a lined face and sharp eyes, silver hair making his age impossible to guess, anywhere between forty-five and ninety.

"Omar! Back again so soon?" the man said, his smile warm.

"Hamid, always a pleasure," Omar said, shaking his hand. "I've brought a friend. We're off to the mountains and need the best you've got."

"Anything you need," the man said, looking Aya over with curiosity. "That terrain challenges everyone."

"Precisely why we're here," she said, stepping forward. "I need sturdy boots, weatherproof clothing, a good pack, a reliable knife, basically everything a serious trekker would have going up Toubkal."

After the man had prepared everything, Aya handed over a stack of dirhams in exchange for two large bags of supplies.

"So, anything else before we leave?" she asked.

Omar hesitated, eyes scanning for eavesdroppers. "Not here," he said. "Follow me."

ELEVEN

THE HUSH OUTSIDE felt oddly flat. The derbs that normally teemed with life stood empty of the daytime crowds who'd either gone inside or headed to the square. Behind them, the tapering glow of lantern light faded. Omar said nothing, and Aya found herself listening to the soft scrape of her boots against worn stones as she kept pace.

After the silent walk, they reached a quiet alley that led to a splintered door. Omar pushed it open, revealing a far more modest courtyard with a single table and two chairs.

"I figured we could take a breather," Omar said, gesturing for her to sit.

Aya reluctantly took a seat, posture tense. "Where are we?"

"A place I keep out of the way. Not everyone I do business with knows about it. There's a chance my place is bugged, but definitely not here, so we can talk freely."

Aya nodded. "So, what else haven't you told me? If you're about to claim there's a dragon guarding this thing, I'm out."

Omar laughed, pausing before responding. "It's about the

people who hired us. I'm telling you this because I like you, but you can't repeat any of it. I'm trusting you."

"Deal. We're the ones putting ourselves on the line, so my loyalty's more to you than to anyone else."

"Well, our employers go by 'Aegis' in certain circles. They're a reclusive organization with a keen interest in artifacts like this one. I don't know much more beyond that."

"The Aegis?" Aya put her elbows on the table. "I need more than cryptic names, Omar. What exactly is their interest in the amulet? And why reach out to me specifically?"

"I'm just their charming messenger. I bring packages, smile at the right people, occasionally dodge a knife, and make the right connections. I don't know much else."

Aya raised an eyebrow. "Really? That's all you wanted to tell me?"

"There's one other thing," Omar said, lowering his voice. "They're mysterious enough, but Aegis isn't the only group said to be interested in the amulet."

Her eyes narrowed. "What do you mean?"

"Word travels fast in circles like this. Others may have caught wind of what we're after—competitors, mercenaries, local treasure hunters. The Atlas Mountains are remote, but not impenetrable. And whoever we're up against is huge and powerful. The dig is funded by an organization named HRF, the Heritage Reclamation Foundation, which sponsors digs all over the world. But they appeared overnight, and there are conspiracy theories that they're a front for some powerful people who don't want to be named publicly. Potentially foreign governments."

Aya tried not to react visibly. HRF. The Heritage Reclamation Foundation. The same organization from Léglise's encrypted files. Her mind raced back to the USB drive and the expedition budgets in the millions, the references to U.S. military contractors, the connection to some energy company called PES. It couldn't be a coincidence.

"HRF?" She fought to keep her voice steady, but Omar caught the shift in her tone.

"You've heard of them?"

Aya hesitated, then decided partial honesty might yield more information. "I've... come across the name recently. They're bigger than just archaeological funding, aren't they?"

Omar's eyes sharpened. "What do you know?"

"Enough to know we're not just up against academics and security guards. If HRF is involved, we're talking military-grade operations, possibly government backing." She paused. "Omar, this changes everything. These aren't treasure hunters; this is a major operation with resources we can't match. We're walking into a potential war zone."

Omar paused, contemplating her words. "Hopefully not, but we need to stay sharp. According to Abdelatif, the operation on the ground is indeed huge. Whoever's bankrolling HRF has endless cash, so our best bet is to sneak in, not try to overpower a massive organization. Luckily, our employers hired the best in the business, Aya."

"I get it, but I hate working blind."

"That makes two of us. It's the nature of this game. That's life, though, isn't it? Believe me, I once dated the most beautiful woman in the Maghreb. I was head over heels, and no one could figure out what she saw in me. Neither did I. I knew it'd end terribly, but it was worth it just to be with her for a while. Then, she set my luggage on fire in Casablanca and flew to Dubai, never to be seen again. Point being, I'm willing to lose my favorite leather jacket so long as it's a good enough reward."

Aya laughed and shook her head.

"Anyway," Omar continued, "Abdelatif has connections to keep us as informed as I can be. I've been as upfront as possible, but if there's something you're wondering, now's the time to ask."

"It's all rumors, myths, superstitions. I don't even know what to ask yet, but I know I'm in too deep already to turn back."

Omar held out his hand. "To partnerships forged in distrust."

She took his hand and shook twice, firmly. "To surviving long enough to collect the reward."

She studied Omar, weighing how much to reveal. Perhaps sharing a little might yield more information in return.

"You know, there is something else I want to tell you," she said carefully, "this isn't only about the payday for me."

Omar tilted his head. "No?"

"My father was an archaeologist, Hassan Amrani. Moroccan-born, though he spent most of his career abroad." She paused, studying Omar's reaction. "He had theories about artifacts with unusual properties, particularly in the High Atlas region. Most of his colleagues dismissed them as fantasy. As far as I know, he never actively pursued them."

"Hassan Amrani?" Omar straightened slightly. "Can't say I recognize the name."

"He died years ago." Aya ran a hand through her hair. "Recently, I found references in his journal to something called the 'Idris Flame' and sketches that match other artifacts I've... encountered. I feel like it aligns with a lot of what you've told me about this Amulet of Idris. Too many coincidences for comfort, and I feel like his last work may have been tied to this job somehow."

"Interesting, so the Aegis conveniently contacts you of all people for a job in the exact region your father was researching," Omar said.

"Exactly. I can't help wondering if his death was really an

accident, or if he found something someone wanted to keep hidden." She met Omar's gaze directly. "You've never heard the Aegis mention him? Or anything similar?"

Omar shook his head slowly. "No, but I'm just the middle-man, remember? You'll want to ask Abdelatif, though. This is his area of expertise. Not Aegis, but the histories. What else did your father's notes say about the Idris artifacts?"

"I can't fully understand his notes, and they're partial, but they align with an ancient power source. He was obsessed with finding physical evidence to support legends."

"A man ahead of his time," Omar said. "Or perhaps just able to see what others couldn't."

Aya nodded, surprised at how easily the words had come. She rarely spoke of her father to anyone. "I guess I'm hoping this job might help me understand what he was really onto. And maybe what happened to him, if there's more to the story."

Omar extended his hand across the table again. "Then we have another reason to succeed—the truth."

She grasped his hand firmly, meeting his eyes. "To the truth."

TWELVE

THE FOLLOWING MORNING, Aya stepped out of her riad to meet Omar again. She had no time to savor its oasis of luxury today. Even in the early morning, the city was already awake and thriving, vendors arranging goods and erecting stalls, the air thick with the scent of freshly baked bread.

She turned into a quieter alley, her steps quickening as she glanced over her shoulder. At first, she saw nothing unusual, just people going about their morning routines.

Then she spotted him: a man in a nondescript blue button-down shirt and jeans, hovering near a cart selling olives. His eyes darted away the moment they met hers, but the damage was done. She had made him.

Her lips pressed into a thin line as she turned a corner, weaving through the narrow alleys. She had no idea who he was or what he wanted, but she refused to let anyone follow her unchecked.

Quickening her pace, she navigated through a series of twists and turns, finally slipping into the shadow of an arched doorway.

Aya waited, breathing steadily. Moments later, the man appeared, scanning the area with a frown. His movements were cautious yet deliberate, almost robotic. Military, or police. His gaze swept over her hiding spot without lingering. She stayed perfectly still, fingers brushing the knife at her waist.

Another figure joined him, a woman this time, wearing a long scarf that partially obscured her pale face. The two exchanged hurried words before splitting up, each heading in a different direction.

Aya exhaled slowly, stepping out from her hiding place. Whoever they were, they clearly weren't amateurs. That was hardly reassuring.

Back to the main thoroughfare, she blended into the crowd. If someone was tracking her, either Léglise had found her or she was walking into a competition for the Amulet that had already begun.

She ducked into a ceramics stall displaying abstract shapes and pretended to examine the wares while keeping an eye on the stream of people on the street.

The stall owner handed Aya a small dish, its vibrant green glaze catching the light. "This design is centuries old," he said in a thick accent, pride evident in his voice. "Passed down from the potters of Fez. Each piece is a story, told in clay and fire."

"It's truly beautiful," Aya said and pretended to look closer before she slipped out again when a couple entered the shop, diverting the owner's attention.

She didn't spot either of her tails again, but tension gripped her shoulders. They wouldn't stop after one failed attempt.

She found shade beneath a nearby slipper stall's threadbare canopy, sagging under the hot sun.

Scanning the crowd again, her gaze fell on a group of teenagers jostling near a café. Harmless, she decided, though she couldn't shake the sense of being watched. A man selling carpets met her eyes for a second too long before looking away. A woman in a patterned scarf vanished into the throng just as she turned toward her. Every face seemed a potential threat, every shadow a hiding place.

Back on the move, Aya entered Le Jardin, pushing through a heavy wooden door into an unexpected oasis. The courtyard café sprawled before her like a secret garden. Towering banana trees and bamboo created a canopy overhead. Wrought-iron tables were nestled beneath the foliage.

A server in crisp white guided Aya to a table in the back, partially screened by bird of paradise plants, where Omar waited with orange juice in hand and papers neatly arranged before him.

"Morning!" he greeted with an exaggerated grin. "You look like you've been busy."

"Not by choice," she replied, sliding into the seat across from him. "We need to talk."

"Sounds ominous. What's on your mind?" Omar gestured for the server to bring another glass.

Aya scanned the room before speaking. "I was followed this morning. Two people, working together."

Omar's grin faded, his expression suddenly serious as his eyes darted around even more than usual. "Details?"

"A dark-haired white man in a shirt and jeans, plus a woman in a headscarf whose face I barely saw. They were careful. They knew exactly what they were doing." She glanced toward the entrance.

Omar took a thoughtful sip of his juice. "If others are tracking you, it might just mean they want to scare us off the job. Whatever it is, it's a headache."

"Glad we agree." Aya paused. "What do you know about rival groups?"

Omar rubbed the back of his neck. "There's always

someone sniffing around artifacts like this—treasure hunters, black-market brokers. The Amulet isn't exactly mainstream, but it's famous enough to the right people."

"Or the wrong ones."

"Exactly. I have a few contacts I can tap. They might have intel on who else is operating in the area. Until we know for sure, stay sharp."

Aya eyed him. "Your contacts can be trusted?"

"As much as anyone in this business." Omar's smile returned, if only slightly. "But don't worry, I won't take anything at face value."

Their conversation paused as the server arrived with a fresh glass of juice for her.

"Thanks, Youssef, you're the best," Omar said.

"*La shukran*, Omar. Enjoy," the waiter replied before leaving.

Aya took a sip. "Damn, that's good," she said, setting the glass down. "But I want to be clear about something because this keeps getting more complicated. I need answers about my father's work, but I won't sacrifice our lives for it. If things go sideways, we retreat, regroup, and find another approach."

Omar raised his hands in mock surrender. "Understood. Though the Aya Amrani I've heard of doesn't scare easily, unless you've changed."

"I haven't, but there's more that I need to share," she said, lowering her voice, "there's still the matter of Philippe Léglise."

Omar's brows furrowed. "The name rings bells on the black-market side. Who exactly is he to you?"

"A billionaire collector who funded half my early career," Aya replied, fingers drumming the table edge. "For years, I lifted artifacts to order, and he always paid. Until he didn't. Last week in Paris, he tried to have me killed and ended up with the Crown of the Moabite Queen, which I'd just recovered for him in Jordan."

"Charming fellow," Omar said. "Let me guess, he's tied to HRF?"

"Tightely. I swiped a drive from his office. Budgets, security rosters, references to the Atlas dig we're walking into. Léglise isn't collecting trophies anymore, he's bankrolling whatever the Foundation is really excavating, and he seemed unhinged, talking about supernatural forces."

Omar whistled under his breath. "Complicated, complicated, complicated. So this isn't just a job or even family business for you, it's also a personal vendetta."

"It's justice," she corrected. "If Léglise gets to the Amulet first, I fear the possibilities."

Omar nodded. "Then we make sure he doesn't. Abdelatif will have dossiers tonight. Names, faces, supply routes. We'll outmaneuver the Foundation and your treacherous billionaire in one stroke."

"Good. Because next time Léglise and I meet, only one of us walks away."

Omar reached into his bag, pulling out another folded map. "Well, okay then, let's dive in. Abdelatif finished mapping our route into the mountains. We're meeting him tomorrow, but I wanted to show you first."

He spread the map across the table, pointing to a marked path through the foothills of the Atlas Mountains. "This is our starting point," he explained. "After we park, it's about a day's hike to our first stop, outside a small village where Abdelatif says there's a great vantage point overlooking the valley."

Aya ran her finger along the indicated route. "And after that?"

"We head straight into the mountains. The terrain is rough, and there's no guarantee the locals will be friendly if they suspect trouble. Abdelatif has connections, but there's only so much he can do."

Aya frowned. "And the archaeology site? Any idea what we're dealing with?"

Omar tapped a shaded area on the map. "Three months ago, a local crew uncovered ancient foundations that supposedly predate known Amazigh sites: massive stone blocks with inscriptions no one's deciphered yet. Word got out. Some big investor from HRF swept in with high-tech drilling rigs and armed security for the archaeologists."

Omar shook his head. "They say it's historical preservation, but rumor has it there's something bigger buried there. An artifact rumored to have some kind of power. Now it seems we have teams descending on the area, competing to harness it. That'd be why we were hired and aligns with what I mentioned last night."

A chill prickled Aya's skin. "Well, the wealthy aren't known for ignoring rumors of 'power,' real or not."

"Exactly. Politicians, CEOs, private collectors, you name it. Whatever's up in those mountains, it's turned the Atlas into a magnet."

They fell silent as Omar stood to pay the bill. Aya stared at nothing in particular until a flicker of movement outside caught her eye. A man was loitering on the opposite side of the street, his posture too deliberate to be random. She tensed. He wasn't just passing by.

"Wrap it up, Omar," she said quickly, joining him at the counter.

Omar's eyebrows jumped, but he didn't argue.

Aya angled her body toward the exit. "We're being watched."

Thirteen

Omar turned casually, his eyes clocking the man outside. "Just one?"

"For now," Aya replied. "But let's not stick around to see if he has friends."

The waiter handed Omar his change, confusion evident in his expression. "Everything okay, Omar?"

"*Moshi moshkil,*" Omar said. "Thanks, Youssef."

As Aya described the man tailing her, Omar's smile faltered. He leaned in, voice dropping to a whisper, adopting a tone she hadn't yet heard. "We can't afford any mistakes."

They exited, and Aya led the way down the narrow alley. She kept her pace steady, ears tuned to the sound of footsteps behind them. The loitering man was definitely following, his shadow stretching across the cobblestones.

"Split up," Aya muttered. "He can't follow both of us."

Omar hesitated, then nodded, and she watched his cavalier demeanor morph into sober professionalism. He veered off, disappearing into the crowds. She continued forward, her path deliberate, drawing the pursuer deeper into the medina.

She took a sharp left, the narrow passage closing in with walls of crumbling cement. Overhead, laundry fluttered in the breeze, and the distant noise of the souks echoed off stone. She moved further in. Behind her, the hurried click of footsteps confirmed he was still on her trail.

When she reached a secluded corner amid the ruins of an old riad, she stopped abruptly, her back against the wall.

As her pursuer entered the alley, Aya stepped forward. Once he was near enough, she pivoted sharply around the corner, the glint of her blade catching weak light from above.

"This way's closed," she said coldly, pressing the blade to his throat.

The man froze, hands raised defensively. "I don't want any trouble."

"Who sent you?" Aya demanded.

"I don't know what you're talking about. I'm looking for a restaurant. Kabana."

She pressed the knife closer, drawing a thin line of blood. "Try again."

He hesitated, sweat beading on his forehead. "I was just told to watch you. Nothing else."

"By whom?"

"I don't know," he insisted. "They contacted me through an intermediary. Said you were important. Wanted reports on where you go, who you meet, what you talk about."

She studied his frightened eyes, her knife unwavering. His breathing came in shallow bursts. "Who sent you?" she demanded again.

He winced. "I don't know anything. They're anonymous."

"I need a name. Now." She pressed the blade harder, more blood spotting his neck.

"They're called PES. I don't know anything else, I swear."

Her hand loosened, shock flaring in her chest. PES. The

same acronym she'd seen on Léglise's stolen USB in Paris, linked to secret budgets and the Heritage Reclamation Foundation.

"PES?" she echoed, her voice low and tense.

"I swear, that's all I know."

"And if I don't plan on letting you walk out of here?" she asked quietly. "What then?"

His eyes darted from hers to the blade. "You're not the only one hunting the amulet. That's all I know."

Before she could respond, movement pulled at the periphery of her vision. Out of the corner of her eye, she caught a small figure watching from a second-floor window—a child, wide-eyed and silent, clutching the wooden sill.

Aya's stomach twisted with regret, torn by the child's presence. Her brief hesitation gave the man an opening. He jerked sideways, scooping up a handful of grit from the rubble and flinging it at her face. She recoiled, blinking hard against the sting, her blade lifting defensively.

By the time her vision cleared, the man's footsteps echoed down the far end of the alley. Aya watched him vanish around a corner, swallowed by the medina's winding streets.

She spat dust and cursed under her breath. Looking up at the window again, the child was gone, shutters creaking softly as they closed.

Omar rounded the bend moments later, breathing hard. "What happened? They didn't tail me, so I doubled back."

"Let's go, before anyone else shows up. Someone's following us, and if I'm right, it's the same people who tried to kill me once already."

"Who are they?"

"PES. Don't know much of anything, but tied to Léglise and HRF."

"Okay, I'll dig deeper, but stay alert."

Back at the riad, after she and Omar parted for the day, Aya locked herself in her room, spreading newly acquired maps across the desk alongside her father's notebook. Her phone buzzed, and she picked it up with reluctance.

A new message glowed on the screen: *The mountains aren't the only danger. Watch your back. We're counting on you.*

She stared at the words, her grip tightening. Whoever was sending these messages knew more than they were admitting, but whether they were friend or foe remained a mystery.

Exhaling heavily, she powered off her phone and turned back to the maps. The Atlas Mountains loomed ahead, offering answers and almost certainly more danger.

FOURTEEN

"Abdelatif prefers to keep a low profile," Omar explained the following afternoon as they turned down a narrow passageway lined with crumbling stone walls. "He's not one for crowds."

"Understandable," Aya said. "Given the nature of his work."

They arrived at a modest, unmarked door in an alley that smelled overwhelmingly of cat piss. Omar produced a massive iron key and, after a few tries, managed to fit it into the lock. Slowly, the door creaked open to reveal a dimly lit interior.

Inside, the space hinted at the former glory of what had clearly once been a bohemian café. Faded posters, their edges curled and yellowed, hung askew on the walls, relics of long-ago poetry readings and clandestine debates. A few overstuffed chairs, threadbare at the arms, formed a loose circle around a battered wooden stage. The entire place felt like a hideout where kindred spirits might once have plotted revolutions in hushed tones, dim corners perfect for quiet scheming. It radiated secrecy and solitude, mirroring the man who owned it.

The business might have been in disrepair, but the air was thick with fresh aromas of cardamom and cloves, mingling with the earthy scent of damp stone.

Wooden tables, polished smooth by years of use, were scattered irregularly across mosaic-tiled floors. Intricate lanterns, their brass frames tarnished with age, cast patterns on the ochre walls. In the far corner sat a lone man in a striped gray-and-blue woolen djellaba, his posture relaxed yet attentive.

"Abdelatif," Omar called as they approached.

The man looked up, his dark eyes sharp beneath a furrowed brow. He appeared to be in his early fifties, with a neatly trimmed beard, flecked with gray, and a weathered face.

"Omar," Abdelatif replied, his voice steady, gravelly. His lips twitched into a smile. "You still owe me for the rugs."

Omar grinned, spreading his hands. "And I'll pay you back after this job. Same as last time, remember?"

Abdelatif shook his head, though the warmth in his eyes betrayed their history. He stood to shake Omar's hand, then turned his gaze to Aya.

"And this must be your companion?"

"I'm Aya," she said, introducing herself, and extended her hand.

Abdealtif hesitated briefly, studying her, before accepting the handshake. His hands were rough and calloused. "A pleasure," he said, though his tone remained guarded. "Please, join me."

They settled around the low table, and Abdelatif poured glasses of fragrant mint tea. As he sipped, he continued to appraise her, his eyes assessing every detail.

"Omar speaks highly of you," he began. "But I'd like to hear from you directly. Aya, what brings you to Marrakech?"

She met his gaze without flinching. "I'm here for work," she said plainly.

"Is that all?" he asked.

"Retrieval," she answered. "We're seeking an important artifact in the Atlas Mountains. I'm here to handle the retrieval."

Abdelatif leaned back slightly. "Yes, the artifact," he repeated. "Many have sought treasures in those mountains, often with unfortunate results."

"I'm aware of the risks," Aya said. "And I'm prepared to face them."

Abdealtif took a slow sip of his tea. "Forgive my directness, but what motivates you? Wealth? Fame?"

Aya's mind flashed to her father, his notes resting in her bag, her abandoned archaeology degree, her growing misgivings, how she wanted out.

"I'm here for more than just money," she finally said, reaching into her bag. She pulled out the weathered leather journal, its pages dog-eared and filled with her father's handwriting. "My father was Hassan Amrani, an archaeologist who spent years researching something he called the 'Idris Flame.'"

Abdelatif's eyes widened slightly. "Hassan Amrani? Your father was Moroccan?"

Aya nodded, carefully opening the journal to pages filled with sketches and notes. "I've come to find out what my father was obsessed with—finding evidence of ancient power sources described in Moroccan folklore, mythology, I guess. Based on these notes and sketches, I think that he believed the stories about djinn and supernatural flames weren't just myths, but references to real technologies lost to time."

She turned to a page showing a sketch of a medallion with a falcon design. "He drew this years ago. It's the same symbol I recently saw on artifacts in Jordan. And here," she flipped to another page, "are his notes about the Atlas Mountains and something called 'the Fire Without Smoke.'"

Abdelatif studied the pages. He extended a finger and tapped the page. "These coordinates here... these might match exactly with the site currently being excavated."

"I think so, too," she said. "The organization employing us, Aegis, claims they worked with my father before his death. They say they want to protect the Amulet from misuse. Meanwhile, a man named Philippe Léglise, who recently tried to have me killed, is funding a massive operation in the same area through something called PES and the Heritage Reclamation Foundation."

Omar shifted uncomfortably.

"My father died in a dig collapse in Colombia before he could finish his research," Aya continued. "I've always thought it was an accident, but now I'm not so sure. Too many powerful people are converging on the very site he identified years ago."

She closed the journal. "I need to know what my father discovered, if it did cost him his life, and make sure whatever it is doesn't fall into the wrong hands. If Léglise is willing to kill for it, it can't be just a historical curiosity. Plus, I wouldn't mind getting a little revenge on him. That's why I'm here."

Abdelatif tugged on his beard. "Your father sounds like a good man. A true scholar. And your causes are worthy."

"So you'll help us?" Omar asked.

Abdelatif's gaze hardened slightly. "You support this endeavor, too, Omar?"

"I do," Omar said. "Aya's the best at what she does. With your guidance, we have a real chance of beating the bad guys."

Abdelatif remained silent for another moment, his fingers tracing the patterns on his teacup. "The Atlas Mountains have always been a place of mystery. The Amazigh call them *Idraren Draren*, or 'the Mountains of Mountains.' Some believe they are home to spirits, guardians of treasures hidden in caves so deep they touch the underworld. Entire caravans have vanished, swallowed by shifting sands and narrow passes. Even today, villagers speak of lights in the sky and voices on the wind.

"But these are not merely superstitions," Abdelatif continued, his voice dropping to barely above a whisper. "The Amulet of Idris is not just an archaeological curiosity. If it is what I suspect, what your father suspected, it could be catastrophic in the wrong hands."

He nodded slowly, his eyes intense. "Our ancestors speak of an ancient conflict between humanity and beings they called the djinn, with powers beyond mortal comprehension. The legends tell that Idris I did not just found a dynasty. He saved humanity by binding the most powerful of these entities using an Amulet forged from metals and rock not of this earth. This binding came at a terrible cost. Many lives were lost in the ritual, and the knowledge was sealed away to prevent it from being undone. But the Amulet itself remained, a key that could unleash them once more upon our world."

"You can't seriously believe—" Omar began, but Abdelatif cut him off with a sharp gesture.

"What I believe is that powerful forces are gathering in the mountains, seeking something they do not understand. Whether the legends are literal or metaphorical, the Amulet contains knowledge or power that should not be wielded lightly."

He fixed Aya with a penetrating stare. "I am helping you because I cannot allow the Amulet to fall into the hands of people who see it merely as a source of profit or power. Whatever it truly is, it belongs to history, to be preserved and protected, not exploited. The future of many may depend on keeping certain doors firmly closed."

"And that's precisely why I'm here," Aya said. "Every risk

we take pushes me closer to potentially understanding why my father never came back from his last dig. And to making sure no one twists his research into something monstrous. If this Amulet can answer those questions or stop men like Léglise from weaponizing the past, that's payment enough. The purse is just fuel for the journey."

Abdelatif glanced at her with curious eyes before speaking again. "Very well. Omar, we have a deal, my friend. I will guide you. But be warned: the journey will test more than just your physical endurance. There are ancient stories about these places deep in the mountains, and we must heed them."

He paused, eyes flicking between her and Omar. "I sense this adventure may unearth whatever you bury inside. Your doubts, your greed, your loyalties. If you're not ready to face them, they'll devour you before you see the end."

Abdealtif paused in contemplation.

"We leave at dawn. That gives us time to make final preparations and allows me to gather intel about our route. And since we'll be working together, I should show you this also." Abdelatif pulled out a worn leather folio and set it gently on the table. "My grandfather passed this down. It's a transcription of Amazigh oral traditions, some centuries old. Might be relevant to what we're after."

Aya leaned closer, studying the intricate Tifinagh script interspersed with archaic Arabic. Omar hovered at her shoulder, eyebrows raised. "I can't read much of that," he said.

Abdelatif traced a faded illustration in the margin: a swirl of geometric lines encircling a small, gem-like shape. "They call it *Al-Naar Bila Dukhan,*" he said quietly, "the Fire Without Smoke."

Aya's heart kicked. "Like my father's work."

Abdelatif nodded. "Yes. It is an old legend often told to scare children away from wandering the mountains alone. But these passages describe a sealed chamber deep in the Atlas, rumored to house djinn. It could be just a story, but if billionaires are chasing it, they must believe it's real. It is wise for us to know everything we can."

Omar peered closer. "Looks like an old riddle. Something about 'one eye sees the truth, and one eye sees itself reflected'?" He shrugged.

Aya scanned it carefully, recalling her father's scribbled notes. "It's incomplete. See how it's missing lines? It suggests a certain path or a specific stone to press before entering the corridor. Otherwise..." Her voice trailed off, the implication clear.

Abdelatif tapped the page. "This legend says the corridor is protected by illusions or curses. I used to think it was metaphorical, but perhaps there is real danger."

"Then we'd better figure it out so we don't trigger some ancient trap," Aya said.

"Yes, we will need to be careful." Abdelatif stood, signaling the end of the meeting. "I will make the necessary arrangements and see you at dawn."

Aya and Omar rose as well, following his lead. "Thank you," she said quietly.

Abdelatif nodded. "May wisdom guide our path."

FIFTEEN

As they returned to the bustling streets, Omar exhaled deeply. "Well, that went better than I expected."

"He's cautious," Aya observed. "But he agreed."

"He's skeptical of what they're up to in the mountains and wants to have a say in what happens to any discovery. He values honesty, history, our culture, far more than the stacks of cash we'll pay him," Omar said, echoing Abdelatif's earlier sentiment. "But you made an impression."

Aya glanced at him. "I wasn't trying to impress. Just being straightforward."

"Exactly," Omar said with a signature smirk. "Now, we've got a little time before the mission kicks off. What are you planning to do?"

"I need to ensure my gear is in order," Aya said. "And I'd like to familiarize myself with any available maps of the region, go over the myths again."

"Always thorough," Omar said. "Well, I'll be hitting every nightclub in the city if you care to join. No telling how long this job'll take."

Aya shook her head with a laugh. "I'll pass this time, thanks."

They walked in comfortable silence for a while, the late afternoon sun casting long shadows through the narrow derbs.

"You know," Omar began, "Abdelatif wasn't always so guarded."

"Oh?"

"He used to be more trusting, I remember. But years of seeing outsiders exploit his homeland have made him wary."

"I can't blame him. People often take more than they give."

"But I think he sees something different in you."

Aya raised an eyebrow. "And what's that?"

"A connection, perhaps. An honesty that's rare. I wasn't so straight up with him when I met him."

She shrugged. "I just prefer not to waste time."

"Well, it's working in our favor."

They paused at a corner where their paths diverged.

"Actually," Omar said, "forget the nightclubs. How about we grab a drink later? One last taste of civilization before we're eating camp food and sleeping on rocks."

She studied him, surprised by the shift. "Sure. My riad's terrace at sunset?"

"Perfect. I'll bring the wine."

Back in her room, Aya immersed herself in preparation, meticulously packing her gear, ensuring every item served a purpose, reviewing the maps, and researching the region's lore. She spent an hour poring over her father's notebook again, trying to crack even a single page of the dense cipher. The Ottoman Turkish elements were beyond her expertise, and the Tifinagh modifications were unlike any standard script. Frustration mounted as she realized the depth of the puzzle her father had left behind.

It was as if he'd anticipated that only someone with both

personal knowledge of their shared history and deep archaeological expertise could unravel it. The irony wasn't lost on her. She had one half of the equation, but her choice to abandon academia meant she might be lacking the other.

By the time the sun was setting, she found herself on the riad's terrace. The city sprawled beneath her, its lights beginning to twinkle like scattered jewels against the gathering darkness. A gentle breeze carried distant sounds of music and laughter, and she felt unexpectedly sentimental about leaving the city with no guarantee of returning. She'd seen so little of it.

Omar appeared right on time, two bottles of Château Roslane in his hands. "Plenty more where this came from," he said, offering her a glass.

She accepted it with a nod. "Thanks. Still can't believe you gave up a night of sweaty, crowded nightclubs and deafening DJs to hang out with little old me."

"You know, it's a large price to pay. Let the record show: I, Omar Bakir, traded strobe lights and thumping bass for moonlight and polite conversation with a friend. Someday, archaeologists, maybe the children of the ones we're about to rob, will dig up my biography and marvel at my restraint."

They stood side by side, gazing out over Marrakech.

"Used to run these streets as a kid," Omar said, a note of nostalgia in his voice. "Back when I thought I'd grow up to be something respectable."

Aya raised an eyebrow. "You say that like it's a bad thing."

He gave a rueful chuckle. "I'm getting old. You know, my mother always hoped I'd be a teacher or architect. Something honest. Instead, I broker deals for plunderers and thieves. Pays the bills, but sometimes I wonder if I'm just digging myself deeper in a hole."

"So why keep doing it?"

Omar hesitated, swirling his wine. "Because I'm good at it. And because I haven't figured out how to stop." He nudged her with an elbow. "Some of us are addicted to the thrill, right?"

"Or we're just running from something else," she said quietly, thinking of her own choices.

"Maybe." He studied her profile in the fading light. "But enough about my midlife crisis. You nervous about tomorrow?"

"Not exactly. It's just been a while since I've worked with a team."

Omar smiled. "I can relate. Solo operations have their perks, but teamwork can achieve bigger things."

"Provided everyone is on the same page."

"True. But I have a good feeling about this. Abdelatif is solid. And you and I," Omar said while starting to dance, dramatically shaking his hips, "well, we're starting to find our rhythm."

Aya laughed. "Optimism suits you."

"Someone has to balance out your stoicism."

"Fair enough."

They sipped their wine in companionable silence, watching the last rays of sunlight paint the Atlas Mountains in shades of purple and gold. The peaks looked both majestic and forbidding, holding secrets that had already claimed lives.

"Can I ask you something, Aya?" Omar said eventually.

"Go ahead."

"Your father's research, do you really think there's something supernatural out there? Or is it all just clever archaeology dressed up in legend?"

She considered the question. "A few years ago, I would have said it's all nonsense. Now? I've seen enough glimpses to know that some artifacts defy easy explanation. Whether that's ancient technology we don't understand or something genuinely otherworldly..." She shrugged. "I suppose we'll find out."

"And if it is real? If the djinn stories aren't just stories?"

"Then we make sure whatever power the Amulet holds doesn't fall into the hands of people like Léglise or these corporations. Real or not, they believe it's powerful, and that alone makes them dangerous."

Omar nodded slowly. "You know, most people in our line of work are just in it for the money. But you're refreshing."

"Don't make me out to be noble," Aya warned. "I want revenge on Léglise as much as I want answers about my father. And yes, the money matters too."

"Still, more honest than most." He drained his glass and set it on the railing. "Well, I should let you get some rest. Big day tomorrow."

As he turned to leave, Omar paused. "Aya."

"Yes?"

He hesitated. "It's good to have you on this team. Whatever we find out there, I'm glad we're facing it together."

She met his gaze. "Let's see how you feel after a week in the mountains."

"Challenge accepted."

When dawn broke, Aya was already awake, her gear packed and ready, finishing a double espresso. She dressed in practical attire for the terrain, looking like nothing more than a hiker on a trek. Durable pants, layered shirts, sturdy boots, and a lightweight jacket.

As she tucked her father's journal securely into an inner pocket of her backpack, she paused, running her fingers over the cover. The morning light caught the faded initials H.A. embossed on the spine.

"I'm finally here, Dad," she whispered. "Where you always wanted to bring me."

She flipped to a page near the middle of the notebook, one of the few sections where her father had written a clear note in English: *The Atlas holds what should remain hidden. But if the seals weaken, if the whispers return, someone must know the old ways. I pray you never need this knowledge, but if you do, find someone who can read the languages of conquerors and conquered alike—the key requires both.*

Her throat tightened. Even in his paranoia, he'd been thinking of her, preparing her for something he hoped would never come to pass. Yet the riddle was still no easier to decipher.

"I'll finish what you started," she vowed quietly. "I'll find what you were looking for, and I won't let it be misused. Whatever Léglise and these corporations want it for, even this Aegis, they won't get the chance to exploit it. Not if I can help it. I'll go along for now, but I work for myself."

Securing her backpack, she took a final glance around the room to ensure nothing was left behind. After descending to the courtyard, she found Omar and Abdelatif waiting beside a rugged off-road vehicle with a top exhaust. Omar was adjusting the straps on his pack, while Abdelatif checked over a list on a clipboard.

"Morning," she greeted.

"Right on time," Omar said with a loud clap of his hands.

"Everything in order?" she asked.

"All set," Abdelatif confirmed. "We have sufficient supplies, and the vehicle is in good condition."

Aya nodded. "Then let's not waste any more time."

They loaded their gear, and Omar slid into the driver's seat, with Aya taking the passenger seat and Abdelatif in the back.

"Next stop, mountain life, baby," Omar announced, starting the engine.

As they pulled away from the riad, Aya watched Marrakech recede in the rearview mirror and eventually disappear behind them, swallowed by the vastness of the barren landscape. She gripped the handle above the window, her knuckles white.

Omar drummed his hands on the steering wheel. "Nothing like a road trip to start the day. Ready, team? Who knows a good car game?"

She buckled her seatbelt. "Just drive."

Abdelatif leaned forward. "Remember, the journey ahead will demand much from us all. Stay focused."

"We will," Aya said.

With that, Omar accelerated onto the open road, the vast expanse of the Atlas Mountains beckoning in the distance.

Part Two

SIXTEEN

THEY ROLLED toward the looming peaks etched against the horizon, each kilometer turning the soil redder and the vegetation lusher. Their Jeep's tires kicked up loose rocks as the smooth city streets of Marrakech were replaced by uneven pavement.

Aya's gaze was fixed on the road that clung to the side of the cliffs, offering little room for error. "So these are the Atlas Mountains."

Omar, at the wheel, seemed unfazed, though the occasional tightening of his jaw betrayed his concentration.

"Yup. And next time," he said, his voice cutting through the steady rumble of the engine, "we hire a helicopter. No offense, Abdelatif, but your shortcuts are going to be the end of us."

From the back seat, Abdelatif's voice was calm. "There are no shortcuts in the mountains. Only paths chosen by necessity. You have known me for a long time, Omar. I will not steer you wrong or take you anywhere you cannot handle."

Aya glanced back at Abdelatif. His face was a mask of quiet

focus, scanning the terrain. The man seemed as much a part of the landscape as the mountains themselves, his movements deliberate and unhurried.

"You still come here often?" Aya asked, breaking the silence.

"Yes," Abdelatif replied. "And each time, the mountains feel different. They have a way of shifting, as though alive. The Almoravids understood this. They built their Ribats, part fortress, part place of worship, throughout these mountains in the 11th century, places where their warriors could practice both combat and spiritual disciplines."

Omar glanced in the rearview mirror. "Like warrior-monks? Sounds intense."

"They were," Abdelatif continued. "The Almoravids weren't just the conquerors of the region. They combined Islamic mysticism with much older Amazigh traditions. Some say the binding rituals we speak of, the ones that supposedly control the djinn, evolved from their spiritual warfare techniques. They believed certain places in these mountains were thresholds between worlds."

Aya's interest sharpened. "And the amulet? Could it be connected to their practices? Is that the myth these people are chasing?"

Abdelatif nodded slowly. "It's possible. The Almoravids were known to guard sacred objects, things they believed held the power to control or banish supernatural forces. If the Amulet dates to Idris I, it would have been exactly the kind of artifact they'd protect in their Ribats."

Omar gave a nervous chuckle. "Great, we can add sentient mountains and ancient warrior-monks to the list of worries."

Aya didn't reply. Her attention was drawn to a cluster of buildings in the distance, a small village clinging to the mountainside.

It was nestled against the rocky slope like it had grown there. Most of the houses were built from cinder blocks and sun-dried mud, with uneven paths worn by years of foot traffic. At the center stood a mosque, its white walls gleaming in the fading sunlight, the single minaret rising above the rooftops.

Abdelatif leaned forward. "We will stop here. The people may have seen something. Unusual travelers, signs of activity. Our mission is intertwined with these people's lives. Any changes in their behavior might give us clues to what we are walking into."

"Might this involve more tea?" Omar asked, glancing at Abdelatif in the rearview mirror. "Not that I'm complaining."

Abdelatif flashed a rare grin. "Tea is always called for, but it is the conversations that matter more."

"You think they'll just tell us? We're strangers," Omar said.

"They will talk to me," Abdelatif said simply.

The Jeep rolled to a stop at the edge of the village, their arrival drawing a few curious glances from the people who lined the street. Aya stepped out, adjusting the scarf around her neck as the wind bit into her skin. A group of children watched from a distance, their laughter subdued, as though even play was a cautious act here.

Abdelatif walked ahead, greeting an elderly man seated on a low cinder block wall with a respectful nod and quiet words in Tashelhit. The man's weathered face brightened at the sight of him. Others drifted closer. Everyone exchanged hushed greetings that carried the weight of familiarity.

"They trust him," Aya murmured to Omar, noting how even those who seemed guarded offered Abdelatif a small smile or nod. "He's not just a random guide."

"He's done this sort of thing for years, bridging the gap between researchers and local folks. They respect that he isn't here to exploit them. He's saved entire communities from property developers, advised village leaders on which 'partners' to avoid. He knows big business, but he always kept his roots."

Aya watched as Abdelatif bent down to speak with a young girl clutching her mother's hand. The girl's eyes widened, a tiny flash of awe, before she broke into a shy grin. Abdelatif patted her shoulder, then rose gracefully, continuing his conversation with the elderly man.

"I'd wager the old man's sharing more with Abdel than he'd ever tell us, even for money," Omar said.

From the short distance, Aya could make out Abdelatif's tone, calm and measured.

Omar leaned closer to Aya, keeping his voice low as he struggled to translate. "I only know a little, but it sounds like he's asking about strangers. Armed men who came through recently." Omar paused, listening intently. "The old man says they arrived in black vehicles, maybe six or seven of them, with what looked like guns. Now he's describing how they questioned people about paths leading deeper into the mountains."

Aya nodded, watching Abdelatif as he encouraged the man to continue.

"The old man's worried," Omar continued. "Says they moved like soldiers, but without uniforms. Made people nervous by taking photographs of the village, writing notes." Omar's expression darkened. "He's telling Abdelatif that after they left, some of the younger men in the village wanted to follow them, see what they were really after, but decided against it."

The older man's posture stiffened, eyes darting toward a shuttered window across the lane as he spoke in hushed tones. Aya saw fear etched in the lines of his face.

Soon, the hush of the village seemed to deepen. A door latched shut, and a trio of onlookers retreated behind a stall, pulling its woven mat cover down halfway. Even the children scattered as though sensing an undercurrent of tension.

Moments later, Abdelatif approached Aya and Omar, his expression grim.

"They came here two days ago—armed men in off-road vehicles asking about old trails. The villagers aren't sure what uniforms they wore, only that they spoke English."

"Fantastic," Omar muttered.

"Did they say where they were headed?" Aya asked.

"They were vague, and the English understanding in the village is minimal," Abdelatif said. "But one of the men mentioned ruins farther into the mountains. I'd have to think the same ones we're looking for."

Aya scanned the village again, noting how quickly everyone had retreated indoors. Doors closed quietly, curtains drawn shut, as though their presence had stirred something unwelcome.

She felt a flicker of guilt as Abdelatif nodded to the elderly man one last time, offering a few quiet words before the man walked away, head bowed under the weight of unease.

As dusk settled over the village, Abdelatif gestured for Aya and Omar to follow him behind an old mudbrick dwelling. There, half-buried in the hard-packed earth, stood a weathered stone pillar carved with faint Tifinagh symbols.

Abdelatif ran his fingers over the etched lines. "When I was a boy, my grandfather told me these markings warned travelers not to wander the high passes after dark. Said the djinn would claim their souls."

Omar crouched down, shining a small flashlight. "Creepy. And is that the same swirling falcon shape we keep seeing?"

Aya's pulse kicked. The symbol was indeed reminiscent of the falcon motif from her father's notes, the same swirling lines around a stylized bird. "Looks like it," she said, brushing off a layer of dust. "And here—" She traced another segment of script. "This symbol references some Iron Gate ahead, this symbol refers to The Flame. That "much of my father's work I've figured out.

Abdelatif sighed, shoulders tense. "Legends say if you enter the Iron Gate uninvited, the desert wind itself comes alive. It is to keep children in line."

"Well, maybe it's not just that," Aya said quietly. She shared a look with Omar. Falcon, Idris, swirling script. Everything pointed to a greater connection that she didn't yet understand. And Léglise's men would soon be there, if they weren't already.

Omar stood, lips pressed thin. "So this is another puzzle piece. Let's hope we're faster than PES."

"Yes, for now it is time to go. They had already seen enough strangers this week. My presence reassures them, for a while, but they are fearful. They sense more trouble ahead."

They climbed back into the Jeep, and Aya glanced at the few people who still lingered, half-hidden behind a low adobe wall. Their eyes followed Abdelatif's every move, as though he were their lone lifeline to a world slipping into danger.

SEVENTEEN

THE VILLAGE FADED into the distance behind them, replaced by the vast emptiness of the mountains. The road ahead seemed narrower now, twisting like a serpent through the rugged terrain.

The roar of the engine filled their silence, and even Omar's usual banter was swallowed by the growing shadows of the mountains.

From the back seat, Abdelatif's voice broke the tension. "We'll stop at the next overlook. It's safer to walk the remaining distance. The Jeep won't make it much farther."

The trail widened slightly, and Omar pulled over onto a rocky outcrop. The overlook revealed a valley awash in orange and gold. Aya stepped out of the Jeep, her boots crunching against the gravel. She leaned against the hood.

Abdelatif joined her, his gaze sweeping across the horizon. "This land remembers more than it reveals."

"What's that supposed to mean?" Aya asked.

"These mountains have seen more than we will ever know,"

he said. "Every path, every ruin, carries the weight of millennia. And not all of it is kind."

"Always cryptic and a little terrifying, Abdel."

Omar slammed the Jeep door shut. "Yeah, I hope history likes visitors, because we're about to leave some footprints. Let's go, guys!"

Aya smirked despite herself, grabbing her pack from the Jeep. The group began to redistribute their gear, Abdelatif taking charge. "We'll follow the trail north," he said, pointing to a narrow path that disappeared between two jagged cliffs. "It should lead us to the ruins by tomorrow, if the weather holds and my intel is right."

"And if it doesn't lead us there?" Omar asked, slinging a pack over his shoulder.

Abdelatif's expression was resolute. "Then we adapt."

They set off, the sun dipping lower as they navigated the uneven trail, the wind biting through their layers as the air grew colder.

Aya kept her steps measured, her boots finding purchase on the rocks. The path was unforgiving, flanked by steep drops that seemed to close in the farther they went, though every glance over her shoulder revealed only empty wilderness.

"You feel it too, don't you?" Omar's voice was hollow.

Aya nodded. "It's too quiet."

The trail wound through a narrow pass, rock walls towering like ancient spines. The shadows grew longer, light dimming to a muted gray. Abdelatif stopped suddenly, raising a hand for silence.

Aya froze, her fingers brushing the hilt of her knife. "What is it?"

"Tracks," Abdelatif said, crouching to examine the ground. "Fresh. Only one, maybe two people. They passed through here recently."

"The people they warned us about in the village?" Omar asked.

"Unlikely. That was a larger group," Abdelatif said. "Whoever it is, they're moving fast, but I can't tell which direction they went."

Aya scanned the cliffs, her instincts screaming at her to keep moving. "We need to pick up the pace. If they're ahead of us, they might already be at the ruins."

Abdelatif nodded. "Stay close. It becomes more difficult from here."

They pressed on, their pace quickening as the last light of day bled from the sky. Aya's muscles began to ache, but she forced herself to keep going.

By the time they reached a small clearing sheltered by a cluster of boulders and a few walnut trees, night had fully fallen. Abdelatif dropped his pack with a quiet grunt, his breath visible in the frigid air. "We camp here. It is exposed, yes, but the higher ground gives us an advantage. No one can approach without us seeing them first."

"Not exactly a Sofitel," Omar said, setting his pack and jugs of water down. "But I'm happy with it; we definitely won't roll off the side."

As they set up camp, the oppressive silence of the mountains pressed in once more.

THEIR CAMPFIRE'S flames were soon flickering against the surrounding rocks. The warmth was a welcome reprieve from the biting cold of the mountain air, but it did little to ease the tension that hung heavy in the clearing. Aya sat cross-legged near the fire, sharpening her knife with slow, deliberate strokes, her gaze darting occasionally to the shadows beyond the camp.

Omar leaned against a boulder, his usual bravado subdued. He stared into the fire, swirling a tin mug of tea. "You know," he said, breaking the silence, "after we complete this job, we could actually open a Sofitel here. Five more of them anywhere we wanted, too."

Aya didn't look up. "Daydreaming about champagne and hot tubs?"

"Yeah, something like that," Omar muttered. "Less frostbite, at least."

Abdelatif, seated on a flat stone, tended to a simmering pot balanced over the fire. His face was illuminated by the flickering light, his expression calm but distant. He stirred with a wooden spoon, the rhythmic motion hypnotic.

"You have both spent too much time in cities," Abdelatif said.

Aya paused her sharpening. "You've been quiet, Abdel. What's on your mind?"

Abdelatif set the spoon down and leaned back slightly, his eyes fixed on the fire. "I am thinking about our role in all of this. What story we are contributing to. What we will leave behind."

"Practical, actionable input as ever," Omar said, taking a sip of his tea.

Abdelatif ignored him. "Have either of you considered what you will do when we find the artifact?"

Aya stared into the flames, her father's journal heavy in her pack. "That's... complicated," she said finally. "I used to think it was simple. Find it, deliver it, get paid. But now I'm not so sure who I can trust."

"Hello, the Aegis?" Omar asked. "Come on, our employer offering untold riches?"

"They claim they worked with my father years ago, that they want to protect the Amulet from misuse. But after what happened with Léglise..." She trailed off, remembering the betrayal in Paris. "People lie about their intentions when this much power is at stake."

"What did your father believe about the amulet's true nature?" Abdelatif asked.

Aya pulled out Hassan's journal, opening it to pages filled with his careful sketches and notes. "I'm not completely sure, but he believed the legends weren't just folklore, that there was real technology involved, something that could harness energy in ways we don't understand." She traced one of his drawings with her finger. "It doesn't seem real, but maybe there's a scientific explanation for something this powerful."

Abdelatif nodded slowly. "And such power, if the stories are true, could unleash terrible evils..."

"Could reshape global politics overnight," Aya finished.

The fire crackled in the silence that followed.

Omar rested a hand on Aya's shoulder. "So what do we do? If the Amulet is what your father thought it was? If it actually has some crazy powers?"

Aya closed the journal. "We make sure it doesn't fall into the wrong hands. Even if that means going against our employers, this Aegis." She looked at each of them. "My father spent his life trying to preserve history, to protect it from exploitation, and I've taken another path, but it's time for a change. I won't let his research, possibly his death, be for nothing."

Abdelatif smiled. "Your father would be proud. The stories say these mountains remember the last time someone tried to claim that power. Entire civilizations rose and fell. The earth itself was scarred."

Omar poked at the fire with a stick. "So if we're journeying into the realm of mythology, we're not just racing other treasure hunters. We're trying to prevent the end of the world?"

"Perhaps," Abdelatif said solemnly. "Or perhaps the legends are just morality tales meant to keep the greedy away. But given what your father discovered, Aya, and the resources being spent to find it..."

"Better to assume the worst and be wrong than the other way around," Aya finished.

As Abdelatif ladled stew into small bowls and passed them around, the rich, spiced aroma filled the air. However, the weight of their conversation had settled over the camp like a shroud, and even the warmth of the food couldn't dispel the chill of what lay ahead.

Omar broke the quiet. "You guys ever wonder if some things are better left buried? Left unexplored?"

"All the time," Aya said. "But that doesn't stop people from digging."

Omar shook his head, leaning back against the boulder. "Well, here's hoping we win this one. Even if the flame is only half real, the leverage is real enough."

EIGHTEEN

LATER THAT NIGHT, beneath a sky bursting with stars, Aya sat near the warmth of the campfire, her thoughts drifting like sparks into the darkness. Beside her, Abdelatif was attempting to read his brittle volumes, squinting in the low light from the fire.

"You're certain about these ruins we'll be exploring, Abdel?" Aya asked. "We're in the right spot?"

He nodded. "As certain as one can be. Old stories, old warnings. New activity, new threats. We are in the right place, and we must be careful."

Aya let the crackle of flames fill the silence for a moment. "Sometimes caution isn't enough."

"You speak again of your father?"

"I wish he could be here to see this, but I don't know what he'd think of who I've become. I—" Her voice faltered. She almost told Abdelatif the rest. How money and cynicism had replaced her youthful idealism and curiosity. Instead, she forced a soft laugh. "I guess I strayed from a path that would have made him proud."

Abdelatif placed a gentle hand on her shoulder. "Sometimes, the path we choose is the only way to survive. Perhaps your father would understand more than you think."

Aya's gaze drifted to the embers swirling upward. She thought of the tombs she'd robbed, the relics she'd sold, the stolen Jordanian crown. *Maybe he'd forgive me. Maybe not.*

She cleared her throat. "In any case, thanks for trusting me to join you. I won't let you down; we'll get that Amulet."

Abdelatif merely offered a calm nod, returning to his reading.

The weight of Aya's thoughts grew too heavy to bear in company. After a few more minutes, she rose quietly, needing space to breathe, to think. The camp felt suddenly claustrophobic.

She walked a short distance, her boots crunching softly against the rocky ground. The clearing opened to a ledge overlooking the valley they'd climbed earlier. The darkness below swallowed all but the faintest outlines of the landscape. She breathed deeply, the cold air sharp in her lungs, and let her thoughts churn.

The artifact. The djinn. The armed men. The mysterious employer. Each piece of the puzzle seemed larger than the last, the stakes growing with every new revelation.

"Aya."

She turned to see Abdelatif approaching, his movements quiet but deliberate. He stopped a few paces away, his silhouette framed by the faint glow of the camp behind him.

"Not ready for sleep?" she asked.

Abdelatif shook his head. "Restless minds."

"And what's keeping yours restless?"

He hesitated, his gaze drifting to the valley below. "The story I told you earlier—it is not the entire truth."

She crossed her arms, her stance shifting. "I'm listening."

Abdelatif sighed, his breath visible in the cold air. "The artifact's power in the myth... it is also said to be a lure, a dangerous lure. Once unearthed, it calls to those who seek it, whether they realize it or not. I believe that is why many have come to these mountains, and why so few have returned."

"A lure? Why didn't you mention this before?"

"Because I hoped it would not matter. These are stories, after all. But the signs are here and growing stronger since ground was broken at this site three months ago. The armed men, the unease in the villages, the whispers that travel faster than we do. The artifact's influence is spreading. More will come."

"You think it's drawing people to it? Like a beacon?"

"Yes. And the closer we get, the stronger its pull will become. That is why we must tread carefully."

Before Aya could respond, a faint sound reached her ears. A distant clatter of something jarring stones loose. Abdelatif stiffened.

"Did you hear that?" she whispered.

"Yes. We are not alone."

Aya moved quickly, signaling for Omar to extinguish the remaining embers of the fire.

The three of them gathered in the shadows, their breaths shallow as they listened. The sound came again, closer this time, a soft shuffle of movement just beyond the clearing.

Omar's hand drifted to the pistol at his side. "Please be just a mountain goat," he whispered.

Aya shook her head. "Too deliberate. Whoever it is, they're trying to stay quiet."

A flicker of movement above.

Aya's gaze snapped upward, locking onto the figure cutting across the ridge. They moved with deliberate fluidity, every shift of weight silent against the jagged terrain.

It wasn't just the way they walked—it was the posture, the unmistakable tension in the shoulders. A woman forged by survival. It was unmistakable.

Amina.

Aya tracked her smooth strides directly toward their camp and watched Amina pause at the crest of the ridge, crouching low, eyes sweeping over their distant camp nestled below. The wind teased strands of her dark hair. Aya's ex wasn't just observing. She was mapping every angle, every escape route.

The last time she saw Amina, truly saw the Amina before things started to come apart, was two years ago on the rooftop terrace of their apartment in Sofia. They had laughed under the stars, wine bottles littering the tiled floor around them, their latest score tucked safely away. The heist had been flawless, like so many before it.

Then there was Egypt and a different Amina, not the one she had grown to love. The sand, the gunfire. A job weeks in the making, and Amina vanishing into the night, leaving her bloodied and empty-handed.

But the memories that surfaced first weren't of betrayal. They were of softer things. Of long afternoons on the beaches of Mauritius, her skin warm against Amina's under the sun, where they hid from the world after a job in Ethiopia. Of stolen glances over maps, plotting their next move from basements in Hong Kong. Of their villa in Phuket, when they'd made love beside the infinity pool, the Andaman Sea stretching endlessly below them, both high on adrenaline and each other.

Aya blinked the images away and pressed her back against the rock wall, out of sight, exhaling slowly as if she could breathe out the memory clawing its way to the surface. She hadn't expected to see Amina again. Especially not here, not like this.

She thought about telling Omar, about alerting Abdelatif.

If Amina was after the same artifact, they were on a collision course.

But the words never came.

Aya didn't need Omar's smirk or Abdelatif's skepticism. She could already hear it: *An ex-lover trailing us through the mountains? How poetic.* No. She would handle this herself. Amina wasn't one to sound alarms. If she were here, she'd slip in like a ghost. There would be no gunfire, no chase. Not yet, until Amina wanted it.

"There," Omar whispered. "I saw movement again."

"Yes," Abdelatif said. "Could be a scout. If they spot us, they'll alert the entire camp."

Aya bit her tongue, resisting the urge to correct them. This wasn't a mercenary sniffing around for intruders, this was a professional who knew the game as well as she did. But she couldn't say that.

"Maybe," she offered. "Let's not jump to conclusions."

Omar frowned. "Jump to conclusions? This isn't a campfire story. If we don't take this seriously, we'll be dead by morning."

Abdelatif glanced at her, his brow furrowing slightly. "No, she is right. We stay quiet, move to a new location, and avoid contact. If it is a scout, they will pass through, and hopefully think we are just locals camping far from them."

Aya nodded. Amina was already gone from the ridge, but her presence lingered.

Omar cursed under his breath. "Great. So much for a quiet night."

Aya stood. "We pack up and move. Now. And Omar, pass me a handgun. My knife won't help if this happens again."

The three of them moved quickly, gathering their gear and extinguishing all traces of their camp.

Nineteen

They pressed on through the night, each step a battle against loose gravel in the moonlight. Aya's calves burned as she and Omar followed Abdelatif along a route chosen for secrecy over comfort.

But her mind was elsewhere. Amina was out there, somewhere in the same mountains, following a similar path. The calm, deliberate way she'd moved along the ridge replayed in the darkness. Aya knew the playbook. She would slip into the camp unnoticed, hide, and take what she came for before anyone realized she'd been there.

"You good back there?" Omar's voice cut through her thoughts.

"Yeah, just watching our backs."

He grinned. "Leave the paranoia to me. You're supposed to be the calm one."

They wove through stunted juniper and half-buried boulders, pausing only twice—once to catch their breath, and once to settle Omar's whispered disagreement over their direction. Neither pause lasted more than a minute.

Finally, in the palest light before dawn, they reached the ridge Abdelatif had promised. Aya could see why he'd chosen it. The land fell away sharply, providing a natural vantage point over the valley below while offering them nearly complete concealment. A few shrubs and low stones offered concealment, and the biting wind funneled through the pass to obscure any errant noise. Best of all, it gave them a clear line of sight.

She crouched behind a cluster of angular rocks, each wedged as if torn from the earth by ancient tremors. Her thighs protested after the long trek through the night, but she ignored the ache. Omar settled beside her, wincing, and Abdelatif joined moments later with no sign of fatigue.

Abdelatif studied Aya's face for a moment, his eyes narrowing slightly as if looking through her. "You carry *baraka*," he said quietly, almost to himself.

Aya frowned. "Baraka? I know the Arabic word, but what are you talking about?"

"It is an old Amazigh-Islamic concept," Abdelatif explained, his voice barely above a whisper. "Some people are born with a connection to the unseen realms. Spirituality, mythology, call it what you like. It runs in bloodlines, passed from parent to child. Your father's journal mentions studying Almoravid spiritual warfare techniques—those warrior-monks, as Omar called them, understood that certain individuals could channel forces others couldn't even perceive. I believe your father may have carried this gift, and now you do. It protects you, Aya. I sensed it when we first met in Marrakech, but here in these mountains, near the old places, it's unmistakable."

Aya absorbed his words, feeling skeptical but oddly comforted by the idea that her father's legacy might somehow protect her. She'd always dismissed such concepts as superstition, but after everything she'd witnessed, maybe there was more to the old beliefs than she'd realized.

"Whether it's baraka or just luck," she said quietly, "I'll take whatever protection I can get."

Even as she talked to Abdelatif in the dim light, she could spot the faint outlines of tents and equipment below. Her target.

Behind her, Omar shifted, wincing slightly as gravel beneath his boots skidded. "I guess that's the site," he whispered. "Doesn't look like the fortress we were warned about."

"We would still be wise not to underestimate the powers behind this," Abdelatif said. "We approach Sidi Chamharouch's domain, "the king of the djinn. Pilgrims come to this mountain to ask his advice, to be cured, to be reborn."

Aya nodded. No matter the mythical underpinning, she was relieved it wasn't a fortress, but a barbed-wire fence that encircled the entire dig, with only a couple of small guard stations near a makeshift gate. Floodlights illuminated every shadow, while the hum of a diesel generator echoed off the canyon walls.

A glimmer of movement on a ridge opposite them caught her eye. Her heart thumped as she recalled the lithe figure she'd glimpsed the night before. She narrowed her gaze, but there was nothing. *I need to get some real sleep,* she thought.

"What was it?" Omar asked, his brow creasing.

"Nothing. Just my nerves," Aya said. She wouldn't mention Amina to Omar or Abdelatif, not yet. One problem at a time.

Abdelatif lifted a pair of small binoculars to his eyes, surveying the fence line. "I see about four guards, possibly local hires or small-time contractors. The real military presence we've been warned about, if it's coming, must not be here yet."

Aya turned to them. "I'll go in posing as a grad student, as we discussed. I should be able to talk my way through. You two watch from this vantage point. If everything goes sideways, I'll signal."

Omar squeezed her shoulder lightly. "You sure about this? You don't want a bit of rest? The plan depends on you staying inside for a while, gathering intel. Meaning no reinforcements from us until you slip back out."

Omar paused, then added, "How long do you think you'll need?"

"Honestly? Could be days, could be weeks. Depends on how suspicious they are and how quickly I can build trust. You have enough supplies?"

Abdellatif gestured to the small cache they'd hauled. "Water for three weeks between here and what's left in the Jeep, maybe four if we're careful. Dried meat, dates, canned goods."

"And we'll rotate between three observation points," Omar added, pointing to the ridgelines. "Never the same spot two nights in a row. If this takes more than a month, we'll have to make a supply run to the village."

Aya studied their faces. "This might be incredibly boring for you both. Weeks of just... waiting."

"Our task is the easy one, don't worry about us," Omar said with a grim smile. "Besides, someone needs to document their patrol patterns from the outside. Might spot something useful."

Aya nodded. "We can't make a successful play for the Amulet until I confirm how close they are to the sealed corridor and what they have planned to reach the artifact. I need to determine what they know, or believe, about it. Also, if I can find a sympathetic archaeologist, I might get more specific details about the artifact's location or the site layout." She paused. "Don't worry, I've handled worse."

Concern lingered behind Omar's eyes. "All right, infiltration queen. Godspeed."

Abdelatif bowed his head in silent prayer, his lips moving soundlessly. When he looked up again, he met her gaze with calm intensity. "The legends around this sealed chamber are not to be taken lightly. If you see any sign of them forcing it open, try to delay. We do not want a catastrophe, either historical or supernatural."

"I'll do what I can."

Without another word, Aya began her descent, moving carefully over the loose rocks. Each breath of cool morning air tightened her chest as she neared the fence. She wore a plain cargo jacket, sturdy boots, and a battered backpack filled with minimal gear and a few personal items. She could pass for a lone traveler.

The closer she got, the more details she observed. Several large crates labeled HERITAGE RECLAMATION FOUNDATION lined one side of the camp, near a pair of parked Jeeps. A small cluster of workers, clad in jeans and T-shirts, lugged equipment around.

At the makeshift gate, a single guard in khaki fatigues carrying a sidearm paced idly. He looked up as she approached. "*Arrêtez*," he called. "Who are you?"

Aya coughed, letting a hint of nervousness color her tone. "Apologies, I—I'm a graduate student at Al Akhawayn University, studying the history of the region. I'm on break, so I thought I'd do some hiking and experience it firsthand. I took the wrong trail and spent the night in the mountains, and ended up... well, here. I guess I don't know what I'm doing. Can you help me?"

He frowned. "This site is restricted. You shouldn't be anywhere near it."

Aya offered a timid smile. "I get it, I'm sorry. I heard

rumors about a big dig out here and thought I could find help." She forced a sheepish shrug. "Could I maybe talk to whoever's in charge? I don't know how to get back, and I'd hate to wander these mountains alone much longer. It's so... exposed out here."

The guard's features tightened, but his gaze flicked over her before he pulled out his radio and mumbled into it. She caught only fragments: "Some girl... says she's from Ifrane... university student, lost... no, no sign of weapon."

Finally, he lowered the device. "All right. Come inside. Dr. Haddad can handle you. But don't wander. Follow me."

Three weeks, Omar had said. They'd brought enough supplies for a month if needed. Dried food, water purification tablets, and camouflage netting for their camp.

"Take whatever time you need to do this right," Abdellatif had insisted. "We know how to wait." She hoped they wouldn't need that long.

TWENTY

A‌YA SLIPPED through the open gap in the fence and swiftly took in the interior of the dig site. Battered tents in loose rows, piles of wooden crates, and metal storage containers dotted the open space, while two large excavators loomed near the center, silent for now. Diesel fuel mingled with turned earth in the cool air.

So far, so good, she thought, her heart hammering.

"Dr. Haddad," the guard called to a slim man crouched over a table scattered with pottery shards. "She's a student at Al Akhawayn. Says she's been researching the area but got lost hiking. For now, she's your problem. We can get her on the supply run back to town if needed, but that's not for another three days."

Dr. Haddad straightened and quickly removed his dusty gloves. In an instant, she sized him up: early thirties with dark, earnest eyes, hair curling at his forehead. A faint smudge of dirt traced one cheekbone. "Right, I'm Karim Haddad, and you?"

Aya was taken aback by his subtle, assessing gaze that swept over her. He looked at her intently, with no bashfulness, as if he were trying to solve her like a newly unearthed artifact.

"Aya," she replied, offering a quick handshake while keeping her eyes steady on his. "I'm a grad student studying North African history, especially anything Amazigh or early Islamic. I, uh, might have gone off-trail, hoping to find something interesting. Guess I found you."

Karim's eyes narrowed. "So you accidentally stumbled onto a dig that, by pure coincidence, matches your thesis work?"

She managed a sheepish laugh. "I know it sounds too perfect, and maybe I'd been tracking rumored sites in the Atlas for a couple of weeks, looking for some inspiration."

"So you weren't just a lost hiker, as you told the guard?" Karim asked, arching a brow.

"I was desperate," Aya lied, scrunching her shoulders. "My advisor approved a month-long field study for my thesis, but all the official sites were either closed for the season or fully staffed. Then I heard whispers about an exclusive dig out here, some major discovery. I thought, what if I just show up and see if they'd let me stay? Even a few weeks of observation would save my research. Granted, it was a gamble, hiking out here alone."

A glimmer of amusement tugged at Karim's eyes. "A gamble indeed. You're lucky you didn't freeze to death out here. We're about two hours from the nearest town." He cast a sidelong glance at the guard, who was wandering off.

"All right," Karim continued, "let me figure out what to do with you."

They stood in awkward silence for a moment while Karim appraised, and the camp's bustle filled the space.

"Karim, when are you expecting Dr. Yazami back?" a voice called from across the site.

"Not for at least three weeks," Karim called back. "He's presenting at the conference in Oslo, then New York?" He turned back to Aya, studying her with his assessing eyes. "As you heard, our senior archaeologist is away, which means I'm managing the analysis tent alone. We're in a critical phase, racing to document everything before..." He trailed off, jaw tightening.

Aya absorbed his gaze, the sunlight catching the faint copper tint in his hair, feeling an unwelcome stir of attraction. She tightened her grip on her backpack strap, forcing herself to blink away the thought. This wasn't the time or place.

Karim cleared his throat. "Look, I can't promise you a warm welcome, but I guess we can't just toss you out of camp without supplies or a ride. If you want to help, maybe I can show you a few things."

"I'll be on my best behavior," she said with a playful smile, "especially if it means learning from the best. Just promise not to make me carry all the heavy equipment."

"All right, Aya. Just stick close to me, keep your head down, and don't get in anyone's way—people are tense around here. If you can do that, you might be a real help and get to jump into some actual fieldwork."

Her heart quickened from the success of the initial approach and from the unexpected draw of his calm authority. "Thank you. This... this means a lot. Really."

"Come on. I'll show you what we're working on."

They walked side-by-side across the dusty ground. Part of Aya wanted to pepper him with questions about the corridor and artifact, but she knew not to press too hard so early. Instead, she studied the site, taking in every detail.

She spotted groups of laborers carefully lifting plastic-wrapped stone fragments from shallow trenches. Stacks of half-labeled crates lined an improvised pathway, some with partial shipping addresses, others bearing only large HRF lettering. A forklift idled near a cluster of steel rods and coiled wires, presumably for reinforcing the deeper excavation. It was all state-of-the-art.

Karim paused by a roped-off area beneath a large tarp. Aya glimpsed a mosaic in the process of being excavated. Blue and white tiles formed ornate geometric shapes, chipped in places yet still striking.

He crouched, beckoning her closer. "We think this mosaic might date back at least a millennium—possibly from Idrisid influence, though we can't confirm yet. What's fascinating is these geometric patterns. See the eight-pointed stars and interlocking hexagons? They're almost identical to the protective symbols found in the Sa'adi Tombs in Marrakech. The Sa'adi sultans were buried with these specific patterns to ensure spiritual protection in the afterlife."

"The Sa'adi tombs?" Aya asked. "The ones that were sealed for centuries?"

"Exactly," Karim said, speaking faster. "They were only rediscovered in 1917. Hidden and forgotten, just like this site. The Sa'adi dynasty believed these geometric configurations had power, that they could protect against evil forces. If we're seeing the same patterns here, it suggests this site had similar significance, perhaps as a burial ground or a place of spiritual importance."

He gestured to one of the patterns with his finger, careful not to touch the ancient tilework. "Normally, we'd painstakingly remove the surrounding sediment to preserve the site context, but the sponsor is pushing us to move forward in search of a deeper structure. We're trying to protect what we can."

Aya feigned wide-eyed curiosity. "But if it's so delicate, won't heavy equipment destroy it?"

Karim sighed. "Exactly. I've tried to reason with them, but they keep muttering about progress and how much they're investing in results. It's irreconcilable." He scoffed. "Frankly, I'm surprised you found us, but I guess word travels even about unpublicized sites. HRF doesn't want official oversight, but they can't hide the trucks and equipment forever. They're planning something big. The president of the foundation himself is supposed to arrive in a few weeks for what they're calling 'the final phase.' Whatever that means."

"Well, I'm glad someone's at least trying to preserve it. My father was big on that; he was an archaeologist too," Aya added softly, letting a pang of real emotion color her words.

"Oh, really?"

"He always reminded me that every piece of pottery or stone he worked on had a voice and that we, as students of history and their descendants, owed them respect and should listen to them."

Karim's expression softened. "He sounds like an incredible man."

Aya nodded.

Something about his careful attention to the mosaic, the way he spoke about history with genuine reverence, reminded Aya uncomfortably of her past life. She caught herself studying the determined set of his jaw as he pointed out details in the tilework, the way his hands moved with practiced gentleness over the ancient stones.

And here she was, lying through her teeth to him.

The realization pressed on her like a weight on her sternum, yet the pull was undeniable. She wanted to stay close, to feel his rare sincerity in her world of thieves and fences.

"Anyway," Karim said, "if you want to help today, I could have you brush off some smaller finds. Just be mindful. Some of the sponsors' representatives are suspicious of everyone. They won't think you're a threat, but they might ask questions and run you off."

She smiled. "I promised not to cause trouble."

As they walked toward the analysis tent, Karim gestured to the various workstations. "Most of the team works on two-week rotations. On-site for fourteen days, then a week back in Marrakech. Helps prevent burnout in these conditions. Since you're here for... how long did you say your field study was approved for?"

"Four weeks," Aya said, matching his pace. "Though I'm flexible if the work requires it."

"Four weeks," he repeated thoughtfully. "That's actually perfect timing. We're expecting to reach the entrance to the sealed corridor within that timeframe, and I could use someone with fresh eyes on the inscriptions we've been finding. Your Amazigh studies background might be helpful." He paused, giving her a sidelong glance. "Assuming you're serious about the work and not just here for adventure stories."

"I'm serious," Aya assured him, and found she meant it more than she'd intended. "Whatever you need documented, translated, or analyzed—I'm here to help."

"Good. Because once we start the deep excavation, things will move fast. The sponsors are impatient, but if we can properly document everything before they break through..." Karim shook his head. "Well, at least we'll have done our duty to history."

TWENTY-ONE

Karim led her toward a row of battered tables where dirt-covered tiles, pottery shards, and corroded metal lumps awaited cataloging.

"Here," he said, handing her a pair of gloves and a soft brush.

He gestured to the artifacts spread across the table: pottery shards, corroded metal fragments, bits of tile. "These are from the upper levels, nothing too sensitive. The really significant finds..." He paused, glancing around the camp before lowering his voice. "Well, let's just say the sponsors have very specific ideas about who gets to handle what. They've restricted access to anything from the deeper excavation levels."

He shook his head. "I can't even show you the inscribed stones we found near the sealed area. They've been locked away in a secure container since yesterday. The HRF representatives insist on 'chain-of-custody protocols' for anything that might be connected to the main discovery."

Picking up a pottery fragment, Karim turned it over in his hands. "So we're stuck cataloging surface finds while the bigger

155

archaeology gets treated like... like corporate assets." He set the shard down. "But these pieces still matter. Every fragment tells part of the story, even if it's not the chapter they're most interested in. If you see anything delicate, set it aside and call me. Meanwhile, I have to check on the next trench. They keep opening new squares like it's a race."

"I'm sorry, that all sounds difficult to work with, Karim. But I can handle this," Aya said, tucking a stray strand of dark hair behind her ear.

His gaze held hers for a moment too long. He quickly glanced downward and stepped back. "All right, I'll be close by if you need me. And... thanks."

"For what?"

Karim offered a faint smile. "For caring about how things are going here."

Before Aya could reply, a voice crackled from a walkie-talkie: "Karim, get to Grid Two. Something's about to partially collapse." He gave her an apologetic nod. "Be right back," he murmured, grabbing the device and striding off.

Left alone, Aya surveyed her surroundings. A few yards away, a cluster of official-looking men in crisp shirts conferred with two foremen. Their voices were hushed, and as she moved around the table, she caught snatches of conversation:

"We can't wait on Dr. Haddad's precious methodology. The deeper corridor is the priority—"

"—but the mosaic—"

"Mosaics don't pay the bills—Léglise expects real results from that sealed chamber; he might show up himself."

A chill pricked her skin at the name, conjuring images of his smooth, cultured façade and the predatory glint in his eyes. Fury flared, followed by a bitter taste of betrayal. Her assumptions, based on the USB file names, were correct. He was funneling money to the Heritage Reclamation Foundation from PES as a cover for whatever he intended to use this artifact for.

Aya swallowed a surge of anger and continued her reconnaissance.

Across the tent, a handful of dusty archaeologists stood huddled around a plastic table and a Nespresso machine. Their posture radiated quiet resentment, as if they'd been forcibly conscripted into a reckless mission. These were the real experts, she thought. The tension between the two factions was almost palpable, the suits pushing for speed and the archaeologists exchanging worried glances.

Her skin prickled as she recognized how precarious this arrangement was. One spark, and everything could collapse, including, perhaps, the corridor itself.

She turned back to the table where she'd been assigned to brush off fragments. For the next hour, she worked methodically, using gentle strokes to clear dust from shards of pottery. Her mind churned with the plan—to determine exactly how soon they'd break open the corridor, what their plans were to do so, relay the info to Omar, sabotage their progress if necessary, and make a play for the artifact. She clenched her fist around the brush handle. *Don't get soft, Aya.*

A warm voice broke her reverie. "You okay?" Karim asked.

Aya forced a small laugh. "Yeah. Just got lost in thought." She hesitated. "How's the collapse?"

He shrugged. "We need to shore up that area with metal beams, but the sponsor's rep is complaining about the cost since it isn't the main focus of the dig. Meanwhile, we're uncovering more mosaics than expected in the easily accessible areas, and they're essentially ignoring half of them to focus on the big prize: the sealed corridor and what it allegedly hides."

She set a dusted shard aside and turned to face him. "I'm

sorry, it must be maddening." Her gaze drifted across his face. Something about his frustration was deeply appealing.

He caught Aya's eyes. For a heartbeat, it seemed as if the camp's noise faded. "Look, I appreciate your help. Even a day's difference might preserve data we'd otherwise lose." His eyes flicked to her lips, then quickly back up.

"Of course. I... I'm really glad I ended up here," Aya said.

Karim's smile was faint but genuine. "Me too." She'd come prepared to charm him as part of her infiltration, which was proving surprisingly easy, but the stirring in her chest felt alarming. *Dangerous*, she warned herself, *yet oddly exhilarating*.

He reached past her and picked up a small, half-cleaned tile, brushing a finger over an etched symbol. She became acutely aware of their closeness. "You see these lines?" he murmured, as if oblivious to the tension. "They might be an early form of Arabic calligraphy merging with local Amazigh script. Hard to say without more context, but every fragment is a clue."

"I love that," Aya replied softly, leaning in to see. Their heads almost touched, a few strands of her hair grazing the side of his face. She opened her mouth to apologize, but at that moment, voices erupted from near the center of camp.

A short, balding man in a crisp button-down called out, "Haddad, we need the final translation by tonight. Mr. Léglise's arrival has been moved up."

Karim's shoulders stiffened. "Wait, when?"

"Didn't say. But they want immediate progress on that corridor, so finish your measurements or whatever it is you do." The man shot her a suspicious glance, then dismissed her presence with an annoyed grunt. "Get it done."

As the HRF rep stomped off, Karim exhaled. "They're

accelerating everything. Sounds like we might be blasting into that corridor sooner than I thought."

Aya's pulse pounded. They're moving up the timeline by potentially weeks. "Is it safe? I thought Dr. Yazami wasn't returning for a while."

He shook his head. "Apparently, Léglise doesn't care about Yazami's schedule. They're bringing their team to force entry if needed. Usually, these sponsors at least maintain the illusion of academic courtesy, but not these guys. Something about them is different." His voice dropped. "They're acting like they're running out of time."

She fought to keep her voice even. "Is there any chance we can delay them?"

"Maybe—if I can prove the site's structural instability. But to do that, I'd need to decode these inscriptions properly, understand what we're dealing with. The fragments we've found hint at something significant, but half the text is in scripts I barely recognize." Karim's eyes searched her face again. "I don't know why I'm telling you all this."

"Maybe because you know I actually care?"

He grinned. "That must be it."

Their gazes locked, the silence thick with more than professional interest. Then he tore his eyes away. "Anyway, I have to get some scans from the deeper trench. If you want to keep helping, maybe bag up those labeled shards and store them in the tent on the left. We can't let them get lost in the chaos."

"I can do that," she agreed. "Maybe I can find you later?"

"I'd like that." He hesitated, then added, "Actually, if you're serious about helping, I've been trying to translate some notebook entries from a previous expedition. The handwriting is... unique. Mixed scripts, personal codes. It's connected to our site, but I can't crack it alone. Maybe fresh eyes would help?"

"I'd love to look at it," Aya said, her mind jumping to the codes in her father's notebook. "When?"

"Tonight? After dinner? The analysis tent should be quiet then." He rubbed the back of his neck, suddenly looking relieved. "I mean, if you're not too tired from your hike here."

"I'll be there," she promised.

Karim grinned, then strode toward the main trench without another word, leaving her alone with a hundred questions.

The analysis tent was filled with the quiet buzz of LED work lights. Outside, the camp had settled into its evening routine, distant laughter from the workers' quarters and the occasional clang of equipment being secured for the night. Aya found Karim hunched over a cluttered table, surrounded by photographs, photocopied pages, and his own sprawling notes.

"You came," Karim said, looking up with a smile.

"I said I would." Aya slid onto the bench beside him, close enough to catch the scent of dust and coffee on his clothes. "So, show me these mysterious notes."

He pushed a stack of photocopies toward her. "These are from the past ten to twenty years. A Moroccan historian named Hassan Amrani was researching sites connected to the Idrisid dynasty. He seemed particularly interested in this area." Karim's finger traced a line of text. "But look at this—the later entries are almost completely encoded. Three different scripts at least, plus what seems to be personal shorthand."

Aya blinked, feeling her vision narrowing. The photocopies were grainy, but she recognized her father's handwriting immediately—copies of the same notebook in her bag. It was impossible. She forced herself to lean closer, feigning curiosity while fearing she might faint.

"Where did these come from?"

"The university archive in Rabat. The Foundation dug them up, apparently. This Amrani donated his research before he died, but no one's been able to fully decode his final entries. He was brilliant, but also paranoid. Believed in wild things. Some say he thought he was being followed near the end."

Aya swallowed hard. "What makes you think it's connected to this site?"

"Look here." Karim pointed to a margin note. "He mentions the 'Corridor of Whispers' and specific coordinates that match our location. And this symbol—" he indicated a small drawing of a falcon within a circle "—appears on several of the sealed stones we've uncovered and photographed."

Aya's hands shook as she picked up the pages. "Yes. The encoding is sophisticated," she managed. "See how he alternates between scripts mid-word? And these numbers might be a substitution cipher based on... hmm, maybe dates? Personal dates?"

Karim turned to face her fully, eyes bright with excitement. "You can read some of this?"

"Not read exactly, but I can see the pattern. My father was a historian too—he used to play code games with me as a child. This reminds me of..." She trailed off, pretending to study the page while her heart hammered. "It would take time to decode properly. Days, maybe weeks."

"Time we don't have," Karim said, frustration creeping back into his voice. "If Léglise arrives soon—"

"Then we work through it together, every night," she heard herself say. "Maybe we can find something to slow them down."

He stared at her. "You'd do that? You barely know me, this isn't even your dig—"

"It's important," Aya said. "I can feel it. Whatever your enigmatic Amrani was protecting, it matters."

They worked in focused silence. Aya carefully revealed just enough insight to be helpful without exposing her intimate knowledge of her father's methods. She guided Karim toward the simpler encoded sections, the ones she could "solve" without suspicion.

"Here," Aya said after an hour, pointing to a decoded phrase. "This part says 'The fire requires three keys—the bloodline, the marked, and the pure of heart.' Whatever that means."

Karim's brow furrowed. "Three keys? But we've only found evidence of one artifact, the Amulet itself."

"Maybe it's metaphorical?" Aya suggested, though she suspected her father meant exactly what he wrote. "Ancient texts love their riddles."

As midnight approached, their heads drew closer over the work, shoulders touching as they compared interpretations. Once, Karim's hand brushed hers as they both reached for the same photograph, and neither pulled away immediately.

"Aya," Karim said quietly, not looking up from the papers. "I'm glad you're here. Not just for the help, but... I haven't felt this energized about the work in months. It's been all corporate pressure and rushed excavations. This, working with someone who actually cares, reminds me why I became an archaeologist."

For a dangerous moment, she wanted to tell him everything: who she really was, why she was here, that the notebook belonged to her father. Instead, she smiled softly, looking into his warm eyes.

"We should probably call it a night," she said. "You'll need rest."

"You're right." But he didn't move away. "Will you... can we continue this tomorrow? The translations, I mean."

"Of course," Aya whispered.

He walked her to the dormitory tent through the cool desert air. At the entrance, he caught her hand briefly.

"Thank you," he said. "For everything tonight. I feel like we're on the verge of understanding something crucial."

If only you knew, she thought, squeezing his fingers before letting go. "Get some sleep, Karim. Tomorrow's going to be another big day."

Aya watched him disappear into the darkness before ducking into her tent, her father's decoded words echoing in her mind: *The fire requires three keys—the bloodline, the marked, and the pure of heart.*

Her father had known more than she'd ever imagined. Now she had to figure out what to do about it.

Twenty-Two

Before long, Aya had developed a routine. Mornings were spent at the excavation, documenting finds alongside Karim. Afternoons brought them back to the analysis tent, where they'd spread her father's photocopied notes across every available surface. Evenings stretched into night as they slowly unraveled Hassan Amrani's elaborate code, getting further than she'd been able to on her own.

The camp had its own rhythm. Teams rotated in and out, supply trucks arrived most mornings, the generators constantly hummed. But inside the analysis tent, time moved differently.

"I think I've got something," Karim said, pushing his glasses up his nose, a habit she'd noticed he only did when truly excited. "This section here, where he switches from Arabic to what looks like medieval Ottoman notation—wait, this isn't just Ottoman. Look at these mathematical progressions. This is based on Ibn Rushd's work!"

She leaned closer, their shoulders pressing together. Each physical contact still sent a jolt through her. "Ibn Rushd? The Almohad philosopher?"

"Exactly!" Karim's excitement was palpable. "The Almohad Caliphate produced incredible mathematical-mystical systems. Ibn Rushd, known as Averroes to the Europeans, and other Almohad scholars believed geometric patterns and mathematical sequences could unlock divine secrets. They developed complex ciphers that combined astronomy, mathematics, and mysticism. Amrani must have studied their methods."

"You're right. And see how the numbers align? They're not dates—they're coordinates, but not normal longitude and latitude."

"What about star positions?" He turned to her, eyes bright. "Maybe Amrani was tracking astronomical events. But why encode them so heavily?"

She knew why. Her father had believed the djinn were bound by cosmic forces, that certain alignments weakened the seals. But she couldn't say that. Instead, she pointed to another passage. "Maybe this explains it. I managed to decode this part last night."

Karim read aloud: "'The fire remembers the stars of its binding. When they return to their houses, the whispers grow loud.'" He frowned. "Poetic, but what does it mean practically?"

"No idea," she lied. "But your Ottoman astronomy theory makes sense. My father—" She caught herself. "My father gave a lecture once about how medieval Islamic scholars were obsessed with the connection between earthly and celestial events."

"Maybe he could help?"

"He passed away over five years ago. Dig collapse in Colombia." The truth slipped out before she could stop it.

Karim's hand covered hers. "I'm sorry, I didn't know. That must have been—"

"It was." She pulled away gently, focusing on the papers. "But he'd have loved this puzzle. He was always creating codes, hiding messages. When I was eight, he made me a treasure hunt where each clue required solving increasingly complex ciphers. Took me three months to find the 'treasure'—an illuminated edition of Ibn Battuta's *Rihla*."

"He sounds wonderful."

"He was." She touched a particularly dense section of code. "This reminds me of his later work. See how he embeds personal references within historical ones? It's like he's having a conversation with someone who shares his memories."

"'*The personal is the key to the historical*,'" Karim quoted. "That's from his margin notes. I've been thinking about what that means."

Her throat tightened. The words her father had written specifically for her. "Maybe he meant that understanding history requires personal investment?"

"Or maybe," Karim said slowly, "he meant it literally. That someone with personal knowledge of his life would be needed to decode this." He studied her face. "You're remarkably good at this, Aya. Almost like..."

"Wait," Karim interrupted himself, eyes widening as he scanned another page. "This reference here—'*The Alchemist's Transformation*.' That has to be about Abu Bekr Ibn Tufail, the 12th-century philosopher from Salé. He wrote extensively about transformation—not just of metals, but of knowledge itself. The legend says he discovered patterns that could transform base elements into pure energy."

"The Alchemist of Salé," Aya said, playing along. "I've heard the stories. Didn't he supposedly hide his discoveries because they were too dangerous?"

"Exactly. And look, Amrani references 'geometric alchemy' in the next line. He's suggesting the Amulet works on similar principles. Not just containing something, but transforming it. Like spiritual alchemy."

A sharp rap on the tent pole interrupted Karim's train of thought. A man's head poked through the flap, his expression serious. Karim shifted away from Aya. "Supply run orders. Anyone need anything from town?"

"Just the usual, thanks," Karim said.

The man's eyes flicked between them, appraising. "Right. Well, the boss is delayed another week. Transport issues. Gives you scholars more time for your... research. So hurry up."

After he left, Karim shook his head. "Another delay. The HRF representatives are furious, but it's good for us. More time to understand what we're dealing with." He turned back to the notebook. "Shall we continue?"

They worked until the late afternoon heat made the tent unbearable, then relocated to a shaded area where the desert wind provided some relief. Other team members drifted past—archaeologists heading to their shifts, laborers taking breaks. Aya knew their names, their routines. Tariq, who brought them mint tea every evening. Sarah, the British ceramics specialist who complained endlessly. Mohammed, the site photographer who'd started documenting their translation work.

"For posterity," he'd said, snapping photos of them bent over the codes. "The day we cracked Amrani's cipher."

If only he knew whose daughter sat in his photographs.

As the sun began its descent, Karim called out. "Aya, look at this!" He grabbed her hand, pulling her back to the tent. "Remember the section we couldn't crack yesterday? I tried applying your father's substitution pattern—the one from the treasure hunt story you told me—and it worked!"

She stared at the decoded text, her heart racing. She'd

planted that story carefully, hoping he'd make the connection. But seeing her father's words emerge still shook her:

The Amulet is not the prison—it is the key to the prison. Three seals were made, three doors that must never open. The fire sleeps behind iron and stone, bound by starlight and sacrifice. But keys can turn both ways. Remember this, habibti. Remember when the whispers come.

"*Habibti*," Karim read. "That's an endearment. He was writing to someone specific."

"A child, maybe?" Aya suggested, voice carefully neutral.

"Must be. Look how the tone changes when he uses it. More urgent, more personal." Karim ran his finger along the text. "Three seals, three doors. We've only found evidence of one chamber here."

"Unless the others are elsewhere," she said. "Scattered across Morocco, maybe. Hidden at other sites."

"If these 'prisons' contain some kind of power source..." Karim trailed off, shaking his head. "Listen to me, talking like I believe in djinn and magical fire."

"Stranger things have turned out to be real," Aya said. "Electricity would have seemed like magic once."

He smiled at her, a warm, unguarded expression she'd come to crave. "You're right. And speaking of magic—we make a good team, don't we? Your intuition with these codes, my knowledge of the historical scripts. It's like we were meant to work together on this."

The words hung between them. She felt the familiar pull, stronger after days of shared discoveries and quiet laughter. She'd told herself she was playing a role, but somewhere between the first decoded passage and their twentieth cup of mint tea, the line had blurred.

"Karim," she began, not sure what she intended to say.

"I know," he said. "This is probably just the excitement of discovery, the isolation of the site. When the excavation ends, you'll go back to your university, I'll move to the next dig, and..."

"And?"

"And I'll regret not doing this," he said, leaning closer and placing a hand on her wrist.

"Dr. Haddad!" A voice called from down the ridge. "The deep trench team needs you. They've found something."

Karim pulled back, frustration flickering across his face. "I should—"

"Go," Aya said, managing a smile despite her racing pulse. "I'll keep working on the next section."

He squeezed her shoulder as he passed, a touch that lingered. "Don't stay too late. You need rest, too."

Alone, she pressed her palms against her eyes. Just over a week, and already she was in too deep. Not just the mission— she'd expected complications there. But her father's notebook. And Karim... He was supposed to be a mark, a source of information. Not someone who made her laugh over terrible camp coffee, who got her genuinely excited about the work, who looked at her like she was a revelation instead of a deception.

In the distance, a muezzin's far-off call echoed across the valley, marking the end of another day. She bent over her father's words, translating warnings meant for her while the man she couldn't have worked to uncover truths she couldn't share.

The personal is the key to the historical.

Her father had been right about that, too.

Aya glanced toward the mountains, barely visible through the analysis tent's open flap. Nine days now. Omar would be getting restless, probably driving Abdellatif crazy.

At least they'd planned for this, rotating watch positions, careful rationing, and keeping their camp signs to a minimum. Still, mountain nights were cold, and she worried about Abdellatif.

Twenty-Three

After two and a half weeks of working side by side, Aya knew Karim's routines by heart. The way he absently pushed his glasses up when concentrating. How he whistled fragments of old Andalusian melodies while cataloging. The precise moment each evening when exhaustion would creep into his shoulders, and they'd take a break for herbal tea.

Aya spent the late afternoon meticulously bagging shards, her movements automatic after weeks of practice. But her mind churned with the morning's news that had been rampaging through the camp: Léglise's sudden acceleration of the timeline despite the delays. After all their careful work, everything was unraveling. No guarantee when, but it was now a matter of days.

She needed to contact Omar. The lack of communication with her team gnawed at her. They needed to know what she'd discovered, needed to formulate a plan before it was too late. Plus, Amina still hadn't shown herself, though she had to have seen Aya no matter what her play was.

But it was the nights that preoccupied her most. Those long hours in the analysis tent with Karim, slowly unraveling her father's secrets while concealing her identity. The way his face lit up when they cracked a difficult passage. How naturally they'd fallen into finishing each other's thoughts, their minds synchronizing over ancient puzzles.

He hadn't gone to kiss her again, but three nights ago, after they'd decoded another warning about the nature of the "three keys," he'd taken Aya's hand across the table. "I've never enjoyed working with someone this much," he'd said. "It's like you were meant to be here."

But nothing changed the fact that at dusk, she'd have to slip out to meet Omar and Abdelatif, share her findings, and plan a sabotage or infiltration of the corridor before Léglise had a chance to show up.

A pang of guilt shot through Aya. She vowed to Karim to do everything in her power to save the site.

Maybe she could steal the artifact first and keep it out of Léglise's hands while, ironically, preserving the site from forced destruction. But that plan carried complications. If she also had to contend with Amina, the stakes would skyrocket.

Just as she sealed the final artifact bag for the day, Aya sensed movement behind her. Spinning around, she nearly collided with the same HRF rep who'd barked at Karim earlier. He was short, his overhanging belly concealed beneath an impeccably clean shirt.

"You," he said, "which department at Al Akhawayn?"

Aya swallowed and forced a meek smile. "North African Studies. Graduate track focusing on early Islamic architecture."

"Got it. Do you have official clearance from our HRF offices, or is Dr. Haddad just bringing random strangers onto a restricted site? We're tightening security."

She forced a nervous laugh. "It was a spur-of-the-moment idea, I admit, but Dr. Haddad said I could observe. I'm sorry if that's a problem?"

He glared. "We have real work to do. If you get in the way, you're done. No transport back to civilization. Understood? We have personnel inbound, so we need you out of the way."

"Yes, of course. I won't cause trouble. I'm here to help."

He stared a beat longer, then grunted and marched off, shouting orders at a forklift driver. Aya exhaled shakily. Had he pressed further, her story might have unraveled.

As daylight stretched, Aya finally saw Karim returning. His hair was damp with sweat, and he was clutching a half-torn blueprint. His face lit up when he spotted her.

"Tired?" she asked as he approached.

"Exhausted. They're drilling test holes near the corridor's entrance, ignoring my warnings. They're about to force it wide open, not to mention trigger any traps the builders may have set for intruders."

Aya parted her lips, choosing her words carefully. "Is there any story about what lies beyond that barrier? Something so valuable it must be kept under wraps?"

Karim glanced around, then shook his head. "I shouldn't discuss the details. HRF has been very clear about information security." He paused, studying her face. "But I trust you, probably more than anyone here."

"I promise, anything you share stays between us. I'm just trying to understand what makes this site so important."

He was quiet for a long moment before he finally spoke in a low voice. "Archaeologically, it should be a burial chamber filled with undisturbed artifacts from a virtually unstudied era, a hidden crypt from a transitional time in the region. The structural engineering alone is remarkable." He paused again.

"But there are other elements that have the sponsors very excited."

"Other elements?"

Karim looked around again, ensuring they weren't overheard. "Local legends speak of this place as a site of binding for energy, for spirits, for djinn. I know that sounds ridiculous to most people, but the sponsors seem to take these stories seriously. More seriously than the actual archaeological value, if I'm being honest."

He rubbed his forehead. "The older villagers believe that meddling here could awaken something fierce. Usually I'd dismiss such concerns as folklore, but given the research you and I have been working on, and how aggressively HRF is pushing to open that corridor..."

Aya recalled Abdelatif's warnings about the myths of the Amulet used to bind the djinn. "What do you think?" she asked.

He offered a rueful smile. "As a scientist, I keep an open mind about lore. Often, myths hold a kernel of truth. But if we set that aside, from a purely structural standpoint, forcibly opening a stone door sealed for centuries is dangerous." Lowering his voice as he stepped closer, he added, "Beyond the science, I can't shake the feeling that this place resists our intrusion."

In the amber light, the familiar warmth in his eyes held something new. Recognition. Understanding.

"Aya," he said softly, "these past weeks... I need to tell you something."

Her heart hammered. Had he figured her out? "What is it?"

"That first night, when you helped with Amrani's notebook, I knew you were hiding something. The way you understood his patterns so quickly, how you guided us toward specific solutions." He stepped closer. "But I also saw how much you cared. About the work, about preserving this history. About what we could do together."

Aya couldn't breathe. "Karim, I—"

"Let me finish." His hand found hers, thumb tracing her knuckles. "Whatever brought you here, whoever you are, these weeks have been the most meaningful of my career. Not just the discoveries, but sharing them with you. The late nights debating translations, the morning coffee where you'd steal my breakfast, the look in your eyes when you have a new idea."

Tears pricked Aya's eyes. He knew. Not everything, but enough. And he was choosing to trust her anyway.

"I've watched you struggle with something," Karim continued. "Seen the guilt in your eyes when you think I'm not looking. Whatever it is, whatever happens when Léglise arrives, if this site is destroyed or pillaged, I want you to know that what we've built here, what we've shared, it's real for me."

The weight of nearly three weeks of lies and half-truths crushed down on her.

"It's real for me too," she whispered, the truth burning her throat. "These weeks, working together, uncovering secrets, seeing how much you care about getting it right... You're incredible; I feel a magnetic draw to you. I don't know why this is the moment, but I can't pretend anymore that I don't—"

Footsteps crunched outside, and one of the laborers called out urgently. "Dr. Haddad! They've broken through to the corridor's outer seal. You need to come immediately!"

Karim stepped back, his expression torn between duty and desire. "I have to go. But tonight, after everything, we need to talk. Really talk, continue this."

"I know," Aya said, touching his face. "Be careful. If they're forcing the seal—"

He caught her hand. "I'll try to slow them down. Buy us more time."

"Go," she urged, stepping back to give him space and forcing a teasing smile. "Guess that's the glamorous life of a dedicated archaeologist?"

"Don't let the HRF team hear you call it glamorous." He hesitated. Then, with one last reluctant smile, he slipped out of the tent.

Late afternoon light slanted through the tent flap as it closed behind him.

Aya's mind swirled with thoughts of Léglise's impending arrival and her complicated feelings for Karim.

Tonight, she'd have to choose. Between the mission that brought her here and the man who'd slowly shown her what she really wanted. Between her father's encrypted warnings, Karim's trust, and revenge on a man who tried to murder her. Between stealing the Amulet and saving the site, along with the horrifying possibility that those might not be the same thing.

Aya gathered the translation notes they'd compiled together, her fingers lingering on pages marked with Karim's handwriting, his excited exclamation points when they'd solved particularly difficult passages, memories in every line.

Finally, she set them down. Time to contact Omar.

She waited until the shift change began, but before Aya could make her move, urgent voices erupted from the center of camp. HRF representatives gathered around a radio, their conversation animated and tense.

"Confirmed arrival at 1800."

"Full perimeter sweep."

"No unauthorized personnel."

Aya froze. Léglise would be here at dawn. She had even less time than she'd thought.

Footsteps approached the tent, and Karim entered again, his face grave.

"They're accelerating everything," he said without preamble. "Full lockdown starts in two hours. No one in or out without clearance." His eyes searched hers. "If you need to do something, it has to be now."

Aya's mind raced. She'd planned to slip out after dark, but if they were locking down the site...

"Karim," she said carefully, "what if there was a way to delay them? To buy more time for proper documentation?"

He paused, conflict clear in his expression. "I've tried everything. They won't listen to archaeological concerns, safety protocols, nothing." His voice carried a note of desperate frustration. "At this point, I'd welcome anything that forced them to slow down, some kind of distraction that made them reconsider the rush job they're planning, but there's nothing left."

It was the opening she needed. "What if I told you that might be possible?"

"How?"

Aya took a deep breath.

"You're right, I wasn't entirely truthful about why I'm here. I have been hiding some things," she said carefully. "I have connections, people who might be able to help create the kind of delays you're talking about. But it would mean trusting me completely, even though I can't tell you everything right now."

Karim stared at her for a long moment. Around them, the camp's activity was intensifying with more lights coming on, more urgent conversations.

"Who are you really?" he asked.

"Someone who wants to protect this site as much as you do," she replied. "Someone whose father died trying to preserve history from people exactly like Léglise. And someone who might be your only chance to prevent this place from being destroyed in the name of corporate greed."

Karim folded his arms, jaw tightening. "What are you talking about? You have friends outside the camp now? What is this... I need to know more about who you really are."

Aya had rehearsed an explanation in her mind, but the raw hurt in his voice made the words stick. "Karim, I'm not a grad student." She looked him in the eye. "I came here with a team, hired to stop the Heritage Reclamation Foundation, to stop Léglise."

"Stop HRF? I thought you didn't know anything about them. I... this entire time..." He exhaled sharply, running a hand through his hair. "So you've been lying to me from the moment you walked in?"

"I'm so sorry. I had to pose as a researcher to get inside. Nobody else on my team could do it—they'd stand out. But I never meant to hurt you or make you a pawn in this."

"So, did you think I'd be grateful to learn you've been using me?"

"I'm not using you," she insisted, stepping closer. He retreated a half step.

Karim paced in the dimly lit tent, fury and hurt scrawled across his features. "So all those late nights we spent together, every breakthrough we celebrated, that time you fell asleep on my shoulder, the times we've almost kissed—was any of it real? Or was I just a convenient source of information for three weeks?"

Aya's eyes filled with tears. "Every moment was real, Karim. Yes, I came here with a mission, but I never expected us. I never expected to care so much about your work, about preserving this place, about you."

"Three weeks," he repeated, voice hollow. "Three weeks of

building something I thought was special, and all along you were—"

"All along I was falling for you," she interrupted. "Fighting it every day because I knew this moment would come. Do you think it was easy, watching you trust me more each day, knowing I'd eventually have to tell you the truth?"

He shook his head, hands clenched. "You told me just enough half-truths to get me on your side, to get me to open up to you."

His voice broke on the final word, and he turned away, shoulders rigid.

"Karim, I never wanted to deceive you," Aya whispered. "But I can't change who I am."

He spun around, eyes shining. "Who are you, then? A thief with an accidental conscience? Or a con artist who found a new mark?"

The silence stretched, thick with hurt. Aya bowed her head. "I don't know. Maybe both."

Karim's eyes searched her for further deception. "You expect me to just accept this? What do you want from me?"

"Listen, there's a reason I'm doing this beyond some paycheck." She pulled out her father's notebook, holding it with trembling hands. "The historian whose work we've been translating, H. Amrani, that was my father. Hassan Amrani. Every night for three weeks, I've sat beside you decoding his words."

Karim stared at the notebook, then at her. "Your father wrote this? Then you already knew—"

"Not everything. Not most of it. His later codes were beyond me. I needed your expertise to unlock them fully. But yes, I guided us toward certain passages because I knew him personally. I used our word games from childhood to help crack his ciphers."

Karim's anger flickered with empathy. "Why didn't you tell me this before?"

"I try not to share it with anyone," Aya confessed, this time offering the complete truth. "But I care about you, Karim, and what you're trying to do here. I can't stomach watching another reckless dig destroy innocent lives, destroy real history, just for the profit of a man I know to be a monster and whatever scheme he's up to."

She pulled out a wrapped bundle from her pack—one of the tablets Karim had shown her earlier. "You mentioned the 'Heart of Idris,' something that 'channels the fire of creation itself.' My father spent years researching what he called the Idris Flame, the same artifact Léglise is after. According to his notes, it's not just a historical treasure. It could be some kind of ancient energy technology, something that could reshape global power if it falls into the wrong hands. It sounds crazy, but my father believed it and so does Léglise."

For a long beat, neither spoke. At last, Karim let out a ragged exhale. "I can't just pretend this is okay, but..." He paused, studying her face. "But I need to know, what exactly are you and your team planning to do? Are you just different thieves competing for the same prize as Léglise?"

Aya shook her head firmly. "No, Karim. We're not here to steal for profit. My father was approached by people I suspect wanted to weaponize his research. He refused them, and I believe that's why he died. Léglise has already tried to kill me once, in Paris. I managed to steal information from his office that may be critical. My team was hired by people who claim they want to preserve this artifact safely. Although I'm starting to question their motives too." Her voice hardened with resolve. "But regardless of who hired us, I won't let my father's life's work become a weapon. If we can get to it first, we can at least ensure it's protected from being misused."

Karim's gaze dropped. Slowly, he reached out, fingers skimming her elbow. His touch was a relief. "I don't know what to think."

She gave a pained smile. "I swear our bond is real. I only wish I hadn't lied about who I was."

He shrugged. "You came here thinking you'd infiltrate and vanish. So where does that leave us?"

"I never expected our connection, or to care so much about what happens to you, to all of this. I don't know where that leaves us, but I'm excited to figure it out after we stop Léglise."

Karim exhaled, stepping closer to her. "I'm still hurt. But I believe you. You want to protect this place because you lost something precious once. And you don't want that tragedy repeating itself."

"Exactly."

His arms slid around her in an embrace. "Thank you for telling me," he murmured against her hair. "And for trusting me enough to share that about your father."

Aya pressed her face to his shoulder for a moment, letting the confession settle, letting his acceptance soothe the ache inside. Then she drew back, meeting his gaze.

"If you think this'll work, I'm with you," he said. "I think it's worth a shot. Whatever it takes."

"Thank you," she whispered.

Karim nodded. "So, what do we do next?"

"Now, we figure out how to stop Léglise's men before they tear this chamber open. I'll need inside help. Someone who can unlock a gate or divert a guard."

"I want to help. But damn, if we fail—"

"We won't," Aya said. "Karim, my plan isn't to fight Léglise's private army head-on. We need to get to the Amulet before they blast their way through and risk destroying everything—the chamber, the inscriptions, maybe even the artifact itself. If we can access it properly instead of bulldozing, we can preserve the site and keep the artifact out of the wrong hands."

She gestured toward the sealed corridor. "You said they're planning to force it open tomorrow. But what if there's another way in? Something the original builders intended? My father's research suggests these chambers were designed with specific entry protocols. Maybe those inscriptions we've been translating contain the key."

Karim's expression shifted from skepticism to intrigue. "You're talking about solving the puzzle instead of smashing through it?"

"Exactly. And while we're doing that, we sabotage their heavy equipment, create delays, and force them to slow down. Buy ourselves time to find the right way in."

He inched nearer. "That seems impossible, or dangerous. I can't ask you—"

"You're not asking," she cut in gently. "I will get it done."

Aya remembered Abdelatif's dire tone and warnings. Even if the reality was purely structural danger and not supernatural, the risk remained colossal—to her payday, to her revenge on Léglise, to her escape from crime, to her father's legacy, and to the man who stood before her now.

"I need you to know something," she said, pressing closer to him. "These three weeks have changed a lot for me. When I arrived, I thought this would be simple. Get in, get the artifact, get out. But working with you, seeing your dedication. You've reminded me who I used to be, who I wanted to be."

"Aya—"

"Let me finish. Tomorrow, when Léglise arrives, everything we've built here will be tested. But whatever happens, these weeks with you were the most honest thing I've done in years, even wrapped in lies as they were."

His thumb traced her cheek. "After everything, you're still

absolutely incredible, maybe even more so. That first week, I told myself the attraction was just proximity. The second week, I admitted I was falling for you. By this week, I couldn't imagine doing this work without you. And now, knowing who you really are." He shook his head. "It explains so much."

His eyes fixed on hers, asking silent permission.

Aya rested her hand against his chest and closed the small distance between them, letting her lips brush his. The kiss was light, hesitant at first, then deeper. For a breathless moment, the world fell away. She tasted the camp's dust on his skin, finding herself craving the connection more than the con.

When they finally broke apart, Karim's breath was unsteady. "Aya," he said, "I know this is crazy. We barely know each other. But I really like you, I really like this."

Aya kissed him again. "I really like this, too," she said softly.

They stood in silence, bodies pressed close, each lost in thoughts of what the next day would bring.

Finally, she eased away, scanning the darkness beyond the tent. The guard shifts would be changing soon.

"I need to go rendezvous with my team to see if I can secure some supplies. Maybe find a place to rest for a couple of hours. You should, too, and I'll keep you updated on the plan."

"Will you be able to get back in? They're locking down—"

"I know another way. Trust me." She touched his face one more time. "Cover for me if anyone asks?"

Karim nodded, his gaze lingering on her face as if memorizing it. "Okay." Then he turned, starting toward the tent exit. Just before he slipped into the gloom, he looked over his shoulder. "I'm glad you ended up here, Aya. No matter how any of this ends, I have one meaningful discovery."

"Me too," she whispered to his retreating figure.

Moments later, like clockwork, the guard shift was changing.

At the far southwestern edge of the perimeter, stacks of crates and a slouching section of fence provided a decent blind spot. She paused for a moment, scanning for roving patrols. The site felt still, almost peaceful. An illusion she knew would shatter soon enough.

Aya slid through a narrow gap in the fence where the wire had been twisted upward. It cut a small snag in her jacket, but she bit back a curse, pressing on into the dark mountains.

TWENTY-FOUR

OUTSIDE THE FENCE, Aya scrambled up the lower slope of the ridge. After another fifteen minutes, Aya spotted two figures crouched behind a broken ridge: Omar and Abdelatif, both scanning the valley below. Relief began to ease her tension as their familiar shapes emerged from the darkness.

Omar was scanning the camp. Upon seeing her, he lowered his binoculars. "Finally. The bosses have been breathing down my neck for updates. They expected action."

"And I told you," Aya shot back, "building real trust takes time. Karim, the lead archaeologist, wouldn't have shared half of what he has if I'd pushed too fast."

Abdelatif placed a calming hand on Omar's shoulder. "She has done well. Three weeks of patience will serve us better than three days of haste. What have you learned, Aya?"

She crouched down beside them. "They haven't the faintest idea who I really am. They think I'm just some wide-eyed grad student with a fetish for chipped pottery. But I've gained more than just their trust." She pulled out a thick folder of photocopied translations. "Karim and I have been working on decoding historical documents related to the site. The Amulet isn't just an artifact—it's part of a larger system. According to the texts we've translated over the past three weeks, there are multiple sealed chambers potentially across the planet, and the Amulet is the master key."

Omar whistled low. "Great. What about how to get it?"

"The inscriptions warn about 'three keys required': the bloodline, the marked, and the pure of heart," Aya responded.

"This is from your father's notebook?" Abdelatif asked, eyes glinting with interest.

"His encrypted notes align with what the team has discovered. He knew about the network of seals, the djinn legends, all of it. But he hid the knowledge in layers of code that took weeks to unravel, even with Karim's expertise and my familiarity. We haven't finished it all."

"This is good," Abdelatif said. "But Aya, are you all right?"

"I'm fine. But we don't have much time. Léglise arrives with a security detail tomorrow night, and then they'll have the corridor open."

Abdelatif nodded. "So, we have only a narrow window if we want to secure that artifact ourselves."

Omar swore under his breath. "They're moving faster than we thought. Not good. Still no idea of who they are? Or more on why they're after the Amulet?"

Aya shook her head. "You know what I know. Karim told me all the same myths we talked through in Marrakech. But if we wait too long, we'll be hopelessly outmanned and outgunned. So I think we need to move at dawn, before their reinforcements get fully established."

She paused. "I have an ally inside, but he's an honest archaeologist, and I won't risk him unless absolutely necessary. He thinks we're just trying to preserve the artifact, which is true. He doesn't need to know more about the Aegis or our backup plans."

"Getting attached to the locals?" Omar's tone carried knowing amusement. "Three weeks is a long time to play pretend."

Aya's jaw tightened. "It stopped being pretend after the first week. Karim is brilliant, dedicated, and genuinely cares about preserving history. We've spent countless hours working together, and yes, I care about what happens to him."

"Complications," Abdelatif murmured.

"No, it's not like that. It doesn't change the mission," Aya insisted, though her voice wavered. "But if we can accomplish it without destroying everything he's worked to protect these past weeks..."

Omar flashed a roguish grin. "Well, as someone you're happy to put at risk, give me the target and I'll shoot it, explode it, smash it. Whatever you need."

Aya rolled her eyes and retrieved a folded scrap of paper from her pocket, smoothing it against the rock as she whispered the details: the generator by the southern fence, the forklift that hauled critical support beams, and the main water pump keeping the trench from flooding. One well-timed disruption could buy them hours or even days.

"But we can't risk harming genuine archaeologists or damaging the site," she said. "And we need to avoid triggering any traps that might further entomb the Amulet."

Abdelatif nodded gravely. "Precision. And the artifact itself —we still plan to take it if we can? You know my concerns, but this may be the only chance."

Aya's mind flashed to Karim's face, forehead pressed against hers. Would stealing it truly save it? Allowing PES to claim it was far worse. And if the legends of djinn and curses held a glimmer of truth, the consequences could be catastrophic.

She exhaled. "Yes. If this delay fails, we can't let Léglise and PES get it, so we'll have to. We might have to go deeper, remove it ourselves, and try to vanish. I'd rather wait it out to have a clearer idea of what that interior chamber looks like and make sure we're safe to go in, but they may force our hand."

Omar nodded solemnly. "So, we finally make our move at dawn. About time. I've got permanent indents from these binocular lenses."

"The three of us are ready, but the question remains," Abdelatif interjected, "whether your archaeologist will truly help when the moment comes. Many days of growing close is one thing, but asking him to betray his employers, his colleagues..."

"He's already conflicted about their methods. Today, he practically asked me to find a way to slow them down. He doesn't know the full plan, but he wants to keep the Amulet out of their hands as much as we do. Maybe more, the more he learns."

Within minutes, they had etched the plan into the desert sand beneath a night sky glittering with scattered stars. In terse, deliberate whispers, they confirmed every detail. Omar and Abdelatif would circle to the southwestern fence. Aya would slip inside and open the gate at exactly the right moment. Karim would cause a distraction, pulling the guards' attention away.

Omar's charge was clear: sabotage the generator by planting a small explosive or cutting the crucial cables to knock out the power. Abdelatif would take on the heavy machinery, disabling a pump to keep them busy on repairs. Meanwhile, Aya would stay within the camp, watching the Amulet's chamber, ready to fight her way through to seize it if the sabotage failed.

There was no room for error.

"We do this before the new security team is fully in place," she reiterated. "Dawn shift, just before 8:00 a.m. We have a small window while the night guards hand off to day guards."

Omar grinned. "You're stressed. Are you sure you're up for this, being the queen of destruction?"

"I've handled bigger jobs," she lied, regretting her confidence as soon as the words left her lips. A man she cared about might stand in the crossfire if it all went wrong, and the memory of Karim's kiss lingered, complicating every thought that raced through her mind.

Abdelatif placed a hand on her shoulder, his voice solemn. "Remember, child, any damage we do tomorrow can likely be undone. But if they destroy that corridor with no regard for centuries of warnings... well, that might be unstoppable."

"I know. Thanks, Abdel."

RE-ENTERING the camp was simpler than leaving, as Aya slipped through the same bent section of chain-link fence under the cover of darkness. She paused, scanning for any sign of guards. None. Tents dotted the field, lanterns glowing like dim beacons. One last check before dawn. She needed some rest beforehand, but doubted it would come easily.

Crossing between silent rows of crates, she reached the small canopy tent from earlier. It was deserted, all lights off except the moon's gentle glow.

She ducked to enter the tent—

Wham.

A sudden impact slammed into her side, sending her reeling. A sharp pain surged up her shoulder.

She stifled a yelp and raised an arm in a split-second block. In the flickering light, a slender figure clad in a skintight black bodysuit grunted as she hooked Aya's wrist, sending them both crashing against a row of crates.

Aya twisted free, eyes widening. This was no clumsy guard. The reflexes, the fluid steps—it was someone well-trained. She pivoted, hooking a foot behind her assailant's ankle to topple them. But the figure was quicker, pushing off the crate to sidestep the attempt. For a heartbeat, both froze, crouched in mirrored aggression.

That was all the time she needed to catch a glimpse of the assailant's face. A slash of sharp cheekbones, dark eyes glinting with contempt, tight black curls reflecting the moonlight.

Ice flooded her veins as the fears buried in the back of her mind took human form.

Amina.

The woman she'd once called partner. Lover. The same woman who had vanished in Luxor and left her for either dead or to face the authorities alone. The memories, sharp and painful, flooded back. And here she was, in the flesh, a smug smile playing on her lips.

"You—?" Aya gasped, fury and shock warring in her voice.

Amina's lips curved into a predatory smile. "Well, well," she purred. "Fancy meeting you here, *habibi*. I've been watching you, wondering when you'd finally notice. Weeks of playing archaeologist—quite the long con, even for you."

Aya felt her neck get hot. "How long have you been here?"

"Oh, I arrived just before you. Just in time to see you get cozy with that handsome archaeologist of yours. Late nights in the analysis tent, those lingering looks. Quite the performance. Or was it?"

The air crackled between them.

The floodlight from the next tent chose that moment to die, plunging them into near darkness. Aya felt Amina shift against the night. She braced herself for another attack as her eyes adjusted to the light, but Amina simply circled her.

Then they were close. Impossibly close. Their eyes met, wide, something unreadable in their depths. Aya remained frozen, unsure of the next move.

Then, Amina kissed the air beside her cheek. "I've missed you. Did you miss me?"

"Don't you dare," Aya said, recoiling. But the scent of Amina's perfume, the fleeting warmth of her breath, unleashed a torrent of memories, a reminder of how much she had lost and how easily Amina could still make her forget who she was.

Amina smirked, letting a quiet laugh slip. "You always liked living dangerously," she taunted softly, stepping back with infuriating poise.

"Egypt," Aya managed, trembling with rage. She'd never prepared her righteous monologue for when she ran into Amina again. She'd never planned to. "You left me. You sold me out."

"That was two years ago. And you know I had no choice," Amina said, her voice softer. "Two years, and here you are, playing the same games with new people. How's that moral high ground treating you?"

"I'm trying to protect something this time, not steal it."

"Are you? Or are you just telling yourself that because you've fallen for the mark?" Amina stepped closer. "I've watched you with him, Aya, and you're in deeper than you were on any job we ever pulled. At least when we worked together, we were honest about what we were."

The words stung because they held truth. "So you were honest with me in Egypt, then?"

Amina shrugged, looking her up and down. "You always did love dramatics, darling. I improvised, I had to. Interpol was closing in, I had the relic in hand, and we both know it's survival first, right? You would've done the same."

"You know that's not true. I would never do that." Aya forced herself to keep the volume low.

"Says the reformed thief. So, who have you convinced these people you are? I've seen you coming and going as you please. Impressive."

"What do you want? You're with Léglise now? His new hire?"

Amina laughed softly. "Me, obeying corporate stooges? Hardly. But I've always been a believer in the open market. Heard rumors of a particular Amulet concealed in a particular corridor. Too much of an opportunity to pass up, especially with the number of people trying to snatch this thing. All the rich psychos really have a hard-on for whatever they believe it can do. Kind of reminds me of that auction job in Maya Bay, such fond memories together. In the shower, beside the pool, in the jungle." She twirled a small blade in her hand, showing it off with unnerving confidence.

"Stop." Aya shook her head, despising the casual cynicism but remembering how Amina's lips felt against hers. The feeling of her body wrapped around her before bed. The look in her eyes when they plotted. The last time she had let herself feel loved.

Then, how easily Amina had vanished, leaving her in police pursuit.

"Look, if Léglise is the highest buyer, I might just sell it back to him. I never discriminate, as long as the money's good. But that's what I'm here for, deal with it."

Footsteps scuffed the rocky ground around the corner. Aya glanced over while Amina froze. They exchanged one charged look, their personal fury momentarily set aside in the face of danger. Wordlessly, they pressed behind a half-toppled crate, forced into reluctant cooperation and even closer proximity.

A guard's flashlight beam swept the dust. He coughed, stepping nearer.

Aya's body was pinned against Amina's, muscle memory threatening to tear her focus apart as she could feel Amina's thighs and breasts shifting against her with each breath. The guard lingered while Amina's face hovered inches from hers, her smile gone.

Finally, mercifully, the guard's footsteps retreated until they were lost.

Amina exhaled through parted lips, winking at her. "Still as stealthy as ever, I see."

"You're arrogant to think I won't just hand you over to the security detail."

Amina tilted her head. "You could try. But I could easily reveal your true identity as well. Plus, you need me more than you admit." Her tone dripped with self-assurance. "Unless you want to watch Léglise yank out that artifact tomorrow. We were always better as a team."

Amina studied her expression before continuing. "Yeah, I can see you agree."

"No, Amina, I don't want your help. I don't want anything from you ever again."

"Then watch these gearheads blow up the corridor, risk destroying the artifacts inside, and ruin everyone's payday," Amina said, stepping away from the crate. "You want to keep it from them, so do I. At least we share a common enemy. Once we have it, we can decide what comes next."

Aya scoffed. "You have no loyalty beyond your bank account. Why should I trust you?"

"Maybe you shouldn't. But I can slip past these guards, same as I always do. And you know it. Unless you think that squeaky-clean conscience of yours can handle a full mercenary squad alone tomorrow, if rumors are true?"

"Enough." The truth was, if they wanted to outrun or outsmart Léglise, Amina was a powerful asset.

Aya felt her nails bite into her palm when another voice cut into her contemplation.

"Aya, who is...?"

Karim strode out from behind a supply pallet a few yards away and stood before them, his flashlight shaky. He'd clearly overheard their hushed voices. Halting abruptly, his gaze flitted between Amina and Aya, demanding an explanation.

"Karim, this is—" Aya swallowed. "An old colleague."

Twenty-Five

The three stood frozen before Amina tilted her head in feigned surprise. "Really, Aya? Is that all I am?"

Beside them, Karim looked pale and uncertain.

Amina gave him a slow once-over. "How sweet, your archaeologist joined. Does he also share your new brand of self-righteous morality?"

A tense silence followed, Amina keeping her smug smile.

"Ah, well," Amina continued, "at least he's cute. I wouldn't mind if you came searching for me in the dark."

Karim stiffened. "Aya... is she one of your friends you went to meet with? What's going on?"

"No. We can't trust her," Aya said, shooting Amina a withering look. "But we might use her." Then, still glaring at Amina, she added, "And you don't need to have anything to do with him."

"If you say so," Amina said. She cast Karim a mocking grin. "Relax, *mon beau*. I'm not your enemy, I'm just passing through, trying to make some money." Her tone turned pointed: "But you do both realize you can't hold them back forever—they will unearth whatever's buried here."

"Yes, we know," Karim said. "I've agreed to help work on that. But Aya, I need to know what's going on."

Aya appraised Amina again. "Here's the plan. At dawn, I'll rendezvous with Omar and Abdealtif, my colleagues. They'll help cause some distractions that should damage enough key equipment so they won't be able to proceed. Hopefully, Karim, that'll buy us a few days to figure out how to safely extract the Amulet. If we can't stop their progress, I'll be in position to steal it before they can get to it."

Amina arched an eyebrow, half-laughing. "Steal the artifact. So sweet to see you returning to your old ways, Aya. I thought you'd gone soft, watching you slave away all day." She circled them slowly. "All those cozy translation sessions. Quite the method acting, or did you actually start believing you were a real archaeologist again?"

Aya's fists clenched. "Some of us evolve, Amina. We don't all stay frozen in our worst versions."

Amina's eyes fluttered. "Three weeks of playing house while the real players position themselves. I've been watching, learning. Did you know Léglise is working with the U.S. military? That PES have satellite surveillance on this site? While you were decoding some old letters from dad, the world kept turning."

Aya stepped closer. "Enough digs, we need to help each other stop these HRF, PES people."

Karim's face was a portrait of reluctance, and Aya could see the questions burning behind his eyes. About Amina, about their history, about what else she might be hiding. "Okay, so she wants to steal the Amulet, and we want to keep it away from Léglise. We share a temporary motive." He paused.

"Though I'm starting to wonder how many versions of you I'm going to meet tonight, Aya."

"The only version that matters is the one trying to save this site," Aya said quietly. "And the one who's been working beside you these past weeks. That's real, Karim. Whatever else you're thinking, that's real."

He exhaled slowly. "But are you sure about this? I'll follow your lead."

Aya swallowed. "I don't know. I see no better path, and we can't go against both her and Léglise's people. Let's just hope she doesn't vanish the moment she touches the Amulet."

Amina's eyes rolled in the faint lamplight.

"But now we need somewhere to talk," Aya said. "We couldn't look more suspicious right now. We need to piece all this together if we're going to work together. Everything that's going on. We need to put everything we all know on the table."

Karim nodded. "Okay. Follow me. There's a half-buried storage shed over by the southwestern ridge. Nobody goes in after dark."

He turned to Amina. "I hope you can move quietly."

Amina raised an eyebrow. "I'm quite good at moving around in the dark. Just ask Aya."

Aya shot Amina a glare, but she only winked and followed Karim.

They proceeded at a crouch, hugging canvas tents and side-stepping a pair of bored-looking guards. At intervals, rotating floodlights forced them to press flat against a crate until the beam moved on.

Eventually, they reached a squat, corrugated shed. Its padlock hung loose. Karim tugged it open with a faint squeak, beckoning them inside. The cramped interior smelled of mildew, and they could make out stacks of discarded and disorganized equipment, lit only by the faint glow of Karim's penlight.

"Hope this is private enough," Karim said. He ran a hand through his curls, exhaling shakily. "So, what do we need to discuss?"

Aya dropped her bag onto an overturned crate amidst the clutter. "I think if we compare notes, we have the best fighting chance to work together, prevent anything bad from happening to this site, and keep the Amulet of Idris out of Léglise's hands. For starters, I have a USB drive from Léglise. I managed to steal it back in Paris. That was a month ago, just before I came here. I've been carrying it ever since, trying to crack it fully during downtime. The drive's still encrypted, and I couldn't get to much of it, mostly just file names. But what I accessed basically reveals that Heritage Reclamation Foundation is a shell. Real money flows from Prometheus Energy Solutions, or PES, as we assumed. They had agents tracking me in Marrakech."

Amina's eyes flashed. "Yes, I know them. Big American multinational that pretends to be a champion of green energy. They're filth." She paused, a tightness in her jaw. "I did a job for them last year, the theft of their competitor's renewable-energy prototypes in Hyderabad. They tried to pay me half of what was agreed, then threatened to kill me if I talked. I haven't exactly forgotten that."

Aya produced the USB from her interior jacket pocket. "The data I could see on the drive implied this dig was funded by them. But we still don't know exactly why they'd be in the antiquities game. If PES is an energy corporation, then what the hell are they doing rummaging for a mythic Amulet in the Atlas Mountains? It implies they definitely believe all this mythology is completely legit."

Karim pressed a fist to his forehead as though a headache

were brewing. "That actually explains something. HRF's upper leadership sometimes demanded bizarre things, like scanning the site with equipment meant for thermal anomalies, not standard archaeology. Everyone on staff was confused, but they just said it was 'special research' we shouldn't question. You can't mean they believe the myths of the Amulet being an ancient source of power?"

Aya nodded. "I think Léglise does. He was going on and on about supernatural powers. And thermal anomalies—maybe they were looking for an energy signature. Some intangible power in the sealed corridor."

"What did they find with the thermal imaging?" Amina asked.

Karim shrugged. "They were thrilled with the findings, which is when other digs in the region began shutting down amid whispers that Léglise himself, the chair of the board, was coming personally. What else do you know of Léglise, Aya? Where does he fit into this?"

"Last time I saw him, he lured me to an apartment in Paris to finish me off. I'd just done another job for him, but apparently, he had bigger fish to fry. My guesses were all swirling: who was backing him? Why did he turn so fast on me? Now I think I see a connection if they believe this Amulet can be used as a source of energy. I read references to these types of advanced scans, but the deeper encryption on the USB might confirm it. Problem is..." Aya grimaced. "I can't crack it. My usual method timed out."

"Wait," Karim said, "there are plenty of HRF laptops here." He walked to a stack of supplies and pulled out a dusty black laptop. "All data on these computers is encrypted with HRF's security software. The data might be readable on an HRF device that's connected to their network if it's encrypted using their protocols."

Aya handed over the USB drive. "Be my guest."

As Karim opened the device, Aya felt the weight of their compressed timeline. A month ago, she'd stolen this USB in Paris.

And now Amina was there, with Léglise arriving at dawn. All the carefully built foundations were crumbling.

Amina peered over Karim's shoulder. "Hurry. My reconnaissance tonight showed increased patrols on the eastern perimeter. They're already tightening security for Léglise's arrival."

As they waited for the system to boot, the shed felt impossibly small. Aya was hyperaware of both presences: Karim on her left, representing genuine connection and possible future; Amina on her right, embodying her past and all its complications.

"This is cozy," Amina murmured, her voice carrying that familiar edge of flirtation and threat. "Just like old times, except with a conscience and a new addition to our team."

"We're not a team," Aya said sharply. "This is a temporary alliance. After tomorrow—"

"After tomorrow, what?" Amina challenged. "You'll ride off into the sunset together? Play happy family like you used to daydream about, pretending the last five years of your life never happened? That's not who you are, Aya. I know who you really are."

"People change," Karim interjected quietly. "Whatever Aya was before, she's shown me someone who genuinely cares about doing what's right."

Amina's laugh was bitter. "Three weeks and you think you know her? I had two years, *habibi*. Two years of hot, passionate—"

"Enough," Aya cut her off. "We have bigger problems than our past right now."

Twenty-Six

Aya watched as Karim booted the computer and inserted the drive. Lines of green code scrolled across the black screen, then the HRF logo. He logged in.

After a moment, Karim was confronted with another black screen of text. He typed a string of commands, and the laptop's fan whirred softly. "Everything looks normal so far," he said.

Seconds stretched. Outside, the breeze shifted the corrugated walls with a dull rattle. Aya felt her muscles tighten. She remembered Léglise's chilling stare in Paris, the memory of his men attacking her. She'd had no clue that behind him lay an even bigger monster: Prometheus Energy Solutions.

The code scrolled faster. Karim's eyes lit. "I think we're getting somewhere—yes... it's decrypted!"

He hit Enter, and the screen blinked to reveal a hidden directory. Aya leaned in as Amina crowded close behind her. "I think we got it," Karim whispered, his brow glistening with sweat.

Aya exhaled. "Open it."

He double-clicked a newly decrypted folder. Lines of text,

scanned documents, and sealed memos filled the screen. A heading jumped out: "PES INTERNAL STRATEGY: ARCH PROJECT MOROCCO."

"So that's what they call it." Amina's smirk was replaced by grim focus. "I've been tracking their movements for weeks, waiting for the right moment. They've been recruiting specialists from around the world—not just archaeologists, but physicists, mathematicians, engineers, people who work with experimental energy systems."

Amina reached over Karim's shoulder and scrolled. "Look—satellite images of the Atlas region. Notes on 'Energy readings'... estimated historical significance... references to shutting down alternative leads in neighboring countries. They've poured everything into this site after what looks like a global search."

Karim clicked on another folder.

"Wait, look at this. *Almohad Mathematics*. They've hired specialists in medieval Islamic mathematics?" He opened an invoice. "These fees are astronomical. They're paying fortunes to experts who study Ibn Rushd's geometric theories and Almohad mathematical mysticism."

"Why would an energy company need *medieval* math experts?" Amina asked.

"Because," Aya said, the pieces clicking into place, "they've realized what we discovered. The Almohad scholars believed mathematical patterns could unlock divine secrets. If the Amulet was created based on those same principles..."

"Then they need the mathematics to understand how to use it," Karim finished. He opened another file. "And here, *Project Spiritual Alchemy: Transforming Intangible Energy into Harvestable Power*. They're not just chasing an artifact. They're trying to recreate the legendary work of the Alchemist of Salé."

"Ibn Tufail," Aya murmured. "The 12th-century philosopher who supposedly discovered how to transform base elements into pure energy."

"Exactly. Look at this memo," Karim said. "'*The Amulet represents the culmination of centuries of spiritual alchemy. What the medieval alchemists could only theorize, the ancient builders achieved. The geometric patterns function as transformation matrices, converting energy from another plane into usable power.*'"

Karim peered back at the screen. "They've spent hundreds of millions. Look, what's this mention of the U.S. ARMY? Codenamed '*Project Muwat Dhahab*'? At this cost, that looks like a private army. *Putain*, and here we are with a half-baked sabotage plan. Is this who's coming with Léglise tomorrow night?"

"I don't know," Aya said. "But we're not just dealing with a greedy sponsor. This is a multinational with infinite resources, led by a delusional megalomaniac, convinced that an ancient supernatural relic can what... hand them an energy supply? Control global energy production?"

"If so, they'll kill anyone in their way," Amina added darkly.

Karim pulled up another file. "Look at this—geological surveys. They've detected energy signatures that shouldn't exist according to conventional physics. Electromagnetic anomalies that spike at regular intervals, almost like... like something breathing."

"Or something trying to escape," Aya murmured, remembering her father's warnings about djinn. "Three weeks of translating those texts with you, Karim. Every warning about 'binding the smokeless fire,' about 'seals that must not break.' What if it's all real?"

"Then we're racing against something far older and more dangerous," Amina said quietly.

"A corporate giant chasing supernatural myths? This is insane," Karim said, throwing his hands up.

"But what if they're right? My father was doing research on the Amulet too, and historians in Marrakech have compiled a lot of suspicious records. I don't know, I'm not saying I believe, but they're willing to put a lot of money and risk a lot to get hold of it. Plus, if they get the Amulet and by some chance they're right, who knows what power they'll wield."

"You're right. It's unbelievable, but they clearly believe it. And I doubt they're going to just let us walk away and tell anyone what we saw here," Karim said.

The text scrolled further. A line made Amina snort in disgust: "Yes, there you are. *'Eliminating local resistance.' 'Neutralizing historical experts.'*" She cursed under her breath. "We are indeed on the kill list. Or at least you are, *mon amour*."

Karim's face hardened.

Aya tapped the laptop closed. "This raises the stakes, but I don't know if it changes anything. Tomorrow, we do enough damage to stall their operation. Meanwhile, we figure out a way to slip inside the corridor ourselves. If PES's reinforcements arrive to find the site offline, they'll be scrambling, so we need to be prepared."

Amina gave a quick nod. "And if we time it right, my buyer might be persuaded to pay top dollar. But I suppose let's focus on not getting shot first."

"But this is about more than money, Amina," Karim said. "The site's value—"

Amina shot him a dry look. "Yes, yes, noble ideals. I'm sure the gods of archaeology will be very proud of you. But I need more than a pat on the back, professor. We can figure all that out after we stop Léglise and this dig."

Aya folded her arms. "So this alliance is what, exactly?"

A flicker of something Aya couldn't place darted through

Amina's eyes, quickly buried. "Look, I'm not asking for your trust, just opportunity. I have reasons to see PES fall on their faces. You need my skill set. So let's call this temporary teamwork." She shrugged, but her voice had an unsteady edge. "You know as well as I do, Aya, that I never do something for free. We'll figure out the price when we've eliminated our shared threats."

For a heartbeat, tension hung thick. Ayacould still remember every detail of that final night in Luxor: Amina's whispered promises for their future, then the cold sting of betrayal. "Fine," she said at last, forcing composure. "But if you betray me again, I'll finish you myself. It will be my life's goal."

"Fair enough. But you'd have done it by now if it were that simple." Amina's mask slipped, revealing something raw beneath. "Look, I know you have every reason not to trust me. But PES... they didn't just stiff me on payment. They had me tortured for three days in a Hyderabad warehouse, trying to extract information about my other clients. I only escaped because their security got sloppy." Her hand unconsciously moved to her side. "But the Amulet isn't their first target, just their most promising."

Amina pulled back her sleeve slightly, revealing faint scars. "They wanted to know about other jobs I'd done, other artifacts I'd encountered. They were building a database, connecting myths and legends across cultures. Whatever they're planning, it's bigger than just Morocco. I've been planning payback ever since. They want to corner global energy markets, eliminate competition, and control governments through energy dependency. They're not just greedy, they're sociopathic."

She straightened, the vulnerability vanishing. "So yes, I want the Amulet's value. But I want PES destroyed more. And if there's even a chance that artifact could give them the power they're chasing..." She met Aya's eyes. "I won't let that happen."

Karim cast her a questioning look, but she squared her shoulders.

"We sabotage PES at dawn," Amina continued, "and buy ourselves time to see what's really in that corridor before Léglise and his team arrive at night. At that point, we renegotiate, but we're completely on the same page until that point."

"Deal?"

"Agreed," Karim sighed. "I can help you get into their generator controls if needed, or distract a guard."

"You're sure? Aya asked. "It's not easy, being a double-agent."

He met her gaze steadily. "I'm not a double-agent. It turns out I was never on their side, just being tricked into thinking this was about history."

Amina cleared her throat. "Lovely moral epiphanies, but we're out of time. We'd best not be found in here."

"Wait. But what about your employers, Aya? Who sent you here? Who else wants PES stopped?" Karim asked.

Aya shook her head. "It's an investment group called Aegis. I don't know much about them. I've never worked with them before, but we can deal with them later, too."

"You can't be serious," Amina said.

"What?"

"The Aegis?"

"I don't know who that is," Karim said.

"As if ancient power sources, djinn, and multinational energy mercenaries weren't cause enough to run. The Aegis is a shadow network, and no one knows who's behind it. Limitless reach, limitless resources, limitless intel. That's the word on the street. Not sure how you got hired by them, Aya, but I suppose

I was otherwise engaged. Either way, rest assured, we will not be dealing with them."

Aya felt a chill run down her spine. "What do you mean?"

"The Aegis has no official existence, no accountability. Word is they manipulate entire countries, start and end conflicts, all in the service of some agenda no one understands. They're not the good guys, Aya, they're just a different flavor of monster." Amina's expression darkened. "I've crossed paths with their operatives before. They make PES look like choirboys."

The implications hit Aya. If Amina was right, then she'd been played from the beginning. The mysterious contact who knew about her father's research, the convenient job offer, the omniscient surveillance. It all pointed to an organization with resources and ruthlessness that dwarfed even Léglise's operation.

"My father," Aya whispered, pieces clicking into place. "Three weeks ago, when I first arrived here, I thought I was just completing his research. But every day, every translation we've done, Karim—it's become clearer. He wasn't just studying the Amulet. He was trying to prevent this exact scenario."

Karim's face paled. "Then his death in Colombia..."

"Might not have been an accident at all. It's what I feared." Aya's voice was hollow. "All these weeks, I thought I was honoring his memory by completing his work. But what if I've been manipulated into finishing what killed him?"

Karim looked between them, his face pale. "So you're caught between two organizations that both might have killed your father?"

"It looks that way," Aya said. "Which means I can't trust anyone but myself to decide what happens to that Amulet. Not PES, not the Aegis, not even..." She glanced at Amina and Karim. "Well, we'll figure that out once we stop the immediate threat. I don't know what else we can do. I came into this wanting to get paid, wanting one last big score, then I was finished. But this isn't just stealing an antiquity and trading it for a new life. I won't let anyone get that Amulet from me if any of this is actually true."

Karim nodded slowly.

"Good for you," Amina said, laced with sarcasm. "Never lacking in confidence."

Aya ejected the USB, tucking it back into her pocket. "We go our separate ways for now. Tomorrow, gather near the southwestern fence right before sunrise. My colleagues, Omar and Abdelatif, will be waiting in the mountains. They'll handle the bigger sabotage while we take the corridor."

"One more thing," Karim said. "If we're going into that corridor tomorrow, we need to be prepared for what we might find. The translations have revealed consistent warnings about protection rituals, about approaching with 'pure intent.'"

He pulled out a small notebook, his personal copy of their translated work. "According to your father's work, the builders incorporated safeguards. Not just physical traps, but something designed to... to read the hearts of those who enter. It sounds insane, but given everything else..."

"My father believed it," Aya said softly. "In his final entries, the ones we decoded last week, he wrote about 'the judgment of the threshold.' He thought the Amulet itself could sense intent, could choose its bearer."

Amina scoffed, but there was uncertainty in her eyes. "Magical artifacts that judge character? Please."

Aya countered, "Look, I don't know what we'll find tomorrow. But if there's even a chance my father was right, we need to be prepared for more than just corporate security."

They agreed to slip out one by one, to avoid raising suspicion if an HRF guard randomly swept the area. Karim went first, breathing shallowly as he hopped out into the night, melting into the darkness until he disappeared around a corner.

Aya exhaled, nerves thrumming, alone again with Amina.

Amina reached for the door, then paused. "Don't think for a second I'll forget about the value of the mythical Amulet of Idris. But if it comes to choosing between that and letting PES seize a global advantage and ruin us all, I will cooperate." She tossed her a half-smile. "Just keep your eyes on me if you're worried I'll run off with it."

She shot her a steely glare. "I plan to."

"Look, I know this sounds hollow coming from me, but..." Amina hesitated, "watching you with him, seeing you actually care about something beyond the score. It's made me remember why I fell for you in the first place."

Aya stiffened. "Don't."

"I'm not trying to manipulate you. I'm just..." Amina struggled for words. "In Egypt, I told myself, leaving you was survival. But watching you building something real with someone who sees you for who you are now, not who you were —it's made me realize what I threw away."

"You threw away more than just us," Aya said. "You threw away any chance of redemption."

"Maybe." Amina's voice was barely a whisper. "But tomorrow, when we face whatever's in that corridor, I want you to know I'll have your back. Not just for the score, not just for revenge on PES. For you. For what we used to be. I miss you."

She touched Aya's shoulder lightly, and for a moment, Aya saw the woman she'd fallen in love with years ago, before the betrayals and before the choices that carved them into different people.

"I miss you too," Aya admitted, the words scraping her throat. "I miss who we were. But that's gone, Amina. Just a few weeks with Karim have shown me what real trust looks like.

What building something meaningful feels like. You and I, we were just two people using each other who happened to fall in love along the way."

Amina's hand dropped. "Maybe you're right. But tomorrow, we're all each other has against forces that want us dead. That has to count for something."

"It counts for a temporary alliance. Nothing more."

"Then enjoy the view, *habibi*. See you before dawn." She paused at the door, back still turned to Aya. "And Aya? Your archaeologist is lucky. You're someone worth trusting. Even if it took you three weeks of lies to get there."

Alone in the cluttered shed, Aya stared into the darkness. Memories gnawed at her composure. Two years since that betrayal, and here they were again, on the brink of a major operation. Shaking off the ghosts of the past, she tucked the laptop into her bag and, with one last glance at the shadows outside, rejoined the labyrinth of tents.

Outside, the generator rumbled like a caged beast. In hours, she would attempt to silence it, to upend the site's entire schedule.

Tomorrow would decide everything.

TWENTY-SEVEN

AYA AWOKE before daybreak to a charged silence. The camp was still cloaked in night, but the first pale streaks of light were threatening to creep over the mountaintops. She rose swiftly, checking her gear.

Her breath clouded in the crisp mountain air as she slipped out of the staff tent.

Karim was already waiting outside, rubbing his arms to ward off the biting chill. He smiled tensely at her arrival. "You're sure about this?"

Aya nodded, looking for guards. "We don't have a choice. The moment they breach that corridor tonight, PES wins."

He led her through the rows of tents. They spotted Amina lurking in the shadows as planned, arms folded in silent impatience.

A faint grunt confirmed she was ready.

Without exchanging words, they followed the path toward the southwestern fence. Just as promised, a narrow tear allowed them to slip through. Aya spotted Omar and Abdelatif, hunched by a ridge of stone a few yards away. Their faces were taut with urgency.

"Rise and shine, sleepyheads. We don't have long. Weeks of sleeping in filth, and it all comes down to this," Omar said, checking his equipment one last time.

"The stars align today," Abdelatif said quietly. "The warnings in your father's notebook, the celestial calculations we discussed. If there is truth to the ancient bindings, they will be at their weakest soon."

Abdelatif nodded in greeting. "No one is patrolling close to this side, at least not yet. But I fear something feels off."

Aya felt it too, a static in the air. She exchanged a glance with Karim before turning to the group. "We do this quickly. Remember the plan: sabotage the generator first. Omar, that's on you and me. Karim, you'll create a distraction near the scanning equipment as soon as the generator goes down. Abdelatif, you handle the forklift or water pump in the chaos, whichever seems more accessible."

Amina arched an eyebrow. "And me?"

"You're with me," Aya said flatly. "We get Omar set up with the generator, then make a play for the corridor before they realize what's happening and can set up a blockade."

For a moment, the five of them stood in a circle, the wind tugging at their clothes. Then, in near-silence, they split off.

A shimmering band of gold spread over the distant horizon, illuminating the rugged outlines of the camp. Most of the archaeologists and guards were just beginning to stir; some clustered around the coffee station or rummaged for tools. The HRF foreman barked instructions, oblivious to the infiltration happening within the site.

Aya crouched behind a tall crate, Amina at her side. Omar had veered left, scanning for the generator's fuel tank. The plan was to disable or destroy it. If they could cut power, the entire operation would grind to a halt, at least temporarily.

Karim was in sight, near a cluster of scanning machines. He faked rummaging for cables, calling out to a half-awake technician. The man approached, confused. Karim gestured wildly at a nonexistent problem on a console.

Abdelatif had broken away to the far end of camp, where a forklift stood, along with a large water pump used to keep the trenches from flooding with groundwater. Aya could just see him unravel a length of tubing. If done right, he'd jam the pump in a matter of minutes.

A single guard paced a narrow alley near the generator, his radio crackling with garbled instructions.

Amina eased forward, pistol readied to eliminate the threat. Aya gripped her wrist, shaking her head. *Too messy*, she mouthed. Aya knew the guard rotations, their blind spots, their weaknesses. This particular guard, Simo, always grew careless during the shift change.

Instead, Aya crept toward a twisted length of aluminum piping lying beside an overturned toolbox. Timing her movement with the guard's slow pivot, she snatched the pipe and lobbed it over the guard's shoulder. It struck a rusted air compressor with a loud, hollow clang.

The guard swore, spinning at the jarring noise. "Who's there?" he barked, stepping off his patrol route and inching deeper into the shadows. She and Amina crouched low, exchanging a tense nod. The moment he was out of sight from the main path, they closed in.

Amina lunged, hooking her foot behind the guard's calf and driving him off-balance. The guard twisted, mouth opening to shout, but Aya darted behind him and snaked an arm around his throat to cut off blood flow.

The guard's eyes bulged. He clawed at her, but Amina

seized his wrist, forcing it behind his back. Within seconds, the lack of oxygen to his brain sent him sagging against them, consciousness slipping away.

Aya eased him gently to the ground, her heart pounding. He was alive, breathing shallowly, but out cold.

Amina's chest rose and fell, adrenaline bright in her eyes. "You're still squeamish about a little pragmatic killing here or there?"

"I do what I must. But I'm not you."

"Right. So we go easy on him and anyone else working for these psychos." Amina took a step closer, brushing dust from her shoulder. "Your call. Just don't regret it if they come back shooting."

"I'll handle it. Let's keep moving before someone finds him."

She gestured for Amina to move behind the generator's housing. The dull roar of machinery drowned out their footsteps. Omar was already prying open the metal panel, revealing a snarl of wires.

"I can rig a charge here. Nothing massive, but enough to break key components in the motor," he said.

Amina peered over his shoulder. "Faster would be cutting the main line." She pointed to a thick cable leading into the ground.

"True, but they might just quickly repair it if we only cut the wire," Omar said, rummaging in a pouch. He extracted a small charge, carefully pressing it against the interior panel. "Thirty seconds, once set."

Aya kept watch.

"All right," Omar whispered. "Stand back." He flicked the trigger device. "Move!"

They ducked behind an overturned handcart, hearts pounding. Ten seconds passed. Fifteen seconds passed.

BOOM.

The explosive roar reverberated across the mountain range. The concentrated blast rattled the air, sending up a cloud of dust. Sparks burst from the generator, and the hulking diesel engine coughed, winding down with a heavy, mechanical groan.

Alarms blared, and Aya's ears rang from the percussion as she scrambled forward.

Inside the camp, the lights sputtered. The hush of the morning shattered as workers shouted in alarm. Over by the scanning machines, a confused gathering indicated that Karim managed his part.

Aya allowed herself a brief surge of hope. For at least a few precious minutes, the entire site was offline. HRF and PES officials would be scrambling. This was the window they needed.

She beckoned to Amina, "Time to move. Corridor entrance."

They sprinted between crates, through the confusion, ignoring the furious chatter of HRF staff.

Karim spotted them passing by and started to follow, but a frantic worker grabbed his sleeve, screaming about the damage. He shot Aya a desperate look over the man's shoulder, but she could only grimace and wave him off.

Up ahead, Omar angled around the collapsed scaffolding near the corridor. "I'll keep watch," he hissed. "If we can get inside..."

WHOP. WHOP. WHOP.

The sudden thunder of rotor blades cut through the morning air. Aya froze and glanced skyward. Two helicopters were descending rapidly over the valley, churning dust into violent spirals. The entire camp erupted in confusion. Some archaeologists crouched in fear, while the nearest HRF suit frantically glanced at his watch.

"Léglise's forces. They're early."

TWENTY-EIGHT

ONE HELICOPTER LANDED with a deafening roar, its side door sliding open. Armored men spilled out, rifles in hand, while a second helicopter hovered overhead, scanning the terrain. Instantly, the site was awash in swirling dust and shouted orders.

Aya ducked behind a stack of sandbags, Amina at her side. Omar crouched low across from them. "Damn it," he hissed. "We only just started. I thought they weren't coming until tonight?"

The second helicopter landed behind the first, and a team of black-clad troops fanned out before quickly spotting the generator wreckage and heading right toward them.

Their lead man barked orders: "Secure the site! What's going on here? Why is everything down?"

"We don't know what's happening, sir," the nearest HRF guard called over the noise. "We suspect foul play—we may have been attacked. The generator and water pump both went down at once. Then we're getting reports of widespread sensor misreads from Dr. Haddad."

Aya could only watch as Philippe Léglise himself emerged from behind the first chopper, wearing a tailored jacket and a calm, almost smug expression. He was flanked by two armed guards, rifles drawn and readied. His eyes swept the chaos with infuriating composure.

Karim had been pinned by a pair of uniformed men along with every other member of the archaeology team. They were being patted down and quickly interrogated.

Aya stifled a curse. If they pulled Karim away or suspected he was up to something, he was in danger. She took a step forward, intending to help, but an echoing crack of gunfire froze her in place.

A sharp voice rang out from a loudspeaker: "This camp is under the jurisdiction of Prometheus Energy Solutions and the Heritage Reclamation Foundation. All personnel stand down immediately while our security forces secure the site. Everyone needs to remain on the ground while we assess the situation."

Across the camp, they could see Abdelatif trying to slip away from the flooding wreckage. A newly arrived soldier spotted him, rifle raised.

Omar bolted upright and shouted. "Abdelatif, get down!"

It was too late. A hail of gunfire rang out, and Abdelatif lurched, clutching his side before crumpling against a forklift.

Aya's stomach twisted. "No!" She sprang out of hiding, ignoring the risk, sprinting across the open ground. More guards swung rifles in her direction. Omar and Amina scrambled after her, each prepared for a firefight.

Another bullet whined past Aya's ear. She dropped into a roll, heart hammering, then dove behind an overturned metal crate, but Omar never broke from his sprint. By the time Aya caught up, he was already crouched by Abdelatif.

The older man gasped, blood staining the front of his shirt.

"No, no, no!" Omar yelled over the commotion, kneeling

beside his friend. He pressed shaking hands over the wound, desperate to stem the blood. "Stay with me, please..."

Omar glanced toward the guard who'd fired the shot. Murder flared in his gaze, but he forced it down, focusing on Abdelatif. "I should've been faster," he rasped. "My friend, I should've protected you."

A frantic moment passed as he continued to put pressure on the bleeding. Abdelatif's eyes fluttered, pained but alive.

Approaching the corridor, Léglise strode forward, ignoring the chaos as his men continued to fan out and secure the area.

More shots rang out as the black uniforms seized control of the dig site: guard towers, the main equipment yard, and the scanning station.

Aya watched as Karim, alongside the others, was forced to his knees by two armed soldiers. They'd come so close to turning the tables, but now PES reigned, unstoppable in their numbers and firepower.

She turned to Omar, who was pressing his shirt to Abdelatif's wound. The older man hissed in pain, but his eyes held focus. "I'm fine," he managed, though the tremor in his voice betrayed how bad it was.

Moments later, Amina reached them. "We can't take them all. At least not now," she said.

"We need to get Abdel out of here," Aya said. "If we stay, they'll grab us all."

Omar shook his head. "We can't just leave the corridor, or Karim."

"We can't help either if we're dead," Amina said. "We regroup, get Abdelatif to safety, then figure out how to rescue your archaeologist and finish what we started."

From across the yard, Léglise's gaze swept in their direction. Aya could almost feel his cold, predatory stare on her skin. She ducked lower. One of the men beside Léglise gestured vigorously toward the area where Abdelatif had been shot.

No time. She and Omar heaved Abdelatif up between them, hooking his arms over their shoulders. He groaned but gritted his teeth, determined to stand.

"Stop right there," one of the soldiers yelled.

"No chance," Amina said. She hung behind them, pistol clenched.

Bullets smacked into crates nearby, sending shards of wood flying. One soldier rounded the corner, rifle raised, but Amina dropped low and fired two quick suppressive shots.

Another soldier rushed through, rifle raised. "Stop! Hands up!"

Amina didn't hesitate. She fired two more rounds, forcing him to dive for cover behind a supply crate. "Move!" she shouted.

More shouts erupted from behind them as additional soldiers converged on their position. Bullets whined overhead, sparking off metal containers and splintering wooden crates around them.

"There!" Omar pointed to a gap in the perimeter fencing, but it was fifty meters away across open ground. "But we'll never make it carrying him."

"We have to try," Aya said. They began a desperate sprint, half-carrying Abdelatif between them while Amina provided cover fire.

A soldier appeared at their flank, raising his weapon. Amina spun and fired, her shot catching him in the shoulder, spinning him around.

"Contact rear!" someone shouted. "Multiple hostiles fleeing southwest!"

The staccato crack of automatic weapons fire erupted behind them. Dirt exploded around their feet as they zigzagged toward the fence. Abdelatif groaned with each jarring step, his weight growing heavier as shock set in.

"Almost there," Omar panted.

A bullet caught the fence post just ahead of them, sending sparks flying. Aya threw herself through the gap first, then helped pull Abdelatif through the jagged wire. His shirt tore, adding fresh scratches to his wounds.

Omar, then Amina, dove through just as a concentrated burst of gunfire raked the fence line. But they were already scrambling up the steep ravine beyond, using the rocky terrain to break the line of sight.

"Keep moving!" Amina urged, glancing back. "They'll send pursuit teams!"

They half-ran, half-slid through the loose scree, supporting Abdelatif between them. Behind them, they could hear shouted orders and the thrum of helicopter rotors. One of the aircraft lifted off, beginning a search pattern.

"There—that overhang," Omar pointed to a rocky shelter carved into the ravine wall. They stumbled toward it, lungs burning, as the helicopter's rotor wash began kicking up dust clouds in the distance.

They pressed into the shallow cave just as the aircraft thundered overhead, its downdraft sending rocks skittering down the slope. For several tense minutes, they remained frozen as the helicopter made passes over the area, its crew scanning for movement.

Finally, the sound began to fade as it moved to search other areas.

Aya ran through weeks of contingency planning. They'd mapped escape routes, identified shelter points, prepared for this possibility, but not with Abdelatif wounded, not with Léglise arriving so far ahead of schedule.

"This way," Omar said. "The old man showed me this

hidden path." He led them down a slope, away from the site, out of view and range.

They kept moving, hearts pounding. Behind them, the camp was engulfed by shouting men, the dual vortex of two running helicopters, and the occasional staccato of gunfire. Their plan had worked for a fleeting moment. Now, PES was in total control, the corridor fully in their grasp.

"Abdelatif, can you try walking?" Aya asked in a strangled voice, sweat trickling down her temple.

He nodded weakly, though his breath came in shallow gasps.

Omar's features darkened. "We can't let them open that corridor. Maybe if we can return and signal to Karim—"

Aya nodded. "We have to." Her thoughts hadn't left Karim, pinned inside.

Amina stepped up beside her. "We'll figure out a way back in. But first, we secure him." She jerked her chin at Abdelatif, who was on the brink of passing out.

They stumbled deeper through the rocky pass. The morning sun was fully risen now, bathing the rugged terrain in harsh clarity. Each step jarred a ragged groan from Abdelatif's lips. Yet they pressed on. No other choice.

TWENTY-NINE

THE PASSAGE HAD LED them through a series of connected caves, as Abdelatif had assured, before emerging into this sheltered ravine. It was invisible from the air and accessible only to those who knew exactly where to look. PES might have superior firepower, but they were operating in Abdelatif's territory.

Aya caught her breath in the narrow crevice. Abdelatif had guided them to an old smuggler's route, a network of caves and hidden passages that honeycombed the mountains.

"My grandfather used paths like these during the French occupation," Abdelatif wheezed as they'd half-carried him through a concealed opening behind a rockfall. "The soldiers... they don't know these mountains like we do."

Behind Aya, Omar cradled a half-conscious Abdelatif. Blood seeped through the makeshift bandage on the older man's left shoulder.

"Don't move so much," Omar whispered, pressing harder onto the wound. His voice trembled with worry.

Abdelatif coughed weakly, forcing one eye open. "I'll be fine," he rasped, though the lines creasing his brow didn't inspire confidence. "You must stop them from unleashing what they do not understand... you may need this in the end." He lifted a hand slowly and reached under his djellaba for his slim leather folio, containing scrawled references to ancient inscriptions, local lore, partial translations. He pushed it toward Aya.

Aya took it gingerly. She'd skimmed this folio before, familiar with its contents and how closely it aligned with her father's own research. "We will," she promised, fingers tightening on the worn cover.

Omar looked torn. "Aya, you know I want to help inside. But he needs real medical attention. I can't just leave him."

Aya nodded. "Of course. Stay with him. Try to get back to the supplies we left at the camp on the ridge. Keep him alive," she whispered, scanning the distance. She glimpsed black shapes patrolling along the fence line. "We'll do what we have to."

"Be careful," Abdelatif murmured. "Djinn... I fear..."

Another coughing spasm stole his breath, but he clung to consciousness a moment longer to shake his head. "I believe in you."

Aya clasped Omar's shoulder. "We'll be back." Then she pivoted, leveling her gaze on Amina, who stood a few yards away with her arms folded, posture rigid in the dusty wind.

Amina's dark hair whipped across her face. "Are we going to make them pay for this, or are we waiting for them to blow it open and find the Amulet first?"

"Let's move," Aya said. With a final glance at Omar and Abdelatif, she and Amina set off along the jagged overhang toward the chain-link fence.

They reached a vantage near the fence where their sabotage's aftermath was painfully clear. A gaping hole in the main generator housing left blackened metal and dangling wires; the ground was scorched from a controlled blast. A lingering haze of smoke mingled with the sharp tang of diesel.

Yet the sabotage also seemed to have forced a more rapid approach from Léglise's crew. His soldiers had roped off major sections of the camp, while some worked feverishly to set up a temporary generator, a smaller unit that whined under strain.

"Léglise is hurrying up," Aya whispered. "We bought ourselves only hours. With this new crew, they'll break through and have the Amulet soon."

One soldier patrolled the fencing near them, scanning the area with a scowl. Aya motioned Amina behind a tangle of collapsed cargo netting. They crouched low, angling for a better look.

In the distance, a group of the dig site's workers was being held under armed guard. Clearly, they were taking no chances at further sabotage or interference. Aya's pulse leapt when she spotted a familiar figure among them: Karim. Even from a distance, she saw the blood on his cheek, the slump of his shoulders.

Another soldier hovered behind the group, assault rifle ready. Karim twisted, peering around, searching for them.

Aya ducked lower, an ache knotting in her chest. She hated the idea of leaving him a captive, but they needed a plan, not a suicide rush.

Amina tapped her elbow. "They're short-staffed on the perimeter. Too many men are busy at the corridor and containing the site workers. Now's our chance." She pointed to the lone soldier at the fence, now with his back to them, struggling with his radio.

"We slip through. If we can free Karim too, all the better."

They inched closer in tandem. The soldier muttered curses under his breath. Aya watched as Amina pulled a knife from her boot, but signaled her to stop.

Amina rolled her eyes but palmed her blade anyway.

They circled behind the guard, using his frustration paired with the acrid smoke and battered crates as cover. The moment he gave up on communications and moved to patrol along the fence again, away from them, they seized the gap.

Amina squeezed through the bent chain-link, then motioned Aya through. Back inside the site, the tension hit Aya. Diesel, burnt metal, fear.

They ducked behind a tent, with a clear path to the central trench that led down to the concealed chamber. Ahead, Karim and the group of kneeling workers, hands pinned behind their heads. She counted ten.

One soldier held the group at gunpoint. Another soldier was making his way through the group, putting cable ties around each of their wrists.

"I can't just leave him," Aya whispered.

Amina exhaled. "Okay, I think we may need him. But we do this fast. One guard in front, the other behind. I'll take the one with the gun."

Aya nodded.

They sprang from cover in unison. Aya's guard whipped around, dropping his zip ties and grabbing for the rifle strapped to his chest, only to be met by Aya's blade slicing across his forearm.

He groaned as blood splattered the ground, and Aya grabbed one of the zip ties before pouncing on him, wrestling her legs around his neck while he fought for air, and forcing his wrists into the restraints.

Simultaneously, Amina launched herself at the second soldier, and he delivered a spray of gunfire that narrowly went wide.

As she closed the gap, she delivered a strong kick to his ribs that knocked him off-balance. She swept his legs and quickly had him on the ground. Amina slammed her forearm into his neck, pinning him to the dirt and starting to cut off air.

In the swirl of dust, Karim lurched upright. "Aya?" he said. "You're insane!" There was still a flicker of doubt in his eyes.

"I had to come back. Now grab a zip tie and help Amina."

He stared at her, then Amina, who was grinning, inches from the soldier's face, as she watched his consciousness fade. Without further hesitation, Karim had the other guard restrained.

Amina stood and extracted the man's gun.

"What are you doing?" Aya asked.

"For good measure," Amina said, before quickly smashing the butt of the rifle into the soldier's head and walking to the second to repeat the process.

"Come on," Aya pleaded.

"We don't want these two knuckle-draggers waking up and coming back to haunt us. I agreed not to kill, but no half measures, especially with this much firepower."

Aya nodded. "Fine, you're right. Let's go, we can't let them blow open that corridor."

Karim gestured at the crates of explosives near the path to the half-exposed trench. "Then we need to hurry. They're early, but the sabotage forced their hand. They'll breach it with bigger charges if needed."

A fresh explosion rattled the camp, sending gray dust geysering into the air. Shrieks followed as the other archaeologists who had watched their skirmish cowered behind a half-collapsed canopy.

Aya, Karim, and Amina all took off toward the chamber and the Amulet inside, giving up on any semblance of stealth.

A voice boomed as they approached: "Hurry up! We don't have all day. Mr. Léglise wants that corridor open now! We need to get out of here, the choppers are running!"

At the far side of the trench. Léglise stood in his immaculate powder-blue suit, on a makeshift command platform, scanning the turmoil with cold fury. Next to him, his commander barked orders at troops hauling crates toward the corridor's stone barrier.

As they reached the edge of the excavated area, the scale of what had been uncovered took Aya's breath away. The corridor entrance, now fully exposed, revealed intricate stonework that had been hidden for centuries.

"My God," Karim whispered in awe. "Look at those patterns—the geometric designs covering the entrance. Those *are* Marinid. I've seen identical patterns in the Bougnaniyyah Madrasa in Fez. The Marinids used these specific mathematical relationships in their schools. It's like I thought, they believed these patterns aided in spiritual contemplation, in achieving higher states of consciousness."

Aya's eyes traced the interlocking stars and polygons that framed the sealed doorway.

"And look there," she pointed to smaller symbols etched into the stone above the entrance. "Those are Sa'adi protective symbols, as we thought, too. They're the same ones found in the royal tombs. Eight-pointed stars within hexagons, just like the ones meant to ensure spiritual protection."

"It's not just decoration," Karim said. "This is a warning system. The Marinid patterns are telling us how to approach: with mathematical precision and with spiritual preparation. Those Sa'adi symbols are barriers, meant to keep something contained. Whoever built this combined centuries of Moroccan mystical knowledge into one defensive system."

"We're too late," Aya whispered.

"There has to be a way around these bastards," Amina said.

Karim's voice shook. "This path to the chamber took us five months to construct, and it's not even stable yet. There is no other way in. Plus, they have half a platoon. When I tried to warn them about the collapse, the commander shoved a gun in my face. Léglise wants that corridor open at any cost. You've seen the way they seized control. They won't hesitate to put us down."

Gunfire raked overhead, and a message came through all of Léglise's men's radios at once. A soldier had found the men they'd taken down.

"This is about to get a lot worse if they're actively hunting for us," Amina said, scanning the corridor entrance, where dust churned in thick waves. "Push forward or we're pinned."

"Push," Aya agreed, hearing the beep of active detonators. "They'll blow it in minutes."

Amina clapped Karim on the back, "Here we go!"

THIRTY

THEY CROUCHED behind a stack of toppled storage containers, hearts pounding in unison. Mangled scaffolding lay strewn across the churned-up earth. Gunfire echoed from around the perimeter. A line of Léglise's soldiers patrolled the open ground, faces concealed behind black face shields and the swirl of dust.

Aya scanned them for a gap. A chunk of rebar pinned half a canvas tent to the ground, forming a ragged passage just wide enough to crawl under.

"Keep low," she hissed to Karim and Amina before leading the way, pressed to the dirt, sliding beneath torn canvas, gravel scraping her elbows.

Someone beyond the tents shouted orders she couldn't make out, and bullets ripped through the tent ahead of them, tearing it to ribbons. Screams followed.

Aya held up a hand. They waited, breath tight, as the soldier stomped past, just outside their cover. The grit of his boots scraped across the rubble, then he moved on.

"We'll never reach the trench if we go head-on," Karim

said. "They're trigger-happy, shooting at anything that moves. They're hell-bent on rounding everyone up after what we did to the generator."

"We'll use the collapsed walkway," Aya said, pointing to a tilted section of platform bridging the crater in the earth to their left. The plank was barely intact, but it might give cover from the line of sight.

"Now!" Aya urged, waving Karim and Amina along as the soldiers were just out of sight. They sprinted over the twisted walkway, ignoring its groan beneath their weight.

They leapt the final gap, rolling behind a shattered column.

At last, the mouth of the trench was in sight, a swirling haze of dust and rubble. The roar of charges thundered again from deep underground.

Léglise's people had managed to divert the flow of water, but Abdelatif's sabotage of the pump had destroyed the scaffolding that once made crossing safe. Now Léglise's soldiers had jury-rigged a route with ropes and stanchions, leading to the broad opening in the rock.

Thick dust hung in the air, but Aya glimpsed the bright blue of broken mosaics that once adorned the entrance. The repeated blasts had reduced them to shards. Through swirling debris, she spotted Léglise stepping back from the threshold of the structure.

Aya counted twelve soldiers with assault rifles in the trench.

Another reverberation shook the site, a charge set inside the chamber. Stones tumbled from the corridor mouth, scattering like ancient bones. Out into the haze stumbled two coughing soldiers.

One shouted, "One more blast will do it, sir. It's barely holding."

Léglise nodded, unsmiling. "Then do it." He put his ear protection back on.

"Set the last explosives!" roared his commander. "Brace yourselves, we breach in one minute."

"There's got to still be a way in," Amina whispered.

Karim's fists clenched. "They're destroying everything, exploding it to get through. Mosaics from the Idrisid era..."

Aya grasped his arm. "Come on, we're too exposed. We stay here, we die. We have to move."

The three of them edged closer, taking advantage of the focus on the explosions. They were only meters away, concealed behind collapsed scaffolding.

Suddenly, a savage crack tore the air. The final explosion rattled the entire site. Aya staggered, ears ringing.

Sunlit dust drifted in a million shimmering particles.

When it had settled, Aya peered through a gap in the scaffolding poles to see the corridor barrier cracked wide, with jagged rocks littering its entrance. A meter-wide gap loomed in the rock, releasing an unnatural rush of icy air. Even meters away, she felt the temperature drop, breath pluming in the desert morning.

An eerie hush fell across the site.

One soldier edged forward, flashlight bobbing. "It's an inner chamber," he called back, voice echoing. "It's pretty empty, but there's a pedestal in there!"

Aya tensed. Across from her, Amina's face was set, balancing between fury and fear.

From behind a twisted section of collapsed scaffolding, Aya pressed Omar's battered pair of binoculars to her eyes and caught a glimpse inside the chamber.

The walls were lined with intricate engravings of falcon silhouettes and spirals of Tifinagh script, each carving flowing into the next like ancient poetry written in stone. Geometric mosaics covered the ceiling in deep blues and golds that seemed to glow even in the dim light, patterns that reminded her of her father's sketches, designs he'd theorized about but never seen.

In the three weeks she'd been here, Aya had seen Karim painstakingly photograph every accessible inscription, treating each fragment like the treasure it was. Now those same inscriptions lay in pieces, ground to dust under military boots. The careful grid system they'd established, the preservation protocols, all obliterated in Léglise's rush.

Karim murmured beside her, "Every warning we translated together, they're coming true."

This was what her father had spent years searching for. Not just an artifact, but a complete historical treasure, a window into a civilization that had mastered both art and power in ways modern scholars could barely comprehend. The craftsmanship was breathtaking, every tile precisely placed, every inscription carefully carved by artisans who understood they were creating something eternal.

And now, thin cracks ran through every carving.

Léglise's eyes glinted with triumph as he descended into the newly exposed corridor, stepping over rubble.

Suddenly, another grinding roar tore through the site.

A section of the corridor had collapsed, preventing any approach from the right. Léglise's soldiers were coughing in swirling dust, stepping back into formation around their boss. A further inexplicable cold was released and lingered in the air.

Karim's face was grim. "This corridor was sealed for a reason. There's an ancient vow never to open it in the mythology. We were trying to find the right way in, following the inscriptions, solving the riddle of 'one eye sees the truth.' But they're ignoring every warning, structural or supernatural, bulldozing through with explosives and brute force. We'll see what price is paid beyond the priceless history destroyed in seconds."

Amina's jaw tightened. "Well, if they think they can keep that Amulet from me, they're sorely mistaken. It's time."

She slid along a half-broken pillar, eyes scanning for an opening.

"No, Amina," Aya hissed, but she was gone.

Beyond the rubble, Léglise emerged from the corridor's gloom, something cradled in his gloved hands, shielded from Aya's sight. Léglise wore a triumphant smile, and Aya knew exactly what it was: the Amulet of Idris.

Léglise raised the artifact high, and sunlight caught it at a sharp angle, igniting a wash of refracted color, icy blues, ghostly whites, a pulse of red glimmer. Every crystalline facet shimmered like trapped starlight, and thin filaments of metal, silver, or perhaps platinum, spiraled around it in the shape of a falcon's wings.

From inside the crystal itself, strange currents of light seemed to flicker and move, as though faint embers swirled in a liquid core. A hush settled over the trench, a pull radiating from the Amulet's center. Even the soldiers fell momentarily silent, weapons dropping an inch, captivated by the eerie glow.

Something about it felt deeply alive to Aya, like static electricity on her skin, or a low hum resonating in her chest. Whether science or myth, it radiated a power that made the air taste heavy with possibility.

A prickle of fear trickled down her spine. She tried to tear her gaze away and found it harder than expected, as if the Amulet wanted to be seen.

"At last," Léglise shouted. His mercenaries parted to give him space. He stared down at his prize, which reflected sunlight that danced across his cold eyes.

He raised the Amulet high in the air. "Behold," he called to his troops. "It's finally ours."

The soldiers around him broke into sporadic applause.

"Hooah," the commander bellowed, before everyone echoed him, and the applause swelled.

A sudden, hollow rumble rolled beneath the ground. Loose pebbles danced over the cracked earth, and a low, grating moan drifted from the newly opened corridor, like the exhalation of something gigantic.

Then the precarious gap in the stone shuddered again, as though straining under an immense pressure.

As the temperature plummeted further, the Marinid geometric patterns that Karim had identified on the corridor walls began to glow—faint at first, like they were submerged in deep water, then brighter, pulsing in rhythmic waves.

"Look at the patterns!" Karim gasped. "The designs—they're activating! The sequences are lighting up in order, like... like they're counting down to something."

The intricate stars and polygons flared with an other-worldly blue-white light, each form igniting in perfect sequence. The glow spread outward from the breach, racing along the carved lines like liquid fire, illuminating centuries of sacred mathematics in a display that was both beautiful and terrifying.

"It is a warning system," Aya gasped.

Even Léglise's soldiers stepped back nervously as the light show intensified, casting eerie shadows that danced and writhed across the excavation site.

Frost began forming on the metal scaffolding nearest the breached corridor, an impossibility under the morning sun.

Aya's pulse hammered as she thought of the lines from Abdelatif's folio describing a hidden vow that once bound fiery djinn to these stones. They had just broken that vow repeatedly.

Movement caught Aya's eye, a flash of dark fabric among the rubble on the opposite side of the trench. Amina had somehow circled around during the explosion, using the chaos to position herself closer to Léglise's group. She was crouched behind an overturned supply crate, maybe twenty meters from where Léglise stood with the Amulet.

Their eyes met briefly across the dusty chaos. Amina held up two fingers. Wait two minutes, then move. She was planning something.

Aya watched Léglise revel in his triumph, the Amulet glinting in his hands. A fierce determination flared: she couldn't let him vanish with the artifact, not after seeing what lay in that beautiful, ruined chamber. Not after thinking of her father's reverence for such places.

"I'm going for it," she whispered to Karim. "Amina's in position. If we coordinate, there might be a chance to snatch the Amulet when they're distracted."

Karim's eyes went wide. "Aya, no, there are too many soldiers."

"We'll never get another shot." In a blur, she bolted from cover, weaving between fallen beams, hoping Amina would see her move and act accordingly.

Aya lunged from behind the debris but was forced to duck as the nearest guard spotted her and peppered the ground at her feet with bullets.

The echo of gunfire ricocheted off the stone. Aya launched herself forward, finding cover under another collapsed beam, inching closer.

Léglise's soldiers, however, were more alert than she hoped. Before she could try to move again, the butt of a rifle crashed into her ribs, sending her stumbling to her knees. Pain lanced her side, and her vision blurred.

Within seconds, two soldiers wrenched Aya's arms behind her back, locking them into a zip tie.

Aya twisted under the rough grip of two soldiers as a rifle

smashed into the side of her head, blurring her vision. They forced her to her knees before Léglise, who clutched the Amulet like a trophy. Debris continued to rain down from the half-collapsed corridor, and dust coated her tongue.

Karim, seeing Aya's capture, rushed forward to help, only to be knocked off his feet by another soldier's savage kick. A paramilitary pinned him with a boot on his back, muzzle of his gun pressed against his head.

In the commotion, a sudden scream rang out across the trench.

Three archaeologists whom Léglise's men had rounded up after the sabotage, two younger men and a middle-aged woman who Aya had worked alongside while cataloging pottery shards, had tried to flee in the troops' distraction. Léglise's commander quickly raised his rifle and gunned the two men down without a flicker of hesitation.

"Stop her," he called to his guards, watching the woman darting for cover by the tents. "She's been warned." One of the guards drew his rifle and fired a single shot that dropped her in a cloud of dust.

Shock rippled through the site.

Léglise stormed forward, the Amulet glimmering like a live ember in his grasp. He glared at the fallen archaeologists, then at the rest cowering nearby, terror etched on their faces.

His voice was a chilling calm: "Let this be a lesson," he announced, letting the echo carry across the site. "I have no use for stragglers or thieves who hide in shadows. You had your chance to comply. My patience is a finite resource."

Then, Léglise turned back to his captives in the trench.

Léglise stared down coldly. "As I suspected, Mademoiselle Amrani. Still alive, I see. Well, there's no doubt who inflicted such futile damage to my equipment, then. I did wonder when I got reports of a beautiful woman who appeared suddenly, slinking around the medina in Marrakech, meeting with all the shadiest people. Pity, I really wished my associates in Paris could have finished you there. Instead, now you appear to have seduced our fine Dr. Haddad to follow you to your death."

He walked closer to Aya, who was still reeling from the soldier's blow moments before. Blood trickled down her chin, but she stood defiantly. He lifted the Amulet, its facets flickering like a storm in a crystal.

"You see this?" He held it high so the survivors could witness. "One piece of history that outshines everything else in these ruins. This is the future, my future. Those who stand in my path will meet the same fate as these pathetic deserters. And if any of you think I'm bluffing..." He gestured to the fallen archaeologists, still warm on the ground. "Take a good, long look."

Horrified silence reigned. The soldiers leveled their rifles at the trembling captives.

Aya struggled, rage coiling in her chest. "If you wanted me dead, you should've done it yourself. But you always stay impeccably clean, eh?"

Léglise raised an eyebrow. "You were merely an inconvenience back then, a loose end. But you seem to have grown into an infestation, crawling into my site, daring to sabotage my discovery." He shoved the Amulet closer to her face, letting her see its hypnotic luminescence. "You have no idea what this truly is, do you? I thought you had evolved, but you're still clinging to naive notions of your father and his sort of idealistic fool."

Anger flared in Aya at the mention of her father.

The corridor behind Léglise lay in ruins, the centuries-old mosaic patterns and the outer chamber's remnants smashed by the repeated blasts. She pictured her father's field log, scrawled with warnings about untested sites. She'd read the same caution in Abdelatif's folio: One eye sees the truth, one eye sees the lie... the vow is never to be broken. She'd always dismissed it as a poetic metaphor. But now, with the ground trembling at random intervals, the air turning to ice, the Marinid patterns still glowing in eerie sequences, the Amulet pulsing, the lengths Léglise had gone to. It felt more like a prophecy.

Léglise flicked his gaze to the rumbling corridor. "Distracted, Miss Amrani? Am I seeing a glimmer of that naive archaeologist I found in Honduras, before I showed you your true potential? The secrets and power buried under centuries of rock and human ignorance?"

"This one was sealed for a reason. In a way you couldn't comprehend."

"And I'm to believe you were here for completely honorable reasons?"

Aya sighed. "It's complicated, Léglise. But what do you know of the myths surrounding this place? The ancient warnings that you've now disregarded?"

He sneered. "We've harnessed nuclear power, sent man into space, crafted artificial intelligence. Do you really think some medieval curse should stop progress? That we can't outsmart some dusty curse? One I've seen little proof of?"

Behind him, the illuminated patterns pulsed faster, their shapes now creating optical illusions that made the corridor walls seem to breathe and shift. Several soldiers looked away, wincing.

Clutching the gleaming Amulet, Léglise turned slowly, letting the dust swirl around him like a coronation cloak. His voice, once silky, carried an undercurrent of triumph.

"You think I fund all these digs and expeditions through Heritage because I fancy myself a collector of dusty trinkets?" he asked, shooting a cold glance at the cowering archaeologists. "Don't mistake my motives for some private whim.

Prometheus Energy Solutions, my enterprise, has spent billions on R&D to capture new forms of clean power. Solar, wind, geothermal. At best, these are incremental steps. But this..." He lifted the crystal relic, its facets refracting ghostly lights across the rubble. "This is a quantum leap."

He paced across the uneven ground. "Centuries ago, the Idrisid dynasty commanded a thriving empire here, powered by this Amulet, though its origins are far older than Idris I. He was just its last master. Before me, that is.

"His people wrote of a 'smokeless flame' that surged through the mountains, an energy beyond mortal comprehension. Superstitions claim it was magic, the domain of djinn, and it was buried and cursed. But we know better. Science has caught up to myth. In this relic is a power beyond our senses, but very much still present, uncharted, ready to be harnessed. Under the right conditions, it could power entire nations with the output of a single mountain's pulse."

A low rumble of aftershocks underscored his words, adding a sinister emphasis.

"Imagine a future where the world runs at the flick of a switch, a planet set free from the tyranny of oil fields and nuclear meltdown risks. No more Fukushima, Chernobyl, OPEC, oligarchs, or BP oil spills. Clean, limitless power, doled out by Prometheus. My Prometheus." His voice dropped. "But anyone in my way will have to be removed, because progress can't be impeded.

"Of course," he added with a mocking half-smile, "some short-sighted fools will claim this artifact must remain locked away, that it's too powerful, or that it belongs to the world. They'll whine about curses and tradition." He raised the Amulet higher, meeting Aya's gaze across the shifting rubble. "But you've seen what I'm willing to do for progress. And for profit. We're finished playing by the old rules. I'm here to usher in the future. "The era of superstition is over. This power is mine. Prometheus, at last, holds the flame of the gods, and the world will beg for a taste."

A deep quake rattled the ground, sending a billowing wave of dust from the corridor. Debris rained down, and the soldier guarding Léglise clutched his rifle anxiously. Another wave of freezing air pulsed from the broken seal.

The Marinid patterns flared brilliantly. For a moment, the entire corridor entrance was outlined in blinding light. Then the glow began to fade, leaving afterimages burned into Aya's vision.

Léglise's triumphant expression flickered with unease.

He recovered quickly. "No matter. You can finally die with your illusions." He straightened, barking orders at his men in a clipped tone. "Finish them. Leave their bodies here. This site is worthless now that we have the Amulet; let it bury her. A fitting end. Hassan Amrani's daughter, dying in a site collapse as well."

Behind him, the corridor continued to emit the cold gust. One of his soldiers stepped back nervously as frost spread across his rifle barrel. "Sir, something's wrong with..."

"Focus!" Léglise snapped. "Natural temperature variance from the underground chambers. Nothing more."

But Aya could see it in his eyes, the first flicker of doubt. The soldier restraining her pressed his rifle to the back of Aya's head, and she felt the force of the hard metal.

"Goodbye, Aya Amrani," Léglise said. "And thank you for your service. I couldn't have gotten here without your help over all these years."

As the soldier pressed the rifle harder against her skull, Aya's mind raced through everything they'd discovered. If the legends were true, if the seal had truly contained something ancient and powerful, then Léglise had no idea what he'd just unleashed.

The Amulet pulsed again in his hands, and for a moment, she swore she saw something move within its crystalline depths, a flicker of fire.

Her father's final decoded warning echoed in her mind: *When the seal breaks, the fire remembers.*

THIRTY-ONE

"COMMANDER!" shouted a soldier near the inner chamber, eyes wide as a crack snaked across the rock, loosening giant slabs of stone overhead. "This whole section is coming down!"

The ground lurched violently, toppling half the scaffolding. A swirling gust lashed the excavation pit. Everyone stumbled, boots scraping for traction.

More stones rained from above, smashing into the half-buried scaffolding. The corridor continued to groan an echoing, unnatural sound.

Léglise scowled, scanning the site. "This corridor's unstable. We need to get to higher ground." His cool gaze flicked over the trembling ground as another rumble shook the debris. "Hurry up, we're leaving." He gestured at the soldier restraining Aya, then at the one pinning Karim. "Leave them to die in the rubble. You can shoot them from above and avoid any complications until we're out of here. We have the amulet, that's all that matters."

In that moment, another quake caused the last standing

section of scaffolding to buckle. Splintered beams toppled behind them, scattering the soldiers' ranks.

Sensing an opening, Aya tried to twist free, but the soldier yanked her arms cruelly.

As she was spun around, Aya saw Amina circling the perimeter behind broken machinery. Her eyes darted from Aya, pinned on the ground, to Karim, forced prone beneath a rifle. For a breath, the scene froze, and Aya pictured Amina disappearing into the chaos.

Instead, she sprinted toward them, brandishing dual handguns.

As the soldier pressed the barrel of his rifle to Karim's neck, Amina fired two precise shots.

The soldier's eyes went wide at the impact, his body jerking as both bullets tore through his torso. He released a guttural cry, reflexively squeezing the rifle's trigger in a final spasm; a single shot cracked skyward before the gun fell from his slackening grip. Gasping, he toppled backward onto the earth, the last traces of life flickering from his stare.

Karim winced, alive.

Meanwhile, Aya's captor spun to face the new threat.

Amina vaulted over a collapsed column, pistols drawn in both hands. One bullet tore into the neck of the soldier holding Aya, and, as he tried to scream, blood sprayed across Aya and the dusty ground.

Another of Amina's bullets ripped through the soldier behind him, dropping him instantly; more blood splattered the churned earth.

A soldier near Léglise barked orders: "Just shoot her!"

Meanwhile, Karim had scrambled to Aya's side.

"There's a knife in my boot, cut me free," Aya said.

Karim quickly found it and cut the zip ties.

Bullets ripped into the ground in Amina's direction,

punching up dirt as she dove behind a chunk of crumbling stone. Before the gunman could take aim at her again, Aya had snapped up her downed captor's assault rifle, swinging it in an arc.

She let off a short burst of cover fire, repelling Léglise's men, already unsettled by fresh tremors underfoot.

"Amina, come on!" Aya shouted over the thunder of rocks collapsing, and then their gazes locked. Guilt, pride, fear, and urgency all tangled in a silent exchange. Then Amina nodded, motioning for Aya and Karim to run.

As they did, another surge of wind roared from within the Amulet's chamber, cold and dry, but carrying a faint, sulfuric tang. The force slammed into everyone within the trench, knocking the two closest soldiers off their feet. Two large boulders from above the blasted opening collapsed, crashing mere meters from where the men were scrambling to their feet.

Léglise gripped the relic closer. He gestured for all his men to follow. "We have the amulet. Leave them for now; this place will take care of them. Get to the helicopters!"

Deep within the revealed chamber, a rippling echo reverberated, low and resonant, like a growl from beneath the earth. Aya's knees nearly buckled at the sensation, a trembling in her bones. Not an earthquake, not the wind. Something else entirely.

Léglise's commander shouted into his radio: "All squads pull back for immediate exfil! The site's collapsing."

Yet another sharp quake jostled the entire dig and spread out across the mountains in the distance as birds alighted in every direction. Mosaics caved in under falling rubble, and several troops rushed to flank Léglise as he retreated toward the waiting helicopters.

"It's collapsing!" the commander yelled again. "Everyone, move out! Both birds, full evac!"

The troops rushed across the battered camp, weapons drawn. Further quakes in quick succession continued to shake the area, collapsing tents and gear around them.

Within moments, the black-clad squad had boarded the two AH64 Apaches. Léglise climbed aboard the first, artifact in hand, and his helicopter took to the sky almost immediately. Then the second chopper followed, lifting off the rest of his private army under a maelstrom of swirling dust. None of them remained.

Aya shielded her face from the rotor wash as the swirling grit stung her eyes amidst the devastation.

The ground roared again, vibrating wildly beneath their feet, sending rubble cascading off the corridor entrance. Thick support columns collapsed with thunderous force, flattening the remaining left wall of the trench.

"Karim, if we stay, we're going to be buried, too. We need to get out of here."

A swirl of stone dust parted, revealing a partial path out. The freed archaeologists were sprinting away or checking on the bodies of colleagues left littering the dig. Aya, Karim, and Amina focused on escaping to their earlier rendezvous point, each step forward shaky on crumbling ground. Gunfire had been replaced by the rumbling of the earth itself.

They stumbled out past the twisted chain-link fence, the hot sun glaring overhead. Yet a ghostly chill from the corridor still clung to Aya's skin.

Not far ahead, the land sloped upward, returning them to the battered ridgeline where they'd parted with Abdelatif earlier. Aya gritted her teeth at each fresh quake rattling the distance behind them, hoping the ancient site wouldn't entomb any of the surviving archaeologists. The wind moaned across the ravine.

As they approached, they saw the older man was exactly

where they'd left him, secured behind a rocky outcropping, while Omar kept pressure on his wound.

Omar glanced up, relief etched across his dusty face as Aya, Karim, and Amina stumbled into view. "You made it," he called. He pressed one palm protectively over Abdelatif's side. "What happened? Where's Léglise? The Amulet?"

Aya dropped to a knee beside Omar. She let out a shaky breath. "He took the Amulet. Flew out on those helicopters before the whole site started buckling. The whole thing's going to collapse. We couldn't stop him, Omar."

"They shot anyone who resisted," Amina said. "Executed them like animals. It wasn't a fight. We barely clawed our way out." Her usual bravado wavered. "And that corridor..." She swallowed hard. "The moment they blasted through, the air changed. I was right next to it. It wasn't just cold—it was like breathing electricity. I kept hearing whispers that weren't there. The Amulet itself..." She shuddered. "When Léglise held it up, I felt something pulling at me, like it wanted to be touched, to be claimed. And the deeper into that chamber you looked, the more it felt like something was looking back."

Karim nodded grimly. "The inscriptions on the walls were moving. Not physically, but in your peripheral vision, like they were trying to rearrange themselves. And that sound when the seal broke..." He ran a hand through his hair. "It wasn't just stone cracking. It was like something taking its first breath in centuries."

Aya shook her head. "Whatever was bound in there, it's been set free, and now Léglise has the key to controlling it."

Omar's hands trembled. "Okay, we lost, but we need to get someone to look at Abdelatif before we lick our wounds." His voice shook with anger and guilt. "We have to get him proper help."

Karim drew in a ragged breath, staring at the path that led

back to the ruined trenches. "Whatever that relic truly is, whatever I helped them find, they can't be allowed to control it. Control the world with it. We have to figure out where he ran with the Amulet."

"We will," Aya said. "We owe it to everyone who bled or died back there, and to whatever's been awakened in that chamber." Her voice hardened. "We're not done fighting, but let's move for now. The old man may be our best bet in stopping Léglise, and I don't know how much longer he has."

Aya and Karim helped lift Abdelatif, and they began their ascent.

After nearly twenty minutes, Aya spotted a rocky outcrop tall enough for partial shelter. They half-dragged, half-carried Abdelatif there, setting him gently against a boulder. The older man's face was drawn tight with pain, chest rising and falling in shallow bursts. Omar rummaged for fresh bandages, pressing them against his wound in frantic care.

Amina leaned against a nearby rock, wincing at her bruised shoulder. At the same time, she and Aya locked eyes.

Amina winced as she rotated her bruised shoulder, exhaling sharply. "Look, I know I said we'd work together, but seeing it all play out..." She paused. "When I saw you pinned on the ground, when I watched those soldiers execute innocent people, when I felt whatever force was radiating from that chamber... this became about more than money."

Amina pressed her fingers to her eyes. "I've done terrible things for profit. We both have. But there are lines, and PES crossed all of them today. That Amulet, whatever it really is, can't belong to these people."

Amina's voice hardened as she continued. "Maybe it's guilt from what happened in Egypt. Maybe it's my pride after PES tortured me, tried to break me. But I'm done letting them crush people to pad their profits. You want to stop them? I'm in. Not just for the alliance, but because it's right."

She met Aya's eyes. "You and I have unfinished business. And I'm not letting you die before I settle my debt with you, one way or another."

Omar watched in surprise, but Amina shrugged, returning to her usual wry tone. "Besides, there's no payday if Léglise torches the world by unleashing whatever tech or curse that is. I'd like to keep living on a planet that isn't haunted by thousand-year-old djinn, thank you."

Aya managed a small nod. "Thank you, you came back for us. That's a great start." She glanced around at their battered group. "Karim, are you okay?"

"The corridor... the mosaic... all destroyed. And did you see that Amulet? What was that? I couldn't save it..." He broke off, a tremor in his voice.

Aya's throat felt raw. A strange, fierce hope welled inside her. She touched his shoulder gently. "Karim... I'm sorry. This isn't what you signed up for. You should walk away from this madness, from me."

He turned, eyes firm. "I can't just forget what happened. I can't forget that artifact or Léglise's men firing on unarmed people. And I can't pretend you don't exist." His mouth set in a grim line. "So yes, I'll follow you, even if it means stepping into your underworld of thieves and fences, danger and secrets. Because right now, that underworld is the only place I might find a shred of justice. Or at least a shred of meaning. Those were my colleagues he killed. My work he destroyed. My history, he ripped apart."

Relief and affection surged in Aya as she reached for his hand, squeezing it gently. "It won't be easy."

He froze, eyes locked onto their hands, expression unreadable. "That's why I'm glad I have you standing next to me, whoever you are."

Omar, tightening Abdelatif's bandage, nodded. "All done here, let's move from these aftershocks. Then we figure out how to track Léglise. He can't hide forever."

Out of nowhere, a swirl of dust rose around their feet. For an instant, it formed a funnel and then collapsed back to the ground. Aya felt a peculiar sensation, like static across her skin. She remembered the partial inscription: *He who breaks the seal unchains the flame. Let the heart weigh the cost, or all shall be consumed.*

Abdelatif stirred, blinking in pain. "The vow... undone," he rasped. "Djinn, like smokeless fire... Freed once more?" He squeezed Aya's hand weakly. "You must stop them from unleashing... the unstoppable."

Aya quickly opened her father's notebook, hands trembling as she flipped to the back. "Abdelatif, wait, we found something. My father wrote about someone named H. Çelebi."

The old man's eyes widened slightly, focus sharpening through the pain. "Çelebi... yes... the Ottoman..."

Karim leaned in, supporting Abdelatif's head. "We translated a section dated 1592. This H. Çelebi created something Aya's father called a *'reinforcement ritual'* after a supposed djinn incursion in Fez. Do you know about this?"

Abdelatif's breathing grew labored, but he nodded weakly. "Çelebi... had his books. He came to Morocco... after the djinn nearly broke free in Fez, so the story goes. The ritual in the story... it requires three." His hand gripped Aya's wrist with surprising strength. "The bloodline, one descended from those who first bound them."

"Three keys," Aya whispered, remembering the phrase

from weeks of translation work. "The bloodline, the marked, and the pure of heart."

"The marked..." Abdelatif's gaze shifted to Amina. "When the seal breaks, the djinn leave their touch on one who witnesses. Look at your arm, girl."

Amina frowned, pushing up her sleeve. Where the cold wind from the corridor had first struck her, faint lines like frost patterns traced across her skin, barely visible, but unmistakably there. "What the hell—"

"The djinn have marked you as their anchor to this world," Abdelatif rasped. "And the pure of heart..." His eyes found Karim. "One who seeks knowledge for its own sake, who has never taken for personal gain. The ritual needs all three, or the binding cannot hold, so the story says."

"But we don't have the complete ritual," Karim said urgently. "We only decoded fragments."

Abdelatif's hand fumbled toward his djellaba. "In this folio I've carried... and your father's final pages... together they might form the whole. But you must hurry. The longer the djinn remain unbound, the stronger they grow. And with the Amulet in Léglise's hands..." He coughed, specks of blood on his lips. "He can direct their rage wherever he wishes."

"We really need to get moving," Omar said.

As they walked, Karim looked back toward the ruined site, confusion in his eyes. "Why do you think Léglise just left us? He had us at gunpoint. With his resources, he could have finished us easily."

Aya followed his gaze to where dust still swirled above the collapsed trenches. "I don't think he had a choice. Look at it, the whole structure's still coming down. Those weren't normal aftershocks. Whatever force was sealed in that chamber, it's not stable now that it's been freed. Léglise got what he came for, but staying there any longer might have been suicide."

"Plus," Amina added grimly, "he probably figures the mountain will finish what he started. Let the collapse bury us and any witnesses to what happened here." She gestured at the unstable ground still trembling beneath their feet. "Bastard doesn't even want to waste bullets when gravity will do the job for free."

Omar grunted as he shifted Abdelatif's weight. "Then we prove him wrong. We survive this, and we make him answer for every life lost today, but Abdel, you're to make it through today, buddy."

At length, they reached the higher path back to where they'd parked the Jeep when the road got too precarious. Below, the entire battered camp lay like a war zone, ready to crumble.

"Abdelatif says we can find a good doctor in the village," Omar panted. "Then we'll figure out what's next."

Aya swallowed, exchanging a look with Karim, his eyes hollow. "Then we hunt the amulet. We can't let Léglise win."

"This is beyond archaeology," Karim said. "Or maybe exactly where archaeology meets mythology. Either way, I'll offer whatever assistance I can."

Amina clasped a hand on Aya's and Karim's shoulders. "We stand together."

Omar shifted Abdelatif, who was fading into unconsciousness. "All of us," Omar said.

THIRTY-TWO

THEY REACHED the Jeep as the sun began its descent in the cloudless sky. The journey back up the rugged slope with Abdelatif had been a slow struggle, but they found the Jeep exactly where they'd left it, now caked with a layer of thick brown dust.

Omar gripped the steering wheel tight, his eyes fixed on the twisting road. In the front, Amina sat scanning the horizon restlessly. In the backseat, Aya cradled Abdelatif's head while Karim braced him, his knees pressed firmly against the seat for stability.

The mountain road was now nothing more than pitted dirt, with treacherous drops at its edges. Every bump drew a groan from Abdelatif. Aya maintained pressure on the wound despite dried blood crusting the bandages.

"Look at this mess," Omar muttered, his eyes never leaving the twisting path. "Those earthquakes shattered the road. It's no longer even a road, it's a battlefield."

Aya peered out. A stream of water burst suddenly from a

deep fissure, racing down the slope with icy force. The mountain itself seemed to be bleeding.

"Nature doesn't forgive," Aya said under her breath.

Small stones skittered off the hillside, pummeling the windshield. A strained silence fell over the Jeep. "Not sure that's the shower this car needs, but it's just a bit farther," Omar murmured as he urged the Jeep forward.

Aya glanced ahead, studying Amina's profile before their eyes met in the rear-view mirror, silent truths flaring for a moment before they looked away in unison.

Abdelatif let out a harsh, rattling cough that shattered the silence in the confined space.

"Abdelatif, breathe," Karim commanded, his voice low and urgent. With one steady hand, he pressed gently against his chest. "Slow down. In and out, steady, now." The old man's labored breaths began to find a rhythm.

"Omar, I don't know how much longer we have," Aya said.

Omar didn't respond, but his shoulders hunched as he put all of his focus into the car, pushing it to its limits.

Minutes later, they reached a narrow gravel road, unaffected by the collapses and landslides, linking the village to the mountain passes. Omar pressed harder on the gas, sending a swirl of dust billowing as the tires hit scattered potholes.

A massive sign in Arabic, Amazigh, and French pointed toward Tizi n'Test, with a cluster of buildings just beyond the sign. Aya recognized the village immediately.

The same crumbling, ancient pillar loomed along the road, its stone carved with the fierce outline of a falcon, wings spread in a silent challenge. The pillar's silent vow, long ignored, pulsed with a promise of retribution: the mountain would not tolerate their transgressions.

Karim wiped sweat from his brow. "If they have a doctor,

they can at least remove the bullet and stabilize him. After that, we can get him to Marrakech, or whatever is necessary."

Amina turned in her seat. "He's strong, he'll pull through," she said, though a flicker of worry betrayed her resolve.

The gravel yielded to a battered concrete road. Low stone and clay walls lined the street, while earth-toned homes clung to the hillside, tilting at improbable angles. A few goats wandered near a communal fountain, their heads bobbing at the noise of the car.

As they parked, the people standing along the road turned and stared, their eyes filled with uneasy curiosity as they took in the Jeep's frantic arrival and the cluster of exhausted faces within. Omar leaped from the vehicle, his hands raised in a universal plea for help.

"*3aawen*!" he shouted. "Our friend is badly injured!"

A young man in a worn gray djellaba ran forward, his face etched by confusion. "Bring him to the clinic, this way," he said, beckoning them with an outstretched hand. "I'll show you, it's just right here."

Aya and Karim carefully removed Abdelatif from the Jeep and carried him. Omar hurried ahead of them with the man, who explained the route to the clinic, while Amina lingered by the Jeep, scanning the perimeter, her hands twitching as if braced for an ambush.

A swirl of local children ventured forward, curiosity lighting their eyes. Women, draped in bright shawls, exchanged glances as the newcomers passed, then quickly resumed balancing woven baskets on their heads.

The young man guiding them pointed to a low, cream-colored building just down from a small mosque. "That's the clinic, quickly now," he urged, breaking into a jog.

As they approached, the village's animals were restless. Goats bleated anxiously, chickens flapped in their coops, dogs whined and paced in circles. Even the donkeys stood with their ears pinned back, eyes rolling white with fear.

Aya glanced at Karim, seeing her own recognition mirrored in his eyes.

Aya felt a chill that had nothing to do with the mountain air. Above them, the sky seemed to shimmer with heat despite the cool temperature, and she could swear she heard a distant rumbling that wasn't quite thunder, more like breathing, deep and rhythmic, echoing from the peaks.

"The atmospheric disturbances," Karim said as they approached their destination. "Remember what your father wrote about the 1995 incident? The same phenomena, temperature inversions, spontaneous vortices, electromagnetic anomalies. He documented it all, but we thought he was being metaphorical."

Aya nodded. "He wasn't. He was trying to create a scientific record of supernatural events. 'The boundary between worlds grows thin,' he wrote. 'What was bound seeks freedom through the cracks.'"

Omar held the door open. "You're saying this is all connected to what we unleashed?"

"Not unleashed, I guess," Aya corrected. "Accelerated. According to the translations, the seals were already weakening. That's why PES moved when they did. They knew the window was opening, and we just helped it along."

As they exited, the clinic exuded a brisk efficiency. White-washed walls bore fading motivational posters, each extolling the importance of vaccines or hygiene. A single row of green plastic chairs lined the waiting area, and a nurse in scrubs manned a reception desk laden with well-thumbed medical forms.

To the left, an open doorway led to an exam room, brightened by the glow of white overhead lights and the glint of stainless-steel trays. The aroma of antiseptic merged with the faintest undertone of herbal ointments.

"What happened?" asked the doctor, who came running to their side from the back room.

Omar replied in quick, halting bursts: "Gunshot. Accident in the mountains. Please. Help him."

The doctor's expression hardened, and he wasted no time cutting away the makeshift bandages, exposing a severe entry wound.

"Watch it, easy now!" snapped the nurse in turquoise scrubs, rushing from the desk as Aya and Karim lifted Abdelatif onto a wheeled gurney just inside the clinic doorway. Another nurse immediately adjusted the bed's collapsible rails and rushed to hook him up to an IV line and blood pressure cuff.

"We have a gunshot wound, high thoracic region," the doctor announced crisply, checking Abdelatif's pupils with a penlight. "Vital signs?" A nurse read off a quick series of blood pressure and pulse numbers, scribbling them onto a clipboard.

"Let's get him into the procedure room," the doctor continued. "We'll prep a local anesthetic and see about removing any bullet fragments. Someone get me more gauze, pressure's dropping."

He gestured for Aya and Omar to step back. "We'll do all we can," he promised, then guided the gurney deeper into the hallway, leaving them at the threshold.

They remained in the lobby, a gnawing helplessness spreading.

Karim paced. "He took that bullet because of me."

"No, because of all of us." Aya placed a hand on his shoulder. "We'll make it right."

Eventually, the doctor returned, wiping sweat from his brow. "I've removed the bullet and stopped the bleeding for now. It tore a muscle, but I see no signs of organ damage. He needs rest and fluids, and we'll watch for infection. He's stable, but I can't promise more unless we get him to a larger facility with more resources soon."

Omar exhaled. "Thank you. Is there anything we can do?"

The doctor shook his head. "Let him rest. I'll monitor him for now. Tomorrow, if you can arrange transport to a better-equipped hospital, that's ideal. We're not set up to be an ER."

"Can we see him?" Aya asked.

"Not now. He's asleep and needs the rest. Come back tonight."

They nodded and poured back into the village's narrow lane, leaving Abdelatif in a medicated sleep.

Rejoining Amina, the group found a quiet stretch alongside the apple orchard on the main street. Wooden benches fashioned from tree stumps encircled a squat trunk. Aya sank onto one, letting the orchard's quiet green embrace her. Apple blossoms wavered in the gentle wind, sending pale petals drifting like confetti around their feet.

For a long moment, none of them spoke; they simply breathed, still thudding with leftover adrenaline.

Amina broke the silence, raking a hand through her hair. "I'm going to find lodging. We'll need at least two rooms near the clinic, more if possible. I'd love a warm shower. And I'll scout around in case PES is trying to track us here." Without waiting, she strode off, boots crunching as her silhouette cut a sharp figure against the orchard's greenery.

"She's right," Karim said. "We can't help Abdelatif if we're all collapsing from fatigue."

"And she's right about the possibility of PES," Omar added, "though I can't imagine they'd care about us now that they have the artifact."

"They might," Aya said, "if they think we'll keep pursuing them."

The weight of their situation pressed down on her. They'd failed their mission spectacularly, the Amulet was gone, the site was destroyed, and they had no leads on where Léglise had taken it.

Worse, they had no idea what their threateningly mysterious employer, Aegis, would do when they learned about the failure. Organizations like that didn't typically accept excuses.

"Omar, I keep thinking about the Aegis," she admitted quietly. "Amina was right, they're not the type to shrug off a failed mission. And we don't even know their real agenda. For all we know, they wanted that chaos at the dig site."

Omar's expression darkened. "I haven't heard from them since yesterday. You think they set us up?"

"I don't know what to think anymore. But staying in one place too long feels dangerous, especially when we don't know who's hunting us." She glanced toward the clinic. "Still, we can't move him yet. We're trapped between protecting him and protecting ourselves."

Omar nodded. "Then let's hope they forget about little old us, or think the mountains finished us off." Omar stood, "But for now, your chauffeur is starving. I'm going to go chase tajine. You guys want anything?"

"Sure," Karim said. "Let us know what you find."

"Right on, you'll have a menu arriving shortly." Omar gave an over-the-top bow and walked back in the direction of the town's center.

Aya's attention lingered on a crooked apple tree swaying in the waning light. There was a time when she felt unstoppable, always the cleverest in any room, the most agile under pressure. Now, each setback, each brush with death, felt like a knife slicing through her certainties.

She blinked hard, struggling against an unfamiliar hollowness. The orchard's hush pressed close. *I used to have all the answers*, she thought. *Now, every question haunts me.*

Karim gently touched Aya's wrist, coaxing her back to the present. "You look like you need a moment away from all this. Would you walk with me?"

She studied his face, still streaked with dust, a bruise forming along his jaw. "I'd like that."

They drifted down a meandering path deeper into the orchard. The rustle of leaves and the faint trickle of a nearby irrigation channel offered a tranquil contrast to the morning's gunfire. Rows of apple trees, heavy with pale-pink blossoms, lined the path, while now and then a walnut fell from overhead, thumping gently onto the soft ground.

For the first time in days, Aya felt the world moving slowly around her, but she still felt the urge to sprint ahead. She inhaled the orchard's fresh, earthy sweetness. Memories of her father's old stories about rural Morocco tugged at her, and she tried to embrace them.

Karim paused by a handmade olive wood fence, leaning against it as he looked back toward the village, his eyes sad and distant.

Aya joined him, resting an elbow on the fence. "We tried, we did. PES came early, and it was more than we could handle. I've never failed like this before," she whispered. "So much was lost."

"I still can't shake the feeling that we unleashed something the world was never meant to see," Karim said. "Did you feel it too, the shift in the air when the corridor broke? It was more than an earthquake. It felt alive. Like the soul of the mountain was unleashed."

She thought of the floating dust, piercing chill, illuminated rocks when Léglise held the Amulet aloft. "I did, I felt it. But I think I know what it means now." She pulled out her father's notebook, flipping to a section they'd translated together in the third week. "Listen to this: '*The djinn exist between states, neither fully material nor wholly spirit. When their prisons crack, they seep into our world like smoke through fissures. First come the signs: nature rebels, technology fails, the very air becomes hostile to human presence.*'"

She looked up at Karim. "We decoded this together, remember? That night, you said it sounded like a description of dimensional bleeding, two realities overlapping."

"I was joking," Karim said weakly. "Trying to apply quantum physics to mythology."

"What if you were right? What if the ancients described in mystical terms, something that we'd call an interdimensional phenomena? The Amulet doesn't control djinn, it controls the barriers between worlds."

For the first time, she truly understood what her father had been obsessed with.

She remembered him, Hassan sifting through a bulldozed Mayan site in Guatemala, his voice breaking as he described how they had destroyed context that could never be recovered. At the time, she'd thought he was being dramatic. Now she felt that same ache, that same rage at the casual destruction and disrespect for history.

"This is the first time I've cared about something bigger than my own survival in a long time," she admitted. "My whole adult life has been about the next score, the next escape, the next reinvention. But standing beside that chamber, seeing what we'd lost... I mean, I lost faith in the nobler side of archaeology. I thought, if I can't preserve it, I might as well profit, right? Well, it appears that led us here, and no one is more responsible for propping up Philippe Léglise than me."

Karim raised his hand, hesitated, then reached out to gently cup her cheek. She leaned into the warmth of his palm. "Aya, I saw how you fought to protect those mosaics, to keep them from bulldozers. That's real. That's you, not some cold-hearted thief. You care deeply."

Aya didn't resist as he pulled her closer. Their faces hovered inches apart, enveloped by the orchard's hush. In the filtered sunlight, she allowed herself a moment of vulnerability, stripped bare as he now knew who she really was.

Her arms slipped around his neck as the kiss began tentatively, each uncertain of the other's reaction. Yet the day's fear and desperation melted away with the press of his lips. A soft breeze ruffled the leaves overhead, scattering pink petals around them in quiet acceptance. Of each other, of past transgressions, of their failure, of their path forward.

Karim's eyes brightened. "Sorry, I realize there's a lot to be said, but I don't know how else to better express how I feel."

Aya felt something give way inside her at the sound of Karim's confession. For a moment, time stilled, and the world receded. She had built so many walls to guard against exactly this sort of vulnerability, yet now every word was a gentle, insistent knock at those walls.

In his eyes, she saw a mixture of hope and fear that mirrored her own.

The cynic inside her fell silent, awed by the earnestness of the man before her. In that heartbeat of silence, Aya felt the last of her resistance crumble softly.

She brushed her thumb across his cheek, wiping away a smudge of dirt. "No, I'm the one who's sorry. For dragging you into this world, for lying to you at first, for failing to prevent this when it was my job. Hopefully, there's still a chance to make some of it right."

Karim set a hand against the fence post to steady himself. "For a while, I hated that I let myself care about you so deeply without knowing who you really were. I felt naive. But every time you spoke, even when you were playing the part of a grad student, there was this undercurrent of sincerity I couldn't dismiss."

He leaned closer, his voice dropping to a hush. "I remember the night after your first day at the dig, when we were both too wired to sleep. We sat under that tarp talking about movies, and you laughed at my dumb jokes about living in dusty tents. That laugh, it wasn't a con, Aya. You were just, I don't know, you. As genuinely as I was me."

Aya felt tears welling in her eyes. "You're right. I didn't plan to open up. But around you, it happened anyway. I care more than I'd like to admit."

Karim let a small, lopsided grin break the tension. "You apologized for bringing me into your dangerous world, but don't you see? I walked in willingly the moment I decided your life was worth risking mine for. That I couldn't stand by while you faced down soldiers with rifles or fought to prevent an evil corporation from seeking mythical treasure."

She gave a trembling laugh, relief and longing washing over her. "So you're not mad anymore?"

"No, I'm not mad anymore. I'm relieved. Relieved that the connection I felt wasn't one-sided or imaginary. You've let me see your heart, and it means more than you know. You're exceptional."

Aya slid her hands over Karim's shoulders and pulled him hard against her. Her lips found his in a desperate kiss that left no room for hesitation, eclipsing the orchard around them.

Karim stumbled, steadying himself. Aya seized the moment to press closer, letting the heat of his body spread against hers. A soft moan escaped his throat as his hands grabbed the curves of her hips and pulled her even closer still.

Moments later, when Aya finally broke the connection,

breathless, she lingered with her forehead against his. A smile tugged at her lips, equal parts relief and triumph at reclaiming the boldness she'd buried beneath regret.

He traced a thumb over her lip. "We face whatever comes next together."

"Together," she agreed softly, interlocking her fingers with his.

Eventually, the rumble of three passing motorcycles snapped them back to reality.

Aya cleared her throat and stepped away. "I can think of quite a few things I'd rather do with you right now, but we should return to Omar and Amina, check on Abdelatif, and help with the plan."

"Yeah," Karim agreed quietly, grasping her hand for one more second.

A sudden gust of wind swept through the orchard. It spiraled upward in a perfect helix, gathering apple blossoms into a column that hung suspended for several seconds before collapsing.

The temperature dropped in an instant, their breath suddenly visible.

"It's getting stronger," Aya whispered. "The disturbances. Just like we read. First, localized anomalies near the breach site. Then expanding outward in waves. Within days, reports from across the region. Within weeks..."

She trailed off, but Karim finished the thought. "Global destabilization. If the barriers continue to erode, these phenomena spread like a virus. That's what Léglise doesn't understand. If we're right, the Amulet isn't just a power source; it's a regulator between planes of existence. Without it properly bound to the seals..."

THIRTY-THREE

AFTER THE WINDS STOPPED, they found Amina chatting with a family outside a large mud-brick house at the orchard's edge. They spoke in a mishmash of Fusha Arabic and French, gesturing animatedly. As Aya and Karim approached, the father, a gray-bearded man clad in a bright blue djellaba with yellow stitching, nodded and beckoned them inside.

"*C'est bon*," Amina announced with a wry grin. "They can rent us this house for the night. Two rooms, enough beds for us to rest. There's an attached cooking area and a big open courtyard. It's cute, a bit rustic, and they're very kind."

"Thank you, we appreciate it," Karim said. "*Shukran khoya*," he added, addressing the man showing them in.

They followed the father through a narrow gate into a tidy courtyard lined with rows of fruit trees and fresh, bright clay soil. Beyond the courtyard's low walls stood a view of terraced slopes cut by a valley that extended into a mist.

In one corner, Omar was already bent over a battered old radio receiver. At their approach, he looked up.

"We're staying?" he asked. When Amina nodded, he

269

exhaled with relief. "Good, they said they have food. And the doctor said we can move Abdelatif here by early evening if his vitals remain stable and he's awake."

Within the hour, they'd claimed two rooms in the mountain home. Thick, brightly woven carpets covered the floors, their patterns echoing Amazigh designs passed down for generations. Cushioned banquettes lined three walls, couch by day and bed by night, while a woven straw lantern cast warm light overhead and a roaring fire kept the cozy space warm. Plastered tadelakt walls were carefully painted in soft teal, chipped in places by the passing years.

The man led them to a central salon where a flat-screen TV quietly aired a local news channel, glowing with footage of damaged rural roads and shaky handheld clips of frightened families gathered outside their homes, narrating how repeated earthquakes had begun rattling through the Atlas Mountains. A calm-voiced anchor reported on mountain villages cut off by rockslides, while a scrolling ticker displayed emergency numbers. Aya tensed at every mention of blocked routes.

"My family will bring you dinner when it's ready," their host said. "I'm sure you're hungry. Please, enjoy, and let me know if you need anything," he told Karim, who translated for Aya and Amina.

"I'll go get Omar," Aya said, before walking to the courtyard and calling to him.

"I'll be in soon," he answered.

Aya slipped to the courtyard's far wall. Against the earthen wall, her pulse finally slowed, and a single thought crowded in: Karim.

The orchard kiss had been brief, half desperation, half relief, yet it kept replaying in her head with disarming clarity: the warmth of his hands, the certainty in his eyes. She'd spent years surviving by never needing anyone, but Karim's steady courage made her wonder whether trust could be strength, not weakness.

Aya was pulled from her reverie when she heard the rumble of an old white station wagon pulling in. The doctor emerged from the driver's seat while a nurse helped Abdelatif out from the back, his IV bag suspended from a makeshift hook by the window. He was pale but alert, blinking in mild confusion at his new surroundings.

"Careful," Omar said, as he and Karim rushed forward to steady Abdelatif. They guided him gently into the courtyard and settled him on plush cushions beneath a sheltered over-hang. The nurse checked the bandages with brisk efficiency, offering instructions about his care. A swirl of dying sunlight glinted against the tiled courtyard floor.

Amina, arms still folded, watched from the courtyard's edge. When Omar gently settled Abdelatif onto a mattress, she stepped forward with uncharacteristic softness. "It's good to see you upright, old man," she said as she knelt beside him.

Abdelatif offered a faint smile. "Always better than the alternative," he said, his voice thin yet carrying a spark of life behind half-lidded eyes.

The nurse set up a fresh IV stand near him, hooking up fluids. "He's stable for now. He needs rest and minimal stress. Keep the wound clean, the bullet's out, but infection remains a risk," she instructed before departing.

Moments later, a trio of women bustled through the court-yard gate, balancing trays laden with fresh bread, amlou, honey, and steaming tagines that filled the space with the scent of slow-cooked vegetables and spices.

The oldest, the mother of the household, offered a pot of mint tea while another carried a bowl brimming with golden olive oil, gesturing politely for them to taste.

"We heard about the wounded man. *Alhamdulillah*, he's okay now," the youngest of the women said softly.

Though they cast curious glances at Aya and her companions, they asked no probing questions, only nodding in quiet understanding as though the mountains themselves kept certain secrets.

They arranged blankets to ensure Abdelatif was comfortable. Omar pressed a bowl of warm harira soup into his hands, coaxing him to sip, which he did gladly.

Night descended gently, draping their sweeping mountain views in silver moonlight and casting soft shadows on the village's mud-brick walls. Their hosts lit a series of lanterns around the courtyard, their soft glow forming pockets of warmth against the cool mountain air.

The group remained gathered around the table, exhaustion etched on every face. Over the meal, conversation drifted in subdued murmurs. The day's horror weighed on them, accompanied by an unspoken question: Where next?

"Abdelatif," Aya said softly once the plates were cleared, "we nearly lost you today. Are you certain you want to keep chasing this madness? We can try to do it without dragging you along. You need to heal."

He exhaled, each breath labored. "I am an old man with regrets. I've devoted my life to bridging the old ways and the new, to understanding this country's hidden histories. I have walked the path of light at times and the path of dark at others, but I have always honored the past. Now, I see what I never wanted to see: the path to destruction. I cannot rest while someone like Léglise wields an artifact of such significance."

He pressed a hand gently over his bandaged side. "And yes, I believe the myths, the legends. That Amulet allows him to wield unspeakable power and unleash unspeakable terror. Yet, you're right, I can't climb mountains or outrun bullets tomorrow. But I can guide you with what I know."

Silence blanketed them.

Amina cleared her throat. "That's incredibly helpful for when we get to that Amulet, but we're going to need more than your knowledge. We need some way to track that bastard and figure out where he's taking it."

Abdelatif shifted, his face drawn with pain. "I know a man... Salah, in Essaouira. He's a musician, a surfer, and a frustratingly unreliable hashish smoker. But also something of a hacker. He was once fascinated with radio frequencies and flight trackers. If anyone can help us locate Léglise's helicopters, it is him."

Karim's brow furrowed. "Essaouira? That's only five hours from here."

"Yes, on the Atlantic coast. Salah can be... eccentric, but he's loyal, if you earn his trust. He is a good man who would oppose Léglise. I believe he's been collecting rumors and conspiracy theories about military operations in Morocco, unusual flights, and restricted zones. We could use that data."

A ripple of cautious hope passed through the group.

"That means we head out tomorrow," Aya said, glancing at Omar, who nodded in agreement. "I'm sorry, Abdelatif, you'd have to remain behind in Marrakech, to heal."

The older man closed his eyes briefly. "No. Let me rest here for a few days. I am fine, do not waste any time taking me anywhere. When I recover well enough, I'll follow. But do what you must, I'll do what I can from here. The doctor and the people in this village will watch over me until you return."

Omar placed a hand over Abdelatif's. "Rest, my friend. We won't be gone long."

He administered a mild sedative as the doctor had

instructed, and soon Abdelatif's eyes drooped as the day's ordeal pulled him into slumber.

A single, inexplicable gust of strong wind swept across the landscape, stirring a wild spiral around the buildings, extinguishing the light in the lanterns.

Amina huddled deeper into her jacket. "Does anyone else feel that? Like a chill around your heart?"

Karim rubbed his arms. "I do. It's not normal."

Time drifted, and eventually Aya found herself alone on the orchard path outside the courtyard gate, staring into the mountains, unable to sleep.

Footsteps behind her made her turn, half-expecting Amina. Instead, it was Karim, arms folded as if to ward off the night's chill.

"You okay?" he asked gently.

"Too many ghosts in my head. You?"

"Same. I thought I'd check on you."

They stood, holding each other and gazing at the moonlit canopy.

Later, when they returned, they found Amina and Omar perched inside by the fire. Amina shot them a knowing, half-teasing glance before pocketing her phone and rising to meet them.

"Ready to compare notes?"

"Yeah," Aya said. "Let's do it."

They settled around the table. Omar had dozed off in a chair, arms crossed over his chest, but stirred when Amina rapped her knuckles on the wood.

"Three priorities," Amina stated briskly. "One: we have to move out tomorrow and find Salah in Essaouira, see if we can track Léglise or his U.S. military stooges. Two: we need gear, explosives, a vehicle that won't break down on the highway, maybe new phones." She cast a meaningful glance at Aya. "I'm running on a battered SIM that might be compromised. You're probably the same. Three: we need to get Abdelatif to a proper hospital in the city."

Aya sighed. "You're 100% right. We can pool our resources. I have some stashed funds I can access once we're in a bigger city. That'll help with equipment. The Aegis, Omar's and my supposed employer, offered large sums, but I'm not sure that's at our disposal anymore."

"Agreed," Omar said, rubbing his bleary eyes. "No way to know how they feel about us right now. They wouldn't take my calls all day. And for getting the money, we're an easy target if PES tracks normal banking channels, but I have some contacts who might do me a favor, for the right price."

"Fourth priority," Karim added. "We don't just want to chase Léglise blindly. We have to prepare for what it means if that Amulet truly channels some unknown force, or if there's another sealed chamber we know nothing about. The corridor we found and the Amulet may be only one clue to a bigger puzzle."

"That's a good point to keep in mind. I've seen the falcon motif and these geometric designs showing up all over, not just in these mountains. My dad's research, Abdelatif's folios, an artifact I stole for Léglise in Jordan. This could be a much bigger commitment than a track, smash, and grab."

Amina tapped the table. "So tomorrow we depart. A short pit stop at the dig site, or do we go straight to the coast?"

Aya ran a hand through her hair. "We should at least check the camp for anything that might help while we're so close. Some archaeologists might still be there, in shock or injured and need help, plus we might find leftover equipment from HRF: maps, data, electronics. I couldn't have read the contents of Léglise's USB without an HRF computer, and that got us so close to the truth. But we're in and out, then we go. And that's only if you're up for it, Karim."

Karim nodded. "I can handle it. We're just burying the dead and gathering intel, not starting a fight."

Omar looked to the door where Abdelatif slept. "Yes. Let's do it quickly—let him rest here, safe with the village—then we move on."

Finally, Aya rose, exhaustion threatening to overwhelm her. "We should get some sleep," she rasped. "We leave at dawn."

Thirty-Four

The following morning, Omar brought the Jeep to a shuddering halt at the dig site's edge, and a heavy silence fell over the car. In the harsh new light, the devastation was heartbreakingly clear. Torn tents were crumpled against bent fencing, and chunks of collapsed rock from the corridor were strewn about in uneven mounds. Bullet casings glinted near a few open crates. It bore the scars of a sudden, chaotic end.

Aya climbed out, a tightness gripping her chest as memories of the bustling dig flooded back. Her mind wandered to those first moments she'd crossed the threshold, feigning academic innocence under the watchful guard's eye. The camp had felt alive then, laptops humming, dust dancing around newly unearthed relics, the quiet thrill of discovery.

Now, the site resembled a battlefield. Amina jumped down on the far side, her eyes narrowing as she scanned the terrain. "So this is what's left of the operation," she muttered, eyes flicking over the wreckage. "Hard to believe we were all sneaking around here not long ago, thinking we had it figured out." She nudged a broken sign with her foot, her tone flat.

As Amina rolled up her sleeve to adjust her jacket, Aya gasped.

"Amina, your arm," Aya said urgently.

Distinct symbols traced across Amina's forearm—angular, geometric shapes that Aya recognized immediately.

"Those aren't just random marks. Those are Amazigh symbols."

Amina frowned and nodded, examining her arm more closely.

"They've been getting clearer since yesterday. Sometimes they burn, sometimes they're cold. It's like ice under my skin."

"Traditional Amazigh tattoos," Aya said. "Women would mark themselves with these symbols, some of them for protection. But this is different. These aren't tattoos—they're appearing on their own."

"Meaning?" Amina asked calmly, though her voice carried an edge of fear.

"Best guess, your body is trying to protect itself," Aya said quietly. "These are ancient spiritual defense mechanisms, manifesting physically. Like the djinn are awakening something primal in you. My father's notes had no reference to anything like this."

They continued walking into the site in silence.

Karim gravitated toward the collapsed corner of the closest tent. "This was my entire project," he whispered, picking up a waterlogged stack of notes.

Aya recognized the notebook, one they'd used during their second week together, when they'd made the breakthrough about the astronomical alignments. She remembered his excitement that night, how he'd grabbed her hands across the table, eyes bright with discovery. Only weeks ago, but it felt like a lifetime.

He stared at the tumble of stones and debris where his workstation used to be: the tables where he'd meticulously labeled ceramics, the crates of newly documented shards. Now, twisted metal beams pinned everything beneath a crumbling wall of rock. Karim crouched, sifting through the wreckage.

"Let's not dwell," Omar said. "We came to help anyone who needs it, gather any remaining gear, and salvage what we can."

They walked carefully, sidestepping piles of toppled crates.

Aya called, "*Bonjour? Il y a quelqu'un ici?*"

A cough echoed from behind a half-collapsed supply tent, and a man in a tattered HRF vest appeared, his hollow eyes blinking as he regarded them. "You, you're one of them." The man took them each in. "And Karim, how can you be part of this?"

Aya raised her hands in a gesture of peace. "I'm sorry. I never meant for any of this to happen," she said gently.

"What do you want?"

"We came to see if anyone's wounded or if anything remains that might help us fix what went wrong. We want to help."

The man let out a bitter laugh. "Help? That's rich. You were with them, maybe not the guys with guns, but you were working against us from the inside. Your sabotage gave them the excuse they needed to escalate. Then they came in, took control of the camp, and shot anyone in their way."

Karim stepped forward. "Ismail, my friend, we tried to protect the site, not destroy it. Believe me."

Ismail faltered, tears welling in his hardened face, "We lost good people. It was chaos. Those men killed anyone who tried to run or to resist at all. You saw."

Aya drew closer and laid a tentative hand on his arm. "I'm

sorry," she whispered, "we never intended for anyone to die. No one could have predicted they'd come so fast or kill so indiscriminately."

"Well, why are you back? You want to take some relics, too?"

"We just want to stop those responsible. If anything remains, notes, files, scanning data, it might help us track them."

Ismail shrugged. "I'll show you the supply tent. A few laptops survived, and some crates remain in the old field lab."

They followed him, and a hush fell as they rounded a corner near the collapsed fence. There, in a patch of disturbed earth, stood a series of small stone cairns, twelve of them, neatly stacked. Strips of canvas and dented field tags were wedged between the rocks, each bearing a name in careful handwriting, the only memorial for those who'd died.

Aya stopped to take them in. From behind her, Ismail cleared his throat, his voice hushed. "We gathered what we could. The rest of us who stayed buried them like this. It's all we could do."

Karim knelt by the closest cairn, gently setting a hand on the topmost stone in silent apology. "They were my colleagues."

Ismail nodded, gaze distant.

As they stood in silent memorial, Amina suddenly gripped her head, a sharp gasp escaping her lips. "Not now," she muttered, but her eyes had already begun to glaze over.

"Amina?" Aya moved toward her, but Amina held up a hand.

"I'm... I'm seeing things," Amina said, her voice distant. "Colors. Distinct colors swirling around everything. I think there are seven blurs. Deep purple around the cairns, like mourning. Angry red on the ground. Gold where the corridor was breached."

Omar's eyes widened. "Seven colors? Like in the Gnawa songs?"

"What do you mean?" Aya asked.

"The Gnawa traditions believe human souls have seven colors," Karim explained quickly, "and that djinn are attracted to specific colors. People who practice it use this knowledge in their healing ceremonies."

Amina's breathing grew rapid.

"There's a voice with each color. The red one is screaming. The blue one is... laughing? And there's something else—a black color I've never seen before, moving beneath everything, beneath the ground, like oil."

"I think you're somehow resonating with the djinn's presence," Aya said, steadying Amina. "You're seeing the spiritual spectrum they navigate. It could be why they marked you."

Amina blinked hard, the vision fading.

"It's gone now, but it's getting stronger. It's happened before, just a headache. But now I see more. Feel more, every time." She looked down at the symbols on her arm, now glowing faintly with their own inner light. "What's happening to me?"

Aya pulled her away from the gathering. "Let's hurry and get out of here," she said. They all followed until they reached a large, tattered tent at the site's far edge, where toppled shelving had scattered artifact boxes. The stench of burnt plastic hung inside.

From outside, the HRF worker coughed, his face drawn with fatigue. "Take what you need. After we finish burying the dead, we're all leaving. There's no work left to be done here."

Karim crouched to inspect a battered laptop. After a failed

attempt to power it on, he sighed and set the device aside. "Maybe we can salvage the hard drive. If the data's intact, we might learn something."

Amina rummaged through scattered crates, cursing under her breath. "Most of this is worthless or destroyed..." she muttered before lifting a small metal box with a bent latch, prying it open with her knife. Inside, a handful of USB drives were labeled in black marker. "Could be scanning results, maybe. Worth a shot." She slipped them into her pocket.

Aya found a crumpled set of printed aerial photographs bearing the HRF logo and the heading "Subsurface Thermal Mapping: ATLAS 7."

As she flipped through the thermal images showing bright patches beneath the earth, she frowned at a margin note: "Depth flux near corridor entrance—possible secondary chamber 15m below primary level?"

"We need to keep these, too," Aya mumbled, sliding them into her backpack.

Karim stepped over, glancing at the printed photos, and sighed. "All that potential, destroyed. But maybe these can reveal something about the deeper layers."

Aya pressed her hand gently to his arm. "Karim, none of us could have predicted this. I had an idea of who was behind this all, and I didn't predict it. You were trying to do real archaeology. This wasn't your fault."

Omar whistled from the outside and yelled, "Let's get going, Essaouira's a long drive."

"I hope we got something worth coming back for," Karim said.

As they climbed back into the Jeep, another wave of vertigo hit Amina.

"The black one," she gasped, gripping the door frame. "It's spreading. It wants... it wants to consume."

Aya and Karim put a hand on either of Amina's shoulders and steadied her as they walked.

"It's going to be okay," Aya said.

Soon, with all safely inside, the Jeep rumbled away from the devastated camp as rising dust further cloaked the site in a shroud of memory and loss.

THIRTY-FIVE

THE FIRST TWO hours of driving were mercifully quiet as they wound through the last of the Atlas foothills. The mountains gradually gave way to rolling hills of farmland dotted with thorny shrubs, olive trees, and sporadic goat herds along the road. A hush settled over the Jeep, each occupant lost in thoughts of the violent days behind them.

Then Aya spotted it, an orange funnel of sand and dust growing in the distance, expanding into the sky over a dry patch of dirt and rocks.

"Did you see that?" Amina asked, twisting in her seat to watch it vanish. "It looked almost alive, the way it shifted direction."

Omar brushed sweat from his brow, knuckles tense on the wheel. "I've driven these roads plenty, hard not to head to Essaouira every weekend when Marrakech's heat settles in. But I've never seen anything like that."

Ten minutes later, another dust funnel rose from the land to their left, swirling menacingly. This one lingered longer, seeming to pulse with its own rhythm before dissipating.

"Another one," Amina announced, craning to look through the window. "They're everywhere."

Each funnel of sand and dust that appeared seemed larger than the last, more deliberate in its movements. The atmosphere in the Jeep grew heavier with each passing mile.

Karim finally cleared his throat. "Amina, you said something about growing up in Cairo. What was that like?"

Amina glanced up. The question seemed to catch her off guard, but after a moment, she drew in a slow breath. "Yeah, I don't like to talk about my personal life. Life wasn't exactly sunshine back then. I'd hang around Khan el-Khalili, that massive bazaar near the old city. Tourists come in droves, pockets heavy, unaware of nine-year-olds with nimble fingers. I got good at theft. Eventually, that got me here. Not much to tell."

Aya twisted halfway in her seat. "You never told me how young you were," she said, voice gentler than usual.

Amina shrugged. "Didn't matter, did it? I learned to be invisible, slipping through crowds, snatching coins or cameras. By sixteen, I was running contraband for bigger players. They taught me advanced infiltration, hand-to-hand combat, and introduced me to black-market channels."

Outside, another funnel spiraled up from the roadside, tracking their movement for several unsettling seconds before collapsing.

"And at some point, you and Aya crossed paths?" Karim asked.

Amina's eyes flicked toward Aya. "Eventually, I wound up on a job in Florence, shadowing a mark for some rare artifact. It turned out Aya was on the same team. By the time it was all over, we figured it was better to team up, that we could rely on each other."

Aya smirked, caught up in the memory. "We had half a

dozen Interpol agents hot on our heels, and you used that city's alleys like you were born in them."

Amina's posture relaxed. "We made off with enough to keep us comfortable for quite a while. That's when we realized our partnership could be... pleasurable and profitable. We stuck together until..." She broke off, biting her lip. "Well, life happens. We parted ways."

"So you've always lived on the edge," Karim said, though his attention kept drifting to the windows.

"I guess I learned early that the world takes what it wants. There's no sense playing by rules that protect the rich, so I found ways to circumvent them."

The Jeep hit a pothole, jolting them back to the present. Through the windshield, the landscape ahead shimmered with heat distortion.

Glancing in the rearview mirror, Omar jumped into the conversation. "What about now? Are you only helping us for a payday from the Amulet?"

"Let's say my motivations have broadened slightly. Call it a crisis of conscience, or maybe I just hate seeing corporations, especially ones that have fucked me over, wage war on everyday people. Plus, there's still a chance for a payday once we have that Amulet, if we can find someone we trust with it. And there's the matter of whatever's going on with my arm and my headaches."

Omar nodded as he shifted gears at an intersection. "I can respect that. I was in the smuggling game full-time for a while until I discovered I had a knack for guiding travelers, too. And that gets me shot at far less. I guess we're all just thieves who are starting to grow a conscience."

Karim laughed. "Well, I was never a thief," he said, then paused and shrugged. "But maybe I am now."

"Cheers to our den of thieves," Aya said.

"Save that toast for when we track down some wine," Omar said with a forced laugh. "But, if we're to be an alliance of rogues and criminals, there's no more fitting destination than Essaouira, or Mogador as the pirates called it."

"I wish it were under better circumstances," Aya murmured, watching three dust funnels now dancing on the horizon, "but I can't wait to see it."

Near midday, they pulled over in a dusty village to refuel at a bright green gas station marked "Bienvenue à Chichaoua." A small open-air market teemed with vendors selling clothes, produce, argan oil, honey, and woven baskets, but everyone seemed on edge. Shopkeepers kept glancing nervously at the sky.

"Getting close now," Omar announced.

Aya stretched her legs while Omar spoke to the gas attendant, watching as the locals hurried to secure tarps over produce stands while the wind whipped the air. An elderly woman selling honey caught her eye and beckoned her over.

"You travel from the mountains, yes?" the woman asked, her weathered hands clutching a carved pendant. She was small and bent with age, but her dark eyes held an alertness that made Aya pay attention. Behind her, jars of golden honey sat arranged on a wooden table, along with various herbs and what looked like protective charms.

"Yes," Aya replied carefully.

The woman's expression grew grave. "The djinn walk again. They are angry. Very angry." She gestured toward the mountains they'd come from, where even now a funnel cloud was visible spiraling against the blue sky.

She reached into a small cloth bag and pressed four etched brass rings into Aya's palm. "For your journey. The old protections may not be enough anymore, but they are better than nothing. And this..." She handed Aya a small vial of what looked like salt mixed with dried herbs. "If the wind speaks to you, throw this into the air and speak your name. Sometimes the old ways still work."

"Thank you," Aya said, moved by the woman's genuine concern. "How much do I owe you?"

The woman waved her hand dismissively. "This is for survival, not profit. But promise me, if you find whatever was taken from the mountain, you will return it. Some things should not be moved."

Omar returned, shielding his eyes from the increasing wind. "All set. Let's push through. If we're lucky, we'll reach Essaouira and find Salah before dark. And hopefully before whatever's following us decides to make another appearance."

As they climbed back into the Jeep, Aya distributed the protective charms to the others. The old woman watched them drive away, her figure growing smaller in the rearview mirror.

They stopped at a small roadside café a few miles down the road to refuel their own bodies. The establishment was little more than a few plastic tables under a corrugated metal awning, but the mint tea was hot and the shade was welcome. Around them, the other patrons seemed agitated, their conversations punctuated by nervous glances at the sky.

Karim blew on his tea, listening intently to a table of men engaged in frantic whispers. After a few minutes, he leaned closer to Aya and Amina.

"They're talking about the storms," he said quietly. "Calling it *nafas al-djinn*, the djinn's breath."

Aya's gaze followed his to the hunched men muttering over plates of olives and bread. Their body language spoke of genuine fear. "Why do they say it's djinn?"

"One man claims sand funnels followed him for miles yesterday," Karim explained. "Says they merged and formed a giant face in the sand. Another swears he heard voices in the wind, speaking in classical Arabic, and threatening." He paused, studying their faces. "The man sounds terrified."

Amina set down her glass with slightly more force than necessary. "Great."

"It might be superstition," Karim continued, "but they swear it's new, never this frequent or aggressive."

As if summoned by their conversation, a gust of unnaturally cold wind swept through the café, scattering napkins and making the metal awning rattle ominously.

"Let's not dwell on that," Aya said, though her voice carried less conviction than her words. "If it's scaring people away from going out, maybe we can slip through to Essaouira unnoticed."

"Yeah, let's go," Amina urged, standing and handing fifty dirham to the owner.

They drove for another hour in silence. Suddenly, the Jeep lurched violently to one side as a massive whirlwind materialized directly in their path, not gradually forming like the others, but appearing instantly, as if stepping through an invisible doorway.

"Hold on!" Omar shouted, yanking the wheel hard right.

The funnel tracked their movement, shifting course to follow them impossibly. Through the swirling sand, Aya glimpsed: two glowing ember-like points where eyes might be, and the suggestion of a massive, shifting form within the whirlwind. This wasn't just wind and sand. This was alive.

The temperature inside the Jeep plummeted. Their breath

misted in the suddenly frigid air, and the radio crackled to life on its own, emitting a sound like distant laughter mixed with the howl of wind through stone corridors.

"That's not weather," Karim breathed, his scientific skepticism crumbling as the entity circled them like a predator toying with prey. "That's not possible."

Aya's hands shook as she recognized what they were seeing. "The myths say when they grow strong enough, they take form within the elements themselves."

"You're saying that thing has a consciousness?" Omar asked, knuckles white on the steering wheel as he fought to keep them on the road. The entity was circling them now, herding them like sheep.

"According to our translations, yes. And it's testing us, learning about us." Aya's voice was barely steady. "It knows we were there. It knows we're connected to the breach."

The funnel suddenly collapsed, sand raining down on their windshield with the force of hail, and Omar skidded to a halt. In the eerie silence that followed, they could hear their own breathing and the Jeep's engine ticking as it cooled. But the silence felt pregnant with menace, as if something vast and alien was studying them.

Then, impossibly, words began forming in the settling sand on their windshield, Arabic script that seemed to write itself: "The seal is broken. The pact is void. The earth remembers."

Amina stared at the message, her face pale as parchment. "Okay," she whispered, "I'm ready to go full mystical now. This is all real."

The words hung there for a long moment, glowing faintly in the afternoon sun, before blowing away as quickly as they'd appeared. But the warning lingered in their minds, along with the unmistakable sense that they were being watched by something ancient, awakened, and very, very angry.

Aya frantically scribbled the message in her notebook, hands shaking so badly she could barely write. "This matches," she said, voice breaking. "This matches accounts from the 1800s of people receiving messages in a similar way. But back then, the seals held. The djinn could only whisper through cracks. Now..."

"Now they can do a whole hell of a lot more than whisper," Amina finished grimly. "And if they keep growing stronger..."

"According to Hassan's calculations, if he was right, full manifestation occurs within seven days of a major seal breach," Karim said quietly. "We're on day two."

Aya closed the notebook. "We need to move. Whatever was unleashed back there, it's not staying in the mountains. It's following us. And it's getting stronger. Much stronger."

Omar didn't need to be told twice. He gunned the engine, and they sped toward the ocean, each of them compulsively scanning the horizon for more signs of their supernatural pursuer.

Behind them, in the rearview mirror, another funnel of sand rose against the blue sky. But this one held its form, twisting in what looked almost like a gesture of acknowledgment.

Or perhaps a promise.

Thirty-Six

As they rounded one final hill, slowing down to pass a shepherd and his flock of goats, the Atlantic came into view, a vast shimmer of deep turquoise and froth with a cluster of low, white buildings clinging to its edge. Carefully plotted argan forests gave way to salt-scrub plains.

The moment the Jeep reached the outskirts of Essaouira, the cool sea breeze ripped through their open windows, tangy with brine and thick with humidity. The whitewashed, crenellated walls of the city's fortified medina shimmered under a sky of fast-moving clouds.

Aya squinted through the dusty windshield as Omar eased their Jeep into a parking lot just outside Bab Marrakech, one of the main gates to the old city. Stretching ahead was an open plaza of neat gray pavers. On the far side, palm trees grew slanted under the gusts of wind. Gulls wheeled overhead in noisy flocks.

"Finally," Amina said, climbing out of the vehicle.

The midday sun had burned away some of the morning's chill, though the breeze still carried a curious tension that pricked at Aya's nerves. She'd expected relief upon arriving safely, but an undercurrent of foreboding clung to her.

She hopped down from the car, scanning the scene: tourists snapping photos, kids playing soccer, a man in a hooded djellaba pushing a cart overflowing with fresh melons. Gnawa music drifted from somewhere within the walls, the metallic rattle of qraqeb mixing with a deep, steady bass line.

Omar cut the engine and stepped onto the pavement. "We'll head toward the walls and find D'Jazy. That's the place Abdelatif mentioned, right?"

"That's what his note said," Aya confirmed. She slipped her backpack over one shoulder, carefully adjusting its weight on her bruised ribs. "He said that's where we'd find Salah."

Amina gave a low laugh. "Let's hope this Salah is easy to deal with. I'm not in the mood for another fight."

They crossed the parking lot, weaving among the field of bright orange Dacias and fading yellow Peugeots.

The path that wound around the outside of the medina walls led them onto a thoroughfare lined with stalls and restaurants. Vendors offered fragrant saffron and gleaming jars of argan oil, women offered hair wraps and braids, while buskers played Bob Marley and Jimi Hendrix at either end. The wind tugged at shops' awnings, snapping the tarps like sails. Every so often, a swirl of sand from the city's outer edges scratched at their ankles.

"We keep going straight around this bend. D'Jazy should be near the ramp leading to the beach promenade," Omar said.

"It's good you know Essaouira," Amina said.

"I'm a cosmopolitan man, Amina. What city don't I know?" Omar laughed. "But no, I come here all the time as a quick getaway. The city's much calmer than Marrakech. Except for these winds." He jerked a thumb at the sky, where thin clouds scudded by at improbable speed.

Beyond the curved street and lined taxis, the Atlantic sparkled under the midday sun. Kitesurfers dotted the distant waves with bright patches of color, their sails tugging them across frothy breakers. On the beach, camels lounged in the sand, waiting for tourists seeking a slow amble along the shoreline and over the dunes.

Aya paused at the vantage. The world was simultaneously bright and precarious: a surfer's paradise with golden dunes overshadowed by the eerie sense that the planet itself was stirring. She breathed in the sea air, letting it momentarily ground her, and watched as a group of kittens chased each other through the tall grass, popping out at random.

Amina touched her shoulder. "There. That mural says D'Jazy." She pointed to a low-arched building with stone columns in front, painted with fluorescent graffiti featuring musical notes, swirling shapes, and the name in bold. A small cluster of stools and poufs ringed the entrance.

D'Jazy faced the busy thoroughfare on one side and an open view toward the wide beach on the other. The exterior was half traditional stone arches, half kaleidoscopic murals. Aya studied the crowd at the door: surfers in boardshorts, travelers in loose linen skirts, a local musician fiddling with a guitar. Overhead was a stylized silhouette of a saxophone player.

Karim exhaled softly. "This place is something else. It's always good to be back in Essaouira."

Inside, round tables sat on colorful Amazigh rugs. On a small raised platform, a man was tuning a guembri, occasionally testing a riff. The air smelled of saffron-laced seafood and lemon.

A tall man bounded toward them, wearing a Hawaiian floral print shirt, flip-flops, and a broad grin. "Hey, hey, hey, *marhaba*! Welcome to D'Jazy," he said. He shook each of their hands and clapped Karim on the back. "Four of you?"

Karim nodded. "Yeah, thanks. But we're looking for Salah. Is he here?"

The host's gaze danced between them, surprised. "He's here, yeah. Surfer with dreadlocks, Salah? How do you guys know him?" He laughed, then motioned them to follow him.

"A mutual friend told us to look him up when we were in town, and said he'd likely be here," Aya said.

"Well, yeah, he's always around, either on stage or behind the bar. Would you like to sit while I track him down?"

"Cheers," Omar said. "Could use a nice relaxing view, if possible. It was quite the journey."

The man led them to a corner near a wide arch that faced the sea in the distance. The strong breeze whipped through from the open entrance and mingled with the café's warmth. Aya took in the details: a worn tapestry draped across one wall, guitars hanging from hooks, and at least three drum sets scattered about. Strings of lights twinkled overhead.

"Essaouira's the best place to escape the stress of the rest of the world and unwind," their host said, leaning back as if the sea breeze itself had soothed him.

"Amen," Omar agreed. Aya tried to smile at the words, but her mind wouldn't quiet.

"I'll go get Salah for you all," the man said with a hangloose hand gesture, disappearing back into the swirl of sound and color while they took their seats.

Essaouira's easygoing charm, its languid cafés and sun-drenched afternoons, urged Aya to relax, but inside she churned with anxiety. No matter how gently the ocean air caressed her skin or how lazily the late-day sunlight draped over the whitewashed walls, she couldn't stop thinking about the conflict she'd been drawn into.

A moment later, a figure emerged from the back. He was a tall man in a loose linen shirt, parted in front to reveal an array of beaded necklaces and chest hair. Salt-and-pepper dreadlocks framed a caramel-toned face, and faded tattoos of waves, guitars, and Arabic writing ran along his arms.

He approached the table and broke into a lazy grin. "What's up, what's up *mes amis*? My friend at the door said you asked for me. I'm Salah." He clapped Omar and Karim on the back before kissing Amina and Aya's hands in turn.

"*Enchanté*. And who might you all be?"

"We're friends of Abdelatif," Omar said. "He told us you might help us with some, shall we say, specialized information."

Salah froze, grin fading. "Abdelatif? No way, the grumpy old man? Oh, it's been too long. That geezer's not in town, is he?"

"No," Aya said. "He's recovering from a gunshot, actually. We just came from the mountains. It's complicated, but he insisted we meet you here."

Salah fell silent, his brow furrowed as he weighed their situation. Around them, other patrons carried on blissfully unaware. Utensils clattered on plates and bursts of laughter rose, the sounds mingling with the distant crash of Atlantic waves. A musician now plucked a guembri beside the stage area, and fragments of its mellow rhythm drifted through the warm air.

Salah gestured at a vacant table away from the stage. "This place is busy. Let's find a corner with less noise."

He led them to a quieter area around the side, surrounded by paintings propped up on easels. Salah waved off a passing waiter, then turned to the group, "So. Abdelatif's in trouble?"

Karim nodded. "We all are, in a sense. There's a powerful corporation, Prometheus Energy Solutions, that just seized an artifact in the Atlas that my archaeology team discovered. They did a lot of damage with their private army, including shooting

Abdelatif. They fled with the artifact by helicopter. Abdel said you're the one who can track them?"

Salah's expression was steady, cautious. "I do some messing around with flight logs, radio frequencies. So you want me to chase corporate paramilitaries?"

"We just need to find out where they landed. Quickly."

Salah studied them, leaning back against the cushion, deep in contemplation.

Aya studied the painting that hung over Salah's shoulder and dominated the space. It depicted a woman's face set against a swirl of emerald-green shadow. One half of the painted woman's visage was rendered in warm, lifelike tones, but the other half was obscured by a haze of bluish-green, as if a second, ghostly face were emerging from or dissolving into the first. The woman's eyes were enormous and hollow, haunted by quiet despair, and a chunky necklace of bright wooden beads hung around her neck, a jarring burst of color against the melancholy on her features.

In that tortured face's fractured duality, Aya saw herself, torn in two. Just like the painted woman, Aya felt as though she wore one face for her companions while another, hidden self, heavy with moral dissonance, lurked just beneath it, silently screaming.

Finally, Salah spoke again. "You do realize if they're as bad as you say, they'll have ways to scramble signals, hush up any official logs."

Aya met his gaze. "We understand. But we also know you have talents. Abdelatif trusts you, and we have no one else we can turn to right now. We also have some of their hard drives that you might be able to crack, full of their operational data, and some of their tech we grabbed from the dig, if it helps."

Salah drummed his fingers on the table's mosaic surface, then shot a glance around to ensure no eavesdroppers were lurking. "Alright, alright. That all sounds right up my alley. But let's not talk details in the open."

He paused before continuing. "And not to harsh the vibe, but what's in it for me?"

"We can pay," Omar said carefully. "Cash is a little tight, not exactly accessible right now, given the circumstances. But we'll figure out a trade if money isn't enough. Abdelatif told us you're a stand-up friend, but that you also like to stay off the radar."

Salah sighed, letting a hand stray to the multiple beaded bracelets adorning his wrist, as though checking each for a hidden meaning. "I do. I also owe Abdelatif more than he realizes. Fine." He inhaled. "I close up here around midnight. We'll talk more then. Meanwhile, eat, drink, pretend you're on vacation. Don't cause a scene. There have been a lotta strange people telling disturbing stories the last couple of days. Avoid them. Later, you'll follow me to my riad. We can discuss specifics there."

With that, Salah stood, glanced at the stage, and rolled his shoulders a few times. "I'm up for a quick jam session. Then I need to pour some drinks, and I'll check on you later. Meanwhile, enjoy the vibe, yeah?" He drifted off, weaving among the tables, dancing, pulled by the rhythm.

At his departure, a heavy silence settled over their table, earlier bravado replaced by an awkward stillness as each retreated into private worry. In the background, silverware chimed and distant chatter continued, but at their table an uneasy quiet reigned.

The waitress returned without being asked and brought out a large platter of grilled fish marinated in chermoula, accompanied by a basket of bread, a tangy tomato salad, and three bottles of white wine.

"Compliments of Salah," she said as she set the food before them and began to pour the wine.

Omar was the first to break. He exhaled a long breath that might have been a sigh or a low chuckle, maybe both. "If I'd known we'd get food and wine this good at the end of the day," he said, eyeing the steaming fish set in the center of the table, "I would have insisted we nearly died every day."

Amina laughed, sharp, genuine, and louder than she'd intended. A few nearby patrons glanced over, while she prodded Omar's arm with her elbow.

"Speak for yourself. Next time you feel suicidal, leave me out of it." Her hand quivered as she reached for her wine glass. Amina tried to hide the tremor by taking a quick sip of wine.

In the gentle light, after a couple of drinks, Amina's tough front softened, her cheeks flushed, and Aya felt the unsettling pull of a familiar attraction.

Karim continued to pour more wine into each of their glasses, the liquid catching the light in shades of yellow and gold. "Tonight, we all deserve this."

He looked around the table at each of them in turn. When his gaze settled on Aya, his dark eyes lingered a half-second longer than the others. She answered his unspoken question with a tiny nod and a small, secret smile.

The first mouthful of food was heaven. Aya closed her eyes as she savored it, the spices dancing across her tongue. Minutes ago, fear had its claws in them all, and now the simple act of sharing a meal and a drink felt like reclaiming a piece of her soul.

Across the table, Omar groaned appreciatively at his plate. "By God, I think this beats my mother's cooking," he said. "Don't you dare tell her," he added quickly, pointing a fork in Amina's direction.

Amina smirked, arching an eyebrow. "Your secret's safe, but hopefully we don't take it to the grave too soon."

"To short memories and long lives," Aya said suddenly, lifting her glass. The words had popped out of her mouth. She felt three sets of eyes turn to her, warm and expectant. "I mean, maybe we don't dwell on what happened. Not tonight. This feels really nice."

Karim was the first to smile, his slow, thoughtful smile that made Aya feel seen. He raised his glass to meet hers in a gentle toast. "To being here together, tonight." Omar and Amina clinked their glasses against Aya's and Karim's, following suit.

"To having something normal," Amina added softly. "And drinking with you idiots."

"I'll drink to all of that, gladly," Omar said.

The world beyond D'Jazy, with its curses, djinn, ancient artifacts, and mercenaries, faded. For the first time in a long while, laughter came easily.

Aya felt Karim's knee rest against hers under the table. The contact was subtle and steady. She leaned in a fraction, drawn to the warmth of him beside her. Their eyes met, a quick, glimmering connection. Her cheeks warmed at the thought of touching him, kissing him, and she took a sip of wine to hide her smile. Across his glass, Karim's eyes crinkled as if he knew exactly what thought had made her blush.

Amina caught the exchange. Her eyes darted from Aya to Karim, and a knowing grin crept onto her face. Mercifully, she said nothing. Instead, she tipped the last of her wine into her mouth.

"That hit the spot," Omar sighed, voicing the sentiment for all of them before turning to Aya. "How are you holding up?" he asked.

She laid her hand over his for a moment, touched by the

care in his voice. "I'm alright," she said. As the words left her lips, she realized they were mostly true. "Better now."

Amina nodded in agreement, reaching over to give Aya's shoulder a light rub. "We all are."

Aya gazed out the large window. The ocean glistened under a nearly full moon. She tried to imagine living a simpler life: traveling here just to soak in the Gnawa festival or watch the sunset beyond the Sqala fortress walls. A romantic getaway with Karim, maybe. Relaxing in a rooftop hot tub, taking in the sea view with a glass of champagne.

At the front of D'Jazy, Salah sat perched on a stool, strumming his guitar with an easy, rolling style. The guembri player joined, forging an upbeat, discordant fusion and building into a rendition of "Zina."

Aya swayed from side to side with the rhythm. Her mind wandered to the flashes of gunfire, the callous ease with which Léglise had killed the archaeologists, the feeling of the rifle pressed to her back. She banished the image, pulling herself back into the present. They all watched the musicians without speaking, and Aya had the sense Omar, Amina, and Karim were wrestling with their own memories.

When the set ended, applause rippled through D'Jazy. Salah conferred quickly with the other musicians, then nodded at their table. "Fifteen minutes," he mouthed and pointed vaguely outside.

PART THREE

THIRTY-SEVEN

SALAH'S RIAD lay hidden behind high, salt-licked walls. A large wooden door, green with age, hid an oasis carved from the centuries-old stone of Essaouira's seawalls. It was after midnight when Aya, Karim, Amina, and Omar finally settled in the courtyard. The Atlantic wind gusted steadily, setting lantern flames dancing.

Around an intricately carved table in the courtyard's center, they sipped from assorted clay mugs of white wine. Chiseled pillars framed the open roof, silence mingling with distant waves pounding the ramparts.

The city of Essaouira, once known for bohemian calm, felt charged by an unseen force.

A battered laptop glowed on a cushion nearby. Salah crouched over it, dreads falling across his shoulders, fingers tapping rapidly as hashish smoke curled upward from the joint hanging out of his mouth.

Finally, Omar broke the silence. "Salah, my brother, anything from the USB?"

Salah exhaled a plume of smoke, then turned to face them.

"Some." He waved them closer. "The encryption's nasty, but I peeled back a few layers. I have mentions of a U.S. military site deep in the Sahara, near Algeria. Looks like your friends at Prometheus Energy might have a secret setup there. If I can find matching flight logs heading that way, we might have them. It's the only lead I see for now."

"That's probably where Léglise will hole up," Amina said under her breath, swirling the wine in her cup. Shadows flitted across her face.

"He'll want somewhere secure where they can retool the Amulet for the bigger scheme," Karim added. "We know from the USB data that they're planning something called 'Operation Smokeless Fire,' mass deployment of whatever power that artifact channels. They mentioned strategic locations across North Africa and atmospheric manipulation on a continental scale. That'd give them a solid base of operations."

Aya remembered the thermal signatures they'd found in the dig site photos. "Those secondary chambers we detected, what if they weren't just storage? What if there are other sealed sites across the region, and the Atlas Amulet is meant to unlock them all?"

"The network of ancient doorways between worlds," Amina said grimly. She shot a glance at Aya. "Three weeks I watched you at that site, pretending to be just another digger while you played house with Karim. I thought you'd gone soft, forgotten who you really were." Her voice carried an edge of something, jealousy, regret, or both. "But seeing what they're planning... you had the right idea all along."

"It wasn't just an act," Aya said quietly, feeling Karim's hand find hers under the table.

"I know," Amina admitted, surprising them all. "I watched you two for weeks, growing closer while I..." She trailed off, then forced a bitter laugh. "While I skulked in the shadows, planning my own score, missing what was really happening. I should have been with you guys all along."

Aya lowered her gaze to the tabletop. Stacks of partially damaged documents lay there, weathered pages of scans from the stolen HRF dig notes. She remembered the day she'd arrived at that mountain camp, posing as a grad student, thinking she could pull off a quick job while uncovering another clue to what her father was working on. She had never guessed how violently it would all unravel.

"It wouldn't have mattered. We shouldn't have gone in so openly," Aya whispered. "We pushed them into a corner. We triggered Léglise's men to escalate faster than we—"

Karim's fingers intertwined gently with hers under the table. "Aya, don't," he said, leaning close. "They were always going to kill anyone in their way. Of course, we had to try to stop them."

Aya forced a nod, though the guilt gnawed at her. "I can still see the mosaic walls crumbling. Now it's like the entire region is reacting, these storms, those vortexes on the road. And we let Léglise fly away. No amulet, no payday, no safety, no preserved history. Only loss."

Across the table, Amina's face hardened. "We can't dwell on what we failed to do. Léglise is one step ahead now, sure, but he's also arrogant. And he's paid others to do the historical and mythological work for him. He doesn't actually understand it. If Salah's right and there's a base near the Algerian border, maybe that's where we corner him next." She began refilling all of their cups. "That is, unless you've got a better idea."

Omar sank against his cushion, crossing his arms. "I'm fresh out of ideas, better ones or worse ones. We're outgunned and outrun, but I'm not giving up. Not after what they did to Abdelatif."

Salah cleared his throat. "Listen, my people, if there's an actual black ops U.S. military site you're headed to on the other side of Morocco, you'll need serious planning. I can keep digging. I'll try to decrypt the last chunk of data on this drive by morning." He patted the battered laptop. "This is the best machine in my stash. Just keep the chatter down a bit. I need to focus."

He put his headphones on and resumed typing, that pungent swirl of hash enveloping him like a hazy cocoon. Only soft keystrokes and the moan of wind disturbed the tense silence.

"Still nothing from The Aegis, Aya," Omar said. "I've tried every contact method we had, just to see what they'd say. Dead silence." He scratched his head. "Organizations like that don't just vanish. Either they got what they wanted from this operation, or..."

"Or we're loose ends they'd probably prefer to tie up, as we feared," Aya finished. "I keep thinking about how convenient it was that they hired us right when Léglise was making his move. Like they knew exactly when and where everything would go down."

"What if it wasn't convenient timing?" Amina said. "What if they knew exactly when Léglise would move because they were coordinating with him?"

Omar's eyes widened. "You think Aegis was working with PES?"

"Think about it. They had detailed intelligence about the site layout, security rotations, and even which artifacts were most valuable. How does their organization get that kind of inside information unless..."

"Unless they were in communication with both sides," Omar finished grimly. "Hiring us as insurance in case their primary operation went sideways."

Amina's eyes narrowed. "You weren't hired to stop Léglise. You were hired as his backup plan, in case he fucked up."

"I don't know what to think anymore. But the timing was too perfect, us getting hired just as Léglise was preparing his assault, Aegis having detailed intelligence about the site, then complete radio silence the moment Léglise succeeds." Aya gulped the wine from her cup. "It makes sense if they were worried about the difficulties of extracting the Amulet, or about others coming. He tries his corporate way, we try our criminal way, Aegis sides with the winner, and whoever is left is a disposable asset who could take the blame if anything ends up public. Léglise was terrified about his public image when he betrayed me in Paris. It makes sense if he felt the pressure."

"And this explains the radio silence," Omar continued. "They don't need to extract us or pay us if we're dead, or exposed to the police, Interpol. Loose ends tied up."

The implications hung heavy in the salty air. They weren't just abandoned; they were targets, too.

Aya's jaw clenched. "And if that's true, then we're not just hunting Léglise for revenge. We're the only ones left who know what really happened at that site. Which makes us very dangerous liabilities."

Aya let her head drop back against the cushion behind her. A rising gust battered the shutters overhead. Her mind darted from one scene to another, Jordan's Wadi Rum. Paris's opulent betrayal. The dire Atlas sabotage. All stepping stones on her path to losing the artifact entirely.

Karim leaned closer. "Still thinking about the corridor?"

"I can't shake it. I hear the wind and remember that swirl of dust roaring out. I see those glowing geometric carvings."

"We'll find a way to fix it," he whispered. "We'll figure out how to reverse whatever's happening in these storms. Or at least stop Léglise from doing worse. You're not alone in this, Aya."

She nodded solemnly and proceeded with another round of refills.

Amina rose abruptly, pacing in an agitated circle. "We can't just sit around. Staying out of sight might be wise, PES or some local authorities might be searching for us, but it feels wrong not to act."

"We only got here hours ago, and there's no way anyone expected us to come here," Omar said. "They'll expect us to have returned to Marrakech if we survived. We need to wait to make a plan until after we have more data from Salah. Rushing in blind is exactly what Léglise would want us to do. He's the type who sets traps, baits you with a clue, then pounces when you arrive."

Amina braced her hands on the table, her knuckles turning white. For a heartbeat, Aya glimpsed the old intensity in Amina's gaze.

"Fine," Amina said. "But with each passing minute, that thing might do more damage. Or Léglise could be hooking it up to some twisted machine, summoning God-knows-what out of the earth, out of some supernatural realm."

From his vantage at the laptop, Salah suddenly raised a hand, beckoning them closer again. "Hey, I've got something, some partial synergy between the stolen data and official channels. A location name is repeated... 'Ain Sidi Rayhan.' Possibly a code for the desert outpost."

He typed furiously, pulling up an old topographical map. "Doesn't guarantee that's Léglise's base, but it's referenced in these PES files multiple times, and the airspace has two hits today."

He tapped a final key, and the screen displayed faint satellite images with red highlight boxes. They depicted stark desert terrain near the Algerian border, a faint geometric shape where no city or known checkpoint existed. Aya felt a prickle of dread.

"That shape looks like it could be a landing pad," Omar said.

Amina shot a glance at Aya. "Okay, we have a lead. What's the plan?"

Salah gave them a guarded look. "Don't treat it as gospel. We're only connecting dots. But it's something, makes sense they would hide in the desert to avoid prying eyes."

Karim tapped the map, frowning. "I know that region, there are few roads, harsh climates. Possibly some old Algerian conflict lines. Breaking in won't be easy, on top of whatever they have at the base itself."

The wind battered the courtyard gate, the sudden gust slamming the wooden door. The flame of the single lamp overhead sputtered, casting monstrous shadows that danced across the walls. A small ginger cat streaked across the courtyard in alarm, hissing at the wind before perching on a surfboard and watching them intently from meters away.

Salah laughed. "That's Marmalade, don't worry about her. She's a street cat that I've grown quite attached to. She comes and goes as she chooses," he said, before switching off the laptop's screen and rubbing his eyes. He stood and walked over to pet the cat, who curled up, purring loudly. "Look, I can do more decrypting, see if there's mention of how many men or what armaments are there. Meanwhile, the rest of you try to rest. My place has enough space if you don't mind a bit of mess. Six bedrooms that I usually rent out to surfers, but they're empty now. Just watch your heads upstairs, some of those rafters are older than my grandfather. And the view from the rooftop over the sea is one of the best in the world. I'll have to take you guys up there tomorrow."

Omar nodded. "Yeah, alright, thanks. It sounds like this place beats my recent digs."

Aya tilted her head back and looked up through the courtyard's open roof. The star-scattered sky was quickly receding behind a surge of ominous cloud cover, swirling faster than the usual Atlantic breeze. Abdelatif's warnings echoed, djinn freed by their mistake, shadows now searching for a way into the world. Karim pressed a warm palm between her shoulder blades.

"To surviving the night," Omar said softly while pouring the last of the wine from the bottle, distributing it among the cups. The others raised their glasses, none of them quite meeting each other's eyes.

Each member of the group nursed their own private fear: guilt, worry for Abdelatif, heartbreak over the dig's destruction, and bone-deep remorse for unleashing a curse the ancients had spent millennia containing.

In the corner, Marmalade hissed again at the unseen night beyond the courtyard wall.

Across the table, Amina exhaled, setting aside her glass. "So," she asked quietly, "we lay low till Salah finishes? No sleepless walks through the port?"

"We stay quiet," Aya said. "First thing tomorrow, we finalize a plan, assuming Salah's decode matches our suspicions."

"We all want to rush out there, but without solid intel, it's suicide," Omar said. "Léglise has firepower; we don't. Plus, it might help to have had some real sleep when we need our wits about us."

Amina gave a nod. "Fine. I'll do my best not to break anything until dawn."

Salah spared them a sidelong glance. "I appreciate that. I just replaced my doors last month." Then he hunched back over the keyboard, a crooked smile on his lips. "Anyway, I'll nudge the code, see if I can pull a miracle from these bytes for you, my lovely new companions."

The hush resumed until finally Aya stood. "Tomorrow, then," she said.

Salah gave her a casual wave as she retreated from the courtyard, heading up the narrow staircase to the small upper rooms.

But in Aya's mind, sleep still felt like a distant horizon. Even as she stepped upstairs to a chilly ocean breeze drifting in from an open shutter, she knew the wind's howling would not relent, not tonight.

As she slipped into a bedroom, the shutters battered once more, a final echoing slam, and the entire medina seemed to inhale, bracing for storms yet to come.

THIRTY-EIGHT

Aya couldn't sleep. Even after the wine and the day's bone-deep exhaustion, rest felt impossible.

After an hour of futile attempts, she slipped out of her room in Salah's riad while Omar snored loudly from the room beside hers. She climbed the old wooden ladder to the rooftop, drawn by the restless nighttime wind and the silent call of the sea and stars.

She stood at the terrace's edge, arms folded over the railing. The moonlit ocean beyond glimmered like dark silk, its surface broken by soft white caps where the waves lapped against the ancient ramparts and rocks below. Overhead, clouds parted just enough to reveal starlight, casting the world in a gentle glow. Aya closed her eyes, enjoying the fresh air, focusing on her breath.

"Couldn't sleep either?"

She opened her eyes to see Karim stepping carefully onto the rooftop, a glowing lantern in one hand. His features appeared sculpted by the dim glow, his tousled hair, concerned eyes.

She smiled weakly. "I tried. But every time I closed my eyes, I felt the gun against my back, heard Léglise give the kill order again. Or remembered the look on his face when he held the Amulet."

Before Karim could respond, more footsteps echoed on the ladder. Salah's head appeared, followed by his lanky frame.

"Thought I heard voices up here," he said, settling cross-legged before them. "That USB data... it's revealing things that keep my mind spinning."

"What kind of things?" Aya asked, grateful for the distraction.

Salah lit another joint, the tip glowing orange in the darkness.

"Your amulet, for one. It's not just some ancient battery. Some reports mention crystalline matrix properties and mineral resonance frequencies. It reminded me of something." He took a long drag, eyes distant. "You know Farid Belkahia?"

"The Moroccan modernist artist?" Karim asked. "He worked with copper and natural pigments."

"Exactly, my friend. Belkahia believed Moroccan earth held memory, that minerals could store and transmit a cultural energy, if you will. He'd grind local stones, mix them with traditional materials, create art that literally contained the essence of the land." Salah gestured widely toward the sea and mountains that surrounded them.

"Now imagine that principle applied to your amulet. What if it's not just crystal, but a specific mineral composition that resonates with... I don't know, whatever was sealed in those mountains?"

Aya's brow furrowed. "You're saying the Amulet is like Belkahia's pigments—it contains the essence of the place it came from?"

"Yeah, but potentially more than that," Salah said, smoke hovering around his dreadlocks.

"Belkahia talked about telluric forces, these earthbound energies that could be channeled through the right materials. Your Prometheus friends seem to think the Amulet works the same way, like it's a conductor, or a lens for focusing whatever power those ancient builders trapped."

"That would explain the geometric patterns we saw work, beyond the mathematics," Karim said slowly. "They weren't just ornamentation. They were instructions for how to align the mineral matrix, to tune it to specific frequencies."

Salah shrugged. "Potentially. And if this Léglise fellow doesn't understand that, if he just sees it as raw power to be exploited..." He shook his head.

"It'd be like taking one of Belkahia's copper pieces and trying to use it as a lightning rod. You might get results, but not the ones you intended."

Salah stood, stretching. "I'll leave you two to enjoy the view. It's restorative in its own way. But think about what I said. Belkahia understood that the earth's natural elements hold power. Your ancient builders understood it too. The question is whether Léglise will figure it out before he unleashes something he can't control."

He headed back to the ladder and disappeared below.

Aya and Karim stood in tense silence for a moment before Karim crossed the rooftop and stood beside her. He set the lantern on a cracked tile ledge. "Every hour, we're getting one step closer to stopping them. But we need to stay sane, and wow, this view might help. Salah didn't overstate it."

"It's one of the most beautiful things I've ever seen. Essaouira itself is incredible."

"Essaouira was always my family's escape from the Marrakech heat," Karim said. "My father used to make up stories about talking cats that roamed the port at night, trading seashells for travelers' dreams and keeping the city safe from malevolent ghosts. I grew up believing that here, anything was possible, from pirates burying treasure in the ramparts, still waiting to be found, to secret passages leading to hidden kingdoms beneath the medina. Even now, I still feel that spark of wonder the moment I enter the city."

"I love that. I wish we had more time here," Aya said.

"We can always come back. After..."

For a moment, they just listened to the wind, the waves, and the gulls. Out on the water, a handful of fishing boats bobbed with their lanterns like weary fireflies.

Aya's voice cut through the hush. "Professionally, I thought I was invincible. I'd never lost before. Now twice to Léglise within days."

Karim reached for her hand, his palm warm despite the chilly sea air. "I can't pretend to have answers. The Atlas site, my friends there, was always a hostage to Léglise's ambitions. You gave us a fighting chance, Aya. And you're amazing. We'll still stop him."

She tilted her head, searching his face. In him, she found a reflection of her anxieties, as though they were bound by the same moral crisis.

"Sometimes I can't help wondering why you're still here," she whispered. "You deserve better."

"I'm still here because I see who you are beneath all of it."

Unhooking her arms, Aya let one hand slide around his waist.

Karim's arm came around her shoulders, drawing her in. "I won't pretend I'm not scared, but as long as we face it together, I'll keep going and feel safe with you by my side. I still think you're invincible."

Aya didn't speak, instead resting her forehead against his

collarbone. The moment seemed suspended, just them above it all, the wind, and the flickering lantern caught between the city's ancient walls and the endless ocean.

"I'm not used to relying on anyone. Needing anyone," she managed finally, eyes drifting shut. "But you make me want to again."

"You don't need anyone. But I'm glad you want me."

The next heartbeat unfolded in a slow, magnetic pull as their lips touched. The kiss was a brush of warmth and trembling breath. Aya felt a rush, as though every jagged piece of guilt she carried might soften under his touch. His hands found her hips, drawing her closer, as her arms slid around his neck.

Above them, the wind gathered, swirling strands of her hair around them like a private veil. In that hush of starlight, his mouth pressed more firmly against hers, and she answered with a hesitant hunger, searching for reassurance in his touch. She let the tension pour out, anger at Léglise, the loss of her father, the fear of curses, all of it receding beneath the surge of feeling alive.

He broke away just long enough to breathe her name. "Aya..."

"I'm here," she whispered. Then her lips found his again. She angled her head, deepening the kiss, feeling the world shift beneath them as though the rooftop itself might tilt out to sea.

Karim's hand slid across her lower back, guiding her away from the ledge, deeper into the shadowed recess by the rooftop's low parapet. The tiles underfoot were cool. She tasted salt on his lips, sea salt, or perhaps the hint of tears, and realized she couldn't separate her grief from this sudden, desperate craving to find solace in him.

He paused, searching her face. "Are you sure?"

She answered by lifting his hand to her heart. Her pulse

pounded beneath his fingertips, the only affirmation she could muster. "I need this. To remember that we're still human, still capable of something besides running or fighting."

Karim's fingers trailed along her jawline. His touch deliberate, every brush of skin a jolt of warmth. She grabbed a handful of his hair as he explored her. They clung to each other, their mouths muffling half-broken whispers of each other's names.

They broke apart with a soft gasp as Karim's hands slid beneath her shirt. She arched forward, helping him lift it over her head and toss it aside. The sea breeze feathered across her bare skin, sending a quick shiver down her spine. Aya reached for his shirt next, tugging it over his shoulders in a single, impatient pull. Beneath her palms, she felt him trembling as she traced the lines of his chest.

He paused, taking in the sight of her naked body in the moonlight. Shadows rippled across them, the lantern's flame swaying in the breeze.

"Should we lock the roof?" Karim whispered.

Aya glanced around at the shadows of the neighboring rooftops along the sea wall and the endless expanse of ocean before them. "No, everyone's asleep," she breathed.

Aya's mind dimly registered the rasp of fabric shifting as they removed the rest of their clothes, the swirl of cooler air on exposed skin, the grip of his hands on her thighs. Their shared breath melded with the sea wind, a fierce urgency unfolding in each sigh.

Aya guided him toward a low lounger on the rooftop's edge. The Atlantic stretched out before them, dark and endless. Heart pounding, she nudged Karim to lie back and swung one leg over his hips, straddling him. Her eyes locked on his, a question in her gaze that he answered by kissing her neck, working his way down to her chest.

She leaned down, pressing a lingering kiss to his lips, her

hands sliding along his arms to his wrists, gently pinning him beneath her. Even with the nighttime wind whipping strands of hair across her face, she'd never felt more powerful, or more exposed. The raw sound of the ocean surf spurred her on, a rhythmic pulse that fueled every shared breath and every touch.

Their movements grew slower and more intimate, achieving a rhythm that devoured her doubts. She sank fully into the sensation of Karim's body against her own, the touch of his hands caressing her body, arching in time with the gentle, desperate cadence they found together. The wind's roar faded into a faint hush, and only this connection remained, skin to skin. She closed her eyes against the swirl of starlight overhead.

Finally, with shuddering breaths, they reached a gentle release. Aya felt a surge of white-hot emotion, joy, hope, and relief, all mingled in a dizzy wave. Karim's hand curled around hers, fingers interlocked, bodies still pressed close as they came down from a breathless high. She rested her forehead against his, breathing fast, her hair a messy halo in the swirling moonlight.

Beneath the open sky, they collapsed into each other's arms, naked and vulnerable but utterly secure in what they'd forged. The quiet that followed felt impossibly tender, the tension in Aya's muscles dissolving beneath Karim's slow, comforting strokes along her back.

"I'm not sure what to say," he whispered, voice unsteady. "That was..."

Aya let out a half-laugh. "Perfect. Exactly what we needed," she finished. "And I can't wait until we need it again."

Aya marveled at how easily they fit together in that cramped space, legs tangled in the hush of night. Even the wind had softened, as though granting them this fleeting respite.

In the dim afterglow, she traced her fingertips across his

chest, the faint stubble of hair. "Karim. This might complicate everything."

His lips brushed her temple. "Things were already complicated for me. And somehow, this feels more honest than anything that's happened to us in weeks."

She listened to the slow, steady thump of his heartbeat. "You're right. We can't predict anything, but at least we have this."

He squeezed her hand. "Aya, no matter what, I want you to know..." He trailed off, as though the words were too fragile to voice. Eventually, he just pressed a slow kiss to her forehead, letting the silence speak instead.

"I know," she whispered.

They stayed entwined under the moonlight, savoring the singular closeness in the face of unstoppable darkness.

Thirty-Nine

Morning light bled slowly into the riad, turning the whitewashed walls to pale gold. Outside, the Atlantic breeze kept its usual vigor. Aya woke with a weightless feeling.

She slipped out of her room and heard movement throughout the riad. Omar, mumbling, was already awake somewhere, rummaging around in search of breakfast. A faint melody drifted through the house, a scratchy old Gnawa album Salah was surely playing. Rubbing her arms, she crossed the courtyard.

Halfway there, she heard footsteps and turned to see Amina emerging from the adjacent corridor. She wore an oversized sweater that she must have found in the room. It skimmed just beneath her hips, leaving her legs and underwear exposed to the morning air. The casual drape made Aya acutely aware of every inch of skin.

There was a raw familiarity in Amina's eyes.

"Hey," Amina said, pulling down on her sweater. The wind tousled her dark curls, revealing faint circles beneath her eyes. She glanced over Aya's shoulder to confirm no one else was nearby. "Got a minute?" She stepped closer, locking eyes with Aya. "Figured we should talk privately at some point," she added, her voice dipping low, as if sharing a secret they might both enjoy.

"Sure." Aya gestured to a side alcove of chipped tile benches, half hidden by a stand of potted palms.

They settled beside each other, neither speaking at first. The warm glow of the morning lit Amina's face, every feature beautiful despite the clear lack of sleep. Amina's thigh pressed against Aya's.

Aya inhaled slowly, preparing for the swirl of old wounds that always lingered between them. But something had shifted inside her since last night. The way Karim made her feel both vulnerable and safe had created a new center of gravity in her emotional world.

Yet here was Amina, beautiful and broken and asking for forgiveness in her own way, stirring up feelings Aya thought she'd buried.

Amina's gaze clung to the floor. "I need to talk to you without Omar or Karim or anyone else listening in."

Aya nodded. "All right."

A sharper gust of wind rattled the windows, and Salah's cat Marmalade darted out from under the bench with a startled meow. Amina's vision trailed after the cat.

"I saw you. Last night, on the rooftop with Karim." She forced a half-laugh. "Relax, I'm not here to scold you for it or give you shit. Actually... I couldn't help thinking about all the times it was me kissing you in the dark. It brought back a lot of memories." Her voice grew softer. "It was like watching the life we could have had if I hadn't fucked it up."

Heat flooded Aya's cheeks with the realization that their moment had an unintended audience. "Amina, I didn't know you could see us."

The truth was, even the tang of jealousy in Amina's voice ignited something dangerously close to desire. Aya tried to quell it.

Amina shook her head. "I wasn't watching on purpose. I just couldn't sleep, feeling anxious about what's happening to me, about everything. When I got up, there you were. But it wasn't just last night, it was all those weeks at the dig."

Aya's chest tightened with memory. "I get it," she said softly. "Amina, we did have something powerful. But we both know how it ended."

For just a second, Aya pictured Amina leaning in, her hand sliding around her waist. There was a time when she would've welcomed that touch, drowned in it. Now, she felt as though she were standing on a precipice.

Amina looked up, pained. "That's exactly it. It ended in the worst possible way. And I..." She swallowed. "I regret it, Aya. Leaving you in Egypt was the biggest mistake of my life."

Silence pressed in on them like a heavy weight. Aya ran her fingertips along the chipped tile beneath her and recalled the mosaic in the corridor, shattered.

Amina's voice quavered. "I did it because I was desperate, afraid. We were cornered. I panicked. I told myself you'd bounce back, that we'd find our way back to each other eventually, because we always have. But as soon as I walked away, I knew I'd wrecked us. And every time I close my eyes, I remember your scent, your touch... I can't shake it, Aya. Even now."

A part of Aya wanted to lash out, to conjure the bitterness she'd harbored for years, but she found only a deep, weary sadness. "And now you want to, what? Rebuild that trust overnight?"

Amina rubbed her forehead. "I know it sounds impossible. But when I saw you with Karim, I realized how much I miss you. Want you." Her voice dropped to a whisper. "Miss us and want us. I keep thinking, if I hadn't messed up in Egypt, maybe we'd still be side by side in every sense." The sunlight sharpened the brightness of Amina's tears. She blinked them away, forcing an unsteady grin. "I guess I hoped that maybe there was a small piece of that bond we could salvage."

"Amina, I can't pretend we didn't have something real, or that I don't still have feelings for you. But that was a different life. Now—"

"I know. Now you have Karim." Amina's expression hardened momentarily. "He's good for you. I've never seen you so… grounded."

"And I don't want to betray him. Not in any sense."

"I'm not here to push you. I just had to speak my truth. That I'm sorry. That if I could rewrite what happened in Egypt, I would. That I still care about you and still want you, Aya. But I know that we can't go back."

Aya let the hush settle over them, letting Amina's words sink in. She saw the regret in her eyes. "I'm sorry, Amina. What we had is over. But—"

Amina looked up sharply. "But?"

"But I do forgive you," Aya whispered. "I can't deny what we had or the pain you caused. But there's too much at stake now for us to dwell on grudges. Maybe we can find something more honest. A real friendship."

Amina nodded.

"I mean it." Aya hesitated, then reached out to fold her fingers around Amina's hand. "You'll always be important to me. Maybe not in the same way anymore. But we need to be able to trust each other and work together."

Amina let out a ragged exhale, then squeezed Aya's hand back. "Thank you. I know I don't deserve a clean slate. But if you can accept me as a friend, that means a lot to me."

A gentle silence stretched between them. Neither pulled away. Aya shifted closer, wrapping Amina in a slow hug. For a moment, Aya let herself sink into that warm familiarity, her pulse racing at the press of Amina's chest against hers. Finally, Amina drew back, eyes shining with unshed tears. "You've changed, Aya. And in the best way."

Aya let out a soft laugh that felt almost like a sob. "You've changed too, or else you wouldn't be baring your soul." She pulled Amina tight again. "We have a lot of darkness ahead. This might be the only way we survive it."

They broke apart as the scraping of footsteps approached. Omar stood at the courtyard's entrance, holding a small tray of breakfast pastries wrapped in paper. He raised an eyebrow. "Am I interrupting?"

Amina flicked him an exasperated smirk, wiping her eyes. "You're always in the way, but we're done now. We just had to have a catch-up chat."

He eyed them both in confusion, then shrugged. "Salah's made some fresh mint tea. Karim's rummaging for coffee beans. Figured you might want something before we look at those new decrypts."

Aya rose. "Thanks," she said to Omar. "You coming?" Aya asked, with a quick look back at Amina.

Amina nodded, wiping her cheeks once more. "I will. You two go ahead."

Omar led Aya out of earshot, confusion still etched across his face. "Everything okay?"

"Better than it's been in a long time."

Together, they headed toward the main lounge where the aroma of strong coffee already swirled.

FORTY

JUST BEFORE MIDDAY, Aya climbed the narrow stairs to Salah's makeshift study, a small room near the top floor of the riad that caught the full blaze of the sun through a single arched window carved into the thick medina wall. She paused at the threshold. The old floor fan did little to temper the rising humidity or the tension swirling in the house.

Salah sat hunched over his laptop. Half-empty mugs cluttered the low table beside him. He glanced up, meeting Aya's gaze with a tired grin.

Aya stepped into the room, followed by Karim and Omar. Amina lingered at the doorway, a slight grimace of pain etched on her features; she'd been nursing a persistent headache all morning, occasionally pressing a palm to her temple.

"Is it bad?" Aya asked.

Amina shrugged, though sweat beaded at her temples. "I'm fine, just nightmares all night, then this headache." She exhaled firmly. "Let's deal with the real problem first."

Karim motioned her to a worn armchair near the window. "Have a seat. If it gets worse, tell us."

Amina gave a grateful nod before settling down. Aya caught the flicker of real pain behind Amina's bravado. She forced herself to refocus, stepping around Salah's shoulder to peer at the laptop monitor.

"Finally, sorry to keep y'all waiting," Salah said, rubbing bloodshot eyes. "I think I've cracked the last bit of that drive." He tapped the keyboard. "Check it out."

Lines of text scrolled, peppered with references to Prometheus Energy Solutions and a series of timetables. Salah clicked through folders labeled in abrupt, coded phrases: *SER_Artifact, OpsCoord, MawtDhahab.*

Omar pointed at the final file name. "Mawt Dhahab, that means 'Golden Death'? Or 'Death Gold'? Something like that."

Salah nodded. "Could be a code name for a project, or a weapon. There's a shocking amount of references to harnessing 'Idris energy' with advanced tech. Honestly, I can't follow what they're doing in terms of the science, but we have access."

He opened one of the newly decrypted PDFs. A schematic popped up, grainy, black-and-white images of an industrial facility. Along the margins were notes in English and French about energy fields, wave frequencies, artifact synergy, and references to a Djinn harness.

"'*Objective: Isolate artifact signals for onsite testing. Final stage: demonstration for strategic advantage,*'" Aya read. "So they plan on using it quickly."

Karim let out a nervous laugh. "I still just can't believe this is real."

Salah scrolled to the next page. A carefully drawn chart labeled *US-PES HQ* took shape, detailing watchtower perimeters, helicopter pads, and certain restricted labs. A small reference read: "*Southern Sector. Approx. 28° N, 6° W.*"

He then opened a folder labeled "*FlightPaths.*" A list of

logs populated the screen, each entry noting a rendezvous time and a landing zone identified as "*H-4*." "These might be the helicopters, and match those airspace hits I found last night," Salah muttered. He opened a satellite view, zooming in on a small clearing inside a barbed-wire fence. "That's definitely a helipad. Based on these documents, they've been using it for regular supply drops every day, but it's impossible to say if this is where they went after they left the dig site."

"Sounds like you were right, way in the Sahara," Omar muttered, recalling the partial coordinates from earlier. "So there really is a secret base out there, some U.S. involvement, with those African Lion drills, or at least a black site for the American military."

Salah grimaced. "This doc calls it '*Facility #4 – Desert Cata-lyst Lab*.' We're looking at a deep collaboration. You're probably right, a black site."

Aya felt a fury run through her. "He'll have the Amulet with him there. This is where they are."

Amina interrupted, letting out a low hiss of pain, pressing her forehead. "Sorry, guys. Keep reading, Salah. We need the full story."

Salah skimmed a new document, face darkening. "Yeah, here's the one I wanted to show you. '*Mawt Dhahab: Proposed final deliverable, weaponization of intangible entity, re-labeled as Smokeless Fire Harness*.' Sounds like they're referencing the djinn as an energy source or machine or something."

Aya's anger spiked. "Weaponizing the djinn for all Léglise's clean energy production bullshit. They're insane. A week ago, I never would have believed any of this even possible."

"The removal of that artifact triggered earthquakes," Karim said. "It created changes to weather patterns, all the strange things we've been experiencing. There may be a scientific explanation at the bottom of this djinn stuff, but it sounds like they intend to keep testing it before they understand it. Thousands, maybe millions, could be at risk."

Omar crossed his arms. "Okay, so we'll go to that base. But how? The place is guaranteed to be bristling with all that armed security. Not to mention the U.S. military. Who knows what resources they have at their disposal, or what torture will be unleashed on us if we get caught."

"Amina and I will figure out infiltration," Aya said.

At that moment, Amina lurched upright from her chair with a groan of pain. She pressed the heel of her hand to her temple, shutting her eyes tight. "Sorry. I'm fine," she insisted to Aya's worried glance. "Just, I feel like something's clawing at my mind."

But as she spoke, her eyes unfocused for a moment, staring at something none of them could see. Her hand moved unconsciously to trace patterns in the air, swirling motions."

Amina?" Karim asked, concerned.

She blinked hard, then snapped back to the present. "What? Oh." She forced a laugh. "Maybe the djinn realize these idiots are messing with them, and they're searching for a link. I keep hearing whispers, in what sounds like archaic Arabic, like the inscriptions in that chamber. Maybe they're trying to show me something, tell me something to help."

Aya exchanged a worried glance with Omar. Earlier that morning, after coffee, they'd caught Amina standing motionless in the courtyard, lips moving silently as if she were having a conversation with someone invisible.

"The dreams aren't just nightmares," Amina continued, her voice taking on an odd, distant quality. "They're... instructions. Warnings. Something is coming, and it's angry."

Salah's brow furrowed. "What's in the visions, sister? What do you see?"

Amina shrugged. "Shapes. Sand swirling in monstrous

forms. Fire that moves like a living thing. I sometimes hear chanting." She grimaced. "Might just be nightmares from everything I've seen, and the lack of sleep. But it's real enough to keep me up all night, and there are the marks on my arms."

Omar set a hand gently on her shoulder. "I'm so sorry, *okti*. We'll get you to the doctor as soon as we finish this, and I have some Doliprane in my bag."

Salah clicked a final command. The laptop screen went black for an instant, then reloaded a map with a distinct red circle near the Algerian border. "We're in agreement then. That has to be the base. If these logs are accurate, they're ramping up for something big, some demonstration in a matter of days, a week at most."

Karim raked a hand through his hair, scanning the map.

Omar tapped the screen. "Well, that's it then. We'll have to find a way in, get our hands on the artifact. That's the only shot at stopping them." He nodded at Salah. "Thank you, brother."

Salah rubbed the back of his neck. "No question. But if infiltration is the plan, I'll come with you. My tech might help, and I can set up real-time hacks on their systems from the inside." He gave a wry grin. "Been a while since I pulled anything that crazy, and I've been missing the big waves."

"Well, we're all set to risk everything," Amina said, her hand still pressed to her forehead. "No hint of payment, and almost certain death. What have you all turned me into?"

They all laughed before Salah dove back into the maps. "Well, we should take a look at old surveys of the area. The base is right on top of where an old village used to be, so there might be a few ways to approach, maybe even sneak in."

Aya opened her mouth to respond, but a thunderous crash from below made them all jump up, instantly alert.

The entire floor trembled from the impact, sending dust

swirling in the sunlit air. A heartbeat later, more noise erupted, heavy footsteps, the sharp crack of splintering wood. Somewhere down in the riad's courtyard, a man shouted.

"I think they found us. Harsh fucking vibes, man," Salah hissed, slamming the laptop lid shut.

Aya locked eyes with Omar. "How? Who?"

Another crash. Shouts. The scuffle of a heavy object being overturned.

"They can't know we're here, but it doesn't matter. They're inside the house. We need to move, now," Karim yelled.

Amina struggled to her feet, leaning against the wall for balance. "I'm ready," she said. She reached under her jacket for the small pistol she carried.

Omar flung the window wide, scanning the rocky beach below, drawing his own weapon. "Good thing I'm paranoid. But there's no telling if more are waiting outside. We might be surrounded."

Without warning, Salah dropped to his knees beside a dusty crate, flipping the lid open. He fished out a pair of well-worn handguns and tossed one to Karim. "Think you can handle this, brother?"

Karim's grip tightened on the gun. "Guess we're about to find out."

Another crack of wood, followed by gunshots, reverberated from the lower floor, then a ragged shout. Aya stared hard at the door. "We fight our way out or jump down to the beach, but it's far, and they might be expecting that. No other options."

Salah yanked the flash drive from the side of the laptop. "Here," he said, pressing it into Omar's hand. "A copy. If something happens to me, you have the data. And there might be more on there. Possibly base schematics in full detail. Enough to plan an infiltration that won't leave us dead on arrival. Hell, if we're clever, we can feed the juiciest parts to a couple of journalists. End this before they even see us coming."

Heavy footsteps pounded up the uneven stairs.

Aya drew her knife and glanced at Amina, who nodded and aimed for the door. Karim and Omar crouched, guns raised, readying for a standoff. Outside, the midday sun glowed bright, mocking the violence about to erupt.

"We've got this," Aya hissed.

Behind them came another crash, closer, rattling the battered door at the end of the corridor. "Man, I just replaced all those doors," Salah groaned. The intruders were down the hall.

Then the doorframe cracked under a vicious kick, and gunmetal glinted in the threshold.

FORTY-ONE

THROUGH A BATTERED OPENING in the door, Aya glimpsed the muzzle of an assault rifle nudging the wood aside.

Omar and Karim flanked her, crouching in the sparse cover they had from the narrow hall. They were trapped in Salah's study with the main stairs blocked by armed intruders.

A low shout rang out: "*Vous êtes encerclés. Se rendre.*" Aya caught the clipped American accent beneath the French. Salah was right about PES's alliance.

More crashes erupted from below, the unmistakable sound of doors being kicked in on multiple levels. These weren't amateurs; they were hitting every floor simultaneously.

"We'll have to take the old servants' stairs, through the connecting room," Salah said. "This way!"

One of the armed men pushed forward into the study. His bulletproof vest glinted. Before he could enter fully, Omar rammed the door from behind. The mercenary jerked sideways, letting out a startled curse as he slammed against the hallway wall. A shot tore from his rifle, ripping through plaster and sending dust spraying.

Another gunman charged into the room at the sound of commotion. "Stay down!" he yelled. Karim lunged from cover, grabbed a leaning bookshelf, and tipped it onto the intruder with a crash of dusty volumes that further barricaded the door. The man stumbled, losing aim. Omar fired a single shot, the bullet pinging off the man's chest plate but forcing him back.

"Move!" Aya yelled, waving them toward the narrow doorway Salah had indicated. "We can't hold this position!"

Amina laid cover fire while they squeezed through one by one into the adjoining room, then a cramped stairwell barely wide enough for a single person. The ancient steps were worn smooth by centuries of use, treacherous in their steepness. Behind them, boots thundered across the study floor.

Halfway down to the second floor, two more men in black tactical gear met them, faces masked except for cold eyes. The confined space erupted into chaos—muzzle flashes strobing in the near darkness, deafening blasts reverberating off stone walls.

The first man fired at Omar, who dove backward, cursing as a bullet clipped the wall beside his head, littering stone fragments onto his shoulder. He pressed himself against the stairwell wall.

Karim, eyes wide, returned a desperate volley from above. In the narrow space, the gunfire was overwhelming, dust and debris raining down.

Aya spotted her opening. The stairwell's confined nature worked both ways, and the mercenaries couldn't maneuver either. She signaled to Karim for a distraction.

He nodded, bracing his borrowed pistol before shouting and firing twice, forcing the intruders to pull back for cover. In that instant, Aya slipped past Omar, her body pressed flat against the wall.

Her pulse thundered as she got within arm's reach of the

closest attacker. She hooked an arm around his rifle, yanking it sideways. He tried to smash the stock into her ribs, but Aya twisted, driving her left elbow into the base of his neck. He staggered on the narrow steps.

The second man tried to aim around his partner, but Aya positioned the man she grappled with as a human shield. Gritting her teeth, she whipped out her tactical knife.

Aya's knife hand swept low, slicing across the second man's arm. He let out a strangled yelp, stumbling backward on the steps. She followed up instantly, using his imbalance to drive him hard against the stone wall.

Without pausing, Aya drove the knife into the mercenary's hand, the blade grinding against bone. His breath escaped in a choke, eyes widening with disbelief before she smashed the hilt into the side of his head. Blood spattered the uneven stone as Aya yanked back, chest heaving, and he collapsed in a slump.

The first attacker tried to recover his footing, but Omar shot forward and cracked him across the face with his pistol grip, sending the man tumbling down the remaining steps.

They maneuvered around the bodies and silently made their way to the ground floor. Salah stuck his head around the corner, calculating their chances.

"There are too many down there for us to break through. We'll have to draw them up and then sneak back down," Salah panted. "I don't think anyone else has found these stairs yet, other than those two. But I need to get to my backup drives if we're abandoning the house to them. Storage room on this level. All my work is there."

"Salah, no—" Aya started, but he was already slinking out into the courtyard despite the chaos.

"Get to the bedrooms!" he mouthed. "Lure them up!"

They ran back up the stairs and burst onto the second floor, ducking into an empty bedroom on the left. Through the arched window, Aya could see that the courtyard below was still swarming with black-clad figures. Her stomach dropped as she spotted Salah approaching the stairwell, arms full of hard drives and documents.

He made it three steps before one of the attackers materialized behind him, rifle raised.

"Drop it!" the man roared, wrenching Salah's arm. The drives clattered across the mosaic tiles. Another soldier rummaged through Salah's pockets. "He's the hacker," the second spat. "He's the one we want."

Salah's furious gaze found them at the window as the tall man pressed his rifle under Salah's chin. "He comes with us," the man growled. "Command wants him alive. Do whatever you want with his hippie guests."

Aya felt paralyzed. Salah's eyes met hers, silently pleading. She counted three more armed men surrounding him in the courtyard, rifles angled outward.

Amina leaned out the window and opened fire from their position. Return fire erupted immediately, forcing them back from the window as bullets chipped the surrounding stone. With the swirl of bullets and shouting, there was no path to save Salah.

One final shout from the courtyard: "Time to wrap up, team, we have what we came for!" The tall man yanked Salah forward, delivering a brutal blow to keep him subdued. "Mop 'em up!"

"Save yourselves!" Salah yelled, his voice cut off by a rifle butt slamming his ribs. The men dragged him toward the main entrance.

"We're trapped," Omar said, checking the hallway. "I can hear more coming up both staircases."

Karim suddenly pointed upward. "The roof! I noticed last night, all these buildings connect. The terraces share walls. We can cross to another building and come down there."

"Better than dying here," Aya said. "Go!"

They raced up the narrow ladder to the rooftop. The afternoon sun blazed overhead, the Atlantic wind whipping their clothes. Behind them, continued shouts echoed up the stairwell.

Aya oriented herself quickly. To the north, the rooftops stretched in an uneven line, separated by low walls and occasional gaps narrow enough to jump. She could see laundry lines and satellite dishes marking other riads.

"This way," Karim urged, already climbing over the first low wall onto the neighboring terrace.

They crossed three rooftops, keeping low, the sounds of the raid growing fainter behind them. On the third building, Omar spotted what they needed—an external staircase, the old stone steps hugging the building's outer wall down to street level.

"Here," he said, already swinging his leg over the edge.

They descended quickly, emerging into a narrow alley three blocks from Salah's riad. The everyday sounds of the medina seemed surreal. Seagulls screeched, waves splashed, children played soccer, life continued as if nothing had happened.

But sirens wailed in the distance, growing louder.

"Keep moving," Aya urged, leading them deeper into the maze of whitewashed streets. They ducked through a construction site, finally pausing behind stacks of bricks and cement bags, far enough from the chaos to catch their breath.

Omar pressed his back to the wall, eyes tight with fury. "Why would they take him?"

Karim hammered a fist against the crates. "He was on the right track. He gave us everything—help, intel—now he's at their mercy."

Aya bent over, catching her breath. "And he inadvertently saved us by drawing them off. I can't believe they didn't even realize who we were. They came specifically for him. We can't let PES keep him or the artifact. We'll rescue him." The vow rang inside her.

"We have his data," Amina said. "That's probably what they feared. So let's use it, find him, destroy them."

"But why did they want him alive?" Omar asked. "PES had no problem putting down anyone in their way in the mountains."

Aya shook her head, but forced composure. "No way to know, but I suspect we'll find out a lot of these answers at the base Salah found. For now, we disappear into the medina and lay low, regroup, then plan our next move. Salah gave us what we need to put together a decent plan. We know where they're taking him."

Omar pulled out the flash drive Salah had pressed into his hand. "He said there might be more on here. Base schematics, security protocols."

"Then we'd better find somewhere safe to review it," Karim said, glancing around the dormant construction site. "And we'll need supplies, weapons, new transport in case the Jeep's been tracked. Everything for a desert assault."

They all nodded in unison. The riad was lost, Salah was captured, and they were fugitives in a city that would soon be crawling with people looking for them. "Let's move," Aya said, leading them deeper into the medina's winding shadows.

Forty-Two

THEY REACHED THE SHORELINE, feet crunching on fine sand as the humid, salt-heavy Atlantic breeze brushed their faces. Even under the sharp midday sun, the wind carried an undercurrent of tension that made Aya shiver.

Seagulls wheeled overhead, their calls slicing the air as if warning the tourists scattered along Essaouira's sweeping beach. Families picnicked under umbrellas, local teens chased a barefoot soccer ball, kitesurfers cut across the choppy waves.

They had fled the chaos of the medina barely an hour ago, each step carrying them farther from the stone ramparts of the old city.

"Karim," Aya called over the wind, scanning the wide expanse of sand. "You said you know a place?"

Karim nodded, shifting the strap of his overstuffed backpack. "Ocean Vagabond. Beachfront beer garden that's usually quiet on weekdays. We can blend in, lay low for a minute, figure out our next move."

Omar paced beside them, jaw clenched. "I hate this.

Running. Hiding. But if we go in half-cocked, we'll get ourselves caught, and that helps no one."

"It's temporary," Aya said. "We'll be on the road soon."

Amina trailed behind, silent, one hand pressed to her forehead. Sweat beaded at her hairline, and they all knew it wasn't only from the sun.

"I'm fine," Amina murmured whenever Aya glanced back. "Just keep going."

As they walked, Aya noticed the symbols on Amina's arm had grown sharper, visible even through the sleeve of her djellaba. The patterns seemed to pulse with each wave of pain across her face.

"Amina, your arm," Aya said, moving closer. "The symbols are spreading."

Amina rolled up her sleeve, and Aya studied the patterns. An intricate network of markings extended from wrist to elbow.

Karim leaned in, brow furrowed. "That shouldn't be possible."

"Nothing about this is possible," Amina said bitterly, rolling her sleeve back down.

They continued barefoot along the shoreline, blending with the crowd. Wet sand cooled their feet; kites arced overhead, surfers skimming the sea.

Aya tried to focus on the beauty instead of replaying yet another bitter loss.

Darija chatter drifted by as they walked through the crowds. Karim occasionally murmured translations:

"'Soldiers in the streets'… 'someone dragged away near the old fort'… 'what's happening to our city?'"

Amina shook her head. "It's worse than we realized. Word spreads fast."

Aya's mind drifted to the terror in Salah's eyes as they dragged him away. "We put him at risk," she said.

Karim's voice softened. "We'll get him back."

The next twenty-five minutes walking along the beach felt painfully long as they passed a string of open-air cafés, loungers to rent, and small stands offering surf gear or fresh juices.

They finally spotted the sign for Ocean Vagabond. The establishment sprawled directly onto the beach itself with a deliberately unfinished quality—part beach shack, part bohemian refuge. Wooden benches were scattered across the sandy deck, some positioned around low tables, others arranged to face the surf.

Tables were arranged between the twisted trunks of old argan trees. The indoor section, visible through large open windows, housed a proper bar and a wood-fired pizza oven that sent aromatic smoke drifting across the beach. Surfers with salt-crusted hair lounged at tilting tables, their boards propped against driftwood posts, while couples claimed the shaded spots beneath the trees, sipping wine.

Karim led them in, raising a hand to catch the attention of a host. "Table for four, please. Something shaded."

They silently followed the man. In front of the restaurant, a string of camels picked their way along the waterline. Their handlers, faces wrapped against the sun, led them while tourists clutched desperately at the wooden saddles, their phones extended at precarious angles for the perfect shot.

Finally, they settled around a table in the shade of an old tree. Aya sank onto the bench, acutely aware of her sweat-soaked shirt sticking to her back. The overhead leaves rustled in the strong ocean breeze.

Amina pressed her eyes shut. "Any chance they followed us here?"

Omar glanced around discreetly. "I don't see any of the

same faces from earlier, and there's been no sign of them. No one who looks suspicious."

A waiter approached, smiling brightly, offering menus, but Omar quickly declined. "Just sparkling water and coffees, *afek*." Once he left, Omar's expression darkened. "But we can't linger too long in one place. I doubt they're going to look for us in plain sight if they realized who we were or got it out of Salah. But the four of us sitting together just makes it easy on them. We need a plan."

Karim tapped his phone, pulling up partially downloaded maps. "So it's most likely that Salah's being taken to the desert near the Algerian border, where he found that base. That's where all the rumors point about '*Mawt Dhahab*.' If we can confirm the route, we might intercept or infiltrate."

Amina grimaced. "But how do we stand a chance? They have an army, endless money, and a huge head start."

"We have a small advantage," Aya said. "They probably think we'll be too scared or disorganized to come after them. But we're lightweight, and sneaking around is our skillset. Plus, we know all about their plans for the artifact, and about the djinn curse." She glanced at Amina, who was nearly trembling. "We also know it's messing with you, and probably them too, in ways they can't control, and we have respect for the power."

Amina squeezed her eyes shut. "Yeah, it's not just random illusions anymore. This pounding in my head, it's like a presence, angry, hungry." She paused, inhaling shakily. "When they forced the corridor open, something got out. It's real, not some geological phenomenon or anything scientific, I swear."

Karim and Aya exchanged an uncomfortable look.

Omar dropped his voice to a whisper. "What you're experiencing, Amina—the marks, the visions, the pain—it all might connect to something deeper, something the old man's always on about. Have you heard of baraka?"

Amina shrugged. "Vaguely."

Omar continued. "Yeah, Abdelatif would love this. He was already putting Aya to sleep, going on about it. Well, as he puts it, baraka is this divine blessing that connects the physical and spiritual worlds. Saints carry it, sacred places channel it, and sometimes, in moments of great need, it chooses vessels to work through. The spirit world recognized something in you, Amina. I think you have the capacity to hold baraka. To be that bridge."

"But I'm not religious," Amina protested. "I'm a thief. A killer when needed. I doubt I carry any kind of divine blessing."

"Maybe baraka doesn't judge worthiness the way humans do," Karim said.

"The pain you're feeling," Aya added, "maybe it's your body adjusting to carrying that energy. Like the Amazigh symbols are a layer of protection, and the baraka is what will allow you to face what's coming, and what drew those symbols out of you, to protect you from these djinn incursions."

Karim drummed his fingers on the table, a contemplative scowl crossing it. "No matter what is true and what is myth, every minute we wait, the danger grows. PES might be actively fueling or weaponizing the problem. We have to move. As we stall, they get more powerful, more secure."

Their waiter arrived with two large bottles of Oulmes and a round of espresso. Aya sipped gratefully. She cast a glance around the restaurant. At a table nearby, a group of surfers, salt in their hair, chatted animatedly.

"Okay, let's get to it. We need to decide who does what." Aya's gaze snapped to Omar. "You know people everywhere. Can you get us a new vehicle? Something sturdy for the desert. Maybe from a contact who isn't going to sell us out, if we're lucky?"

Omar nodded. "I have a cousin in Imsouane who rents out

off-road SUVs under the table. It might take a few hours to get up the coast, but he owes me, so no questions asked."

"That's great," Aya said. "Any chance you have the black-market connections for gear?"

He nodded. "Yeah, I know an old Army guy outside Asfi who sells, well, probably anything. Guns, bulletproof vests, that kind of stuff. We'll have to be discreet, though. They're probably still looking for us. And I hate to say it, but we're running low on cash since we paid Salah. It's probably still sitting in his riad, but I don't think we can go back there."

"We have enough left for essential supplies," Aya said, though the confidence in her voice felt thin. "If we can muster enough to arm ourselves and get the SUV, we can drive out after them. We'll adapt from there."

"What about putting together infiltration intel?" Amina asked.

Karim flicked through his phone. "Salah managed to decode a lot." He grimaced. "I can keep digging. My skills are far from Salah's, but I might be able to help."

A sudden gust of wind rattled the hanging bulbs overhead, sending a few menus and packs of cigarettes skittering across the deck. Patrons gasped, then laughed nervously, startled by the sudden gust. Kite surfers were ripped out to sea or thrown sharply into the water.

Amina's nails dug into her palm, and she let out a hiss of pain amidst the roar, the headache spiking. "It's starting again," she said through gritted teeth, eyes half-lidded. "Like something's shifting in the air. Not just this breeze."

Karim reached for her shoulder. "Can you describe it? You said it's like a burning behind your eyes?"

She nodded, swallowing a whimper. "Feels like it wants me to do something, but I don't know what. I don't understand." Her breath trembled.

Aya remembered a passage from her father's notebook. "'*The marked ones will hear the whispers first,*'" she quoted quietly. "'*Through them, the djinn test the boundaries of their prison.*'"

Karim looked up, recognition dawning. "And the next line, '*As the seals weaken, the marked becomes a bridge between worlds.*' Aya's father discovered something about this, Amina. Whatever's happening to you, it's not random. You're connected to them now, like it was prophesied."

Amina's voice cracked. "I don't want to be connected to anything supernatural. I just want this to stop!"

"But it might be why we need you," Aya said gently. "Remember what Abdelatif said about the three keys? The bloodline, the marked, and the pure of heart. You're marked. The ritual won't work without you, if Abdel can figure it out."

The wind died as abruptly as it began, leaving everyone in the restaurant and on the beach glancing around in mild confusion. The surfers in the water took advantage of the new calm, paddling back out. Life returned to normal in moments.

But at Aya's table, the tension was palpable. "Okay. We gather what we need today and leave by nightfall. Even if we're not fully stocked."

Omar offered an uncharacteristically grim nod. "I'll get in touch with my cousin about the SUV, and my contact for the supplies. I'll try to keep a low profile."

Karim leaned in, voice hushed. "And I'll find a hotel room to get this gear set up and see if I can uncover anything further in the meantime. Let's meet at the parking lot near the ramparts of Bab El Marsa at sundown. We can blend in with the fishermen ending their day and head out from there."

Aya studied Amina. "You'll come with me. We'll keep out of sight. If your headaches worsen or if something, I don't know, supernatural, flares up, then I want to be there."

Amina managed a weak smile. "Don't worry. I'm too stubborn to let a headache kill me."

"Good," Aya said softly before her expression hardened. "Look, we also need to talk about the reality of this mission. We might have to take more lives if cornered, potentially many, and it's not something I take lightly. We all need to be prepared, mentally and physically."

"No one wants more bloodshed," Karim said. "But if it comes down to them or us..."

"I know," Aya whispered. Her gaze dropped to the table. "But it still matters."

Omar cleared his throat, glancing around at the boisterous surfers nearby. "We should get moving before we draw attention. Are we set on meeting up at sundown near Bab El Marsa?"

"Yes," Karim said.

"And if something goes wrong, we need a fallback plan," Aya said. "Worst case scenario, regroup when possible by those dunes to the left, where all the camel herders are hanging out."

Beyond the café's barrier, camels trudged past over the dunes. Aya rose from the bench, the wooden planks creaking underfoot. "Let's settle up."

"Already taken care of, my lovely dates," Omar said, tossing two hundred dirham on the table. He cast a fleeting glance across the other tables. "Stay alert on your way out."

As they stood to leave and made their way back onto the sand, Aya kept her head low, scanning for suspicious faces, but saw only carefree beachgoers.

Once they were a few paces from the café, Omar spoke. "We'll split here. Karim and I will double back into town along the corniche. You two keep moving along the beach, maybe circle into the medina from the far side. We'll all blend in more easily if we're not together as a group."

Aya nodded. "Got it. And guys... be safe."

Karim touched her shoulder. "Same to you."

Omar and Karim strode off, weaving through a group of teenage girls skateboarding on the pavement.

Alone, Aya turned to Amina. "Think you can manage another walk?"

Amina's eyes squinted, but a spark of resolve lit behind them. "I'm not exactly myself, but I'll live. Let's get away from the crowds and the noise."

They wove through a scattering of sunbathers, lying and reading on bright towels.

"Wishing that was us?" Amina asked.

"I can't think of anything I'd like more than to have stayed at Ocean Vagabond for a few beers, then gone for a swim and a lie on the beach. But, it feels like it's the refrain of my life—once this work is done, I'll try that."

As they curved away from the busiest stretch, the city's fortress walls loomed at the edge of sight. Beyond that, the rest of Essaouira sprawled, a maze of alleys and secrets.

Amina stumbled, her legs giving out without warning as if her muscles had suddenly forgotten how to coordinate. Aya caught her arm, feeling how Amina's entire body trembled.

"Let's rest for a second," Aya insisted, guiding her to a stone wall, half-buried in the sand. As they sat, Amina's hands began shaking uncontrollably, and she muttered rapidly under her breath.

"Amina?" Aya gripped her shoulder and shook her. "Amina!"

Amina's entire body tensed, then she blinked hard, seeming to return to consciousness. "Sorry, I... I keep losing time." Genuine fear flooded her face. "I don't know where I just went."

Aya took Amina's hand. "It'll be okay, I promise. You're here with me, and we can rest here now as long as you need."

They sat and gazed out at the large islands that loomed off the shore and the endless ocean beyond them. The horizon shimmered, slightly blurred by the midday heat.

After a few minutes, Amina steadied her breathing. "Let's go. I feel fine now."

They marched forward into the city's outskirts.

FORTY-THREE

THE AFTERNOON WAS a blur of nervous movement through Essaouira's backstreets. While Omar and Karim handled supplies, Aya guided Amina through the medina's quieter quarters, staying away from the main thoroughfares where PES might have watchers.

The last light of day clung to the sky as Aya stepped onto the narrow, windswept road outside Bab El Marsa, her arm around Amina as if it were old times.

Over her shoulder, she could still see the fading sweep of the beach. Her thoughts refused to settle while she squinted through the deepening twilight, anxious to see Karim and Omar safe.

Finally, a battered Land Rover with a dusty top-exhaust rumbled into view. Omar leaned out the driver's window, waving them over. The vehicle was littered with dents and scratches.

As they approached, Aya saw that Karim was already in the back seat and sighed with relief.

"*Yalla!*" Omar called. "Let's go!"

Aya tossed her small duffel into the trunk, then climbed into the back beside Karim.

"Figured it'd be best to give Amina shotgun," Karim said. "Might be a bumpy ride."

"Thanks," Amina said. "Head's pounding, and I've lost vision a couple of times, but I'll manage. Let's move before someone takes note of us."

"I haven't run into any complications all day," Karim reported.

"We haven't either," Aya said.

"It's like those grunts didn't even realize who we were. Better for us," Omar said before shifting gears. The SUV picked up speed on the steeply inclining road, leaving the beach behind. "Oh, one other thing. We're picking up someone else first."

"What?" Aya asked. "We don't have time, Omar. Who?"

"Oh, just Abdelatif. But if there's no time—"

"Abdelatif," Aya repeated, incredulously. "Is he even in any condition to come along? He was shot!"

Omar made a face, half regretful, half resigned. "You know him, he refused to stay idle. As soon as I got in touch, he insisted on joining. Says he can't bear to watch from the sidelines after what he's seen. What he fears. He's wracked with guilt. Can you believe the old man has the audacity to say we might need him and his knowledge?"

Karim laughed. "He does have a point. He knows more lore than any of us. I can handle the history, but the mythology of our predicament is a bit beyond me."

Aya stared out the window, torn between concern for Abdelatif's health and the knowledge that he might be crucial. She rubbed the back of her neck. "All right. If he's sure, then let's go."

The city's lights fell away behind them like dim stars. Soon they were surrounded by rolling hills and the occasional orchard of argan trees, cast in moonlight. The air grew cooler, thinner.

Just before midnight, they pulled onto a familiar dirt road. At a bend in the track stood a cluster of low houses, earthen walls bathed in silver-blue starlight. A single donkey cart rattled past. Across the road, an old man squinted at their vehicle but offered a polite wave. The hush of late night blanketed the village.

"Abdelatif said to meet him behind the communal oven," Omar said, guiding the Land Rover around a corner, past a crumbling stone arch.

They spotted Abdelatif, seated, wrapped in a heavy robe over his typical gray striped djellaba. He rose carefully, gripping a walking stick, and a bandage showed under his collar. When the vehicle stopped, Omar and Karim hopped out to help him load his small bag.

Aya climbed out and walked over to him, taking in his careful movements and the way he favored his left side. "You look like shit," she said with a smile.

Abdelatif laughed, though it visibly pained him. "Always direct, but I can not lie in bed while evil forces consume the land." He gestured to the vehicle. "Now help this old fool into your chariot before I change my mind."

Karim gently steered him into the back seat before Omar turned the car around and headed south, dust clouds rising behind them. After a few minutes, Abdelatif began rummaging through his bag.

"I did not waste my time sitting around. I may have found a solution, consulting with the elders in this village, who still tell many of the old stories, of the times before Idris, tales of the djinn." Abdelatif held up a book, bound with carved wooden covers, the etched symbols reflecting the moonlight. "It is older than any script I've studied, but... see here?"

He traced a spiral design that enclosed a stylized falcon, then tapped a line of swirling symbols. "I think it describes a rite of containment. A binding, maybe the one I mentioned. The region's ancestors believed only someone 'of the bloodline,' a direct descendant of the original men who stopped the djinn, could finalize it, because of an ancient pact that was reached between mortal and spirit."

Aya exchanged a glance with Karim. "So there's a way to lock down the djinn? Stop everything? Because the weather's getting worse, Amina's getting worse. That has to mean PES is getting closer to harnessing the power, pushing this opening between realms wider."

Abdelatif swallowed hard. "Supposedly, if performed exactly as described, but this text warns that the price is high, 'the vessel must stand at the threshold of the flame.'"

A shiver ran down Aya's spine.

"I will continue to study this so that we are prepared when it is time. Once we have the Amulet."

A collective silence settled over the vehicle. "One more thing," Abdelatif said before focusing on the volume. "It is really good to see you all."

They traveled for over an hour on a modest tarmac that gradually gave way to rough patches.

After a while, Karim pulled Hassan's notebook from his bag and opened it on his lap. One margin note that Karim seemed particularly focused on read *"Ottoman travelers, synergy with desert phenomena, 16th c. expedition?"*

Noticing Aya's eyes on him, Karim cleared his throat. "Your father left a lot of interesting questions when it came to his research in Morocco. Something about Ottoman scouts who ventured this way. Seems they documented bizarre phenomena in the Moroccan deserts, maybe similar to these alleged djinn phenomena."

Aya nodded, leaning in to read the page. "But, I assume, struggled to match those legends to any actual historical record. Probably why he never managed to get an actual dig off the ground."

Amina twisted around in the front seat, wincing. "Any idea how that helps us now?"

Karim shrugged. "It might show how this power manifested in the past. If PES is replicating an old method of harnessing it, we might find a weakness. We have some records from the drive Salah cracked, but no explanation of the specific methods or how their engineering is supposed to work. Or maybe we'll confirm nobody can truly control it at all."

Abdelatif offered a tired smile. "Your father was thorough. Ottoman or Amazigh, it does not matter. Once the desert chooses to rage, no empire can tame it. That much is always known."

"He was onto something about these legends, though, Aya. It's wild the connections he's able to draw, from Morocco to the Ottoman Empire to Southeast Asia," Karim said. "Maybe this isn't just in Africa. Once we've rescued Salah and confronted whatever Léglise and PES are unleashing, once this has all died down, maybe we can pick up where he left off."

"Maybe." Aya felt a complex mix of emotions as she watched the desert landscape roll by. She caught Karim's eye in the rearview mirror and offered a small smile. There would be time later, if they survived, to figure out where they would go next.

BY THE TIME the sun began its rise, they had covered over 400 kilometers of cracked asphalt, dust swirling until the horizon blurred in a dry haze from their headlights. Omar, Aya, and Karim had taken turns on the driving, mixing naps in between shifts. They all slowed whenever the wind whipped too fiercely, dropping visibility to near zero. As they continued to notch kilometers, they twice spotted partial convoys on distant roads. Each time, they killed the engine and waited, hearts hammering, until the vehicles vanished.

Eventually, they rounded a bend and spotted a small nomadic encampment beside a shallow wadi. Two low tents stood beneath the scorching sun, the fabric rippling. A figure in a tagelmust pulled tight against his face waved them down. A goat was tethered, bleating and shifting nervously.

"Stop," Abdelatif said. "They might be in trouble. These storms are intensifying."

Omar braked gently. As the dust settled, Aya saw a woman emerge from one of the tents.

Amina exhaled. "Yeah, the storms are definitely worse. Feels like static in the air. I can see it, shapes moving like smoke."

Abdelatif placed a hand on Amina's shoulder, and they exchanged a short smile. "You have a gift that comes at a great cost. It will be okay in the end, child."

Karim and Abdelatif climbed out of the SUV. The woman who emerged from the tent greeted them. Abdelatif answered, and Karim joined the conversation.

Aya stayed back, scanning the desolate surroundings for anything suspicious. Omar hung by her side.

"You paranoid too?" she asked.

"Well, I don't speak Sahrawi, so I doubt I would be much help. Surprised Karim does."

"Yeah, he's full of surprises."

Omar raised an eyebrow but said nothing.

After a short exchange, Karim returned and filled them in. "They're seeing more convoys lately," he said grimly, "armed men in military vehicles, helicopters overhead, usually heading south. Rumors of a prison in the desert, like the years of lead. Also, dust tornadoes have been devouring parts of the wadi at night."

"Devouring?" Aya repeated.

"Yeah, odd choice of words, but apparently they've been snatching entire herds of animals, even tents of people," Omar said.

Abdelatif returned, muttering a prayer under his breath, then spoke softly. "The woman said it's as though the land wants to spit out these intruders, helicopters at night, strangers stomping around. Even the desert animals are on edge."

Aya's mouth felt dry. She gave the couple a nod of thanks, watching as the pair returned to their tent while a swirl of dust chased their steps.

Solemnly, they reentered the Land Rover.

After another hour of driving in silence, Amina opened her eyes, wincing. "That corridor. I can see it clearly, but as it was, when it was new. Fresh carvings, torches, golden decorations. Every few minutes, I see a flash behind my eyes." She inhaled shakily.

"Until we reseal what has been undone, your visions may worsen," Abdelatif said carefully.

Omar reached over to pat Amina's arm. "We'll figure this out, *okti*. We won't let them use you."

Karim cleared his throat. "Yeah, it's about time to come up with some kind of plan. If we just show up at this base, we'll be sitting ducks. PES will have guards, patrols, maybe aerial support. But I think there's a hidden way we might be able to use to slip in."

Aya's voice was hushed. "Right, what did you find in Salah's materials?"

Omar slowed to maneuver around a series of jagged rocks, and the vehicle rattled.

"I think I found an abandoned well shaft near PES's base," Karim said. "Might be a place to hide, and it could lead underground. Salah had the satellite images, but the base could have changed since they were taken. We'll have to confirm once we're in range."

Abdelatif's gaze was distant, but he nodded. "Old wells sometimes connect to aquifers or caves. Could be your best route in."

Aya rested a hand on his arm. "You sure you're up for this? You're in pain, I can tell. No shame in staying behind if it gets worse."

He smiled weakly. "I'm stubborn, Aya. And I owe the desert a debt for what we couldn't stop. What we played a part in awakening."

FORTY-FOUR

A BLOOD-RED GLOW bathed the plateau as Omar brought them to a stop on cracked gravel, nestled behind a pile of boulders and dangerously close to the drop-off. Beyond it, the desert sloped into a vast stone basin dotted with endless scattered dunes and painted in the fading fire of dusk.

At its center stood the base, its perimeter lined with floodlights and encircled by tall, razor-wire fences.

From the back seat, Karim leaned forward, eyes narrowing against the windshield's dusty glare. "Salah didn't exaggerate; they threw this base together quickly. Look at those watchtowers. They can see for kilometers."

Omar cut the engine. "We're on borrowed time," he said quietly, scanning the horizon. "Sun's almost gone. It took us nearly a full day to get here."

Abdelatif opened his door with a stiff groan. "I will check the surroundings," he said, gingerly stepping onto the rocky ground. He retrieved a battered rifle from the back seat, testing its sights with a determined nod.

Aya slid out behind him. The base loomed large below

them, rows of squat prefabricated buildings, a radar tower sweeping in slow arcs. She'd broken into plenty of secure facilities before, but never anything military.

They gathered behind the Land Rover. Omar propped an elbow on the vehicle, binoculars to his eyes. "Guards on every corner," he observed. "At least four towers. Plus, they've got two helicopters if needed."

"The front gate looks locked down," Amina said, raking windblown hair from her eyes. "There's no way we can bluff our way through that." Worry pinched her features. She glanced at Aya. "So, are we going with the well plan?"

Aya swallowed hard, gaze fixed on the horizon. "Yeah. We'll have to hope it connects with an old khettara system. Based on what Karim found, there should be a disused underground water channel there, running beneath the southern perimeter from when this was an old village."

Abdelatif smiled. "Yes. They were all built centuries ago, back when men coaxed water from under the desert. Most have collapsed or been forgotten. But the land remembers more than men suspect, and these opportunists in the base do not care about this land or its history. I think we can safely hope they overlooked it."

Karim nodded, unfolding a printed map. "And they built this base in a hurry. If there's a khettara tunnel that leads inside, or under the base, that could be our way. But there's no way of telling exactly where it leads."

The group fell silent, turning over the idea.

Eventually, Omar lowered his binoculars and pointed toward a patch of ground near the fence line, halfway up the basin's far side. "From here, you can see a slight depression in the terrain, there." He squinted into the sunset. "Could be an old access point."

"So hope's alive," Karim said.

"I'll head that way," Aya said.

Amina sighed, brushing damp hair from her forehead. "But the second we get close, they'll have patrols all over us. We need a distraction."

Karim pinned the map on the hood with a rock. "You're right. How about one group sneaks in, the other creates enough of a diversion at the gate to pull the guards' attention away from the southwestern quadrant. If we time it right, half their soldiers should rush the front, never suspecting an infiltration from below."

"I'll go with Aya," Omar said. "Amina, I know you can whoop me in a fight most days, but I don't think you're in the right state. We can try to pass for local workers or farm laborers if anyone sees us. With some tools and a beat-up cart, they might buy it."

Aya nodded and looked to Amina. "So you and Karim handle the gate diversion?"

Amina's gaze was steady. "I always liked putting on a show, and people usually can't look away. Works for me."

"I think we play it as lost travelers looking for Merzouga or one of the tourist camps," Karim said to Amina, "then we set off a charge and get out of there. We just have to avoid getting pinned by return fire."

"Solid enough for me," Amina said.

Abdelatif leaned on his cane, scanning the violet-streaked sky. "And I will take the vantage point up here. That plateau west of the base might give me a clear shot with the rifle, in case it is needed. A well-timed bullet could save your lives, and I will be of more use once you have retrieved the Amulet."

"You sure? You're still recovering," Omar said.

"Each of us has a duty tonight," Abdelatif said quietly. "Mine is to watch your backs. I will not let pain overshadow necessity."

Just then, the wind rose, stinging Aya's cheeks with sand. She shielded her face, blinking grit from her lashes. As the gust faded, the desert air crackled with static, an electric charge skimming across her skin.

Then it was gone.

"I hate when it does that," Amina spat. "Like a spirit crossing the land. But I saw wildfire consuming a mountain, consuming everything, leaving shadows behind."

Karim exchanged a glance with Aya. They all felt it, something stirring. Something old.

"Any reason to wait any longer? The sooner I can get my head fixed, the better for us all," Amina said.

Karim folded the map. "If we move after twilight, we can use the darkness for cover. Amina and I will approach from the northeast, near that outcrop, pushing the car and asking for help. We'll rig a small charge to make it look legitimate. While they're distracted, you two hit the khettara."

The sun clung to the horizon, a burning disc half-submerged in clouds. Darkness would soon claim the basin.

"Let's get our gear ready," Aya said. "Maintain complete radio silence unless it's urgent. We'll aim to rendezvous near the southwestern fence after infiltration."

Omar rubbed his palms together. "Works for me. That second ridge might help us get out, just don't actually destroy the car."

"Yeah, don't worry, that's not the plan."

"So we strike as soon as it starts getting dark," Aya said. "If Salah's inside, we don't leave without him. And if we find anything like what we saw at the Atlas dig site, we shut it down and recover the Amulet. It has to be here."

Quickly, Omar distributed handguns, Kevlar vests, and small explosive charges.

Before zipping the supply bag up, Omar pulled out a small

box. "Body cameras," he explained, holding up small, discrete devices. "Military grade. We can monitor each other's progress on the monitors and coordinate timing. They sync with the radios. Plus, if something goes wrong…"

"We'll have evidence," Aya finished. She clipped the small camera to her jacket. "Good thinking."

Karim tested his device, the tiny LED blinking green. "The moment we see you're in position underground, we'll know when to approach the gate."

"And we can see if you run into trouble," Amina added. "Assuming my vision stays clear enough to be useful."

Silence ruled as they climbed back into the vehicle and descended from the plateau, leaving Abdelatif in his position.

Below, the plateau gave way to a barren expanse speckled with black shrubs. The base's floodlights flickered on, slicing through the dusk like blades.

Just before the final stretch, Karim killed the engine behind a rocky outcropping.

Omar and Aya climbed out to change clothes, trading travel gear for dusty, unassuming outfits: scuffed boots, plain tunics, headscarves. Aya's was a coarse linen dyed dull brown; Omar's had frayed edges that hinted at hard use.

"In the old days," Karim said while they changed, "the people who worked the khettara were called *muqannis*, those who revealed hidden water. They saved entire tribes of people, whole towns." He smiled at Aya. "Now, a thousand years later, we'll do some saving too. It's really fitting."

"Let's hope the desert sees our cause as worthy," Amina said from the passenger seat before shaking her head. "God, what have I become. There's some serious treasure in there being held by some serious assholes who deserve what's coming to them. Let's take care of business."

Omar laughed. "There she is! Rock and roll."

They parted ways as night fell for good. Stars slowly blinked into view as they walked, strewn across an infinite sky that dwarfed the fortress's glow.

Aya paused, glancing back at Omar, who walked a pace behind her. "No turning back. You ready, *khoya*?"

"As ready as I'll ever be, partner. Whatever the Aegis really is, whatever they actually hired us for, I'm glad it brought us together, that we're on the same team."

Aya smiled, despite the tight knot in her stomach. "Me too," she said. In the distance, searchlights swept the fence line like giant mechanical eyes.

The base loomed ahead, hidden just beyond the ridge.

A swirl of static-laced wind swept the plateau. The moment had come, the djinn-charged air whispering its warning: *Hurry*.

Forty-Five

Aya crouched behind a half-collapsed wall, minutes later. The faint buzz of mechanical generators filled the air. There was no movement, no voices.

Beside her, Omar adjusted the scarf around his head. In the stillness, the soft rustle of fabric sounded thunderous. He cast Aya a quick, determined glance. "You good?"

She nodded. "Let's approach before they shift any patrols this way."

They eased away from the crumbling walls, skirting what had once been an irrigation channel. Dry reeds crackled underfoot. In the distance, the base's floodlights rotated in sweeping arcs. But here, at the southwestern rim, the light barely touched the remnants of old farmland.

Aya nudged aside prickly vegetation. Half-hidden under debris and tangled vines lay the mouth of the ancient khettara. "Exactly where Karim said."

She crouched, peering into the opening. The upper stones had partially collapsed, leaving just enough space to slither through. Inside, the faint smell of damp earth mingled with a centuries-old staleness.

Omar reached into the sack he carried over his shoulder, retrieving a rusted pry bar and some rope. "If the owners of this channel are watching from the afterlife, let's hope they're cheering us on."

Aya pressed a hand to the cool stone. "I think they'd rather we use it than let PES corrupt their land."

He gave a gentle nod. Then they ducked inside, sinking into darkness.

Immediately, the temperature dropped. A musty chill enveloped them, and their flashlights revealed walls lined with stonework, blocks fitted snugly, forming a sloping passage that lay silent, forgotten.

They inched forward, crouched low. Water dripped from cracks in the ceiling, the plip-plop echoing eerily. Grit and slime clung to Aya's palms each time she braced against the walls.

In her flashlight beam, she glimpsed faint carvings etched into the stone, abstract swirls and names along with rusted piles of Flag Spéciale cans. "Well, that tells me this definitely isn't a death trap," she said. "Looks like some teenagers were hanging out down here at some point."

"Not a death trap, but where it will lead us is all that matters."

They pressed on. A sagging support beam forced them to crawl, scraping knees and elbows over loose rocks. The corridor branched into side passages, most caved in. Twice, they retraced their steps.

"Damn, let's hope we don't get lost," Omar cursed, sweat forming on his brow despite the chill. "This time of year, we only have a few hours until sunrise."

"We'll make it," Aya said. She pictured the armed fortress, hopefully above them, and she thought of Karim dealing with the guards on the surface, with only a shadow of Amina to help him.

Aya pressed a hand against the tunnel wall as her radio crackled to life. "We're in position," Karim's voice whispered through the static.

"Check the monitor," Omar said, adjusting the small screen clipped to his pack. "Let's see what we're dealing with."

On Karim's camera feed, Aya watched him roll the Land Rover to a stop a couple of hundred meters from the gate, then throw it into neutral. Through his camera, she heard him say, "We're close enough to push it the rest of the way."

"Time to get into character," Karim continued. "Sorry, our romantic getaway didn't work out as planned, honey."

Amina's voice came through the audio as she moved into frame: "Let's do it. And don't worry, my favorite kind of vacation involves a lot of getting sweaty together."

Aya smiled at the banter. But her stomach tightened as she watched the guards at the checkpoint straighten through Karim's camera, hands moving to their rifles. Floodlights adjusted angles, and she could see scopes tracking from the tower.

"Just look broken," she heard Amina mutter through the audio feed. "No sudden moves."

Through Karim's camera, Aya watched him pop the hood and wave. "Salaam! Hi! We need help, the engine overheated, and has been stuck for hours!"

The first guard raised his hand cautiously. "Step back from the vehicle."

Aya saw Amina stumble into the camera's field of view in feigned exhaustion. "Please. We're stranded. No water. Started giving us trouble kilometers back."

The second guard mumbled into his radio through the

feed. This was going exactly as planned, but seeing it unfold made her realize how exposed Karim and Amina were.

Through Karim's camera, she saw him lean over the engine. "Come take a look, it might just be a belt. Is there any chance you have parts? Or could you call someone?"

The first guard approached slowly, rifle half-raised, his posture tense as he circled the hood.

Then he paused.

Aya's breath caught as she saw the guard's gaze land on their bags in the trunk through the camera feed.

"I'm going to need you to open your bags," the guard ordered.

"Sure thing," Karim's voice came through the audio, but Aya could hear the tension beneath his casual tone.

The guard lifted his radio. "Car trouble out here. Couple on a trip, it looks like. Awaiting orders."

Amina moved back into frame, her hand moving toward her pocket.

The explosion hit harder than intended.

Karim's camera feed went white with the blast, then filled with smoke and chaos. The small screen shook violently before cutting to static.

"Shit," Omar muttered, staring at the dead feed. "That was way bigger than we planned."

The explosion rolled above them through the tunnel ceiling, muffled thunder followed by the tremble of shifting earth. Sirens shrieked in the distance, confirming what they'd just witnessed.

"Time to move, fast."

They pushed forward, deeper into the dark and the damp. Aya nearly lost her footing on slick algae, as a shallow pool soaked through her boots. Omar steadied her.

The corridor narrowed. Decayed wood jutted from a

collapsed support beam. "We'll have to squeeze through this," Omar said.

They crawled beneath, dust coating their clothes, spiderwebs in their hair. Aya's breath came fast, claustrophobia rising.

The tunnel curved.

"Do you hear that? We have to be close, maybe even under the site," Omar whispered. Faint whirring echoed from above.

"Let's hope there's an opening."

Finally, they emerged into a bricked alcove and could stand. An overhead metal hatch sat corroded, rusting. Aya pressed her ear against the cracked ceiling. Nothing but the clang of distant machinery. She let out a slow breath, wedging the pry bar into the hatch.

Grains of sand trickled through the rim the moment she applied pressure.

"Careful," Omar whispered. "Get ready for a shower."

Aya dug her heels in and pried again. The hatch collapsed inward with a groan, releasing a rush of sand.

"Down!" she hissed, bracing an arm across her face. For several moments, they were lost in swirling sand as the Sahara poured in.

Then the flow subsided, and Aya hoisted herself through the gap, boots sinking in the fresh mound of sand. She beckoned down to Omar, who was still partially buried. "We're inside the fence. Hurry."

Alarms echoed, and an overhead speaker blared between the buildings. "All units to Gate Sector Bravo, this is not a drill!"

Aya and Omar emerged above ground and moved fast before ducking behind the nearest building. Footsteps approached as two soldiers rounded the corner, rifles reflecting in the fluorescent glow.

Aya sprang, snatching the first soldier's weapon at the barrel. Before he could register what was happening, she twisted it aside, smashing the stock into his chin. He staggered and crumpled with a groan.

The second soldier lunged at her, but Aya rolled low, hooking her leg around his ankle and yanking him off-balance. He hit the ground with a thud, rifle clattering away. Aya pinned him, wrapping her legs around his neck and cutting off airflow. She squeezed her thighs tighter as he put up a futile struggle and eventually passed out.

Behind her, Omar snatched the first soldier's sidearm. "Record time, nice work."

Aya wiped her brow. "We're in a hurry. Zip tie them, let's keep them out of our way."

Aya scanned the compound while Omar finished securing the unconscious men. "Let's go, this way."

They passed a block of doors labeled "Barracks," "Armory," and "Canteen."

As they hurried past a door marked "Experimental Lab. Authorized Personnel Only," Aya caught a glimpse through a reinforced window. The room beyond was filled with strange equipment—copper vessels connected by glass tubes, crystalline chambers glowing with internal light, and what looked like modern spectrometers linked to ancient alchemical apparatus.

"My God," she whispered, pulling up abruptly. "Omar, look at this."

Omar pressed his face to the window. "Those copper vessels... they look like the illustrations in the old texts about the Alchemist of Salé. It's as we feared."

"That's what I thought. Ibn Tufail," Aya whispered. "Transforming spiritual energy into physical power."

"And trying to industrialize it," Omar said grimly. "Mixing

modern technology with medieval mysticism. And the Amulet is probably the key component the alchemist used, the catalyst that makes the whole system work."

"We need to keep going. There are too many possibilities. Salah could be anywhere, and keep your eyes out for the Amulet," Aya said, forcing herself to move on.

They advanced until a reinforced door appeared. Overhead, the sign read: E-Wing, Maintenance & Holding.

Omar tapped the sign. "They didn't kill him, so they need him for something. If it's computer work, they'd stash him in a smaller annex. Secure holding sounds like a good bet. Might be plenty of space in Maintenance as well. Should we try E-Wing?"

Aya nodded. "This might be it, then."

Omar tested the knob. Locked.

"Let me," Aya mouthed, extracting a small electronic bypass from her boot.

Click.

They slipped inside. A sterile hallway with doors lining the corridor lay ahead of them, fluorescent lights buzzing overhead. The place smelled of disinfectant.

They checked the first two, which were empty. Then, as he threw open the third, Omar whispered, "Salah."

Slumped behind bars, Salah blinked. "Who's..."

"It's us. Omar. Aya. We're here."

Relief filled his bruised face. "No, how? I told them nothing."

"No, we're not captured. We're here to break you out, but we have no time. Come on, let's go."

Aya got to work picking the padlock, and moments later, they slipped inside to help him up.

"They wanted me to create a digital black hole," Salah said. "Not just erase traces of this place, but build a system that would automatically scrub any mention of 'Mawt Dhahab' or this location from internet searches, satellite databases, even government records. They needed someone who could hack deep enough to reach classified archives."

Aya's jaw tightened. "So you were their cover-up guy."

"Exactly. They needed someone who could navigate the dark web and government back-channels without leaving fingerprints. And someone they could throw to the dogs and deny any culpability if they got exposed. I'm just an outsider they could control and then dispose of." Salah rubbed his shoulder and winced. "I tried to stall, told them I needed specific hardware, lied that the encryption was more complex than it was, but they started to suspect when I kept asking for another day."

Omar nodded grimly.

"If you hadn't shown up, I would've been dead the moment I finished their digital clean-up," Salah said. He trailed off, eyes shining with gratitude.

Omar slid an arm under Salah's, helping him stand. "Don't thank us yet," he said. "We still have to get out of here in one piece."

Another alarm blared while a voice echoed through the speaker system: "Emergency alert, explosion at Gate Sector Bravo. Secure perimeter. Secure the artifact location."

Aya froze. "Secure the artifact."

"Think they realized we're here?" Omar asked.

Aya exhaled. "Sounds like they suspect the blast might have been a distraction. But it doesn't matter, we can't linger either way."

"They must think..." Salah began.

"Whatever it is has to wait," Aya snapped. "We move. Now."

Omar hobbled with Salah. "Southwestern corner. Or the tunnel, if we can."

Another blast shook the building.

"There was only supposed to be one explosion," Omar said.

"Fuck," Aya said under her breath as she tried to push thoughts of Karim and Amina far from her mind.

Shouts erupted outside in repetitive bursts, unrelenting.

Aya peered through the exterior door. "Stay close. If we're fast, we can slip past. I don't think they're in full lockdown yet."

Then the lights shifted to red. Sirens wailed. The intercom screamed: "Condition Delta, we are under attack. Secure all exits from Subsection E! Secure all artifact labs! I repeat, under attack in Section E. Contain at all costs."

Aya locked eyes with Omar.

"If we don't get out now," he said, "we never will."

"I can't leave without the Amulet," Aya said. "I refuse, not when we're this close. You two go, get out of here. I can get it myself and still make the rendezvous."

"It's in the secure lab, one of those buildings on the left," Salah said. "Good luck, sister."

Omar offered no resistance to Aya's plan, and he and Salah hobbled through the sirens, tremors, and chaos, back to the ancient kettara system.

The fortress was alive, and it wanted to crush them.

FORTY-SIX

AYA PRESSED her back against the cold steel wall, forcing her breathing to steady despite the piercing alarms echoing through the base. Waves of red emergency lights pulsed overhead, painting every surface in anxious crimson.

A shrill announcement burst over the speakers: "Intruder alert in Sector Charlie. Deploying response teams."

Aya pressed forward across the compound, keeping to the shadows cast by the blocky buildings. The desert wind whipped grit against her face as she darted between buildings, each one looking frustratingly similar in the pulsing red emergency lights. She checked a supply depot that was empty except for vehicle parts. Then, a barracks, but voices inside forced her to retreat quickly.

Meanwhile, a storm was building on the horizon, dark clouds roiling as lightning flickered within them.

She crept along the perimeter of what looked like an administrative building, then past a motor pool where engines sat silent under canvas covers. Her boots crunched on gravel as she moved from shadow to shadow, watching for patrol routes, listening for the sound of approaching footsteps over the howling wind.

Time was running out. The base was locking down around her.

As she turned another corner, progressing further into the base while slinking against the wall, Aya spotted a battered metal sign ahead, half ripped from its mount, that read LAB ACCESS. She skidded to a halt. *This has to be it.*

Storage crates lay scattered across the floor once she pushed inside. Some were split open, revealing half-assembled coil apparatuses, others brimming with slender cylinders etched in circuit-like patterns. Twisted clamps and tangles of wire formed mechanical intestines all over the passage.

Aya's flashlight flickered across cryptic PES labels. A scrawled note on the nearest crate read PHASE 3, EXPER-IMENTAL.

Ahead, a muffled voice echoed, accompanied by rapid footfalls.

Heart pounding, Aya snapped off her flashlight. She flat-tened herself behind a toppled supply locker. In the flickering red emergency lights, she spotted a lone guard in black tactical gear posted near the next bend, rifle at the ready.

He was jittery, scanning every shadow. The alarms had everyone on high alert. Still, Aya had no time for stealthy detours; the only path to the lab was through him.

Suddenly, he swung his rifle toward her position and fired two rapid bursts. Bullets tore through the locker's upper edge, flinging metal shards across the concrete. Aya pressed her cheek against the floor as sparks showered over her.

"Show yourself!" he barked, voice taut with fear and adrenaline.

From the corner of her eye, Aya found a splintered piece of wood beside the battered crates. Slowly, she palmed it, staying low, and tossed it into a side corridor. It clattered loudly, echoing off the steel walls.

The guard whirled toward the sound, muzzle aimed, finger tense on the trigger. Aya lunged from cover, slamming her boot into his rifle and knocking it upward. The next shot went wild, blasting a chunk from the ceiling.

He recovered with startling speed, driving an elbow into her ribs. She twisted, but not fast enough; pain flared where an old bruise lingered. She stifled a cry, staggering back. The soldier pressed forward, swinging the rifle butt at her jaw. Aya ducked, and the blow whooshed past her ear, stirring stale air.

With a grunt, he kicked low, catching her shin. Her knee banged the metal floor, agony jolting up her leg. He moved to hook an arm around her neck, doubling her over, muzzle scraping her shoulder. Aya struggled to breathe. She had only an instant.

Bending low and planting one palm on the floor, Aya spun her torso despite the protest in her ribs. She yanked her body sideways and kicked backward, hard. Her heel cracked into his kneecap. He hissed, grip loosening, and she seized the moment to spin. A rapid roundhouse kick slammed into his midsection, driving the air from his lungs.

He staggered momentarily, eyes wide, and she followed with a fierce kick to his jaw. His head snapped back, helmet rattling onto the floor.

Gritting his teeth, he delivered a wild jab with the rifle butt. Aya blocked with a forearm, pain flared through her muscles, and then kicked his leg out from under him. He crashed onto his back, rifle skittering away. Gasping, she dropped her elbow onto his temple, and he went limp.

Bent over him, Aya sucked in slow, pained breaths. Another half-second and he might have pinned her. With trembling fingers, she pulled a zip tie from her belt pouch and secured his wrists.

The overhead lights changed to a pulsing white. A voice crackled over the loudspeakers: "Reinforcements en route. Secure the lab. Repeat: secure the lab."

Aya glanced down the corridor. The artifact had to be in this lab.

She forced herself onward. Another corridor branched right, footfalls echoing in the gloom. At the far end, under the harsh strobe of alarm lights, she spotted a massive reinforced door labeled CONTAINMENT LABORATORY in bold letters.

Showtime.

A blinking keypad demanded a code that she didn't have. Without hesitating, she pried the panel open, cutting two tangled wires, ignoring sparks and frantic beeping, then she slid in her short override key. Each beep hammered her nerves as she waited for soldiers to flood the corridor at any moment.

Hurry... hurry...

With a final hiss, the lock released. "Old reliable," Aya muttered under her breath.

A gust of pressurized air brushed her face as the door slid open. Cool lab light spilled into the corridor, and Aya slipped inside.

A domed chamber greeted her, partitioned by glass walls and scaffold-like rigs. Monitors flickered along one side, streaming real-time data in glowing lines of text. An unsettling hum permeated the air, a thrumming pulse that crept under her skin, raising every hair on her arms.

Near the center rose a platform crisscrossed with cables and coiled rods. At its heart rested the Amulet of Idris. Its veins glowed ember-red like living coals, and Aya felt its invisible pull stirring a tingling static across her scalp. She wasn't alone.

A frazzled scientist in a heavy vest peeked from behind a console, sidearm shaking in his grip. His lab goggles sat askew on his sweaty brow.

"Stay back!" he cried. "You don't know what we're about to accomplish! We're..."

"Enough, Renaud," came a harsh voice from deeper in the lab. Footsteps echoed between the scaffolding. "This particular intruder is my business."

Every muscle in Aya's body ached. *Léglise.*

He emerged from behind a half-assembled coil, wearing a tailored black suit undone at the collar. His eyes gleamed wide, manic. All the polished calculation she remembered had vanished.

"Aya Amrani, again," Léglise said softly. "How predictable that you'd show up here. Still chasing illusions of heroism? Or is it revenge you seek, my dear?"

Her instincts screamed to keep him talking, to buy a moment. She glanced around the chamber: dozens of screens, arcs of electricity dancing off metal rods, swirling chemical fluids sealed in thick tubes. Everything looked precariously close to a disaster she couldn't comprehend.

"I'm shutting this abomination down, Léglise. You have no idea what you're doing."

He gave a cold, humorless laugh. "Too late for that. We're about to harness the greatest power known to humanity, the djinn's spirit, I call it. Long believed to be a mere myth, but I have discovered its truth. A pathway between worlds, to harness unheard-of energy from another dimension. Enough to reshape the world order on our terms."

His gaze flicked over her battered clothes, the bruises above her collar. "You've come a long way from the naive archaeology student I found rummaging around dusty tombs. In fact, I regret ever giving you the impetus to step beyond them." He shrugged, mouth curling in disdain. "I should have ended you long ago, and now twice I've allowed you to escape. I fear I created a monster."

"You never created me," Aya said. "Whatever you think you did, you have no idea who I am."

"On the contrary, I know exactly what you are." He stepped closer. "Don't you see, Aya? We're not so different, both shaped by forces bigger than we realize. What separates us is that I embrace it. You still fight it, foolish girl."

A new alarm rang, and the overhead lights dimmed for an instant. Dr. Renaud, trembling behind the console, inhaled sharply. "Sir, the capacitors aren't ready," he warned. "The meltdown threshold is climbing. We can't just ramp..."

"You're losing control of this facility. Surrender," Aya shouted.

"Silence," Léglise snapped, rounding on Renaud. "You know nothing of the djinn's true power. These systems can handle a small surge." A savage glint lit his eyes. "We start the harnessing process now, for Ms. Amrani to watch. Let's see Aya try to interfere then. No, instead she can watch her own failure."

Renaud's eyes bulged. "But the stabilizers... Sir, Mawt Dhahab protocols require at least another hour of preparation..."

"I said, do it!" Léglise roared, voice echoing off the glass partitions.

Dr. Renaud reached for a lever on his console. Aya lunged forward, determined to stop Renaud from throwing the switch.

Léglise blocked her in a sudden rush. He drove a knee toward her torso, and she twisted aside just in time, boots squeaking on the slick floor. Overhead, sparks rained down around them from the equipment.

"I should have killed you the moment you served your purpose." His blows came hard and fast, forcing Aya to block or dodge. "But I was intrigued. You overcame every test, pried open secrets not meant for amateurs. I thought I could keep using you. But now, now you stand here, against me, against the future."

They careened past precarious stations, monitors flaring from green to orange to red. Something began beeping shrilly behind Dr. Renaud. Léglise's footsteps rattled on the grated floor as he chased Aya.

She ducked as his arm grazed her ear. "You're deranged," she yelled, kicking low. He dodged nimbly. "Whatever you think you're harnessing, it's not going to obey you. The djinn bows to no one, certainly not you! These are real forces at work, not just an energy source to tap into."

His laugh was chilling. "We'll see."

Behind them, Dr. Renaud threw the lever, fear contorting his face. A roar of energy ripped through the chamber, coils humming with blinding light. The arcs of electricity blazed from faint blue to sizzling gold. Alarms began swirling in discordant unison.

FORTY-SEVEN

AYA FELT something shift almost immediately in the air. The Amulet of Idris flared, sending out pulses of energy that rippled across the lab floor, shaking desks and rattling cables.

Léglise yelled and swung at Aya again. She blocked, groaning as her bruised ribs flared in protest. "You can't stop what's begun," he hissed. "The djinn's power will soon be the only resource that matters on the planet. And I will be its master."

Without warning, a coil behind him exploded, showering molten debris across the rafters overhead. Aya ducked just as a chunk of searing metal flew overhead.

With a roar, thick black smoke poured from vents near the ceiling, filling the entire lab with a haze, while red emergency lights mixed with surging arcs of gold-white electricity.

"Sir!" Dr. Renaud shouted, eyes wide with terror. "The meltdown threshold is off the charts! We can't contain it..."

Léglise cut him off with a glare. "Then we push forward. Divert all power to the harness array. Now!"

As Renaud frantically worked the controls, Aya noticed something on the monitors—a star chart overlaid with geometric patterns. It pulled her back to the Atlas Mountains, hunched over a series of numbers and guessing at their meaning. A puzzle, one she and Karim had been unable to figure out.

They're star navigation patterns. Ancient people had used these celestial maps for centuries, not just to navigate the Sahara, but to track whatever was going on with the Amulet and these forces at work. So, her father had theorized that the Amulet's power fluctuated based on star positions.

Aya studied the overlay closer. They were nearly aligned.

No wonder Léglise had accelerated his timeline. He wasn't just racing against Aya and her team. He was racing against the cosmos. The Amulet would achieve full power when the stars matched the pattern the navigators had encoded centuries ago.

"That's why the djinn are growing stronger," she whispered. "The star patterns reveal when the boundary between worlds is at its thinnest."

Aya lunged behind a toppled console. If she didn't get the Amulet out, it wouldn't matter if Léglise lived or died; the artifact's power threatened to tear the entire desert apart.

The clang of shifting steel shutters echoed from above. She glimpsed banks of monitors shutting down in waves, flames licking at the lab's edges. The stench of burning plastic filled her nose.

The artifact glowed a vicious orange, arcs of energy snapping across it like writhing serpents.

Léglise took no notice and advanced again, debris crackling underfoot. Aya braced, fists raised. He struck low, feinting before hammering a punch toward her shoulder. She twisted, restraining his wrist. They grappled, each straining for leverage as the meltdown hammered around them. The floor quaked, toppling racks of equipment.

"Do you think you're some kind of hero?" Léglise shouted. "You're nothing but a pawn. You should have realized that by now. Even I'm just a foot soldier for the truly great powers, but now I can rise to the top of the new order."

Aya slammed an elbow into his ribs. He staggered, letting out a guttural snarl of pain.

A massive pop jolted the lab as one of the giant glass tubes shattered, spewing thick chemical fluid across the floor. Sparks continued to rain, igniting pockets of flame. Dr. Renaud scrambled to avoid the spreading fire, screaming in terror.

For a beat, Léglise and Aya froze, transfixed by swirling arcs of raw energy racing along the overhead rig. The entire base seemed to shake with unstoppable force. Overhead lights died in bursts of glass, leaving only sporadic neon strobing from half-dead circuits.

In that wild tableau, the Amulet shone, beckoning from the dais, both deadly and seductive, the key to controlling or destroying everything in the facility.

Aya's skin prickled, feeling something tugging at her consciousness. Léglise tore his gaze from the artifact back to Aya.

"Don't even think about it. You can't handle that power," he said, before lunging with renewed ferocity, trying to take her down.

Aya ducked behind a toppled table, heart hammering. She could feel desert wind roaring through a breach in the wall while acrid smoke stung her throat. *I'm running out of time,* she thought. Léglise was too dangerous to take on with brute force alone, not in this swirling inferno. She had to separate him from the harness rig, disrupt the meltdown, if it wasn't already unstoppable.

Keeping low, she crept behind a battered desk while Léglise prowled the lab's center, searching for her. "Come on, Aya, I thought you were fearless!" he yelled over the howling chaos. "Face me!"

"Sir!" Dr. Renaud shrieked from the far side. "It's gone too far! We have to shut everything down or we'll..."

"Silence!" Léglise snapped, pulling out a sidearm and turning it on the scientist. "Do your job, divert the meltdown away from the harness array if you can. Focus the surge into the desert. We're taking the djinn. Move!"

Renaud stumbled toward a bank of flickering screens, hands moving in a frantic blur.

Meanwhile, Aya readied one of Omar's explosives from her belt.

She jumped up from behind the desk, fighting through the blur of heat and smoke, and hurled the explosive at a coil of cables near the dais.

"No!" Léglise roared, darting forward.

The charge went off with a thunderous crack, and cables snapped through the air. Sparks flew in a blinding shower of violet and orange. Léglise was shot backward, arms raised to shield his face from debris. Dr. Renaud cried out, dropping to the floor.

Aya seized the opportunity and rushed for the dais. She vaulted a toppled beam, ignoring half-formed flames licking at the edges of her vision. Overhead, a chunk of ceiling collapsed in her wake, sending chunks of cement crashing near the rigs.

She reached the Amulet, still anchored by thick wires and now glowing an intense electric blue. A single coil beside it spat bright arcs of electricity, strobing the lab in bursts of harsh light. The relic pulsed brilliantly.

Her fingers hovered over it, a primal fear warring with her resolve. She had no choice.

As she grabbed hold of the Amulet, a brutal jolt blasted up her arm, forcing Aya to freeze, straining every muscle. She stifled a scream, nerves on fire.

Then, a shockwave radiated outward, toppling lab tables backward and shorting nearly all of the lights. Still, she clung to the relic, refusing to let go, even as images, illusions, flared behind her eyelids: a rocky corridor full of moving shadows, chanting voices in an ancient tongue, her father's notes consumed by fire, Abdelatif's stern face, melting. The physical destruction around her merged with hallucinations in a swirl of light, fear, and energy.

Her vision began to clear just in time to see Léglise ambling toward her, contorted in fury and desperation. "You stupid girl," he rasped. "You have no idea what you're messing with."

Gritting her teeth, Aya yanked the artifact free, snapping the last cable. The rig that had held it collapsed in a shower of sparks. A shriek of twisting metal reverberated as the system lost its main anchor. The lab quaked violently. Fresh flames erupted from a workstation near Dr. Renaud, who stumbled away with a cry.

Amidst the new round of destruction, flames and swirling dust half obscured Léglise. From within the smoke, he fired his handgun wildly. Aya dove aside, rolling behind a mangled lab station.

Shots continued to ring out, ricocheting off metal.

Aya clutched the artifact to her chest, ignoring the stinging burn in her fingers and crackling electricity coursing through her body. When Léglise had seemingly run out of bullets, she crawled out to find him coughing in a swirl of black smoke, one hand pressed to a bleeding cut on his scalp. Power cables sparked around him, slicing the air, zapping anything they touched.

"Stop, for your own good!" he screamed. "You have no idea

what it means, you won't be able to contain it. The work I've completed to be able to control its power. Its connection to the djinn, to entire other realms of existence. How I could use it."

"You think you can control the djinn? How naive are you? Have you not seen the storms, the earthquakes, the environment on the brink of destruction across the country?" Aya shouted back, forcing herself upright. "No one can control the djinn, or this power."

A fresh explosion rocked the facility, pitching them both sideways. Aya caught herself on a bent railing. Overhead, the main power grid bellowed its death knell.

As Léglise struggled to stand, a pipe in the ceiling groaned, and with a hideous shriek, it snapped free and crashed down in a storm of steel and steam.

Aya watched as Léglise tried to wrench himself loose. For one harrowing moment, his face twisted in panic and pain. Fire raced across the spilled chemicals. He fought to break free as arcs of electricity danced in the swirling inferno, and flame enveloped him.

A fleeting pang of closure seized Aya. His monstrous ambitions had been crushed by the very power he sought to control, but with trembling breath, she realized she felt no triumph in his death, only cold, hollow relief.

An alarm shrieked anew: "Containment failure in Lab Sector. Security teams to your stations."

Aya doubted the base, let alone any security, could survive now. It was time to leave. Smoke choked her lungs as she stumbled on shaking legs, the Amulet clutched tight in her hand.

Suddenly, Dr. Renaud staggered into Aya's path, eyes bulging with hands pressed to his temples. His lab coat was torn, charred. Black ash had consumed his flesh from the extremities inward, creeping up his arms and legs like some terrible blight. His hands and feet looked carbonized, the skin transformed into something resembling burnt paper that should crumble at the slightest touch. The ashen death climbed past his wrists and ankles, leaving behind flesh that had turned to brittle char. Where the blackness met healthy skin, the boundary pulsed with faint energy.

"Dr. Renaud?" Aya called, stepping closer.

A deep chill swept the lab, cutting through the roar of flames and sizzling electricity.

Then Aya saw another black haze seeping from the cracks in the floor, coiling around Renaud's ankles like living shadows.

He jerked upright, spine arching backward. His pupils glowed with a bright white light. When he spoke, his voice reverberated, layered with a guttural undertone.

"The vow has been broken," Renaud uttered, possessed. "Ripped me from centuries of peace."

Aya clutched the Amulet, still pulsing against her ribs. "Who, what are you?"

A low laugh rumbled from Renaud's lips. "I am the eternal flame. I am the hunger of the desert storms. And you," The scientist's face twisted, expression shifting between pain and ecstasy. "You hold what was not meant to be disturbed. You have breached the boundaries between our worlds. You dare think you can force me here, and then control me?"

Aya's mind flashed to the corridor, the howling winds, the swirling illusions. "I didn't want that to happen. We never intended this. It was these people. Léglise, Renaud, PES. I'm here to take the Amulet back, restore the bonds put in place, and end all this. Surely in your power you can see this."

"You were there. I see all, and I care not for your human distinctions," the djinn snarled through Renaud's mouth. "An ancient agreement has been broken by modern man, so all modern flesh must pay, to be reminded why our worlds are best apart. Why we should not be disturbed. And why the idea that any can be our master, harness our power, carries the sentence of death by eternal flame."

The scientist's body took a lunging step forward, arms raised as if preparing to strike. Aya retreated and watched Renaud's features contort again, terror etched within the blazing eyes.

For a moment, the real scientist surfaced, tears carving paths down sooty cheeks. "P-please," Renaud's voice gasped through the deeper resonance before falling into a coughing fit. "Help me... I didn't know."

Then his head flew back, neck snapping. Another roar filled the chamber as the black haze in the air collected, thickening around him, entering his nose and mouth.

Flesh crackled. Renaud's torso glowed from within as his clothes caught fire and burned away. White lines of sizzling light crawled up his throat and along his arms. He screamed and screamed again, as the djinn's power consumed him. Renaud's body hit the floor with a lifeless thud. Scorch marks covered his body.

The black haze shot upward from his corpse, like a living whip, spiraling near the ceiling. A hissing whisper raked across Aya's mind: "The fire breathes free, and consume it shall..."

Then the shadowy form dissolved.

Aya stood rooted in shock. Fresh alarms blared overhead and jolted her alert. She limped toward the exit, away from the twisted remains of Dr. Renaud and the charred corpse of Léglise. Sliding doors along the far wall hissed half-shut, fire clawing at the edges. The heat battered her; each breath tasted of copper and dust.

The corridor beyond was a collapsing maze. Alarms wailed,

echoing off scorched walls. Aya coughed in the haze, eyes tearing amidst the thick smoke. Overhead horns blared, metal shutters slamming somewhere in the distance.

She cradled the Amulet against her side and rushed through the chaos. Its pulse thrummed, static crawling under her skin. Soldiers' shouts reverberated nearby, but the clouds of dust and smoke obscured nearly everything. She caught glimpses of black-clad figures scrambling.

A deeper siren blared: "Fire containment protocol. Complete base lockdown in sixty seconds." Heavy shutters thundered down from the ceiling.

Aya knew she had mere seconds to find an exit before she was sealed inside the inferno.

She coughed, lungs burning, ignoring the raw pain in her fingertips where the Amulet's energy still crackled. Half-blinded, she forced herself back in the direction of where she'd first entered.

At the corridor's end, the door hung half off its hinges. Through the gap, Aya glimpsed a night sky split by lightning. Thunder rumbled like a distant drumroll. She shoved the panel, inching it wide enough to slip outside, hot metal burning her and she squeezed through.

The air glowed orange from the base's raging meltdown. She stumbled for a moment before collapsing to her knees in the sand, panting, getting fresh oxygen.

A distant fury roared. Metal shrieks echoed across the dunes. She thought of Léglise's final scream. Clutching the Amulet, she found it heavier than any relic she'd ever stolen. She'd won, for now.

Léglise was destroyed, but the machine behind him wasn't, and what he'd awakened had yet to be put to rest.

She squared her shoulders against the wind, tucking the

Amulet into a small bag at her hip. All that mattered was meeting Karim and the others.

She turned and fled into the swirling night, the meltdown's infernal glow at her back. Red lights strobed on watchtowers as they collapsed, one after another, entombing the facility, and Léglise's ambitions in a cataclysm of their own making.

But night, it seemed, had only just begun.

FORTY-EIGHT

SAND-LADEN WIND ROARED across the compound, driving stinging grit against every patch of exposed skin as Aya raced to reach the others. She could see the outline of their Land Rover by the front gate.

Through the swirling dust, she could also make out what looked like two figures. Aya darted in their direction, hoping to see Karim, Amina, Omar, or Salah.

"Thank God, you're both okay!" she shouted over the howling gale as she got closer.

Omar had an arm looped under Salah's shoulders, helping him limp forward. A ragged tear in Salah's pants revealed a bloody mess of mangled flesh, but he wore a determined half-grin. Wind whipped his dreadlocks, and Omar's headscarf flapped against his cheek.

Omar's reply was breathless. "Barely. The way we came was blocked off, so we had to cut through two sealed corridors... I almost got pinned under a collapsed roof, but Salah pulled me free." He sucked in dusty air. "And then..." Omar glanced down at Salah's leg.

"You can thank Léglise for all this," Aya said. "He forced a power draw from the Amulet. I guess the djinn chose to tear the entire facility apart instead, Léglise included."

Salah's eyes widened. "You saw him?"

She nodded. "But he's gone, consumed by the fire."

Omar's gaze immediately dropped to her small bag. "And the Amulet, did you get it?"

Aya patted the bag at her hip, feeling the artifact's continued pulse through the fabric. "Yes. But it's not over. It's worse than we feared. A djinn that was bound to it, that the Amulet and all the dig site's protections held back, is free now and vowing revenge for humanity breaking an ancient commitment. I watched the djinn possess one of their scientists before killing him."

Before either could respond, a boom reverberated through the compound, followed by a flash of eerie, green light snaking through the storm-torn sky. Sparks erupted from the nearest half-toppled watchtower, arcs of electricity whipping across broken antennae.

The crackling energy coalesced into a cloud, swirling above the main lab like a desert phantom. For an instant, a twisted visage seemed to glower across the compound before dissolving into roiling smoke.

"Is that... the djinn?" Salah whispered, voice shaking. "Taking shape?"

Aya swallowed hard. "Yes. They're real, Abdelatif was right. It's not some anomaly that can be 'scienced' away. I... I spoke to one."

The phantom overhead let out a distorted howl, flinging electric fury into the ground. Flames danced an infernal waltz across the courtyard, consuming the last remaining structures.

They'd gone only a few yards when frantic shouts sounded ahead. The wind briefly parted, revealing Amina and Karim.

Relief flooded Aya's chest. She rushed forward. Amina's face was ashen, eyes pinched with pain. Karim supported her from the waist, an assault rifle over his other shoulder. A trickle of blood ran down his temple.

"Aya!" Karim called.

As she reached them, Aya threw her arms around both him and Amina, pulling them into a fierce embrace. "I thought I might have lost you both in there," she said, her voice breaking with relief. She held Karim's face in her hands for a moment, her thumb brushing away the blood from his face. "Are you hurt badly?"

He shook his head, covering her hand with his. "Nothing I can't handle. When that whole place started coming apart, I kept thinking about you, about how we never got to finish our conversation about what comes after all this, for us."

"We can finish it soon," she said firmly, squeezing his hand. She pulled back slightly, her eyes bright with urgency. "I have the Amulet. I got it. And Léglise is dead."

Karim's eyes widened. "You actually—"

"And there's more," Aya interrupted frantically. "Inside the lab, I saw their equipment—astronomical calculation devices, star-tracking instruments. It all looked exactly like the diagrams in my father's notebook, the ones we couldn't decode. Those coordinates we struggled with for weeks? I think they're connected to the stars, to what's happening now, to when the djinn can be... pulled between worlds." She gestured helplessly at the supernatural chaos around them. "I need to study the notebook again, but I think my father knew this was coming."

Amina coughed, pressing a shaking hand to her forehead. "Good work, Aya, like always. We couldn't let them salvage anything. So I triggered the last explosives we had after we blew the SUV... then a squad ambushed us. We barely..." Her voice faltered as she clutched her temples, some invisible force pounding in her skull.

Aya helped Karim, reaching an arm under Amina's shoulder. "You both did great. But we have to go."

Lightning snaked across the courtyard, forcing them to duck. The djinn phantom above extended a shadowy arm, compelling wind that whipped debris into a swirling funnel of sand, embers, and twisted metal.

Karim stared up at the malevolent shape. "Yeah, let's go. If the destruction doesn't kill us, that thing might."

They broke into a limping run for the perimeter, supporting Salah and Amina, each step a battle through shifting sand. Whatever gates once stood were in piles of flaming rubble. Instead, they aimed for a side breach where the chain-link fence lay twisted on the ground.

A fresh roar rose from the base's center, a final, cataclysmic surge. Columns of flame shot skyward, forming a blazing funnel. The domed lab caved in, hammered by a percussive force. A shockwave rippled outward, toppling the three remaining towers completely, carving jagged fissures in the desert floor.

Overhead, the djinn's formless shape shrieked in a guttural language none could comprehend. Then, in a bone-shaking convulsion, it collapsed, drawn inward by the facility's catastrophic destruction. A brilliant flash seared their vision.

Blinking, Aya realized she was on her hands and knees. Pain stung her elbows where they scraped the sand. Nearby, Karim hauled Amina upright while Omar supported a coughing Salah. Around them glowed rivulets of molten metal, tracing through the wreckage, spreading outward.

Silence fell, broken only by the crackle of flames. The compound had devoured itself, leaving a ravaged husk. The domed lab, Léglise's dream of power, was now a blackened crater.

"Go!" Aya shouted, struggling to her feet. The others followed, battered figures retreating into the Sahara's dunes.

They found refuge behind a U.S. ARMY patrol vehicle, flipped on its side.

Karim exhaled, wiping grime from his cheeks. "What now?"

Aya peered at the horizon, blinking away smoke. "We find Abdelatif." She felt the weight of the Amulet against her side. "We need his help to stop this djinn for good, put things back the way they were."

As they walked through the sand, the stars began to peek through the clearing sky above them. Aya needed to study his notes more carefully once they reached safety.

The Amulet pulsed against her side, and she resisted the urge to get it out, to hold it.

Forty-Nine

By the time they reached the ridge and found Abdelatif waiting and watching, the desert night had grown cool and quiet. Smoke lingered on the horizon like a dark bruise beneath the moonlit sky. Otherwise, only silent dunes stretched away in every direction, their pale curves gleaming under the moon.

As soon as Abdelatif spotted them approaching through the darkness, he rose from his vigil, relief flooding his weathered features. "*Alhamdulillah*. When I saw the flames on the horizon, the explosions... I feared the worst."

His eyes quickly assessed their battered state. "What happened? Did you retrieve the artifact? And Léglise?"

"We got it," Aya said. "And Léglise is dead. But Abdelatif, what we witnessed... the djinn, the supernatural forces. Everything you warned us about was real."

Abdelatif's expression darkened as he studied Amina more closely. "And the price of that encounter shows itself already," he murmured. "We must act quickly."

Salah pressed a hand to his ribs. "I'll try to get a fire going, enough for warmth and food, before we get rolling. I can still manage that." Every word seemed to scrape his throat, and fresh blood stained the makeshift bandage beneath his fingers.

Aya's eyes lingered on him as he hobbled over to their supplies.

"I'm still in this, Aya," he said.

She gave him a quick, worried nod. They were all battered in one way or another, but Salah's wound looked especially raw.

Abdelatif resumed his silent watch, scanning the dunes as though expecting further trouble at any moment. His weathered hands gripped his cane with white knuckles. Amina only sank onto the sand and cradled her head.

Before long, a small campfire had been coaxed to life, casting flickers of light on their exhausted faces. Sparks drifted into the darkness overhead, vanishing among the stars. The six of them huddled close in the fragile glow.

Salah grimaced, raking a shaky hand through his dreadlocks. "Far out, right? One minute I'm chilling with you guys, the next I'm locked up, then I'm dodging bullets like some trippy action flick. And here we are. Listen," he tapped his injured thigh, "I'm pretty sure it missed the big stuff, but I can't call it." He forced a laugh while sweat gleamed on his forehead. "I owe you all for dragging me out of that twisted base. If that means limping through a cursed desert, guess that's my new vibe."

"I'll do what I can to bandage it better," Omar said, digging through his backpack again. "You saved me back there."

As Omar tended to Salah, Aya saw the lines on Amina's wrist glow with unsettling luminescence. Dread crept through her. "Let me see," she whispered.

The sight jolted Aya with a flashback: Dr. Renaud, his eyes possessed, his sleeves scorched away to reveal the same creeping patterns. She could still hear his final scream echo off the lab walls. Aya shut her eyes, picturing Renaud writhing as that black haze poured into him. He was consumed from within, she thought. If this thing were the same, did they have only days, hours, before it tightened its hold?

Reluctantly, Amina lowered her hand, revealing spindly lines radiating from the juncture of her forearm. But it wasn't just the marks. Amina's movements had become sluggish, almost mechanical. When she'd walked from the base, there had been moments where she'd stopped mid-step, staring at nothing, before Karim had to guide her forward again.

Aya pressed her palm against Amina's arm, noting the heat beneath the skin and the way Amina's pupils seemed to dilate and contract independently of the firelight.

"Aya, I'm scared." Amina's voice cracked, and for a moment she sounded completely like herself again. "Sometimes I feel like I'm watching someone else control my body. Like I'm a passenger."

Aya wrapped her arms around Amina and held her, catching the familiar scent of almond oil in her hair beneath the smoke. "We'll fix this."

As she held Amina, Aya's mind drifted to another loss that had been gnawing at her since their escape. Her father's notebook, his work, had been in her bag when the explosions started. In the chaos of fleeing the facility, she hadn't dared to hope it had survived. The thought of losing those precious pages, especially now when they might hold the key to stopping the djinn, made her stomach clench with dread.

Amina rested her head on Aya's shoulder, and they shared a few deep breaths before Abdelatif approached, his cane scraping faintly against the sand.

The firelight sharpened the worry etched in the man's brow. "This is precisely what I feared," he said, studying

Amina's markings. "I don't know exactly what it means, but if we don't act, I fear there may be dire consequences for us all."

He gestured at the bag beside Aya, where the Amulet lay wrapped in her sweater. "And if we keep that with us, the curse remains half-awake, always present with us. These experiments unleashed more of the djinn's presence, I fear."

"But why me? Why is no one else affected?" Amina asked.

Abdelatif shook his head, his expression grave. "The djinn cannot manifest fully in our realm without a willing vessel—or one they can corrupt slowly, like water wearing away stone. You were one of the closest to witnessing the seal's breaking. In that moment, when the barrier cracked, you became... visible to them. Marked."

"I saw it happen to another, but without any protective markings," Aya said. "There was a scientist in the lab with the Amulet. When I was stopping their work, taking the artifact, something happened to him. Like the djinn possessed him and was speaking through him. Before it tore him apart from the inside."

Amina's hand shot to her mouth. Her panicked eyes darted to the faint lines creeping along her arm. "Fuck."

Abdelatif nodded. "I believe Amina has time before this fate awaits her, but we must restore what centuries of caution held back. Léglise and his people cracked the barrier between planes of being. Now we must seal it again. There is no choice." He straightened, leaning heavily on his cane. "This is a burden our ancestors carried millennia ago, and now we bear it. If we stand aside, the djinn's wrath will devour more than just the people in that facility."

Karim crouched by the flames, adding another handful of dry brush. "So, we have no choice but to return to that corridor in the Atlas. We have to re-bind the djinn. But how?"

Abdelatif nodded slowly. "According to the old texts I was

able to decipher, the myths passed down, the ritual requires three elements: the sacred site itself, the corridor where the original compact was made, at a key location where the gap between our world and theirs wears thin. Then we will need the proper incantations in the old tongue, in Old Arabic. And...” He paused, his gaze moving between Aya, Amina, and Karim. “I’m sorry to say, three participants, each representing a different aspect of the divine connection, the keys.”

“What do you mean?” Omar asked, wincing as he stood.

“They are called the three keys,” Abdelatif said quietly. “One of the bloodline, descended from those who first made the compact with the djinn. The old families who bound them to protect humanity.” His gaze found Aya. “One who has been marked by the djinn themselves, who can serve as a bridge between worlds.” He looked at Amina. “And one pure of heart, who seeks knowledge for its own sake and can anchor the ritual in human intention rather than selfish desire.” Finally, his eyes settled on Karim.

Omar’s eyes widened with sudden understanding. “Baraka,” he breathed. “That’s why it has to be you three. It’s not random. You’ve been touched in different ways.”

Aya felt a chill that had nothing to do with the desert wind. “The ritual doesn’t just need three people. It needs three vessels, each representing a different aspect of the divine connection.”

Abdelatif nodded approvingly. “Without all three keys, the binding cannot hold. The djinn will break free again, stronger than before, especially now, if what you found about the alignment is correct. Djinn will be able to pour through the collapsed barrier between worlds when alignment is achieved, if your father’s coordinates are correct.”

They exchanged uneasy glances in turn. Even the wind seemed to hush, as though some unseen presence listened.

Aya brushed her gritty hair off her forehead and nodded. "Then it's settled, we have no choice. Abdelatif, you'll guide us?"

"I will share what I have learned and lead it, but the three keys must perform the ritual. As best I can, with the fragments of knowledge I've collected or can guess at."

"We'll need a vehicle to get there," Karim said. "Our Land Rover is toast, sorry about that. But there is that old transport truck near the southwestern perimeter. We hid behind it, flipped over from the explosion, but it could be operational."

Salah laughed. "I haven't hotwired a car in a few years. Let's pray there's half a tank of gas."

Omar tried to smile, the corners of his mouth twitching. "Better than trekking on foot."

Their eyes turned to Aya. "All right," she said. "The sun should be up soon. At dawn, we look for that truck. We can't risk the main roads. PES or local police will be watching, especially after that explosion. Who knows what they'll think happened. Side routes, small villages."

One by one, they nodded and settled into silence.

"Aya, can we talk?" Karim asked, finally.

"Of course," Aya said before walking away from the fire with him.

Karim handed her a scuffed backpack. "I managed to grab your bag from the SUV wreckage before we left the area," he said gently. "Your father's field log was half-buried, but it seems undamaged."

She pulled out the notebook, its edges crusted with dust. "Thank you," she whispered, holding it protectively against her side.

She flipped a few fragile pages, seeing her father's research in a new light after Abdelatif's revelations about the bloodline. "I admired him, but I'm not sure he'd say the same about me."

"You've risked more in the past week, trying to do the right thing, than most people do in their lives. Trust me, wherever he is, I'm sure he sees how fierce you are, how determined you are to prevent catastrophe."

Aya swallowed and meekly nodded.

She flipped through the familiar pages, relief washing over her as she saw her father's careful notations still intact. "There might be more here that can help us understand the ritual," she said. "But right now, just having this back, it feels like having a piece of him with us, helping."

She turned to a scrawled note referencing Ottoman travelers seeking cosmic synergy and astral engineering. The words felt outlandish given the night's danger, but after everything they'd witnessed, her mind kept coming back to it.

Karim peered over her shoulder, curiosity creeping into his exhausted features. "I'm fascinated by this, too. Maybe there's a connection between Morocco's legends and Ottoman scholars. They never conquered this far; the Sa'adi held them off, but there was still a significant exchange."

Aya closed the notebook, her gaze sliding toward Amina, who huddled near the fire. "Something to investigate once we've dealt with the immediate crisis. One supernatural threat at a time."

Karim touched her forearm, a gentle, grounding gesture. "I'm by your side, as long as you'll have me. I couldn't come to terms with the thought of losing you back there."

Their eyes met, and a silent understanding passed between them. Aya slid her arm around Karim and pulled him tight. "Thank you. For everything. And you have no idea how much I want this. Us."

Breaking apart moments later, Aya walked back and addressed the group. "Whatever ritual or vow we need to seal this djinn for good, we'll do it. But let's try to get some good rest and be ready."

"Oorah. And just in case we're not a match for immortal, supernatural forces with a few centuries of pent-up rage?" Omar asked.

A weighted silence fell before Amina ended it. "We have to be."

"Then let's rest while we can," Salah said, clapping his hands. "Tomorrow's another hill to climb, and I don't know about you cats, but I'm beat."

Sleep soon dragged them under one by one. The low crackle of fire and the wind's relentless hush became a lullaby, though Aya's mind churned with unanswered questions. Astral engineering... cosmic alignment... The phrases tugged at her, but she pushed them aside. Enough immediate threats lingered.

In the fire's glow, she cast one final look around the camp. *Don't let them break*, Aya prayed into the void. The Sahara stretched endlessly, the vastness offering small comfort against the weight of what lay ahead.

FIFTY

DAWN BEGAN to break over the scorched desert, illuminating twisted fragments from the collapsed PES base. As the sun rose above the horizon fully, they were already approaching a battered truck, leaning at a precarious angle among metal roofing and debris from the base, exactly where Karim and Amina had said it would be.

Omar eyed the wreckage. Sparks still glowed faintly along severed beams and bent steel. "We'll have to yank that roofing off first. Karim, take the left side with me. Aya, see if you can pry the rear panel free."

They all moved in a chorus of grunts and scraping metal.

Karim wedged himself under a jagged corner of corrugated metal. "On three," he called. They heaved in unison, grunting as the roofing peeled away from the truck with an ear-splitting shriek.

Bit by bit, the truck inched free from the debris, pieces clanging on the ground, leaving the battered vehicle partly upright, rocking unsteadily.

Aya pushed to test the truck's balance. "If we all push from the driver's side," she said, "we might be able to tip this thing back on all fours. Lucky it's a tiny Suzuki."

"Wait until we're all crammed in it," Omar added. "See how lucky we are."

Metal creaked ominously as they synchronized a push.

For a second, nothing happened. Then Omar let out a guttural yell, digging his boots deeper into the sand. Aya echoed him, teeth gritted in pain and determination. The truck began to shift.

Gravel clattered beneath them, and with a final surge, the truck bounced upright. Its suspension jolted, rocking, as all four tires thumped against the earth. Karim nearly lost his footing as the momentum sent him stumbling forward.

They huddled around the newly righted vehicle, catching their breath.

Omar patted the dented hood and held his arms up in a flex. "Let's hope the engine's as tough as we are."

Salah limped forward. "I've hotwired worse, brother," he said as he dropped into the driver's seat. "Trust me, I got this."

He leaned under the dashboard, rummaging through wires with calloused fingertips. Sparks shot, and the engine gave a protesting cough. Undeterred, Salah fiddled with another knotted cluster of cords, eyes narrowing in concentration.

"There we go," he murmured, giving a final twist, and the dashboard lights flickered to life. The engine roared. "See? Piece of cake."

"The fuel gauge is nearly full," Karim said. "It'll easily get us to the nearest station." His eyes scanned the wreckage. "No telling what we'll run into, but I think we need to move."

Aya nodded.

"Let's go." Amina approached the cab. She tried to hide a tremor as she touched the car door.

"Another headache?" Aya asked.

"Worse," Amina whispered. "It just... crashed into me." For a moment, Amina's pupils rolled back. Her body went rigid. Then her gaze snapped wide. "I see the corridor again, but deep inside this time. I've never been here. Dust swirling in a cavern. A moaning wind, calling me deeper."

Aya took Amina's head in her hands, fighting back tears. "Stay with me. You're going to be okay. Breathe."

Omar and Salah looked on, alarmed, but Aya lifted a calming hand to keep them back. Gently, she guided Amina so she could lean against the truck's fender.

"Amina. Listen to me. Whatever visions the djinn is sending you, they aren't real. You're not alone. We've overcome so much. You're never alone."

"The corridor is screaming, like it wants me to come back. Like I'm a part of it."

Karim approached, placing a steady hand on Amina's shoulder. "We'll go back. But on our terms, and we'll finish this once and for all."

"The spirits cry out," Abdelatif said. "Let us go from here. Look." He pointed to a cluster of stars still visible in the lightening sky. "The alignment has already begun."

Aya followed his gaze, squinting at the constellation. "What am I looking at?"

"The Seven Sisters, or what you call the Pleiades," Abdelatif said, his voice heavy with concern. "And there, Al-Dabaran, the Follower. See how they form an almost perfect line with the morning star? This alignment happens rarely, perhaps once in a generation. It matches the astral coordinates you and Karim were working on."

Karim nodded, pulling out Aya's father's notebook from her backpack. "Yeah, he predicted this exact alignment. The stars are moving into the same position they held when the djinn were first bound, if your father was right. We thought these were coordinates on the earth, not in the sky."

"We have perhaps thirty-six hours before the alignment reaches its peak," Abdelatif calculated. "After that, if the djinn could remain unbound, they're said to have enough power to manifest physically in our world without needing human or animal vessels."

Aya studied the star chart in her father's notebook, pieces of his astronomical calculations finally making sense.

"Look at this," Karim said, pointing to the page. "I was studying it last night. Your father mentions this scholar, H. Çelebi, multiple times. Always with question marks, like he suspected a connection but couldn't prove it. This is the Ottoman stuff you were mentioning last night, Aya."

He pointed to a marginal note: "'Çelebi's expedition coincides with local legends of the Great Binding. Coincidence?'"

Aya studied the cramped handwriting. "I don't remember him ever mentioning this name specifically. He talked about Ottoman influences in general terms, but this seems more focused."

"And here," Karim continued, turning another page, "he writes 'Çelebi's astronomical instruments found near corridor site, purpose unknown.' Your father was onto something specific about this Ottoman scholar and the djinn binding. Like this Çelebi figured out whatever it is we need to know, what your father was looking for."

"Could he have been involved in creating the binding?" Aya asked.

"If the dates and myths are to be believed," Abdelatif said, "Çelebi would have come after a great djinn incursion in Fez, seeking the old knowledge to prevent future breakouts. So not the original performer of the ritual, but a protector hundreds of years later."

"The ritual we need to perform, it's based on Çelebi's work?" Aya asked.

Abdelatif nodded. "The binding ritual requires the three keys we discussed, but also perhaps the proper astronomical timing. Perhaps."

"Okay, and we need to understand our specific roles," Karim said. "The bloodline, the marked, and the pure of heart—what exactly does each of us need to do?"

Abdelatif shifted, wincing as he adjusted his weight on the cane. "The bloodline, Aya, must speak the binding words and provide the ancestral connection. The marked one, Amina, serves as the conduit, channeling the djinn's energy back to its source. And the pure of heart, Karim, you anchor the ritual in human intention, preventing the djinn from corrupting the process. You support the others. The ritual fails if any one of the three falters. Which is why we must prepare carefully once we reach the corridor."

"I'm ready—let's cruise north," Amina said. "Sounds like we're low on time."

Abdelatif rapped his cane once on the rear tire. "Yes. Let's go quickly."

The sun rose higher, casting harsh shadows across the desert wreckage.

"Then we go," Aya said. "North, back into the Atlas. Let's end this."

The engine roared to life, and they began their journey toward a confrontation that would determine the fate of multiple realms.

FIFTY-ONE

NINE HOURS in the car passed in almost reverent silence as Aya spotted the first jagged silhouettes of the High Atlas Mountains on the horizon. They had taken turns driving, resting, and contemplating.

The winding track grew rougher, pitted with deep ruts left by recent storms. The battered transport truck rattled and groaned, each jolt sending flares of pain through Aya's ribs, but she knew it was mild compared to Salah, Abdelatif, or Amina's plights.

Karim sat beside her, clutching a well-worn map. His brow was furrowed in concentration. "We're close," he murmured. "Another hour, maybe two. Then we may have to continue on foot if the roads have continued to erode."

From the driver's seat, Omar gave a tight nod. The hush resumed inside the cab as they climbed higher, a chill wind slicing through the open windows.

They found the final stretch of road all but erased. The asphalt was broken into jagged fragments, forcing the truck to grind along what was now barely a trail. Fallen boulders crowded the road, some perched precariously at the cliff's edge as if any breath of wind might send them tumbling.

Aya tensed, peering through the cracked windshield as pebbles from the mountain pinged off the hood of the vehicle. Far ahead, one colossal rock had entirely caved in the pass, creating a blockade. The track beyond vanished into a landslide.

Omar eased the truck to a stop. "This must've happened after the quakes. No way around it." He hopped out, crunching across the debris.

"Yep, the road's done," Omar concluded, returning to the driver's side. "We'll never navigate these chunks in the truck. We'll have to hoof it. We're not far from where we camped out on that first night, Aya."

"On foot it is."

"Oh, what memories," Omar said. "Simpler times of being a humble Aegis employee, trying to steal some old hunk of rock."

Aya laughed and patted him on the back.

"All right, who can I help?" Omar called. "Salah, piggyback time?"

TIME BLURRED INTO STEADY FOOTFALLS. The mountain air grew thinner as they climbed, each breath requiring more effort. Loose scree shifted treacherously underfoot, occasionally forcing them to catch themselves against the rocky slope to avoid a dangerous stumble.

Amina struggled the most, stopping frequently to press her hands against her temples. The dark lines on her arms had spread again, now reaching past her elbows in thorny, vine-like patterns of Amazigh symbols.

"The closer we get, the stronger it becomes," Amina whispered, her voice taking on a distant quality. "I can hear them calling through the void. Multiple voices now, not just one."

Eventually, they caught the first glimpse of stone rubble near a deep ravine, the scattered remains of the collapsed excavation. Aya's heart picked up pace. *They'd returned.*

The final approach to the dig site felt surreal. What had once been an organized archaeological excavation was now a chaotic sprawl of overturned equipment and scattered debris. The neat grid lines that had marked their careful excavation were replaced by jagged gouges in the earth, torn through the ground.

They picked their way carefully through the wreckage. Aya recognized pieces of their former camp, remnants of the life they'd built during those weeks of painstaking work.

"It's like looking at what's to come if we fail," Karim said quietly, nudging a pile of rubble and tent fabric with his boot.

Aya faced the corridor's entrance, once a half-buried tomb carved into the rock, now barely recognizable. Its outer arch stood partially collapsed, the stone marked by deep cracks radiating outward. Blocks of masonry littered the ground, as though some colossal beast had battered the walls from within, sending the blocks shooting outward.

As they approached, Karim suddenly stopped. "Look at these damage patterns," he said, running his hand along a fractured stone. "Yeah, the cracks, they're following Sa'adi geometry. See how they radiate in perfect octagonal patterns from each impact point?"

Aya moved closer. Karim was right. What seemed like random destruction actually followed precise mathematical relationships.

"They built their tombs and sacred spaces using these principles," Abdelatif said, leaning heavily on his cane. "But here, the patterns are inverted. Instead of containing power, they're releasing it, undoing the magic."

"And look at the arch itself," Karim continued, excitement mixing with dread in his voice. "The collapse isn't random either. It's creating resonance chambers for the energy."

"It's a lock that's been broken from the inside," Aya realized. "The original builders used the Sa'adi and Marinid mathematical principles we studied to create a perfect prison. Now the same mathematics that kept the djinn contained are helping them escape."

Amina shuddered. "I think it wants me to cross through the void."

A low, unnatural hum tickled Aya's ears. Across the ravine, half-solid shapes flickered at the edges of her vision, vague silhouettes drifting through the dust. Whenever she tried to focus, they vanished, leaving nothing.

Karim gestured at the jagged corridor mouth. "See those cracks? The entire entrance might shift if we're not careful. Even if we find stable footing inside, it won't be easy."

"I brought climbing gear. We can rope off, just in case," Omar said.

Abdelatif, cane in hand, walked to the edge. "We cannot delay. But before we enter, there is something else you must know, something I have been studying during our journey." His weathered face grew grave. "This place... it sits in the shadow of Sidi Chamharouch."

Omar's eyes widened. "The sanctuary of the djinn sultan? Another legend, sure, why not?"

"No legend, Omar—just as none of what we have seen or experienced is mere legend," Abdelatif said firmly. "Sidi Chamharouch, Lord of the Djinn, has watched over these mountains for centuries. The shrine that bears his name is only a few valleys away. This corridor, this binding—it would have been done with his permission, under his authority."

"Which means?" Karim asked.

"Which means we are not just dealing with random djinn," Abdelatif explained. "These are Sidi Chamharouch's subjects, contained by ancient treaty. When the seal broke, it was a violation of Sidi Chamharouch's law."

"Is that why they're so angry?" Amina asked.

"These djinn would be loyal soldiers; they are not seeking freedom or passage into our world—they're seeking justice for a betrayal. And only by acknowledging Sidi Chamharouch's authority can we hope to restore the balance." Abdelatif looked at each of them in turn. "When we perform the ritual, we must invoke his name. Without his blessing, I fear no binding will hold. We are at his mercy."

Abdelatif paused, studying their faces to ensure they understood the gravity of what lay ahead. "Remember what we discussed. The three keys must work in perfect harmony. Aya, when the moment comes, you must speak the binding words with the authority of your bloodline. The djinn will test you, try to shake your confidence. Hold firm."

Aya nodded.

"Amina," Abdelatif continued, "you are the bridge between worlds. The djinn will try to overwhelm you, to possess you completely, to enter your body. But your connection to them is also your strength—use it to guide their energy back to its source."

Amina's hand trembled as she touched her arm. "And if I can't control it?"

"Then Karim anchors you both," Abdelatif said, turning to the archaeologist. "Your role is to maintain intention throughout the ritual. When supernatural forces threaten to consume the others, you ground them in purpose, in the knowledge that this must be done for humanity's sake."

Karim straightened. "So if either of them falters…"

"You become their lifeline back to our world," Abdelatif confirmed. "The ritual requires all three, working as one. The moment any of you lose focus, the binding fails."

Omar stopped beside Salah. "Let's be smart," he said. "You and I stay up here at the entrance, keep the rope system secure. You shouldn't climb too deep with that leg, and we need someone out here as a failsafe."

Salah didn't protest, though frustration flickered in his eyes. "Fine. But if you need me…"

"We can help anchor or haul people out if things go south," Omar said. "We can't risk you bleeding out in a cave-in, and they need a backup plan to get out."

Nearby, Amina, Karim, and Abdelatif gathered by Aya, who hoisted her pack. She unzipped it just enough to check the artifact. A new orange gleam brightened at her touch, another ripple of energy coursing through her palm.

"It's reacting," Karim murmured, leaning in. "The closer we get to the original altar, the stronger its resonance becomes."

"Which means the djinn are feeling it too," Amina said, her voice tight. "They're getting agitated. They think we're shattering the barrier as alignment approaches."

Abdelatif's expression darkened. "They will fight us with everything they have to make us pay for betraying humanity's pact—for trying to use them. Be prepared for the chamber itself to resist us. The illusions will be stronger, more convincing. They may show you things from your past, your fears, your regrets—anything to break your concentration."

"We have to put the past, any regrets, behind us," Aya said. "We focus on the present, each other. No matter what we see, we remember why we're here."

Amina put a hand on Aya's shoulder and nodded before walking ahead.

Moments later, they stood at the broken threshold. The opening was littered with jagged, great slabs of stone. A rush of stale, ice-cold air still poured out, carrying a deep, throbbing moan that set Aya's teeth on edge.

"All right." Omar exhaled, checking the rope knot around a fractured pillar. "Safe travels. Watch yourselves. If you don't come back soon, we'll—I guess Salah and I will figure something out. Just keep hold of the rope."

Salah tapped fists with Aya, his voice tight. "We'll be waiting, *okti*."

"Thank you."

Then she, Amina, Karim, and Abdelatif eased past the fallen stones. The corridor swallowed them in creeping darkness, illuminated only by their flashlights. Before Aya's second foot had touched the stone ground, she glimpsed half-formed illusions: walls that rippled like heat mirages, shadows skulking at the corners of her vision. A faint scraping sound in the distance sent her heart racing.

"Stay focused," Abdelatif warned, voice echoing off the stone. "These illusions feed on fear. I see them too, but they are not real. It is the thinning of the barrier between our worlds. It is nearly dissolved in this chamber."

Karim took point, scanning the floor with a small geologist's sensor that beeped near unstable rock. He pulled up abruptly. "*3andek!* Watch out, everyone. The next few meters are cracked. Step exactly where I do."

They advanced in single file. Drips of water resonated through the gloom. A distant whistling rose and fell, like pained sobs reverberating in the stone.

"This is so much bigger than it looked from outside," Aya said. "Léglise's men got the Amulet so quickly."

"I do not think it was always this big. There are strange powers afoot here," Abdelatif said.

Karim ran his fingertips over the rope tethered to his waist. "This can't keep us linked much farther," he said quietly.

Amina wavered, swaying from side to side. "Then we leave it behind. We can't let some rope hold us back now."

They unfastened their harnesses in tense silence. Each pop of a carabiner sounded like a gunshot in the hush.

"Stick close," Aya said, eyeing the corridor ahead, with no end in sight. "Omar and Salah can't help us now. We only have each other."

They paused when Karim motioned to a fresh collapse blocking the corridor's left side. "We can squeeze through on the right. Watch for loose rocks overhead."

They inched forward, scraping their shoulders against rough stone. The corridor moaned again, a hollow, resonant wail.

Abdelatif muttered in Arabic, shining his flashlight into a side chamber. The beam revealed nothing, but Aya felt watched, as though invisible eyes were observing their every move.

At last, the passage opened into a grand antechamber. Aya's flashlight revealed walls once richly carved, now riddled with fissures. Parts of the domed ceiling had caved in. Stone falcon statues lay cracked on the ground, and ancient columns buckled precariously. At the far end stood a smaller arch leading deeper into the tomb.

Abdelatif glanced from Aya to the others. "That tomb is our destination. Remember, each of you has a role that cannot be filled by another."

They all nodded. Anxiety silenced through them as they pressed on, the corridor's darkness clinging to them, its eerie reverberations rising into a half-whispered chorus. Step by step, they neared the half-collapsed arch.

Abdelatif lifted one hand. "From this point on, every step lies fully in the djinn's domain. We will be trespassing. If we falter, the djinn may find the opening it needs to break free completely."

Aya rested a hand over the bag containing the Amulet. "Then we don't falter."

A final gust of frigid air rushed down the corridor, carrying a guttural moan. They stood at the threshold of the tomb's inner chamber, three keys ready to unlock humanity's salvation or witness its destruction.

FIFTY-TWO

KARIM PAUSED, shining his flashlight on a series of half-exposed carvings. "Look."

Fractured lines depicting robed figures, now so eroded by centuries and recent upheaval that only ghostly outlines remained.

"They're beautiful, but haunting," Aya said.

"I can't think of a single historical comparison," Karim said.

A shrill hiss echoed in the darkness behind them. Amina gasped, stumbling before gripping Aya's shoulder. Panic flickered in her eyes. "I—I saw... I'm not sure. A city, maybe? Towers carved from reflective black stone." Her breaths came in quick, shallow rasps. "It vanished, but I think we're there, in another dimension or something."

Aya steadied her, tightening her grip around Amina's waist. She glanced at Abdelatif. "We need to hurry."

The floor sloped downward to the wide, low archway. Beyond it, an orange glow shimmered.

Abdelatif stepped forward, his cane tapping gently on the

stone. For a moment, he stared at the faint light in the next chamber. "We shall see what is required of us. The moment any of you loses focus, all is lost."

They followed the path toward the arch that glowed with ghostly light. The illusions thickened, forming blurred shapes at the edge of Aya's vision, shadows of the ancient city Amina had described. Aya forced herself not to flinch, focusing on the tangible: the pace of her breath, the gritty traction of stone beneath her boots.

Once through, the archway opened onto a sprawling sub-chamber with steps leading down. In the center, a raised platform waited, its surface carved with swirling patterns that perfectly mirrored the lines on Amina's arm.

"Oh great," Amina gasped. "What does that mean?"

The glow was originating from the platform. A slow pulse emanated, keeping time with each step of their approach, recognizing the artifact in Aya's bag.

The swirl of energy felt like a gravitational pull, but Aya moved forward slowly, resolutely, heart pounding faster with every step.

Amina let out a soft cry, stumbling into Karim. "It's like it's pulling me apart," she gasped. "I see them, tall spires, robed figures chanting." Her eyes were fully dilated. "They all turn to me, arms out. What am I supposed to do? It's burning."

Aya fought to stay upright as the floor lurched beneath her feet like a ship in a storm. Dust rained from the ceiling as it started to fracture, and every breath tasted of crushed limestone.

As Amina stood trembling at the platform's edge as the marks branched along her skin, morphing into a fiery red.

Aya's mind raced through everything they'd learned. "The sketches," she breathed, remembering the hours she'd spent in Karim's tent, struggling with her father's cipher. "Karim, remember when we couldn't understand why my father drew those spiraling patterns next to Çelebi's name?"

Karim's eyes widened. "The ones that looked like…"

"Like the marks on Amina's arm, on that platform." Aya's voice cracked. "He wasn't just documenting them from legend. He was trying to tell us something about the connection between the marked and the binding."

Abdelatif turned sharply. "What connection?"

"I don't know exactly," Aya admitted, frustration bleeding through. "The cipher for that section was different, more complex. I only figured out fragments. Something about 'channels' and 'returning to source,' but I couldn't piece together the full meaning."

Amina looked between them, the patterns on her arm pulsing. "So we're gambling my life on half-translated notes?"

"Not gambling," Abdelatif said slowly. "Aya's father's research confirms what the old stories only hinted at. The marked one becomes the conduit. That's why the djinn chose you, Amina. You were already connected, somehow. But the task before us, the choice we face, may prove most difficult for you."

Karim steadied her, his voice calm despite the chaos. "Amina, it's like Abdelatif said, you're the bridge, you channel their energy back to its source. You don't fight them, you guide them home. You've got this."

Abdelatif limped to the front of the raised platform, his weathered face set with determination. "Let us begin, you all know your roles. Aya, when you are ready."

Slowly, Aya stepped onto the platform beside Abdelatif, facing the pedestal where the Amulet would be returned. The artifact pulsed so powerfully now that it felt alive, shaking, longing for its resting place. Behind her, Amina moved to the center of the chamber, directly between the platform and the corridor entrance. Karim positioned himself to their right, where he could see both clearly.

With trembling fingers, Aya lifted the Amulet of Idris from her bag. Its carvings matched the shape of the pedestal precisely. Energy crackled like bolts of lightning between relic and altar.

"Place it, Aya," Abdelatif called out.

As she moved, a massive slab of stone crashed behind them with a thunderous boom that shook the entire chamber, sealing off the arch completely. The sound reverberated with the gravity of a death sentence.

"No!" Karim spun around, rushing to the fallen stone barrier. He pressed his hands against it, pushing with all his strength, but the massive block didn't budge even a millimeter. "We're sealed in!"

Aya's eyes widened. "Omar and Salah can't reach us now, and there's no way back."

The chamber's orange glow pulsed brighter, as if responding to her words, the boundary between realms dissolving around them, pulling them further in.

"This isn't just a trap," Amina whispered, her marked arms beginning to glow. "The djinn, they're not just trying to escape our world. They're trying to drag us into theirs. I can feel it."

Abdelatif straightened himself, leaning heavily on his cane. "If there is no way back, we can only go forward. We must do this now, for everyone."

Aya placed the Amulet at the center of the narrow pedestal. When it touched the stone, it instantly blazed with blinding light, searing her vision to nothing but white, and the corridor roared, drowning out all sound, all thought.

Amina collapsed to her knees as the chamber sizzled with energy.

Fully formed djinn materialized around them, towering

shapes of smoke and flame with eyes like burning coals. Their voices rose in a cacophony of rage and ancient pain.

"They're fighting the binding!" Karim shouted over the chaos. "Aya, now, we need you! You can do this!"

Aya stepped forward again and raised her voice, speaking with the authority of generations: "By the blood of the first compact, by the covenant sworn beneath these very stones, I call upon you to honor the ancient treaty!"

The djinn turned their burning gazes upon her, testing, probing. She felt their power pressing against her mind, seeking weakness. But she held firm, rooted in what she represented.

"I am Aya Amrani, daughter of Hassan, descendant of Idris, and keeper of the bloodline that first bound you to peace. You know my right to speak!"

Meanwhile, Amina rose to her feet, her arms blazing with silver light. Instead of fighting the djinn's presence, she held her arms high and opened herself to it, becoming a conduit for their rage.

"I hear you," she gasped, her voice layered with harmonics that didn't sound entirely human. "I feel your betrayal, your fury."

Amina's marked arms illuminated like silver torches as she spread them wide, her body becoming a living bridge between worlds. The djinn's energy poured into her in visible streams of fire and electricity, writhing around her arms and through her hair.

Her feet left the ground as she levitated between the pedestal and the entombed entrance.

With the energy, she began to trace complex patterns in the air. Each gesture redirected streams of the djinn's energy away from the chamber walls and toward the waiting Amulet.

She let out a guttural scream of pain, her entire body trembling as she fought to control forces that could tear her apart from within. "I am your bridge," she growled, her voice echoing with distortion. "Through me, you return home!"

The effect was immediate and dramatic. The towering djinn around the perimeter began to waver, their solid forms becoming translucent as Amina's weaving pulled their essence toward the Amulet.

Streams of golden fire flowed from their bodies into her outstretched hands, then were redirected onward to the pedestal. The chamber's oppressive heat began to lessen.

But the more djinn energy that flowed through Amina, the more she began to change. Her skin glowed like molten gold, and when she opened her mouth to speak, flames flickered between her teeth.

"I can... see everything," she yelled, her voice layered with the voices of the djinn flowing through her. "The burning cities, the endless desert of their realm. It's beautiful. Why did we ever fear them?"

The marks on her arms spread rapidly, covering her neck, her face, transforming her into something that looked no longer entirely human.

"What's happening to her?" Aya shouted, before continuing her incantations but watching in horror.

Amina's control over the energy streams began to falter. Instead of directing the power toward the Amulet, she started pulling it into herself, feeding on it. The wild energy lashed out at the chamber walls, sending columns of rock crashing down around them.

"Why bind them?" Amina asked, her eyes now glowing like coals, her feet floating further off the ground. "Why not join them? The fire realm calls to us all..."

Karim sprinted forward and wrapped his arms around Amina's transforming form, pulling her back down to the ground. The moment his skin touched Amina, he screamed in agony, her flesh burning him, but he held on, becoming a human anchor.

Karim pressed his forehead against hers, screaming as djinn fire scorched his skin. "Feel what it means to choose, Amina! These djinn don't choose. They just hunger and consume! But you can choose to help us, choose to save people, choose to to do the right thing, to not abandon us. Choose your humanity."

As Karim maintained contact with her djinn-touched form, the transformation began to reverse. The golden fire faded from her skin, the flames died on her lips, and the alien voices in her speech grew quieter.

Amina shook her head, blinking rapidly as if awakening from a deep sleep.

"Karim?" she whispered, her voice returning, confused and frightened. "I almost... I could see their realm. I wanted to stay there, to become a being of pure energy."

"But you chose to come back. You didn't leave," he said, still holding her despite the pain. "You chose us. You chose humanity."

FIFTY-THREE

THE WILD ENERGY streams gradually stabilized, and Amina's human consciousness fully reasserted. The djinn fire still flowed through her, but under control, obeying her will rather than consuming it, coursing in perfect streams toward the waiting Amulet.

The Amulet pulsed with power, yet the djinn remained partially manifested, their forms wavering but not dissipating. The wind rose in intensity. Stones rained down from above. Aya threw an arm over her head, eyes stinging from dust and panic.

Abdelatif limped forward, his face grave with understanding. "It is not enough," he said, his voice carrying over the supernatural chaos. "The binding demands more than energy and words. It is as I feared, as Sidi Chamharouch would demand, any ritual sealed with a life willingly given."

"No!" Amina cried, still channeling the djinn fire. "There has to be another way!"

"A soul must seal the vow," Abdelatif said solemnly. "This is my burden. Do not worry, I am an old man and I have been given much. It's time to give back, and for me, there is no greater honor."

Before anyone could stop him, Abdelatif stepped forward into the stream of energy flowing between Amina and the Amulet. He grasped the blazing artifact with both hands, wincing as arcs of power coursed through his body.

"No!" Aya cried.

Energy crackled around Abdelatif, raising a barrier of sparks.

As the Amulet's brilliance swelled, Abdelatif raised his cane toward the ceiling and shouted: "Sidi Chamharouch, witness this covenant renewed! Accept this offering made in your name!" He drove his cane into the stone floor.

The chamber shook with a deafening boom.

"This ends with me," he said, his voice carrying across the melee.

He raised his head, chanting in a low, haunting cadence that Aya couldn't understand. Each syllable sent a fresh jolt of power through the artifact. The djinn howled overhead, their burning forms beginning to waver more substantially.

Suddenly, lines of flaming script raced across the floor and walls, forging a net around the djinn's manifestations. Stalagmites of flame erupted upward, tangling with the writhing shapes overhead.

Clinging to the artifact, Abdelatif braced himself as a fresh scorching current surged through his body. His chant broke into ragged gasps, but he refused to yield. The glyphs swirled closer, tighter, confining the djinn's power.

"Stop!" Amina pleaded as Karim and Aya held her back from the scorching dais. Jagged spears of gold-white flame erupted around Abdelatif.

With a final, harrowing invocation, Abdelatif pressed the artifact into a carved recess at the pedestal's center.

A searing white light blinded them as energy reversed like a tidal wave.

Then came a thunderous crack. The artifact imploded, absorbing centuries of contained power in a single, devastating burst. Receiving all the energy, slowly at first, and then all at once.

As it did, shards of blazing crystal shot through the air, colliding with Abdelatif, ripping a wet gasp from his throat. Lines of light traced across his robes. For an instant, the platform glowed with unbearable radiance, then faded, the glyphs paling to dead stone.

Aya watched as Abdelatif fell, striking the edge. Overhead, the djinn vanished completely. The chamber fell silent, leaving only broken stone.

Amina tore free of Aya, stumbling to Abdelatif's side. "No, no, no!" she choked.

Abdelatif coughed weakly, flecks of blood staining his lips. Crystalline fragments still glowed in his chest, each ragged breath seizing his body. "The flame is sealed, and the Amulet is gone, never to tempt humanity again," he whispered, his eyes finding each of them. "The three keys... you all played your part. It worked because you stood together, because you sought the good of all above profits or pride. Never forget this."

His eyes slid shut.

"Abdelatif!" Amina's voice echoed across the chamber.

Aya knelt beside them, pressing shaking fingers to Abdelatif's wrist. There was no pulse.

The floor quaked again, blocks in the ceiling shifting. One by one, pieces of the corridor's roof crashed down.

"We need to go!" Karim shouted.

He and Aya dragged Amina away from Abdelatif. She shook violently, tears streaming down her face. Leaving Abdelatif's body behind in the roiling dust, they fled as the entire sacrificial altar of the djinn disappeared under a torrent of stone.

The chamber then shuddered again, as waves of energy rippled outward from where the Amulet had imploded, each pulse cracking stone and buckling the floor beneath their feet.

"The archway, it might give way!" Karim pointed through the swirling dust. The massive slab that had sealed their exit tilted, groaned, then crashed backward as another energy wave slammed into it.

"Now's our chance!" Aya grabbed Amina's arm, pulling her toward the partially cleared opening.

Amina's legs buckled. "Everything's spinning."

"I've got you." Karim swept her other arm around his shoulders.

They stumbled across the ritual chamber as the room crumbled behind them, collapsing in upon itself. The sprawling space that had felt vast moments before now pressed inward, walls seeming to close like a fist as the supernatural expansion into the realm of the djinn closed.

A column toppled, blocking their path. Aya vaulted over the debris, pulling Amina over. "This way, hurry!"

They squeezed through a gap in the damaged archway and reentered the antechamber beyond. The falcon statues they'd passed earlier lay shattered, and the carved walls rippled like water as reality reasserted itself.

"To the right," Karim gasped, recognizing only traces of the route from their descent.

They plunged deeper into passages that twisted back on themselves. The illusions were fading. Glimpses of impossible architecture flickered and died, replaced by solid stone that groaned under the mountain's weight.

"Cold," Amina whispered, her arms trembling. "I can't go on. Leave me."

The supernatural chill was retreating, but Amina was shaking uncontrollably.

"No, we're not going anywhere without you. We're so close, Amina," Aya insisted.

They proceeded as fast as they could, putting space between themselves and the collapse, until Amina collapsed on the floor.

"Don't worry," Karim said. "I'll carry you."

Karim hunched down, and Aya quickly helped Amina wrap her arms around Karim's neck and hoisted her onto his back.

Karim stood as the roar of grinding, cracking stone grew deafening. "We have to move!"

They ran while dust flooded the air and fracturing rubble nipped at their heels, making them cough and obscuring their vision.

"We're not going to make it," Karim yelled through his panting. "I can't tell which way is out."

"Can you hear that?" Aya shouted, listening.

"Hello!" Omar's voice echoed from ahead. "Anyone alive down there?"

"Here!" Aya shouted, her voice cracking. "We're here!"

"Keep talking!" Salah called back. "Follow my voice!"

They navigated by sound through a final corridor choked with dust and debris. The mountain bucked around them as the deepest chambers collapsed, sealing Abdelatif's sacrifice in stone forever.

"Keep coming," Omar continued to call, his voice growing steadily louder.

"Almost there," Karim gasped. "I can smell fresh air."

Light from the outside world cut through the dust ahead, and Omar's silhouette appeared in a narrow breach.

"Got you!" His hands seized Aya's shoulders, hauling her,

then Amina, through the opening. Karim tumbled out behind them.

As they collapsed on the rocky slope, gasping for fresh mountain air, a final roar thundered from behind, and the corridor caved in completely, dust billowing out in a suffocating wave. Where the corridor entrance had been, only solid stone remained.

Omar put a hand on Aya's shoulder, eyes shining with exhaustion and heartbreak. "Where's Abdelatif?"

A tear slid down Aya's grimy cheek. "He... he sacrificed himself." She paused as the words sank in. "And I think he always knew he would have to."

Amina let out a ragged sob, burying her face in her hands. "It should have been me, it was supposed to be me," she whispered. Omar slid an arm around her, tears shining in his own eyes. Salah sank to his knees, clutching his side with a trembling hand.

Ash still coated Aya as Karim's hands found her shoulders, pulling her in. She didn't resist. Their bodies collided in the hush of the aftermath.

His breath brushed her ear. "I worried I'd lose you down there."

They lingered before the rubble in silence, each lost in their own mourning, taking in the final resting place of Abdelatif El-Sa'adi.

No illusions tormented them now, no blasts of flame or swirling shapes. The corridor's final fury had died as well.

FIFTY-FOUR

It was finished. A dull rumble rolled through the Atlas Mountains, the last echo of the storms that had ravaged the region for days.

Salah exhaled shakily. "We can't stay here. People will come. Police, soldiers, or just frightened locals wanting answers we can't give. About this, about the base. They'll move quickly."

Aya nodded, forcing herself to move. Any chance of recovering Abdelatif's body, of giving him a proper burial, had disappeared with the final cave-in. The corridor's walls had sealed themselves around his last, heroic act.

They were gathered a short distance from the rubble, where the sun was rising again above the peaks. They had been underground for far longer than Aya assumed. Amina leaned against a boulder, arms trembling as tears welled in her eyes, pressing her palm against her forearm where the djinn's mark still showed faintly beneath her skin, now inert but permanently etched there.

"We have to do something," Aya said. "We can't just leave him down there."

Omar pressed a hand to her shoulder, tears welling in his eyes. "The corridor's closed. Even if we tried, we'd only risk more cave-ins, one of us joining him."

"We can still honor him," Karim said gently. He limped across the rocky ground, selecting a few flat stones fallen from the ridgeline. One by one, he stacked them to form a small cairn on a stable patch of ground before the collapsed entrance. "He'll always be in the mountain's memory. I think he would have liked that. This can be our memorial."

They joined him, each placing a stone onto the makeshift cairn. Omar pressed his forehead against the topmost rock, whispering a surah.

Salah bowed his head. "Thank you," he said quietly to the cairn, voice shaking with gratitude and grief. "You gave us a future."

For a long moment, no one moved. The hush stretched, a stillness settling over the valley as though even the mountains grieved.

Amina finally broke the silence with a tearful exhale, brushing dust from her eyes.

Aya looked around at the remaining group. They had proven they could work together to face the impossible. "He taught us something," she said quietly. "About standing together when everything seems hopeless. About the responsibility that comes with knowledge."

Karim's hand found hers. "We can't bring him back, but we can make sure his sacrifice means something."

Amina rose from her crouch, the tears on her cheeks mostly dried. "He bought us time," she whispered. "Let's not waste it."

They stood in silence around the small memorial, each lost in their thoughts and grief. The wind had stilled completely, leaving only the vast quiet of the mountains, the weight of what they had accomplished, and the realization of what it had cost them. Aya closed her eyes and tried to imagine Abdelatif's spirit at peace, finally reunited with the ancestors whose knowledge he had carried forward.

Minutes passed without a word. One by one, they placed their hands on the cairn, a final farewell to the man who had given everything to save a world that would never know his name.

Salah glanced up at the sun's climb. "We should go," he said hoarsely.

The walk back to the truck felt longer than their approach. Without the urgency of their mission driving them forward, exhaustion settled into their bones. Salah leaned heavily on Omar's shoulder, his wounded leg struggling with the uneven terrain. Amina moved like someone walking through a dream, her eyes distant.

The battered vehicle rattled down the narrow path, weaving through sharp switchbacks, leaving the dig site behind. Aya drove, gripping the steering wheel, exhaustion pinching her eyes. She flicked on the radio to escape from the oppressive silence.

"...initial reports indicate another series of potentially seismic events, with an epicenter in the Atlas Mountains. We're being assured there are no concerns for future aftershocks, but they are investigating the surprising development with suspicion that it could have been triggered by an archaeological dig in the area..."

Omar's laugh was hollow. "That's how they'll bury this?"

Aya switched the radio off. "Takes any attention off us, I hope. They control the narrative now. HRF, PES, Aegis. Whoever's really in charge, above Léglise. They'll claim it was an excavation accident."

Her father's notebook sat heavy in her pack. All those years of research, finally understood, finally used. But at such a cost. The pages about H. Çelebi and the network of supernatural sites seemed more important than ever now.

"We can't let this happen again," she said, her voice gaining strength. "Abdelatif said the djinn threat is contained, but the people who unleashed it are still out there, and my father's work tells of other potential sites, other artifacts that could potentially do the same."

Behind them, the High Atlas sank into haze, the corridor's secrets buried with Abdelatif. Yet a single certainty settled in following Aya's words: although the djinn were bound, the shadowy powers above Léglise who had orchestrated everything were still out there. They had resources, connections, and now they knew that ancient powers could be harnessed. The djinn threat in the Atlas was contained, but the human conspiracy behind it remained intact and dangerous.

Unless someone stopped them.

Karim turned in his seat to face her. "What are you thinking?"

"I'm thinking about those notes in my father's journal that we kept coming back to. The ones about Çelebi creating a network of sealed sites. If there are others like the corridor, someone needs to find them first. Someone who understands what they're dealing with."

Aya looked in the rearview mirror at her companions. They were battered, grieving, but united by what they'd experienced.

"I'm in for whatever comes next," Karim said, squeezing Aya's hand. "We can start by tracing the historical connections. Follow Çelebi's path through the archives."

Amina leaned forward from the back seat. "I can still sense things, feel energies that others can't. I might be of some help, now that I know I can control it."

Omar and Salah exchanged glances. "You know I'm in,"

Omar said simply. "After everything we've seen, everything we've lost... we can't just go back to normal life, no matter how much I'd love to while away my days with a heavily stocked wine cellar."

"A mission, my people," Salah said. "Not just revenge. Prevention. You have me."

Aya felt something shift inside her, the grief and exhaustion giving way to determination. "Then we don't stop here. We find the other sites. We make sure no one else can do what Léglise tried. And we end whoever was behind him."

Behind them, the mountains kept their vigil. Ahead lay a world that didn't know how close it had come to destruction, and the shadowy forces that would try again if given the chance.

FIFTY-FIVE

A TENSE HUSH clung to the sprawling villa they had rented in Marrakech's Palmeraie. Lanterns glowed amid lush palms and manicured gardens, their light flickering over mosaic-tiled walkways. The façade, arched doorways, carved wooden balconies, and terracotta pillars felt like a fortress for them.

Outdoor seating dotted the central courtyard, where half-finished cups of mint tea sat abandoned alongside scattered cushions. Aya perched cross-legged on a colorful pouf beside a low table.

She frowned at the muted television's newscast coming from her laptop: an English-speaking reporter outside a chain-link fence, the headline scrolling on the bottom of the screen read "Classified Accident at U.S. Desert Facility Sparks Global Outrage." Grainy footage looped behind him, showing the meltdown's smoky ruin. Any mention of the djinn, Léglise, Aegis, or the unimaginable phenomenon they had witnessed was conspicuously absent, as it had been for the two days they'd been staying at the villa.

Across the courtyard, Omar was scrolling news sites on his

phone, each bulletin parroting the same official statement from Prometheus Energy Solutions: a "routine test" gone wrong, no further comment. He dropped the phone onto a cushion with a frustrated huff.

"All that destruction... reduced to a 'tragic mishap,'" he complained.

From the far end of the garden, Amina rose out of the pool in a scarlet one-piece, its cutouts revealing the fading lines of her ordeal. She paused, allowing the water to slide off her body. "No surprise. Léglise's meltdown nearly exposed what they were actually up to. They'll blame it on sabotage or mechanical failures, some military thing, whatever covers up the truth."

Salah sat under one of the villa's sweeping arches, the bandages around his injured leg stark white against matching beige linen. He turned a small USB stick between unsteady fingers.

"We're ghosts in our own backyard," he said. "Word I've seen circulating is that they're sniffing around for 'foreign agents' in connection with the meltdown. That's us."

"No movement on the security monitor," Karim announced quietly as he entered the yard, glancing at a small screen on a side table. "You all still hoping for some actual justice?"

Aya opened her mouth to speak, but stopped when her phone buzzed. She snatched it up, an unknown number displaying on the screen.

"*Allô*?"

Everyone turned to watch Aya.

A smooth male voice drifted through the line. "Aya Amrani. I'm so glad you picked up." She gestured for everyone to come closer to listen as she turned on the speakerphone.

"Who is this?"

"We've spoken before, Miss Amrani, and I believe you

know who we are by now. The Aegis Foundation, I believe you consider us your former employers."

Omar's face went white. "You bastards. Where have you been?"

"Exactly where we needed to be. Managing a very delicate situation. You see, our relationship with Prometheus Energy Solutions was multilayered. Dr. Léglise was always a useful asset, but unpredictable, as I'm sure you experienced. We needed insurance."

"Insurance. Yeah, that's what we were," Aya said. "You're welcome for cleaning up Léglise's mess. Your mess. How much is that worth to you?"

The man on the line paused. "Initially, yes, you were our safety net if things went south. We hired you to retrieve the artifact if Léglise's operation failed or became too public, and we had to end our relationship with him prematurely. What we didn't anticipate was how spectacularly he would overreach."

"You were playing both sides, leaving us blind to which one we were on," Omar said through gritted teeth.

"We were simply managing risk. Léglise had the resources and obsession necessary to locate and extract the artifact. But his methods were crude. When his operation inevitably collapsed, we needed someone capable of salvaging the situation."

Aya's voice shook with rage. "You let all those people die. The dig team, the base personnel..."

"Léglise let them die. His actions went against our original plan, I can assure you. That's not how we conduct ourselves. Now, the fact that you not only survived but actually contained a supernatural threat? That makes you far more valuable than we initially projected."

"So what, you want to pay us? Give us a raise?" Aya asked.

"Now we want to offer you an enduring partnership. Your

father's research, your proven capabilities, Mr. Haddad's growing expertise, and of course, Miss Said's unique... conditioning. We have other sites to investigate, other powers to understand. With proper backing this time, and no rogue elements. You'll be in charge on the ground. What happened in Morocco has been proof of concept."

Aya shook her head. "And if we refuse?"

"Then you remain hunted fugitives, tied to multiple international incidents, which we may be happy to let slip. Or you could work with us and help ensure these forces are properly contained and studied. Your choice."

The line clicked off. Aya stared at the phone, heart pounding.

"They know... everything," she said quietly. "And they're not even hiding it anymore."

Amina's shoulders sagged. "They fed Léglise intel and let him do the dirty work. Now that so much was destroyed, Aegis wants us, and any data we have, to complete their plans. Not fucking happening."

"But how are we supposed to face them? They seem omniscient," Karim said.

A heavy pause fell, and they could hear the rippling pool. The hush felt charged, as though something else might crash down on them at any second.

Aya's phone buzzed again, another unknown call. Everyone tensed. She hit the speaker.

The same cool voice. "Well, Miss Amrani, I assume you and your compatriots considered our offer? Time is rather precious."

"What exactly do you want from us?"

"Specifically, your father's research notes, any remaining data or artifacts you may have recovered, and most importantly, you and Miss Said. Her unique relationship with these powers makes her invaluable for future operations. As does your proven ability to navigate these supernatural threats, and your connection to Hassan and his work. Mr. Haddad's historical expertise could also be a great addition. Omar, I'm sure you're listening. We're also happy to continue our working relationship; we've always been impressed."

Aya's jaw clenched. "Why do you want Amina so bad? Are you planning to weaponize what happened to her now?"

"Nothing of the sort. We want to understand it. There are other sites, Miss Amrani. Other powers waiting to be harnessed. With your team's expertise and Miss Said's enhanced sensitivity, we could revolutionize how humanity interacts with these forces, ushering in a bright future for humanity."

"I'm done being your pawn." She hurled the phone at a nearby marble column. The device shattered on impact, clattering to the courtyard floor. Silence.

Omar was the first to speak, voice low. "They'll come for us. We're in real danger."

Aya closed her eyes, taking a series of deep breaths. "We have to vanish again, then find them first. We can't let them do whatever it is they want if this was all part of a bigger plan."

Karim placed a reassuring hand on her shoulder. "We'll stand with you. The last few days have proven they're not invincible. What we accomplished proved we're stronger together."

"First, we survive. Then we bring the house down on them," Omar said.

Amina traced the fading marks on her arm, the designs now permanent reminders. "They want to use me as some kind of supernatural detector. But maybe..." She looked up with fierce determination. "Maybe that's exactly what we need. I can sense these energies now. We could find the sites before Aegis does. They'll have nothing like me. Plus, Aya, they're desperate to get their hands on your dad's work. We have a lot stacked in our corner for this fight."

She paused, exchanging a look with Aya. "We can't pretend anymore that the world is anything like what we've assumed. There's so much more... and if they stay in control of it..."

A weighted silence followed as they each registered the new world order.

"Exactly," Aya said, finally. "Djinn aren't just legends. We saw that. We fought it. Who knows what other legends are far more fact than myth. And this secret war will keep growing if we don't push back. We owe it to Abdelatif, and everyone else they've trampled, to fight."

She pivoted toward a low table by the courtyard fountain, where her father's battered field log lay open.

"I've been studying these pages more carefully," Aya said, running her finger along a hand-drawn map. The others followed her and crowded around the table.

"During those weeks at the dig, when you helped me with the more complex ciphers," Aya continued, glancing at Karim, "we only decoded about sixty percent. But now, with what we learned from the binding ritual, more pieces are falling into place. Look..." She pointed to a section they'd struggled with before. "This wasn't just gibberish. It was star charts, overlaid with geographical coordinates, that much we know. But that also means all these other ones are as well. My father wasn't just documenting legends, he was tracking a pattern."

She spread the pages wider, revealing the full scope of her father's research. "Look at these sites: Morocco, Turkey, Cambodia. All places where H. Çelebi traveled, all locations where 'celestial anomalies' were recorded."

Karim leaned in, studying the interconnected lines her

father had drawn between locations. "Each site is connected to the others."

"Exactly. And here..." Aya pointed to detailed notes in the margin. "He writes about 'astral lenses' and 'cosmic keys.' Çelebi was studying these sites and mapping them systematically. He was creating a network of sealed ancient powers that could be accessed under the right conditions."

Her finger traced a specific route on the map. "And here's what we missed before. Çelebi's ritual that saved us in the corridor wasn't his first. He allegedly performed similar bindings at each of these sites. My father must have known our past, the heritage that allowed me to initiate the ritual. I think he was tracking Çelebi's path because he realized something crucial: the Ottoman scholar wasn't just a researcher. He was a guardian, sealing these powers one by one, but also creating a comprehensive system to protect or preserve them."

Salah whistled low. "And if Aegis gets their hands on that system..."

"They could do what Léglise tried, but on a global scale," Amina finished grimly.

Karim's eyes flickered with recognition as he studied the astronomical charts. "Your father believed Çelebi left Morocco for Istanbul, following specific celestial events. Look at these calculations. If they're right, the next major alignment occurs in Turkey."

Omar's expression turned grim. "Do we chase them there? Haven't we lost enough?"

Aya looked around at her companions.

"We can't let them repeat this," she said firmly. "If they're after something in Istanbul—some 'astral lens' or cosmic key— another tragedy is waiting to happen. But this time, we'll be ready for them."

Amina's nod was firm. "I'm in. They want to see my

connection to the supernatural? Fine. We'll use it against them."

"Then I guess we ride again, together," Salah said.

"For Abdelatif," Omar said.

Karim walked beside Aya and put his arm around her. "Together, whatever comes next."

The villa's arches cast long shadows as the fury Aya had carried in her chest crystallized into something sharper, more focused. "Okay. We go underground," she said. "We heal, we plan, we learn everything we can about Çelebi's network. And when we resurface..." She looked at each of them, seeing her resolve reflected in their faces. "We take the fight to them."

As if responding to her words, a warm breeze stirred the courtyard, rustling the pages of her father's notebook. For a moment, Aya could almost feel Abdelatif's presence, or her father's, offering approval for their choice to continue the work he'd begun.

A secret war was just beginning, but they were no longer the pawns they'd once been. They were the players now, and they intended to win.

Epilogue

A PALE CRESCENT moon silvered the ancient stones of Galata Tower. Below, Istanbul sprawled, its twinkling lights divided by the dark silhouette of the Bosphorus. A robed figure stood at the tower's highest balcony, hands gripping the weathered marble ledge. A hot breeze blew in from the water, unusually warm for midnight.

Lowering his hood, he revealed sharp cheekbones and eyes that caught the moonlight with a predatory gleam. On the ledge before him were crinkled schematics on thick parchment pages. The top sheet bore an intricate diagram labeled Project Astral Key. Tiny star symbols dotted the margins. He ran a gloved fingertip over the swirling lines, exhaling with quiet satisfaction.

He lifted his phone to his ear, speaking in a low, clipped tone. "Don't worry. Morocco was only the beginning. What happened was... unfortunate. But everything here remains on schedule." He paused, listening, then allowed a small, humorless smile. "Perfect. Proceed with the acquisitions; no further delays. Aegis has come too far to falter now. We've waited too long."

A gust of wind rustled the parchment at his side. Pressing one hand to keep the pages from blowing off the ledge, he gazed out at the city's skyline. Minarets and modern towers stretched in every direction, while cranes sat idle, ready to add more. It was a collision of centuries, reminding him how easily history could bend beneath the will of those who knew its secrets. Clouds drifted in tattered shapes across the moon, their shadows rippling over Galata's ancient bricks.

"Yes," he murmured into the phone, "I'm fully aware of the fiasco in the desert. Léglise's failure cost us the Moroccan site, but the binding's energy signature gave us exactly what we needed to proceed: proof that the energy exists and can be tapped. It's confirmation that Amrani's daughter has her father's gift for unlocking it. She'll come to Istanbul—we just have to wait for her, and it won't be long."

He ended the call and set the phone aside before he unfolded another sheet of vellum, bearing the emblem of a falcon. His hand traced it reverently, then his eyes slid shut, as though sensing an unseen force stirring in the night air.

A still hush fell over the balcony, broken only by the distant horns of ferryboats crossing the Bosphorus. Lightning flickered along the far horizon, illuminating storm clouds massing over the Black Sea in the distance. The figure's smile sharpened, a triumphant curve to his lips.

His phone buzzed with an encrypted message: *"Amrani team spotted in Marrakech. Sultan's residence under surveillance. Awaiting instructions."*

He typed back: *"Let them run. Istanbul's web is already woven. When they arrive seeking Çelebi's trail, we'll be waiting. They will join us."*

Then, casting one final glance at the symbol, he drew his

hood over his head again. In a moment, the phone, the papers, and his presence disappeared into the tower's stairwell.

Galata Tower kept silent watch under the moonlit sky. Far below, the city's narrow streets remained unaware of the shadows gathering overhead.

If you've enjoyed Into the Atlas and the beginning of Aya's journey, continue the adventure and see what awaits in Turkey with the second book of the Aya Amrani Adventures: WITHIN GALATA'S SHADOW.

Please enjoy the following excerpt of the novel.

CHAPTER ONE

A hooded figure stood motionless amid the flowing river of pedestrians, watching.

"Karim," Aya whispered, holding her gaze firmly on the table. "Three o'clock. Don't be obvious."

The blue neon of Yana Café cast an electric haze across the tiled terrace, transforming the evening crowd into silhouettes against the amber glow inside. Aya Amrani lifted her Turkish coffee, inhaling the cardamom-laced steam before taking a careful sip.

Karim stiffened. "I don't see anything," he whispered. "We only landed a few hours ago. How could they already be onto us?"

"Building corner. Hooded figure. I have no idea if he's Aegis or if I'm paranoid." Aya tilted her head toward Amina on her right, who was scrolling through her phone with affected boredom. "Amina, do you clock them?"

Amina Said glanced up, her expression bored as she scanned the street with practiced nonchalance. The faded markings on her forearm, remnants of their encounter with a djinn in Morocco just over two weeks ago, were visible beneath her pushed-up sleeves. She took a long sip of her mint tea before answering.

Before flying to Turkey, the three of them had witnessed the opening of a sealed crypt in Morocco's Atlas Mountains and watched djinn materialize before their eyes from another plane of existence. Aegis had funded the dig, hoping the Amulet of Idris could tap raw energy from the djinn's realm to rewrite the world's power grid.

Instead, the unleashed spirits pushed Morocco to the brink of environmental collapse, took their friend Abdelatif with them into the void, and forced them to destroy the amulet before the death toll spread beyond Morocco. They escaped with scars: Amina's permanent mark that still tingled like static, Karim's nightmares of being trapped in the collapsing tunnel system beneath the Atlas Mountains.

Aegis had lost its super-battery as their base went into full meltdown in the Sahara, but not its appetite. Now, the shadowy organization that had pulled their strings wanted another relic, and Istanbul's streets were the next hunting ground.

"Yeah, I've noticed him," Amina said as a roguish grin shot across her face. "He's been there since just after we arrived. Hasn't moved. I'll deal with him, habibi."

Amina moved to stand, but Aya's hand shot out, gripping her wrist. "Don't. Too many witnesses."

"I wasn't going to create a scene," Amina argued, but settled back into her chair. "I hate sitting around waiting."

Karim, unable to resist, turned his head fully toward the figure. By the time his eyes found the spot, there was nothing but empty space where the watcher had stood. "I think they're gone," he said, turning back to the table. "Did you see where they went?"

"No. Damn," Aya said, banging her fist on the table. "It's probably nothing. We can't go looking for Aegis on every corner."

"Yeah, but Salah warned us they'd be here," Karim said quietly. "Aegis doesn't let go."

"They're afraid we'll beat them to their next power play." Aya's jaw tightened. "The Lens."

Amina's hand drifted toward the markings on her arm. "We beat them to it. I'm not interested in a repeat of Morocco."

"Neither am I," Aya said. "That's why we're here."

The waiter, a lanky kid with a long ponytail and a barrage of silver earrings, glided up, carrying a sweating pitcher.

"Başka bir şey ister misiniz?" he asked.

"Şimdilik sadece su, teşekkürler," Karim answered.

The waiter refilled their water glasses and was gone.

"Nice Turkish," Aya said, pushing Karim's shoulder.

"A couple weeks of intensive study will do that," Karim replied with a smirk. "But it's really not good. Still, the basics might be useful, and there wasn't any more research I could do until we were here on the ground."

"Better than my pathetic attempts. I can't even speak Darija, and I'm half Moroccan." Aya leaned forward, lowering her voice. "So, are we going to talk about the plan here?"

"Dismantling a global shadow organization that's hunting ancient artifacts of immense power with only your father's incomplete research as our guide? What is there to talk about? It's not complicated," Amina said dryly. "Just another Tuesday."

Karim laughed. "Oh yes, and just the simple revelation that djinn are real, and who knows what other supernatural terrors await..." His voice trailed off, but they all felt the weight of his unfinished thought.

"That's why we're here," Aya said. "To make sure it never happens again. The Astral Lens, if we're right and that's what they're after in Turkey, stays out of their hands."

Amina's dark eyes flicked to Aya's face, then away. "Quite the career change we've had. Though I'm not sure I like the new benefits package."

"People do change," Aya said, fingers drumming the handle of her cup. "Six months ago, I'd have stolen the Lens and sold it to some megalomaniac like Léglise."

Amina's mouth curved into a half-smirk. "Radical rebranding: Aya Amrani, inconveniently heroic."

Karim laughed again. "Hero or thief, labels are flexible. I, for one, still consider myself an archaeologist and historian. But what matters is we're a team now, and we have an enemy to stop. The three of us here, plus Salah and Omar."

"Then I suppose we won't waste time arguing old résumés. Or thinking about past experiences too much." Amina's gaze lingered on Aya before sliding away. Amina rubbed at the markings on her arm, which looked to any outsider like a series of Amazigh-inspired tattoos.

"How have they been?" Aya asked quietly, nodding toward Amina's arm.

Amina's hand stilled. "Manageable."

"That's not what I asked."

"They hurt sometimes," Amina admitted. "More when I dream. It wakes me up."

Aya felt an urge to reach across the table, to offer comfort, to wrap her former partner in an embrace. But that was the past. Before everything had changed. Before Karim. The murky waters of their new dynamic made her hesitate, her hand hovering momentarily before retreating to her coffee cup.

Karim cleared his throat, clearly sensing the sudden shift in atmosphere. "Should we head back to drop off our things? It's time to check into the apartment, and there's still daylight to explore our new neighborhood. Who knows how long we'll be here."

"Always the practical one," Aya said. "Yeah, it'll be good to at least enjoy the area before we have our next steps."

They settled their bill and stepped out onto the tiled street-side terrace of the café, now getting much busier than when they'd arrived. The early evening air carried a hint of salt water from the nearby port, mixed with the aromas pouring out of restaurants' open windows.

A ten-minute walk later, they were climbing the stairs to the fourth floor of a hilltop Ottoman building near Moda. The trendy neighborhood on Istanbul's Asian side was a world away from the tourist-packed streets of Taksim across the water. The apartment door opened to reveal a stylish living space with a blend of contemporary furnishings and traditional architecture. Three comfortable sofas surrounded a wooden coffee table, with floor-to-ceiling windows offering sweeping views over the sprawling city.

"Omar outdid himself," Aya said, moving immediately to the windows and pulling one open to let in the breeze. The rooftops of Kadıköy spread before them, the Bosphorus glittering in the distance, and beyond that, the silhouette of Istanbul's European side with its minarets and towers puncturing the darkening sky.

Somewhere out there, hidden in the bones of this ancient city, lay the Astral Lens, the device her father had spent years researching before his death. Çelebi's masterwork. Capable of channeling energy from deep space itself, focusing power that made the Amulet of Idris look like a spark beside a bonfire.

If Aegis found it first, Morocco would indeed be a footnote.

The plan was simple: find the Lens before they did, then

vanish. Leave Turkey. Hide the components somewhere Aegis would never reach. Guard them forever if necessary. No activation, no catastrophe, no more supernatural fallout.

Her father had died before finishing his research. Now it was hers to complete. And to bury.

"Not bad for a carpet salesman," Amina said.

"Well, he's always been just a bit more than a carpet salesman," Aya said with a laugh. "And hopefully his connections are as invaluable as he thinks."

Karim threw open the sliding terrace doors. "So far," he said, taking in the view, "I have complete faith in him."

"I'll take this room," Amina said, claiming the bedroom closest to the fire escape.

"Three exits," Aya noted. "Not bad."

Karim tilted his head toward the next room, with another terrace and views out over the Bosphorus. "That one's huge. Care to share?"

Aya smirked. "You need to ask?"

He shrugged and scratched his head. "Professional courtesy."

Amina's voice drifted from her doorway. "You two negotiate sleeping arrangements; I'm testing the fire escape, just in case."

Aya tossed her a salute, then turned to Karim. "Try not to steal all the blankets this time."

"No promises."

They stashed their passports in a hollow book, slid their notebooks and research beneath a couch cushion, and rigged Amina's micro-tripwire across the terrace door.

Karim snapped the last sensor into place. "Perimeter secure. Time for some street reconnaissance? I've been reading about Tellalzade Street," he said. "It's not far, and it's known for vintage shops and record stores. And Kadıköy Square is supposed to be amazing this time of day. We could check those out, then get dinner?"

Aya took a long look, surveying the apartment and their security measures. Satisfied, she nodded.

"Lead the way, Professor," Amina said.

They spent the next hour wandering through Kadıköy's streets. The district felt crowded and alive, but relaxed. Students with colorfully dyed hair moved between cafés, street musicians competed with the sounds of conversations and laughter, vendors sold everything from antique books to hand-crafted jewelry, while packed bars and restaurants dotted every corner.

The streets themselves were a maze. Some wide boulevards were lined with plane trees; other narrow alleys were barely wide enough for two people to pass, but all sloped dramatically toward the Sea of Marmara below. When they reached Tellalzade Street, it charmed them with narrow passages lined with shops selling vintage clothing, antique cameras, and records from decades past.

Aya watched with amusement as Karim excitedly examined a collection of Ottoman-era photographs, remarking on every detail. "So you're in your element?" she asked when he finally tore himself away.

"A couple of months ago, I was analyzing pottery shards in the dust and heat with no prospect of it ever meaning anything," Karim said, taking her hand as they walked. "Now I'm on an adventure in Istanbul, a place I've always wanted to visit, tracking an ancient Lens with mysterious powers, along with two beautiful master thieves. Life is not bad."

Amina was several paces behind them, either examining a shop window with intense focus or deliberately giving them space. Aya couldn't decide. The distance she maintained wasn't just physical. Since they had defeated Léglise and sealed the djinn away for good in the Atlas, Amina had kept an emotional barrier firmly in place.

"I don't know what's up with her," Aya said quietly. "She has flashes of normalcy, but then she's so distant."

"She's still processing. And aren't we all?" Karim said. "She'll come around."

They continued to Kadıköy Square, and the energy intensified. Street performers drew crowds, and food vendors filled the square with grilled meat and spices. Near the tram stop, a man in a red fez rang a brass bell, flipping elastic ice-cream cones just out of reach of giggling tourists.

A clarinetist accompanied by a saz player threaded a haunting Anatolian melody through the square; every so often, the clarinet swooped into a jazz-like riff that set the crowd clapping. A drummer with a worn davul kept the pulse, his heel stomping the pavement.

As they walked through the square, taking it all in, the sun began to set, painting the city in gold and amber.

"There's a traditional meyhane nearby that Omar has on his list of recommendations. Piraye Taş Plak. Apparently, they play classic Turkish records while you eat, and the food's good."

"Sounds perfect," Aya agreed. "Amina?"

Amina, who had been photographing a wall of street art, nodded. "I could eat. Do they have alcohol? I could really go for a drink."

"Indeed, they do," Karim said. "Let's go."

The meyhane was warm, intimate, with walls covered in vintage travel posters and shelves laden with old records. A phonograph in the corner played traditional music, the crackling quality of the recording creating an atmosphere out of time.

They were seated at a corner table and presented with

menus. Karim ordered a selection of mezze and a bottle of anise-flavored rakı, Turkey's national drink.

The bottle of rakı arrived, clear as spring water, with tall, narrow glasses alongside a pitcher of still water.

Karim filled their glasses and lifted his own first. "To finding the truth before Aegis does."

They clinked. Aya took a cautious sip, eyes watering. "Tastes like a black-licorice bonfire."

Karim laughed. "Come on, you've been to Turkey before." He tapped the water pitcher.

"I'm not usually somewhere long enough to enjoy the culture." She added water, and the liquid bloomed to a milky white. "Ah, science is magic."

Amina raised her untreated glass of pure rakı. "Here's to the woman who convinced thieves to play heroes! Try not to get us killed, Amrani."

Karim banged the table. "Şerefe, cheers."

More clinks, bigger swigs, and rounds of laughter.

Aya exhaled, cheeks flushing. "Why do people drink this voluntarily?"

Karim laughed. "We're probably supposed to pace it. Mezze, water, conversation."

"Well, too late for that," Aya rasped, still smiling.

Servers covered the table in waves. Glossy eggplant smothered in garlic sauce. Midye dolma, mussels snapped open and stuffed with cinnamon-scented rice and pine nuts. Tender, raw çiğ köfte rolled in crisp lettuce. Grilled octopus drizzled with olive oil and lemon.

They devoured the feast in near silence until plates were cleared and a bottle of wine appeared.

"Oh, thank god. I'll switch to some wine, and you two can finish the rakı," Aya said, pouring a large glass. "Omar's contact should reach out tomorrow. Someone who's been tracking Çelebi's work for years. Until then—"

Her phone buzzed against the table. She glanced at the screen, then sat up straighter.

"Salah?" Karim asked.

Aya nodded, scanning the encrypted message. Her expression darkened.

"What is it?" Amina leaned forward.

"He intercepted new Aegis communications. They've confirmed a recovery team in Istanbul. At least six operatives currently, more soon." Aya scrolled further. "And they're not just looking for the Lens. They already know it was built in pieces. Multiple components, hidden separately. Çelebi scattered them after the Sultan destroyed his observatory."

Karim refilled his rakı glass. "So it's a race for fragments."

"A race we have to win." Aya set the phone face down. "Who knows what happens if they assemble even part of it..."

"They won't," Amina said, taking the rakı bottle from Karim's hand and topping off her own glass. "We got to the Amulet first. We'll get to this."

"Salah says one more thing." Aya's voice dropped. "They've got a lead we don't. Something about Çelebi's original workshop location. He's trying to intercept more, but—"

"But we're already behind," Amina finished.

Silence settled over the table. The phonograph crackled through a song change.

"I'm getting worried about Omar's contacts. And they're going to notice Salah poking around in their system again. We need to move," Aya said.

"Well then, may Omar hurry the hell up," Amina said, lifting her glass. "But for now, here's to the plan, whatever's left of it."

After three more rounds of drinks and two record changes,

the album switched to Barış Manço's deep voice. Aya felt a knot between her shoulders loosen.

Karim drummed his fingers on the table in sync with the bass line. "Feels good not to sprint for our lives."

Amina leaned back, swirling her rakı. "A quick ceasefire with reality." Her eyes locked on Aya, light but firm.

Aya lifted her glass in reply. "Then here's to savoring the armistice. Tomorrow we're back in the trenches. But for now, there's nowhere I'd rather be."

Amina locked eyes with Aya, flashing a wide grin that she couldn't help but return. Aya looked away, then back, unable to break their eye contact before Karim placed his hand on her knee under the table.

It was nearly midnight when they finally left the meyhane, pleasantly full and slightly drunk. The streets of Kadıköy were still alive, but they opted to head back to the apartment, aware that the next day would be full and heavy.

They climbed the stairs to their floor, Karim fumbling with the keys, Amina still humming the last song from the phonograph. For a moment, standing in the dim hallway outside their door, Aya let herself enjoy the simple pleasure of the evening. Good food, good company, the promise of real work ahead.

Tomorrow, they would begin the search in earnest. But tonight belonged to rakı and laughter and knowing they weren't facing it alone.

Thank you for beginning this adventure with me! If you've made it this far, you know that some adventures are too good to end.

Get The Prequel For Free
Want to receive your free copy of Beneath the Andaman, the Aya Amrani Prequel? Join my newsletter at zackhacker.com for updates on the Amrani Adventures series and more.

Help Others Discover This Series
If this story kept you turning pages, please consider leaving a review on Amazon or wherever you purchase books. Whether a single sentence or detailed thoughts, your review helps other adventure seekers find their next great read. This will take you there:

Continue The Adventure
If you thought the Atlas mountains held secrets, wait until you discover what's hidden in Turkey, from the fairy chimneys of Cappadocia to the shores of the Aegean. See you in Istanbul!

-Zack Hacker

ACKNOWLEDGMENTS

In the throes of Covid, I moved to Morocco after I accepted a job teaching in Marrakech. I'd never set foot in the country or continent before, and I had little idea of what to expect. That risk quickly ignited a love for going on 5 years, and doesn't look to fade any time soon. From Marrakech rooftops to Essaouira beaches to Atlas treks, Morocco has inspired me, and this work is the biggest testament. Into the Atlas is my love letter to Morocco, and I hope I did it justice. Thank you to my adopted home.

To my partner, Maria Tedesco, I can't thank you enough for your unending support, partnership, and encouragement, for your infectious creativity, and for living this exciting journey side-by-side, from Morocco to Moldova to Svalbard to Singapore. Thank you for always being happy to read drafts, talk through complications, celebrate breakthroughs, and somehow never tired of hearing me ramble on. I love you and your belief in me and my writing kept me progressing when I lost confidence in myself or the story.

Karima Kaddouri, thanks for being the best friend anyone could ask for. You brainstormed more possible plot ideas over drinks at Tabz or chats at Ocean Vagabond than any human should ever have to endure. You read the earliest, roughest drafts of Aya's journey and saw potential where I saw only problems. Your enthusiasm for this story and my work exceeded my own at times when I needed it most. Thanks for always being there for me, making me laugh, and inspiring me.

When the 2023 earthquake hit Morocco, I found myself spending an increasing amount of time in the Atlas Mountains, rattling around in the back of a truck on the side of a cliff, or lying on a mattress under the stars on a village road. Those countless hours, experiences, life stories, and culture shared alongside Brittany Stone, Jacqueline Kinney, Abdeljalil Igassi, and Abdelatif Qassine have laid much of the groundwork for the story I wanted to tell in Into the Atlas. Eternal thanks to the people of the Atlas Mountains.

Additional thanks to Jacqueline Kinney, who has been on this process parallel to me, launching a new writing project, and has never failed to offer enthusiasm, curiosity, or support that helped me progress when I felt I might be losing sight of the bigger picture.

Thanks to my editors, Lucia Dupliak and Ruchi Daven, who polished my work and helped shape it into something worthy of my readers. Your keen eyes and thoughtful guidance elevated every aspect of this story. Thank you for everything you've taught me and for making this book shine.

More friends and family than I could ever list have cheered on this new series or kept me motivated from day one, thank you! This book wouldn't exist without your encouragement, support, or curiosity.

Special thanks to Ayoub Zkhiri for helping me with Darija spellings in the Latinate alphabet.

And I can't forget my cats, London and Marmalade, who might not be able to read but always kept me smiling and motivated throughout the writing process.

All the love to anyone who's supported my work. Cheers until the next one.

ABOUT THE AUTHOR

Zack Hacker is the USA TODAY and international bestselling author of the reality TV thriller Cut Reality, the action-adventure travel series Aya Amrani Adventures, and the coming-of-age fantasy saga Magic's Erosion.

Originally from Cincinnati, Ohio, Zack now lives in Marrakech, Morocco, along with his wife and their two cats. Connect with Zack, sign up for release notifications, and get free books via his official site at zackhacker.com.